AQUILA BOOKS

THE DEED'S CREATURE

DAVID FROST was born at Hayes, Kent, and educated at Dulwich College and St John's College, Cambridge, where he was elected to a Fellowship after a short spell lecturing in University College, Cardiff. He taught for ten years as an English don at Cambridge, and since 1977 has been Professor of English at the University of Newcastle, New South Wales. His numerous books, articles, short stories and poems include a study of Shakespeare in relation to his contemporaries in the drama, *The School of Shakespeare*, and an edition of the Jacobean dramatist, Thomas Middleton. But he is best known for his extensive contributions to church services in modern English, having served for ten years on the Church of England Liturgical Commission, and a further eight years on a similar body in Australia. His version of the Psalms for *An Alternative Service Book* has exceeded four million copies in various editions, is incorporated in service books in England, Ireland, Australia, South Africa and India, and is in use throughout the English-speaking world.

DAVID FROST lectures and broadcasts extensively, is an enthusiastic amateur actor, and a keen organiser of the arts. As Chairman of the Hunter Orchestra, Australia's most recently founded symphony orchestra, he has administered collaborations with the Australian Opera on productions of *La Bohème* and *La Traviata*; and in 1981 he was Administrator for the Christ Church Cathedral staging of *The Chester Mystery Plays*, for which he also played the roles of Lucifer and Herod. He is married to Christine Mangala, who is also a novelist, and who also holds a doctorate in English Literature from the University of Cambridge. They have four children.

The Deed's Creature

David Frost

AQUILA

CAMBRIDGE - SYDNEY - NEW DELHI

First published in Great Britain in 1990
by Aquila Books Limited
P.O.Box 293, Cambridge CB5 8AU

Published in Australia in 1991
by Aquila Books,
42 Homebush Rd., Strathfield, Sydney 2135

Aquila Books,
23 Ajit Arcade, New Delhi -49

Distributed in Australia by
Magpie Distribution,
27 Tyrrell Street, Newcastle NSW 2300
Tel. (049) 264215

© David Frost
Portions of this book originally appeared in
Southerly and *The Eagle*

All rights reserved

Printed and bound in Great Britain by
Billing & Sons Limited, Worcester

A CIP catalogue record for this book
is available from the British Library

Hardback: ISBN 1 872897 00 2

Paperback: ISBN 1 872897 01 0

Push! Fly not to your birth, but settle you
In what the act has made you, y'are no more now;
You must forget your parentage to me:
Y'are the deed's creature; by that name
You lost your first condition, and I challenge you
As peace and innocency has turn'd you out,
And made you one with me.

Middleton & Rowley   *The Changeling*, III. iv

CHAPTER ONE

'Mr Lepage?'

'I presume this isn't a parochial visit—unless the clergy have also taken to going in pairs.'

'We have a somewhat personal matter to discuss with you. May we come in?'

Lepage stepped out on to his front path, half-closing the door behind him. From within came the sound of a woman's voice coaxing a pet. The young man looked hesitant, and glanced appealingly at his superior.

'I do not come here of my own volition,' said Dr Kemberton, 'but because I was asked. It is not my practice . . . to open windows into men's souls.'

The younger man looked pained, as though betrayed already by such an admission. A tide of undivulged misery seemed to spill over from the priest and lap at Lepage's insides.

'There's a great gulf between us,' Lepage insisted. 'Nothing you say can cross it.'

The young man looked frightened. Dr Kemberton swayed slightly.

'Nevertheless,' he said, 'I have a duty to perform.'

Lepage heard the kitchen door click open behind him. It would not be safe to keep them standing longer.

'All right. If you insist.' He stepped back into the house, holding himself against the latch for them to pass. The younger man deferred to the elder on entering, as he had done earlier in speech. They stood together in the hall, looking round at its walls and ceiling.

'In here.' Lepage threw open the door of his sitting-room. Dr

Kemberton teetered in and stood unsteadily in the centre of the room, awaiting an invitation to seat himself. Whether he pined for the theological college of which he had once been principal, or for the wife whose infidelities were said to have caused him to leave it, his manner as he went about his parish duties was of the most flat and utter joylessness, as if only his mind were engaged, and anything that might have given body and pith to his actions taken up elsewhere, far distant. His voice, even the cut of his clothes, exuded depression.

The wheedling, coaxing tone in the kitchen turned suddenly to a high-pitched yell.

'I don't know . . .'—the young man reddened—'but I think you're being called.'

'That would be my call-sign,' said Lepage. He left them sitting side by side on the sofa.

His wife was ironing, head down, a two-foot pile of damp clothes on the chair beside her. She gave no indication of having called.

'Why are you screaming?'

'I need more money.' She agitated the iron from side to side, head still down, concentrating on the weave of the cloth.

'Show me the book.'

She ironed two more yellow dusters.

'Show me the book, woman. I've got people waiting.'

'Who are they? What do they want?'

'One of them is old Kemberton. I don't know the other; I imagine he's the new curate—or whatever.'

'The one that lives in St Botolph's old Rectory? What are they after?'

Lepage held open his palm, and stood waiting.

'Why do they call him the vicar?' She took a tiny pair of ladies' briefs from the pile, holding them up for him to see before she ironed them.

'I don't know—anymore than I know why they call St Botolph's the "Minster". It's an anomaly. Some historical accident.' He caught her ironing-hand above the wrist, and guided hand and iron together to the stand. 'No book, no money.'

She fetched her account book reluctantly from the dresser. Lepage drew up a chair and sat at the kitchen table, scanning the small items. He made a calculation with a pencil on the bloodstained back of an old butcher's bill.

'You must have a joint uncooked.'

For answer she walked into the pantry, threw open a wire

meat-safe, and brought out for display a half-shoulder of lamb lying on an enamel plate in a circle of dried blood.

'Why do you make me do it? How can you be so mean?'

'If I pay you one penny more than you need for eating, you'll squander it on detectives.'

'A woman can always save out of housekeeping.'

He stood up, took a wad of notes from his wallet, and counted out two pound notes and a ten shilling note, dealing them like cards side by side on the table. On consulting his calculations again, and after precise deliberation, he resumed the smaller denomination, returning it carefully to his wallet.

'One of these days,' she said with fierce defiance, 'you'll make a mistake; and then I'll take you to the cleaners for this house, and everything you possess.'

'One fine day,' he sneered, smiling in her face. He took a rayon slip, heavy with damp lace-edging, from the top of her pile, spread it on the ironing-board, and put the iron to lie face down in the cloth. She caught up the iron again and recommenced smoothing, as if that had been her intention, and he had only made things ready for her. He returned to his visitors, carefully closing both doors between them and the kitchen.

The young man was studying a photograph of men in uniform as Lepage entered the room; he looked embarrassed to be caught, and hastily resumed his seat. Lepage took a high-backed chair in the window facing them, with his back to the light. His chair was by intention considerably higher than the sofa on which the two men were sitting; the elder seemed to feel this, and got with difficulty to his feet. His curate put a hand to his elbow to assist him, and then withdrew it quickly, like someone who had touched electricity.

Dr Kemberton began walking about the room in his unsteady, rolling gait, putting down each foot as if uncertain where exactly it would come to rest. He leant forward in imminent danger of falling, rocked back on his heels, swayed and turned; but neither of the two men made any move to support him. The young priest sat on the sofa beside the other's hat, leaning well forward with his slim white hands stuck out in front of his knees, his wrists resting upon them. He looked as if he would have liked a book to clasp. Lepage waited, following the old man with his eyes, but otherwise not moving.

No one spoke, and the old man continued walking. As he staggered a second time into his turn, Lepage could see him clearly in the light from the window. He was obviously overweight, almost dropsical, and his head in profile was near egg-shaped, except for a corrugation of chins that blended face and neck into each other. A thin wisp of hair, dark grey with grease, was plastered from one ear over the top of his otherwise bald head; some attempt had been made to splay out the strands, but it still lay in a single straight band, like a girl's ribbon. His complexion, as far as the light enabled it to be judged, was pallid, but suspiciously purple on the cheeks and where his spectacle-frames pressed on each side of his nose. The spectacle-frames were specially thin and delicate, the heavy lenses rimmed in gold wire; and as he came closer to the window Lepage could see that the lenses had the effect of distancing his grey eyes, making them small and unnaturally abstracted.

The young man looked at the older priest as if seeking permission to begin, but received no answer. It appeared to Lepage that Dr Kemberton was attempting deliberately to heighten the atmosphere into a solemnity in which he could speak. He had passed the age when manners were compulsory, and seemed to be taking advantage of the fact to be as impressive as possible. He still said nothing. Lepage was determined not to let himself be caught up into the clergyman's mood; he removed some newspapers from another chair, pushed them into a corner and then returned to his seat. Dr Kemberton blinked at the now vacant chair, and flopped down into it. There he regained his breath, making little masticating noises with his lips, and staring into space with an oddly withdrawn expression. The young curate looked at Lepage with a gaze that was at once curious and apologetic.

When Dr Kemberton at last began to speak, with a faint Scots accent, pausing and stumbling over his labials, Lepage found his hostility checked by the drained sadness of the voice. There was no relief in being angry with a man present only in mind. He had previously decided to break off the interview as soon as they gave him excuse; but instead he found himself waiting till the old man had finished, and preparing his answer without animosity. He knew instinctively that whatever he replied Dr Kemberton would accept, since the priest lacked the power to feel whether his answer were true or no; so he listened without impatience.

Dr Kemberton sat to one side of him, staring into space, and mumbling at some imaginary audience. It was some seconds before Lepage could gather the gist of his remarks; and by then he had finished his preamble. His voice grew still softer, and he stumbled more frequently over his words. '... Whether unchastity in w-woman', he was saying, 'is more blameworthy, I do not know ... seeing that nature has given them less temptation, and the ability, if they would, to resist ... or what b–blame attaches to the man who succumbs to such a woman I must not judge.' He shook his head as though to clear it, and continued more strongly. 'But it is a course which must lead to the destruction of the body and the death of the soul ... for it sets up a swamp between man and his Maker, through the mists of which no eye can see. ... It deadens our natural feelings—an overwhelming madness, in the pursuit of which everything that is valuable is trodden underfoot as if it were pig-swill, of no relevance or account. There is no joy or satisfaction anywhere ...'

Again he shook his head, and for the first time looked at Lepage with his distant grey eyes, the tired lids hanging heavily over them. 'The family lives in my parish ... and my duties have made it necessary to call on you, since her relatives asked me. I shall not speak to the girl again unless she wishes to see me ... but I p-promised to come and visit you, and to ask you to cease meeting her. ... What to say to you I do not know; I cannot understand how a police-officer ... whose daily labour requires him to maintain virtue ... can find himself in such a situation that a priest must come and beg him to remember who he is, and on what his livelihood depends. I do not know how persons who have been married many years can throw away their secure affection as if it was of no value. The family care for their daughter; they do not wish their child to be the gossip-fuel of the town. They have asked me, the representative of Christ, to beg you to give her up, for her sake and for your own. ... It is a force which deadens the eye and the mind and the heart ... cuts off everything that makes man a rational animal, sucks the taste from every p-pleasure ... dries up b-blood and bone ...' The eyes were withdrawn again, and the priest finished speaking; he did not seem to be waiting for any particular answer.

The room was silent except for the old man's laboured breathing. The younger priest sat in the same position, intent, still leaning forward with his wrists upon his knees, but pushing the knuckles of each fist against the other, so that the bones showed ivory-white through his pale skin. Lepage felt that he, at least, was demanding an answer; but he experienced none of the animosity which he had felt when they entered the room. The old man was so far removed that the whole matter could be got through as if it were a game of chess; Lepage positioned his argument coolly, with the intention of clearing the house of both of them as quickly as possible.

But before he was ready, Dr Kemberton began speaking again. 'They tell me I must advise . . . that we m-must all guide the flock of Christ. But they do not tell me there is a different kind of animal now, who is not a man as I knew him . . . whom I do not know how to talk to, with whom I have nothing in common, who cannot understand what I say.' He lifted his heavy lids again and peered into Lepage's face, trying to find his eyes in the shadow. 'Are *you* that animal, Mr Lepage?'

'I do not understand.' Lepage's voice was clear and controlled. 'My profession is irrelevant, for the girl is legally capable of making her own choice. I see that she is well-fed and healthy— my conscience is perfectly clear on the matter.' He glanced across at the younger priest, whose fair hair and chiselled features made him appear unpleasantly feminine. 'If I was rude to you on entering, I apologize; I did not realize that the cause of your intervention was a mistaken sense of duty. There is nothing more you can say.'

The old man blinked. It seemed he wished to speak, but could not make up his mind. Suddenly he leaned forward and gripped Lepage above the knee with a big-boned but emaciated hand, supporting his weight on it, his grey eyes behind the spectacles scanning Lepage's face. Lepage could feel the hand trembling under the strain.

'Tell me one thing, Mr Lepage. . . . The girl: I have seen her, she is intelligent, friendly, and she has a happy home . . . she says she is not in love.' He had ceased stumbling, and his speech was quick with the irritable excitement of old age. 'Why does she behave so? What is it that drives her?'

The grip on his knee did not relax and the priest's eyes, no longer distant, were obstinately seeking his own. Without shifting his gaze Lepage was conscious of the younger man watching him intently. He felt trapped, embarrassed, and spoke without thinking. 'Nothing but the itch for fornication,' he said, and laughed.

The old priest sat back suddenly, withdrew his hand, but made no other movement. His jaw muscle tensed rigid below his ear, and a vein on his left temple stood out in all its tortuous convolutions. But his breathing remained steady, and his eyes once more appeared rather to be looking inward than at anything in the visible world. There was a long silence during which no one moved. Lepage was still conscious of the younger man's stare, but did not turn and face him. At length Dr Kemberton moved a hand half-consciously to his head, separated the strand of grey hair as if some touch of vestigial vanity still remained, and pulled himself unsteadily to his feet. He began crossing the room; but although the young man made as if to offer him assistance, he did not appear to notice. He picked up his hat from the sofa, turned shakily, and spoke to his companion.

'That is all, Mr Cathcut. We have done our duty, and I did not expect it to be otherwise. Will you walk with me?' Nothing more was said, and the two men went out into the hall.

CHAPTER TWO

Lepage decided against any attempt to allay the kitchen-demon. Instead, as soon as the front door had shut behind his visitors, he returned to the room they had just left, and, taking his chair in his hand, paced diagonally from one corner of the room to the other, counting the paces. He divided the paces by two and set the chair down at mid-point, where it was furthest from every wall, without inclining in any direction towards another.

Having assured himself that this was the case, he sat down astride the chair, leaning his elbows on its back and staring out of the window at the two priests as they carefully secured the latch of the garden gate and moved off to the right. Without any particular intention of turning his back on his guests, he reversed his chair and remounted, facing a blank, featureless wall. The sheer blankness of the wall eased the slight irritation in his mind, a vague sense of humiliation, which was not, however, related especially to the activities of the two priests, who had after all only been doing what they conceived of as their duty. Despite the relief which this action afforded, and a certain satisfaction at having eased out his visitors with only one minor incident, he felt oppressed by a pang of loneliness, which nevertheless had at its core something at once both painful and pleasurable.

He might have sat like this indefinitely, absorbing the bittersweet pleasure of isolation, until such time as his mind, unable to take in enough to keep it sinking, popped back like a cork to the surface; but a hesitant tap at the front door obliged him to answer it before his wife was tempted to break out of her kitchen-confinement. It was the younger priest, his forehead perspiring as if he had run back from the street corner.

Despite a slight effeminacy, there was something appealing about this young man: his forehead, from which the hair was already receding, the strongly defined nose, both had a marked forward thrust that imparted to his features an air of sensitive, delicate energy. Lepage was by no means as resentful of the intrusion as he had anticipated.

'Mr Lepage . . . I can't leave matters there.'

Lepage took him back into the room they had just vacated, and sat him down at the mid-point.

'What can't you leave?' He circled the central chair.

'I'm young; just out of theological college. In my first parish.' He looked up appealingly, following Lepage's perambulations with his eyes. 'But if what you said was true . . . nothing I've been taught, nothing I've believed in, can stand up. I might just as well pack my bags and go home.'

Lepage took a second chair, and again straddling it, sat facing him.

'I'm impressed to be such a blow to faith. But,' he said, reaching out and placing his hand gently on the young man's knee, 'perhaps we are not as far apart as you think.'

Cathcut was not ready to tolerate a touch: he moved his knee quickly outwards from under Lepage's hand, but looked frankly into his face, as though to make it clear that he had not interpreted the gesture as some homosexual advance.

'I hope so. I hope so very much.'

Lepage again propped his elbows on the back of the chair, and pressed his upper lip into his clasped hands.

'I'm not averse to helping a young man in his first post. —What about me so disturbs you?'

The young man tried to evade his stare by glancing first at the window, then round at the handful of photographs, before consenting to return it.

'That can't be true.'

'What can't?'

'What you told Dr Kemberton.'

'Oh. —The "itch for fornication".' Lepage smiled gloomily in recollection of the priest's reaction. 'How would I know what is in it for her?'

Cathcut licked his lips nervously. 'But you know what is in it for you. And that can't be true. A mere animal itch.'

Lepage fixed him with his yellowed eyes. 'Why not?'

'You wouldn't risk a long-standing relationship—a mature affection—for something so trivial.'

Lepage considered for some seconds, looking him over austerely, as though debating whether to expend the truth on him.

'I *have* no relationships.'

The young priest began to be flustered.

'But surely,' he said, 'surely you loved your wife when you married her?'

Lepage looked at him. It seemed that he answered more for the sake of his own, unspoken question.

'It was early days. I was naive.'

'You mean you discovered she had faults?'

'Faults? . . . I didn't notice faults. —Only those incident to women, I suppose. She couldn't hold on to the flame.'

The priest looked puzzled.

'Mr Lepage, I beg you . . . if you knew how important it is to me . . . I must know the truth.'

Lepage scrutinized him again.

'Could you bear the truth, if you knew it?'

'I believe I could . . . I am sure I could. After all, *"the truth shall make me free".*'

Lepage smiled ironically. Cathcut shifted uneasily in his seat, pulling at his jacket shoulders as though they had settled badly.

'The truth *binds* me,' Lepage said.

'Binds?' But Lepage gave no sign of elucidating his comment. 'You mean you're tied to a woman you no longer love?'

'I don't know what you mean by "love". I married her because she moved me.'

'Moved you? To what?'

'To whatever it is that makes life bearable. Bearable because it borders on death—like a variant of death.'

'But life is so worth living.' Yet Cathcut's voice was beginning to falter. 'The joy of music . . . the beauty of the natural world. You seem so extreme.'

'I *was* extreme.'

'In your relationship, I mean.'

Lepage turned his head aside in irritation. 'It wasn't a relationship. That was not its function.'

'That makes it sound as if you used people.'

Lepage looked weary, bored. 'Little man, I'm like an addict with a drug. You don't blame a man for consuming his drug. Or for discarding its container.'

'But you blame him for his addiction.'

'Do you? But that presumes he has an alternative. What is my alternative?'

The young man began to flounder.

'I don't know. Concern for other people . . . self-discipline, restraint. Love of God.'

'I'm addicted to a glass of water. He made me to want water. It's there, just out of my reach. And when I stretch out my fingers towards it, he would pull my hand back, tell me to do without. Why should I love God?'

'"He shall give them rivers of living water".'

Lepage laughed. 'Now that *would* be a God.'

Cathcut looked shocked. 'You can't remake God in your own image.'

'Nor can I remake myself to suit you.'

'But it isn't for my own sake,' protested Cathcut, beginning to redden, and making little agitated pleadings with his hands. 'It's for you. You're going against the grain, against the law of your own nature. You must be, if you are anything like the kind of man I take myself to be.'

Lepage smiled sardonically. 'I don't think I am. I think you may be a very cowardly little man.'

Cathcut grew indignant. 'I don't think it's cowardly to have come here.'

'I don't mean that. I mean all the little dogmas and doctrines you take to yourself, to avoid facing up to things as they really are. That's cowardly. The people out there'—he waved a hand toward the window—'they break your natural laws with impunity.'

'But they don't!' Cathcut cried. 'Look at them. What they do starts to react on what they are. *"On every face I meet, marks of weakness, marks of woe."* They can't do ill without suffering the consequences.'

'There might be natural causes. Poor health. Poor feeding.' But Lepage sounded unconvinced. Then his eye brightened. 'But there are exceptions. They don't last, but there are exceptions.'

Cathcut began to look frightened. 'But that means endless pursuit,' he protested, 'jumping from one person to another. It's a hell on earth.'

'But nothing to the hell of not feeling.'

Cathcut's expression softened. 'Not to feel love,' he said earnestly, 'just to be hard and unyielding, that's the hardest thing in life to bear.'

Lepage got to his feet, and began walking about the room in irritation.

'Keep your love,' he said.

'Mr Lepage,' insisted Cathcut with passion, 'when I talk of love, or the joy one feels at an altruistic moral action . . . of the beauty of the world, of the sheer fascination of the animal kingdom . . . music, the delight of colours and sounds, let alone God—do you mean to tell me you have no inkling of what I am talking about?'

Lepage stopped in his tracks, white with anger.

'I don't say I have no inklings. But I regard them as a weakness.'

'You must be mad.'

Lepage came towards him.

'I *am* mad, my pretty priest.' Cathcut moved sharply, but Lepage forced him down from behind with one hard hand on his shoulder. 'When you come here, what do you think goes on behind these eyes of mine? Do you see them laughing at you? What do you think I mean at the level where politeness doesn't go, where I can't talk, where I think and dream? Talk to me of beauty, but down there I have a black snake, shining and sinuous with patterned gold. Have you never felt that snake, twisting softly round those pale white limbs? Have you, my pretty priest? Tell me, there's no one here to overhear.'

'I don't understand.' Cathcut was white and puzzled. Lepage stood behind his chair, both hands on the top, leaning forward to speak. Cathcut averted his head.

'Does my breath sting you, Cathcut? Sulphur—the Devil's own tang: the theologic nose scents it out instantly.'

'The Devil is rarely conceived of in such terms by modern churchmen.'

'It's a pity, Cathcut; because he lives for me—so very beautiful. Have you never felt him, in the darkness of your theologic dormitory, come gliding out of the ecclesiastic night, my own soft snake, whirling and coiling back on itself in the darkness, pure fire, and bathed in musk? Like the smell of joss-sticks—do you find joss-sticks pagan, Cathcut?'

'I find your conversation nonsensical.'

'Do you, my little priest? Do you?' He was gripping Cathcut's shoulders hard with both hands. 'You sought this conversation, you forced us out. Do you like me when I come out, Cathcut? *Am* I your species? *Am* I your man?'

'You are. You must be.'

'"I must be." The Devil's man, Cathcut, the Devil's own true man. Pick up your wares, put the church socials, the Sunday flower-hats, the enthusiastic hymns, put them all back in the pedlar's pack. They have no currency here. This is devil's ground.'

'Mr Lepage, although the medieval age is a glorious period in the Church's history, it's a mistake to try and live in it.'

Lepage came round to the front of the chair, and tipped up Cathcut's chin.

'You understand me, don't you?'

'I find your snake image disturbing.'

'Why?'

'I don't know. It reminds me of something.'

'It reminds you of nymphs black as ebony, with supple glistening limbs, clothed in silk, slight and diaphanous; of heavy perfume, crushed flowers, the lithe and subtle panther: all the things they don't allow in theology.'

'I think theology is better without them.' Cathcut's voice was dry and tense.

'But you aren't without them, Cathcut. Theology doesn't understand what I mean, but you do. Listen to me, and when you have finished listening, run as hard and as far as you can, because you are the Devil's man too and can understand as well as I. Don't speak to me of the beauty of the world because I can't see it, or of the joys of music because I don't feel them; among the tangled relics, the rusting machinery, your neat streets, or your macadamed roads, I see one thing, one being; and her limbs are lined with blue fire, flickering and darting.' He paused and drew breath sharply. 'I know only one pleasure, one interest, one joy: to bury myself in that fire, to feel its electric tongues engulfing and consuming every part of me. There is no gain to equal that loss; and my only desire is to lose again and again until the abyss will bury me for ever. The light moves and changes, glows in one being, then another. But where it goes there I must follow, until it will accept me for its own. Do you understand, ascetic? "Cut"'s the word for "gelded". Do you understand, Cath*cut*?' Again Lepage tipped up the priest's chin, but his hand was forced fiercely away.

'Don't ask me. I refuse to be questioned.'

'Are you afraid, little priest? You asked me to be honest. Answer me. It is the host's privilege.'

'You have no privileges.'

'If I was a devil, no. But as I am your fellow sinner, yes. It is your duty. Answer me, or I shall think your God has no answer at all.'

It was some seconds before Cathcut replied. His fair skin was dotted by small glisters of perspiration.

'It is true. God forgive me. I do understand.' He dropped his head, but lifted it immediately in a sudden burst of speech. 'But to make yourself over to it is spiritual, moral, physical death. You must kill off what longs for the abyss, if you are to live at all.'

'But I have chosen the abyss. Will you leave me now?'

CHAPTER THREE

The sun reached Seshton with melancholy face—a doctor who regrets, in thrusting back the curtains and releasing the overbreathed air, that light must be so harsh to angular features, to grey and gritty complexions. But well before his bedside appearance, the dawn had worked a transformation on the sleeping town: first outlining the flats on Seshton Hill against a back-cloth of bluish-grey, then wreathing dark clouds, intermingling bars of pale yellow light behind the gaunt, silenced monoliths. A little later, and the eastern sky flashed orange; so that if there had been anyone awake to see it, he might have known a pagan temple, a lonely henge, black before the rising sun. A few tradesmen covered their rounds in the streets below, purring along avenues in discreet vans that chinked their bottles over the ruts at corners—half a round still to go. The paper-boy was too conscious of a keen November wind biting under his armpits to look at clouds. Cathcut might have admired their dark, rain-heavy shapes, tinged at the base with pink and orange; but Cathcut was cycling at speed down Seshton Hill, his cape ballooning behind him, too intent on correcting the bucks and capricious twistings of his antiquated machine to bother admiring scenery.

Three months had passed since his interview with Lepage; but his anxious expression and appearance of perspiring haste would have precluded any attempt to judge the effect of Seshton upon him. His front wheel twisted, struck the kerb a glancing blow, and rebounded. In an effort to keep balanced he wrenched the handlebars round and shot out into the centre of the road. Fortunately, there was no traffic in the fast lane. His determined zeal, of which Luther himself might have been proud, seemed to overbear the violence necessary to control his rebellious steed. A milkman whose van he brushed laughed coarsely but not unkindly; indeed, it might have been St George riding the dragon bare-backed. Cathcut had surprised the tradespeople by taking a room in the poorer area beyond Seshton Hill. They felt there was no 'side' about him; and though his gesture did not make them any less uncomfortable when he spoke to them, it earned him some goodwill.

With a timely flick of the handlebars and some luck, Cathcut diverted his onrush out of the main road and into a parallel backwater before a terrace of Georgian houses. Apart from the church, they were the only surviving buildings of architectural merit in Seshton, and most of their façades were discoloured by a bloom of green lichen which lay upon the stone. In all conscience, they would have been poor enough to satisfy even Cathcut: charity flats administered by the church council, inhabited by the detritus of a population, who had drifted through tenement after tenement, finally to lodge and accumulate there because at last nobody troubled that they could see no point in cleaning or maintaining a property. Whole families had been marked down as educationally subnormal. The children were inordinately friendly, darting out to grab the hands of passers-by, hanging on till they had extracted a smile or a word of recognition, and sometimes permitting themselves to be dragged off their white, bowed and puffy legs by the effort to toss them aside. In contrast, their elders appeared sullen, bodies unstrung, their faces rucked and hollowed by the fatigue of matching intolerable demands, of unravelling recurrent complications whose solution slipped through the memory; so that their many children seemed more the product of exhausted despair than of the self-indulgence with which the parents were credited.

Battered prams, which served as need arose to transport coals or children, cluttered the open hallways. Dustbins emptied that morning exuded a smell of dead ash and stale vegetable trimmings; for one of the dustmen, perhaps in ironic recall of some Hollywood epic, had hung their lids at intervals all along the terrace railings, like so many shields upon a Viking long ship. Scraps dropped by the refuse collectors were fast blowing into the wells that admitted light to the basement windows, joining unswept leaves, discarded orange wrappers and rubbish blown down from the street, all left to decompose at their varying rates. And yet Cathcut had not chosen to live here among this obvious squalor. Partly, he felt that as a gesture it would be too flamboyant, self-dramatizing rather than self-effacing. More than this, to live in such proximity would have pointlessly aroused in him questions capable of no answer. He was grateful that the Church acknowledged a special duty to tend those so botched for life by their Maker; but he recognized that in its pity was a wish to compensate, an element of atonement for the creator by his creation. To live among them, so exposed, to maintain faith on such a seaboard, would necessitate that one's defences be continually re-built, holding, containing doubts, resisting the scour of contrary impressions. He knew that the strain of counteracting such erosion would impair the efficacy of his ministry.

He admired the Georgian style; and yet he regretted that, to differentiate the end-house from its neighbours, the church council had cajoled Dr Kemberton into accepting a scheme of renovation. A working party had picked out in white the windows of the Rectory and the pillars of its portico, painted the front door a contrasting black, and re-glazed the fine, semi-circular fanlight. The decoration was tasteful, unassertive, its sole extravagance an angel with a leer, a knocker in brass discovered by the vicar's warden in the Lanes of Brighton, polished by him, lacquered and presented. But all such touches were in vain; the effect was ruined, for Dr Kemberton had refused to replace or even to raise his blinds from the upper windows: brown blinds, faded by the light into reddish-pink eyelids, and protruding through the cracks in their outer surface a fuzzy material like horsehair. With a jarring application of brakes and a spurt of gravel, Cathcut dismounted, hauled his bicycle across the pavement and leant it precariously against the Rectory railings. He rushed up the steps, left the fallen angel to spread its wings undisturbed, and stabbed at the door-bell.

A measured tread pounded the boards of the Rectory hall, and his heart jumped to time with it—Mrs Avling, the vicar's house-keeper. He could not understand her. Her opening of the door was echoed by a sick cavity which yawned in his midriff, making it difficult to regain his breath. The angular shoulders that filled the doorway were square like a man's: unnatural, as repellent to him as the bristles that poked through the pore-holes of her chin and fringed her upper lip, causing him to feel wretched that he was thus repelled.

'He is at his orisons. He is not to be disturbed.'

Orisons. What kind of word was that? Cathcut attempted to smile her into affability, but she contracted her brows at him till the tufts mingled, then blinked and relapsed into vacancy. Orisons: a word archaic by several hundred years, dug from some play or rubbishy novelette, no doubt one of the books he had seen bending their soft covers over the narrow shelves of the kitchen dresser, and only kept from falling by the weight of others stacked on top of them. Did she know what she was doing? Stupid, pretentious. No, that was uncharitable—quash these sudden eruptions. An old woman, nervous—and he should understand nervousness—using language as a self-defence, a stockade against the incursions of others, surely that was it.

'I fear it's most imperative that I see him.' His words came in a rush of breath.

'At this hour it is quite impossible. The spirit must have its hours and its seasons.'

He wished he could think it true of her. Her life seemed singularly lacking; nor could he ever conceive of her with a husband. Perhaps he had died young; he remembered something of the sort. The Bishop had told him, in his precise accent that rolled swiftly and lightly off the tongue, during that long afternoon in which they had pretended that an interview was a social event. '. . . A strange fish, Kemberton, something of a scholar . . . somewhat contemptuous of a Lambeth degree, I suspect, if the truth were known. Have you met his housekeeper? Have you not?' And like an eager three-quarter the Bishop had gathered his opportunity of an anecdote, to rush triumphantly downfield and deposit it behind the touch-line. 'Well then, what is her name?— no, of course you wouldn't know, but a fish odd enough to frighten the others out of the aquarium you understand, quite the diocesan Medusa. Reminds one of my Oxford tutor, who read so much Johnson that he began to talk like him—though with her it's quite undiscriminating, you understand, *the most disparate authors yoked by violence together*.' He had paused to emphasize the allusion. 'Well then, it seems on one occasion there was a garage hand— my suffragan claims to have been present—who wanted a reference of some sort, so she had to go and see if it was convenient. And when asked to describe him, she had some phrase about a "rude mechanic"—which was all very well, except that the fellow was waiting in the hall and it was strident enough for him to hear every word. He was most upset, took it in quite the wrong way. . . . No doubt apocryphal, I'm sure it is, but "rude mechanic" . . . Ha *ha*, very *good!*'—and the Bishop had slapped his thigh so that the loose fat shuddered, at the same time throwing back his head in a disyllabic laugh, the second tone louder and higher, but cut suddenly short as he eyed Cathcut askance through the lower segment of his bifocals, for fear lest he had not registered the point. And Cathcut had also laughed, though he was alarmed, and wondered at the ease with which the Bishop converted the souls in his cure into an anecdote . . .

But at the last moment Cathcut diverted his thoughts from so customary a channel: Mrs Avling must not be allowed on this occasion to drain his emotional energies. She had already cost him enough, when work had increased in the printing works beneath his flat, and the rhythmic clash of the presses into the small hours had harmonized with and remorselessly prolonged the wash of his mind against the problem of Dr Kemberton's housekeeper. He was not content, nor could it be right, to leave her as he found her; but he must mortify himself now for a greater project by temporarily accepting the opaqueness of her tragic stare. He smothered a distaste that only sharpened his anxiety to comprehend, and set aside her wooden expression, her affected language and theatrical gesture, the addiction to print that he suspected was her substitute for living, shelving them for future consideration. It remained to clear the way, for she held the edge of the door in a large red hand, determined to protect the privacy of her employer. From earlier probings he had learnt that she was sensitive to any reference to her pursuits, and what had previously baffled him he suddenly realized might be turned to account.

'If you went back to your books, Mrs Avling, I'm sure you must have something to do, and I could go up to the Doctor by myself.'

Immediately, he felt remorseful. She maintained her stare for some seconds, scraping discoloured foreteeth several times over her lower lip, pinching it between upper and lower teeth; then, the colour rising in her cheeks, she averted her eyes, and after seeking confidence from the floor for a moment, turned clumsily on a very built-up heel and retreated altogether down the hall, banging the kitchen door behind her as if in some dissatisfaction with herself. Smothering the suspicion that ill-will as much as necessity had conditioned his action, Cathcut ran upstairs to the first landing, took breath, and with more toil climbed the reverse flight up to the first floor.

The speed with which he hurried to consult his superior came more from habit than from conscious intention. It was not that he really expected help. Dr Kemberton oversaw his reading, tailored his sermons, drily set in order points of doctrine, and even (which

Cathcut found supererogatory) trained his intonation of the church services: it was natural that he should go first to him. He found such supervision irksome; but he underwent it in the hope of having his pride crushed, like a body under masonry.

He crossed the linoleum of the corridor and gently opened the door of a room which Dr Kemberton had converted into a private chapel. Air heavy with the grease of extinguished candles lunged out at him, but inside it was dark and empty. Mingled with stale wax there was a warm, felty smell of blinds beginning to be touched through by the wintry sun playing on them from outside. A little early-morning light leaked in round their edges, but insufficient to light the room. Dr Kemberton's joylessness dispirited him, for he seemed able to use the talismans that aroused so much for Cathcut without any sense of awe, of the numinous, of the infinite God who yet presented his meaning in a cold metal cross upon an altar. His superior worshipped in gloom; and when he abased himself before the Host at communion, even that had an air of dry formality, of a frozen attitude, the mannered control of some El Greco saint hitting off a posture of adoration.

A liquid choking sound of catarrh being dislodged reached Cathcut from the study adjoining the chapel. He listened, and heard the drawn-out slither of soles dangled and scraped idly across linoleum, rising quickly to a high, loud tone, then sliding and fading slowly down the scale. Rapping a knuckle painfully against the door, he went in. The vicar was seated hunched among his books, annotating desultorily the yellowed margin of a volume of religious writings, identifiable by its bold, heavily inked typeface, broken by lighter lines which were italicized quotations from the scriptures. The whole room was walled with books, brown Victorian bindings and modern coloured cloth, but all order or system had been abandoned, so that Cathcut noted, on the shelf above the clergyman's head, Aquinas hob-nobbing intimately with collected Freud.

'Dr Kemberton, please excuse my interrupting, but a most urgent matter has arisen. I sorely need your advice.'

The clergyman half turned, fixing on him eyes still red and clouded by the night's rheum.

'Ah . . . let us go downstairs.'

'It's quite unnecessary, I assure you.'

'No, no, I insist.' He laid down his pen and rose unsteadily from his chair. His manners were fads rather than courtesy, and one of them was that he would receive visitors nowhere but in his drawing-room. Stumbling to the head of the stairs, he waved aside

Cathcut's proffered assistance, thereby compelling him to watch a spectacle which agonized him. The old man clutched on to the banisters with two quivering hands that were a knot of intersecting blue veins sprinkled with brown, wart-like discolorations of the skin, and lowered himself step after step, recovering his semi-upright stance each time he had both feet together. An image thrust itself at Cathcut, eluded his control: some black, sag-bellied ape, hauling on the bars, swarming downstairs, a gibbering, gesticulating creature, its wrists dark with hair, its face contorted as if by human emotions, so that one scanned its bloodshot eyes for signs of intelligence behind the mimicked actions. It looked like some Satanic parody of God's creation, a mockery pushed at man to persuade him that he too was brute, and might scratch, slobber and rut like the beasts. No more, no more—clearly, he was in an overwrought state. Old age was reverend, old age was beautiful, he was going towards his Lord; oh hurry and grant him the spiritual body that shall outstrip the beauty of this husk. . . . Once in the hall, Dr Kemberton was senile but human; yet Cathcut would not rid himself for some while of the guilt this image invariably aroused.

The delay seemed interminable before Dr Kemberton was settled, for the Indian carpet of the drawing-room, though faded, retained much of its hairy pile and thrust up tufts like patches of coarse grass, so that he had to pick up his feet and negotiate them carefully. He reached an immense and rounded armchair, whose loose cover fell to the floor where it was bunched and pleated in a skirt-fringe.

'The woman insists on packing these chairs with w-wadding.' He threw out several cushions and lowered himself into its lap.

Cathcut brought himself to sit also, on a low, straight-backed chair, and to wait until the Doctor should indicate that he was ready. He felt that his skull confined an over-accelerated grindstone, turning over and over, whirling by its own momentum, brushing off attempts to restrain it or bring it to bear on any object, but sparking sudden images, little snatches of prepared speech. A succession of brief scenes rehearsed themselves in his mind: himself explaining his plans, his motives to his superior, laying his soul open to the quick for the inquisition and approval of this grave listener, having his emotions vetted; and again, confessing how the event which gave this saving opportunity was so terrible that he hesitated to take advantage of it, fearing lest the taint should transfer from the act to whoever made use of it, however aseptic and remedial his purpose. For he noted in himself a satisfaction at the state of affairs that presented itself, whatever the means by which it had arisen: a relief that Lepage had now moved into an area of mind of which he himself had cognizance, a pleasure that Lepage was more bearable, more approachable.

He pictured to himself the happy accord of minds to which his understanding would convert Lepage, and for a moment he dwelt with joy on the notion of Lepage kneeling at the brass altar-rail, gladly submissive to the God he had defied, flanked by unknown women whose sisters he had degraded and defiled, but with whom, though strangers, he was now in equal communion of the Spirit, as Cathcut placed the healing Blood between his lips and in the place of Christ accepted him back. And he imagined himself conducting Lepage through the fabric of the Church, stripping off before his eyes the accretions of vulgar piety that overlaid and obscured it, exposing foundations of hard, historical fact, pointing to the verified lives of the saints who buttressed it; until Lepage recognized that within the precinct there was sufficient satisfaction for all the yearnings of men, that there were no real restricting walls, that they were not repressive but a kindly barrier to ward the soul from dangers and corruptions, from all that could exist outside—beyond whose protection lay bogs exhaling a cold, isolating mist, offering only a queasy footing from which a man would sink, drowning, to die encased in mud, mouth stopped with weed, alone.

He turned to contemplating the delight that would grow like a bud between them, as each came to recognize that the bonds of doctrine were no encumbrance, but life-lines. He anticipated how, through the mazes, and in the giddy, exhausting climb towards the Godhead, he would in the darkness lead Lepage's hand to the life-line, put it to grasp on a guide-rope of rule or on the experience of the mystics. And he saw himself at last explaining to Lepage, when his sorrow was assuaged, the dangers, the grief, the dissatisfaction inherent in partial comforts which please only to cloy or decay. He would point out to him the unwisdom (as Augustine had found) of trusting in created things rather than the Creator: the needless pain of loving what must die. He would advise a wise distance between Lepage and others, to whom he would be bound by links of *caritas* rather than by eddies of affection. It was a religion infinitely demanding, harsh on the emotional and on women. But he would explain that the resultant sadness, the ache of deprivation, was a necessary preliminary before the inundation by the Lord; a preliminary to be endured unless one was to suffer a recurrent downward coil—of sadness, indulgence in vain palliatives, despair, circling down to the dead water where the soul committed sin in the hope of rising to the dignity of any feeling, good or evil. And in such an attempt, though Cathcut foresaw no active aid, Dr Kemberton was commissioned by faith to be his one sure ally.

'You seem rather distraught, Mr Cathcut.'

Immediately, Cathcut felt a steel shutter close, isolating the fire inside him. The spinning in his brain slowed. He realized at once that he was totally mistaken, that there could be no understanding, no dialogue of minds here; he must act completely alone, unsupported. But he had committed himself so far that he must tell part at least of his story.

'It is something I have just learned at the other end of town. Something very terrible has occurred.' He watched the vicar's face, but, as he feared, there was not the slightest flicker of interest.

'It must indeed be important to b-bring you out so early.' Often it was almost impossible to catch Dr Kemberton's words. 'Go on.'

'You will remember, Doctor, about a month after my licensing, you took me with you to interview a Mr Lepage, a police officer.' By no gesture or comment did his superior show that he recalled the encounter.

'The girl with whose welfare we were then concerned . . . was found dead this morning.' A pause, then a question.

'How did she die?'

'By violent hands.'

'By violent hands . . . you mean she was m-murdered . . . excuse me one moment.' Without further comment and with surprising swiftness, he was gone. Cathcut heard him shuffle the length of the hall and claw his way painfully upstairs. Then silence. From the next room came sounds as of dusting, the displacement of furniture and tableware and the drawing of curtains. He waited for some minutes, his thoughts in suspension, not caring to plan further, until the elapse of time convinced him that Dr Kemberton was in no eagerness to return or to give advice.

At this realization he felt suddenly free, conscious of himself as a deliberating agent, weighing and balancing possibilities, staking his chances on one single line of action, then judiciously nursing events as they ran their course. His faculties tautened to meet the challenge, stringing him to a pitch of nervous excitement that demanded to be released, to impart its impetus. From the main road, now thickening with traffic, a continuous rumble and the smell of oil and petrol reached him through the open window. He wondered where that smell and this emotion had coalesced before. Another gust, and it was on him without his thinking further: the gravelled area in front of the door of his home, and cars arriving for one of his parents' interminable parties; the skid of tyres as they pulled to a halt, a faint smell of scraped rubber, drowned by their exhaust-pipes pouring out white fumes into the afternoon air till the engine was switched off; then a pause until the doors burst open, disgorging guests who crowded in through the door, laughing and calling. His father, unsmiling and detached, was standing chest-high in children, organizing a game to keep them occupied whilst their respective parents were elsewhere. It was to be 'Smugglers and Customs-Officers', and an elder sister had had thrust into her hands a ball of wool. She was the umpire and the wool was the 'lives': when somebody got your 'life', you had to go to her and she would tie another one round your arm—and she kept a score. Father had made her do it, but she wanted to be in at the party. The limits were the perimeter of the grounds. His father was arranging two balanced sides, dividing up Cathcut's friends from school, his cousins, the strange children, and those boys from the village who were permitted because they were suitable. And unthinkingly, assuming that his son would be dominant, his father had made him leader of the customs men. After a shock of surprised fear, a fierce joy had swept him, with the same nervous excitement; but his side looked sullen at the imposition, resenting the apparent favouritism. He knew he ought to resign, but he would not, though he knew they did not want him. With the first flush of authority he had asked his father:

'What trade are we suppressing?'

And his father, glancing over at the visitors spilling from freshly arrived cars and standing watching him, had said:

'The white slave traffic, I should think.'

The onlookers guffawed, but Cathcut had ignored them, for a trade in white men seemed even more unnaturally evil than that in negro slaves, with which he was familiar from his reading. The smugglers scuttled into the distance, in their grey shorts and brightly striped school belts, to hide and defend their contraband; and he was already planning the disposition and manoeuvres of his side, at a pitch of nervous tension, longing for his father to give the signal to begin, for the adults to withdraw, leaving him to his unaccustomed command.

And now he felt something of the same emotion; he must launch off alone, while the tide was running his way. He would wait another five minutes and then leave an apology with the house-keeper. The car fumes became worse and, combining with his excitement, made him more than a little sick. He moved over to shut the window, wondering as he did so if he detested the smell for itself or for its associations. The cars crawling bumper to bumper were like protozoa, clogging the arteries of the town, multiplying, and poisoning the parent organism with their evil-smelling toxins. He pulled down the lower sash and shut them out.

The sound of the window being banged down brought Mrs Avling from the other room. She glanced at the sash, then at Cathcut, and, ignoring him, began rubbing polish into a heavy occasional table, whose legs were sunk into the carpet as if it grew there and the tufts had sprung up round it.

'Mrs Avling, where is the vicar?'

She assumed a pose and pointed upwards.

'*Doctor* Kemberton is above.' The slightest of emphases reproved him.

'Then would you please persuade him down from the heavens, because time is getting short.'

She continued polishing for some seconds, bending to one side to catch the shine off the wood, then painstakingly rubbing more wax along the length of the grain in those places which dissatisfied her. And he in turn practised floating over his irritation and excitement, flattening out and rebuffing the wavelets of emotion, as though he were a broad piece of mahogany wallowing in a choppy sea. In her own time Mrs Avling forsook her polish-tin and, duster in hand, made a leisurely and dignified exit. Cathcut heard the stairs creak under her weight, and her stately tread across the upper corridor. Then all was quiet. Though he strained to catch any murmur of voices he could hear none.

At last there was a sound of feet placed very cautiously on stair-treads. Someone was descending the stairs, faster and faster, in a tumbling crescendo of sound, so that Cathcut leapt up, afraid lest the vicar had fallen headlong. But the footsteps clattered along the hall and into the drawing room: without her dignity, without her blank tragic stare, Mrs Avling was a rather pitiable old woman.

'A fit! Dr Kemberton's having a fit in the chapel!'

Cathcut ran to the door, but she hung on to his arm with both hands, digging the fingers in hard and shaking with fright. Despite the thickness of his sleeve and the yellow duster which she still clutched in one hand, both sets of nails seemed to penetrate through to his forearm.

'Leave him alone! Let him be!' she shrieked.

'I must go up there,' he said, trying to shake her off, and then more gently, to prise her fingers from his arm.

'I can tell you, I can tell you,' she cried again, holding on still harder, bringing herself closer under his shelter and appealing to him, her eyes wide with childlike terror. 'He's singing, and rolling his eyes and shaking all over as if he's going to fall apart. Don't go up there. It's a fit, I tell you.'

He judged that it was serious, for she had forgotten all affectation: he had never heard from her so long a speech in natural language. She seemed to collapse under the strain, and Cathcut got free.

'Don't let him hear you, don't let him hear,' she implored.

Tenderly he pushed her into a chair and gently but firmly held her down by the shoulders. The duster had slipped to the floor; she snatched at it, jerking her shoulders out of his grasp, but sat back immediately with her hands on her lap and the duster between them, leaning backwards, neck outstretched, drawing in her breath with repeated hiccupping sounds. At first he feared that she was crying; but she brought the duster up to her lips to muffle the sound, then bit on the material to stifle it. He took this as a sign that she might become more composed, and went swiftly and softly upstairs.

Before he got to the landing he heard Dr Kemberton's voice, or such he presumed it to be. He did indeed seem to be singing, but the voice was so off-key and punctuated by convulsive shakes that it was impossible to guess either words or tune. The Scots accent which Cathcut had always noticed was now so pronounced that it hid all but the odd phrase.

'. . . *of the Lord divideth the flames of fire.*' It dawned on Cathcut that the old man was not singing but chanting—chanting a psalm. The daemonic energy with which the word 'fire' was hurled out stopped him on the point of rushing in; but he was relieved that he had to deal with mental unbalance, rather than some physical convulsion needing immediate attention. The door of the chapel was slightly open, and Dr Kemberton had not heard him coming. He looked in.

The segment of the room which he could see was ill-lit, for the blinds had not been rolled up; but on a table which served as a makeshift altar were two tapers, recently lighted, for the melted wax had not yet disturbed their regular outline. Presumably, the Doctor must have been steady enough to put a match to them. They cast a glow of yellowish light up the wall, illuminating a dark crucifix from which the head of an ivory Christ bent towards the worshipper below. Dr Kemberton was kneeling at a prie-dieu; or rather, he was supporting himself by clasping it with both hands.

His whole body was shaking as though with fever, and as he fetched breath his frame seemed to heave up, falter and subside. With the violence of his outbursts the candles smoked and guttered. For a moment he stopped singing, released his hold briefly on the prie-dieu, and turned over the pages of a prayer-book with fumbling hand. The vein in his temple whose convolutions Cathcut had noticed before seemed to contract and expand like a snake struggling to break free. He found his place and began again, chanting in a voice cracked and tremulous with age, but enforced with insane energy. It was a psalm, rendered with horrible enthusiasm.

'God is a righteous Judge, strong and patient; and God is provoked every day.

'If a man will not turn, he will whet his sword; he hath bent his bow and made it ready.

'He hath prepared for him the instruments of death; he ordaineth his arrows against the persecutors . . .'

The old, crippled body shook with sobs and the singing ceased. Again the flutter of pages, and again the chanting resumed. The enormity of what was happening struck Cathcut suddenly. Somehow it was the death that had brought the dead to life and given this joy: from cracks in some dry-earth dam that shuddered under the impact, water was bursting, boiling with rage at its long imprisonment, crushing its barriers, issuing in a tumult of unholy song. Cathcut was terrified at the violence unleashed; he could not trespass in the room, or stand face to face with a man thus unprepared. He must go back as if nothing had happened.

He returned along the corridor and went softly downstairs; but halfway down Dr Kemberton's voice again stung his ears—or rather the sense, for the sound now came to him from a distance.

'Mercy and truth are met together; righteousness and peace have kissed each other.

'Truth shall flourish out of the earth; and righteousness hath looked down from heaven.'

Anger and bitterness overwhelmed him: it was not his truth or his righteousness. All the while they had been serving different gods, and this barbarous tribal deity was attributing to him its primitive nature, enlisting him as a devotee, oblivious to the complexities of the situation, to his remedial motive, disregarding his lack of desire for blood. He hurried down the remaining stairs to escape from so intolerable an imposition.

There seemed only one way to differentiate his own motives: by carrying the news immediately to Lepage, before he could receive it at some other, less charitable hand. Cathcut surprised himself by feeling no anxiety, no inclination to try his message over in his head; the Spirit would give appropriate words when the time came. He felt oddly dispassionate about it, like a sword of God, but a sword of truth rather than vengeance, pared down to a thin, cutting edge. He could offer Mrs Avling only the austerest of comforts: the assurance that there was nothing physically wrong with her employer—his emphasis implying an uncharted spiritual depth which he was not competent to fathom. The same austerity led him to abandon his unreliable machine and walk by the most direct route to Lepage's villa, from which he had retreated three months before in such disarray.

CHAPTER FOUR

That morning, early, Lepage came to the attic room; up five flights of stairs from a grey street, blinking in the darkness. She was dead; he knew so, and tried to convince his imagination and his heavy loins. But every step crushed out images of habitual pleasure: the dust of the landings had absorbed his passion and sent back tart scents that tickled anticipation and set the muscles of his hams a-quiver.

Cathcut hung at his heels. Lepage climbed higher, grasping the coarse-grained, rounded wood of the banister-post, wood which he had always touched with mounting excitement, prolonging and enjoying the throbbing in his nerves, yet longing to drive on to a conclusion. She was dead; and yet he yielded to pleasure, consciously encouraging the images which welled up and spilled over like oil from a pit. His body felt heavy, as though each vein was clogged with fermenting honey, a glutinous, swelling tide that moved through its passages in violent spasms, then slow flowings, as each convulsion of the heart pushed out the artery walls and then relaxed. The net of intellect ceased its intolerable sifting, began to admit images the more titillating in that they lacked particularity: diaphanous silks, concealing yet revealing, rounded limbs, moulded and pendulous breasts, thighs muscular yet soft to the fingers—images not enticing in themselves, but clamouring promises of an annihilation to which they themselves were the barrier to be crushed and broken in the leap toward his peace. His lust had scooped a channel in his interior self and tumbled down it sharp-edged, hurling each pared fragment over the rim.

What did it matter that she was dead? Cathcut, the ascetic, who had waited for the news to break him in pieces to his hand, was powerless to exorcize. Hadn't he too admitted that he knew?—

and knew the pleasure of sinking below mind and fellow-feeling into that subterranean channel which mined under them, floating in that current with all creatures toward the flood which received identity into forgetfulness. Personality had no importance. The girl was but a pathway and had sunk out of sight. His energy lay within him. What if she were dead? He conceived the idea of embracing the corpse while it was yet beautiful. The image maddened him, the spasms in his veins quickened. To hold the unresisting body, to die into death, seemed more annihilating than anything he had every conceived. Half in earnest he began to plan, in imagination to persuade Cathcut and the others to leave him alone with his mistress.

Cathcut was climbing the stairs close behind. Lepage wanted to cry out to him what was in his mind, to burn his images into that ivory face, to let the blood in. He could foresee Cathcut's horror, his disgust and fear—fear of himself, and of that dark conduit which linked him to Lepage and to the mindless flood. But would he not be released? Released from the interminable Seshton which dragged at his heels; for Cathcut, though he might squirm and protest, was Seshton, and his god the simpering Jesus of altar-frontals and soft lights, Jesus of the smooth veneer, Jesus all order and light, gentle Jesus beaming bright. His dead hand denied him Cathcut. Lepage was not afraid for himself, but wanted to take that soul in his hands, to plunge it in the stream, to see the lust-light in its eyes, inhuman, pulsing and racing under his hands, driving to the madness that is peace and happiness, below Seshton to the root of the world.

It was not as it should have been. On the highest landing stood a figure in uniform, lit by a small window, who seemed unbearably tall as they climbed towards him. Seshton had extended over his private bolt-hole. He stopped at the topmost step. Cathcut pushed past and reached the landing. The door in front was shut, but from within came a mutter of activity and quick commands.

Cathcut stood on one side of him and the policeman on the other. Before him was the tribunal. Yet Cathcut could not understand that he was not a soul brought to judgement. If the other had not been there he would have told him that he was not afraid, that the death meant nothing to him. Could this pale ascetic understand that he was proud of having bought a human being to his will, of using and possessing; that to cut her out of the grasp of Seshton by corruption and defilement gave him joy, that he exulted to ride the fallen, crushing and destroying whilst remaining untouched? In his pursuit of the dancing flame he became most truly himself, devoid of the least contamination of others. He longed for purest isolation, and was savagely glad that she who had entwined her body around him like poisonous ivy was dead, defunct, rotting, whilst he remained the same. Use becomes necessity; he was free of her—free of the lingering kiss as he descended these stairs, the slobbering pull at his lips, the disgust as her tongue dribbled in at his teeth. She had fallen from him like a leprous skin; he was alone, white metal, new-minted. Only Cathcut could not understand: he was fed on watery, self-denying pleasures.

The door opened, and Lepage could see into the room. But it was not as he was accustomed to picture it. It appeared darker, filled with figures and shadows. Someone was standing by the window, blocking out the light. One of the uniformed officers addressed him by his rank. 'Inspector, Superintendent Care sends his apologies. Will you take charge of the preliminaries and report to him?' Inspector. Familiar faces danced in front of him, photographing, measuring, taking the room apart piece by piece. The whole of Seshton was looking in, and he was the 'inspector', directing them: 'Come, gentlemen, this is my private lusting-ground. Here are some of the garments and little knick-knacks I bought for her, and over here . . .' Nudges of the body and faint pressure of hands were urging him towards the bed. They were frightened children, looking for a leader. As he moved forward, others straightened up from their tasks and crowded gratefully in behind him. Lepage with a dry comment, Lepage with a business-like command, Lepage would disperse the fear of death.

'Far too many in here. . . . Stand away from the window, will you?' Too many. Too many making him their inspector, looking in. Too many in awe of death. They would not let him alone to be himself. And Cathcut stood by the door, waiting for his soul to drop. 'Will those who have finished their business here get out.' The photographers left, and a uniformed constable. Be angry, their eyes said. We prefer live anger, be angry.

Seshton had broken in on his fantasies, was urging him forward to see what it had made of his imaginings, his joys, his delights. People were all around, talking at him, demonstrating, puncturing his lust. The beauty of the world was dead, the dark flood sunk underground, while police officers kicked the dust of their boots into it.

Who had done this? Cathcut was kindly: he explained quietly that Lepage had a slight acquaintance with the family, that he would prefer to face her alone. One by one they left, and only the police doctor remained. Cathcut was kindly for his own ends, but he had got him what he wanted, solitude.

The doctor was merciless. He picked up one white, softly moulded arm, and twisted it to show where the settling blood within had stained the underside the colour of lead. Nine hours dead. He indicated where the blood had drained from the wax-white forehead to the nape of the neck and lobe of the ear as she lay on her back. The lower part of the ear was blue-black. He drew back the bed-clothes and kneaded the muscles of the thighs. No rigor mortis as yet, but underneath, the tell-tale stains. Nine to ten hours. The muscles of the face were beginning to stiffen, her body temperature was low—perhaps nearer ten than nine. The doctor left to call an undertaker.

In life she might have been provocative to him, for she was poorly clad; but she had gone past provocation. He was not afraid, but in deep awe of her. The images he had conjured up of embracing the dead body seemed childish, irrelevant. He felt no grief, no sense of loss, no joy at his release, but only a silence which spread from her, up through his body, smoothing the wrinkled brain, a silence that he wanted to continue unbroken for ever. Cathcut, over by the door, never moved. He was afraid and had nothing to say. Lepage scanned her whole body, moving his head slowly from side to side. He sat down on the chair by the bed and savoured the silence, letting it reach into every corner of him. He had lived only in his passion before; yet this awe seemed more powerful, more deeply pleasurable.

Her beauty was changing, decomposing before his eyes. The doctor had said she had been forcibly suffocated; yet her eyes which stared up, receiving everything, seeing nothing, had no hint of fear. The whites were beginning to discolour, but he was not angry. She had never been his; he had not possessed her, and now she had withdrawn silently, leaving this corpse as a wall between them and a memento of his passion. He felt only awe and silence. Her whole body was frozen, the vital blood had sunk down, and, as if there was still some connection between them, the cold immobilizing ichor which flowed in her veins ran into his own. He wanted only to be still, and to live in the stillness.

He looked at her hair as it clung in dark ringlets to her neck and spilled on to the pillow. He remembered its soft texture and the warm scent as he pressed into it, and suddenly put out a hand. It was ice-cold, oily and brittle to the touch. He recalled the strange tenderness which he had felt in spite of himself as he lay spent, her warm hair in his face.

He felt her neck, her arm, her breast, soft and cold under his touch like the skin of a toad. He could feel himself crying; not superficially with tears, but beneath his conscious mind, a shrivelled, buried being sobbing to itself. Its tears were suffocating him; there was no way out for them, he could not connect them to his will or let them flow through his eyes.

He could not be sorry for the loss of a mistress: she was but a pathway, and had sunk out of sight. It was not his will that was weeping—only the blind, mole-like creature: his body crying for what his will despised, crying because it had felt warmth pulsing in living flesh, had known the embrace of limbs, the brush of lips—crying too because the beautiful was collapsing before its eyes, hollow, a sham.

The will was prisoner of the body's act. He could not go back on what he had done. He had made his body over to another, and even in death it was exacting its price, in sorrow, in sympathy, demanding that his flesh die with her. He told himself that, as there had been before, so there would be again, other passions, other mistresses. But his physical pain insinuated the fear that, once dead, the flame moved no more; that he would never again feel the exaltation which kindled another into fire, making her body flash with light, supple, desirable. In every imaginable embrace, the clasp of the dead, on each lip a mortal slime. In his despair he sobbed audibly, breaking through the barriers of will in a paroxysm of misery and self-pity.

* * * * *

Cathcut could hold off no longer. A force sucked out his stomach, his lungs, his throat, drawing water from the soft flesh, pulling him towards Lepage. He knew that it was good in a sense that he had not known existed: a calcifying fire, purging and cauterizing the ulcerations that clustered inside him, cleansing and burning. He shook as though a white-steel brush had plunged through his body and returned from his entrails. His will abandoned itself to the bubbling flood and floated on a tide of fire, dancing and plunging itself in the stream. He had struggled in a morass of rule and order, fighting emotion every way, and now his rules and petty statutes of morality were burnt in the flood like so many scraps of paper. The pain of sympathy was a greater joy than he had ever known.

He examined his intellect as it floated above him in the top crust of his skull, and saw in that white light his moral actions mean and proud, springing from nothing that knew the force in him. His pursuit of Lepage, which he had thought so just, seemed the action of fear, of the lust to dominate. And he saw his will as a scrawny and avaricious spider, extending its clutch over the minds, bodies and thoughts of others, strangling out with bristled tentacles their selfhood. He was ashamed, and the shame was happiness and purification to him.

He laid a hand on Lepage's shoulder, trying to communicate through his flesh to the coiled spirit beneath. It was a touch of fellow-feeling that he had never before given. He felt strangely quiet and powerless. The temptation to dramatize himself, to act out his emotions, was never further from him. He was no prophet-king, but mean, stunted Cathcut. He could only wait and hope that Lepage might honour even him. The girl's eyes were still wide open: the doctor had left the office to Lepage. Cathcut leant over and pressed the lids down, round the curve of the eyeball till the lashes mingled.

When he turned again to Lepage, he saw that his eyes were shut fast. Cathcut began talking smoothly and swiftly, paying little attention to words, but by the tone of his voice preventing Lepage slipping away from him. Lepage's face was alien and expressionless as the dead girl's, but his eye-balls pulsed under their membrane, the raw lids threaded with blue. Cathcut fought off his fear and continued talking, grappling him with words and feelings as he would a plunging whale. He could feel the weight of Lepage's mind, burrowing down into solitary darkness. Out of his self-discovery he offered pity and companionship; he felt words to be inadequate to carry the weight of feeling. He wanted to sing, some wild formless melody that might come pure from emotion without the refraction of logic. The tune rose inside him, forcing him to utter it.

Lepage drew back his lips, uncovering his teeth. His eyes remained shut, but his tongue flickered over his gums. Cathcut began talking once more, wildly and urgently, until Lepage's voice cut across him, hard and solitary, rising from great depths.

'Let me go, Cathcut; free me of your concern. Let me be alone.'

'Brother, forgive; forgive us all.' The words came naturally, without his thinking. For a moment there was no movement, as if a spring gathered energy. Then Lepage's body stiffened in his chair and jumped as if filled suddenly with scalding metal. He cried out once, like an epileptic. The rigid shoulder-muscle stood out under Cathcut's hand; but he could see water seeping from under the closed lids. Lepage was crying; Lepage had broken.

Cathcut stood by, feeling humble yet elated. Emotions of the kind he had just experienced were new to him; he savoured the pity he felt as he watched this lonely, abject figure, and delighted in a sense of fellow-feeling. It was delightful to abase oneself, to realize one's kinship, to be free from judging. He felt a desire to place his hand on the elder man's head and say 'My child'; yet it would not be he who was speaking but a greater power using and possessing him. So this was the power of the priest, making him at once paternal and child-like.

He found his emotion ebbing, and his dislike and fear of Lepage returning; he let his hand drop, but made a conscious effort and thought again of the miseries of Lepage's condition. The emotion flowed again, but not as strongly or as unalloyed. He tried to remember his reasons for thinking his pursuit of Lepage to be wrong, but could feel only satisfaction at the progress of events. He felt once again that he was the preserver and director of men's souls. The victory was won; and yet he felt dissatisfied and at a distance from what he had been a minute before.

There was a movement beside him, and he realized that Lepage was rising from his chair. This was undesirable; he moved to prevent it, and met Lepage's eyes, red-rimmed, wild and obdurate. Turning from Cathcut, Lepage half-knelt upon the body and began tearing at it with his hands. His nails left long lacerations on the flesh. He fumbled and tore at the hair, missing his clutch at intervals because of the spasms which shook him. From his tight-shut lips came little, sharp cries, like an injured animal. Cathcut seized his wrists from behind and exerted all his strength against him. He could hear Lepage's jaws moving at his ear and felt the gasps of his breath. His disgust at the mutilation reinforced his strength; he tightened his grip until Lepage's hands became purple, and the nails purple and white. The pain distracted Lepage, forcing his spasms to subside, and he allowed himself to be hauled back into the chair. The crisis was over in a minute. There had been no time to call for assistance and Cathcut was glad he had not done so. He felt for a handkerchief and began to wipe saliva from the corners of Lepage's mouth.

Lepage sat, and after some minutes became calmer. He regained his breath and began talking, inaudibly, holding a savage dialogue with himself. Cathcut told him to stay quiet; instead, he spoke to him. The voice was hard and factual, but his body was strung rigid.

'I wish there had been some wax to seal my eyes and every other vent and cut me off from sense and sound. But since you compel me back, it is right that you should know to what you call me.' He paused, drew breath. 'I find nothing in life that is worth the living. As for this corpse, I ask only for a knife to open it from the womb to the breasts for the pain caused to my body and the cheat put upon me. She has died out of my knowing; and for the beauty that died with her I could tear this drab city brick from brick. I have one remaining desire: to hunt down the author of this; and when I have found him, to visit upon him every subtle and diabolic torture that ingenuity can devise.'

CHAPTER FIVE

Words and feelings; for next morning Dr Kemberton received a telegram. And for these Mrs Avling was searching in the retreats of her kitchen, thumbing through worn folios, looking for definition. He had shut her out. Fourteen years she had cooked, swept, beaten and cleaned, and the study door was shut fast, because she had failed in words. There were none suitable in all the life she could remember; nothing sprang to lips like knife to hand. Plays contained words, fine feelings, but the word was a point in the scene and the feeling geared to the action, so that the words alone seemed deflated balloons, sheep's lights. She had hit Dr Kemberton with a sheep's light, spongy, inflated. He had rammed the door in her face.

There was no one in Seshton to whom she could go for help. One might not discuss such intimate matters with neighbours. But it was hard to live with a shut door, not able even to clean the room. Where was the word that would charm open locks, interior and exterior? You might lay a hand on his shoulder, but how was it to be done? How make the right gesture, the sympathetic pressure, the chosen moment? In literature word and gesture lived at the level of emotion; in life they fell far short. Without words, and the thoughts to give them body and pith, feeling could not begin to run; it remained an untapped capacity when her employer had need. The word was communication, but also definition and discovery.

With the allowed liberty of servants when their masters become senile, she had opened his telegram. It was from his wife, the first for seventeen years: *'Charles dead last month. Will you give me a home?'* And Mrs Avling, whose feelings took origin from the printed word, sensed the insensitivity, the criminal want of sympathy in the choice of that final noun. She had handed the telegram to Dr Kemberton in dread, afraid lest he might once again throw a fit, and she should not know how to cope. The vein on his forehead whipped like a compressed snake, pulsing blue. She had said something dramatic and foolish, something which she could not now remember, although the embarrassment of it made her blush red. It was always that way with words; literature was analogous, running parallel, needing remoulding by experience before its words could express one's emotion. He had shut the door in her face.

She did not consider that, if Mrs Kemberton returned to her husband, Mrs Avling might be superfluous. She had lived there too long for the thought to enter her head. She was concerned only that Dr Kemberton should not falsify his image. The venerable patriarch, the father of his people, heavy with learning as with years, must not fall into an analogy, run beside his first self, or branch off into tracks that led him from the line of the prophets to regions of lesser men. Dr Kemberton was literature; a refusal to forgive would be more terrible than the betrayal of words.

A word from her, of sympathy and understanding, and he might now be on his way to week-day Communion, secure in the knowledge that he had forgiven, fit to dispense the rite of absolution. She had failed in her duty.

The verger had arrived, for a bell began ringing for the eleven o'clock service. Dr Kemberton had been locked in his room for two hours. Surely he must now come out? She had never known him unpunctual in performing his duties. Before she was prepared, or had ready speech or action, he was on the stairs: the slow, deliberate tread, punctuated by suspenseful pauses as he teetered from one step to another. His cane clattered against the banister rail. He was taking his stick; he had been drinking. She dreaded the inadequacy of the man to the situation.

She pulled on an old coat, but dithered for some seconds about whether to go out into the street in carpet slippers. By the time her mind was made up, Dr Kemberton was half-way between the Rectory and the church vestry, and passing the railings on the west side. She thought she might overtake him before he turned in at the north gate. Two small boys, aged about nine and ten, came towards her, wrestling one another over the pavement, and blocked him from her sight for a moment. They glanced back over their shoulders occasionally as they fought, to see if they had attracted the Doctor's attention.

'Know what my dad says about old Kemberton?'

'No,' breathlessly.

'Give him a jog with your elbow, and he'd dig his teeth in the mud.'

They collapsed laughing, bending over and pressing their hands into their stomachs. The elder boy straightened up, saw Mrs Avling, and looked suddenly furtive. Then, realizing he had been overheard, he smiled knowingly, as if hoping that she would share the joke. She felt she ought to resent it, but only stared blankly back. 'Old loony,' they called to her, and ran off.

The carpet slippers were an encumbrance, but she overtook the Doctor before he reached the gate. He was walking fast, his head hunched into the wrinkles of his neck, staring intently at the pathway and concentrating on swinging his rubber-stopped cane round in time to arrest his forward movement. With the exercise he was breathing noisily, short snatches of air. She called gently 'Dr Kemberton'; but the voice was so unlike her usual theatrical tones that he failed to recognize it and continued walking. She came almost abreast, spoke more loudly and pulled at the sleeve of his cassock. This threat to his balance attracted his attention. He must have known already that she was there, for he answered thickly, without stopping or turning round.

'Woman, go away.'

He carried a fog of spirit-vapour along with him, but had drowned his speech-impediment. Tears came into her eyes, and she was terrified lest the Doctor should see them. His drinking had never worried her, but after his recent outburst it began to make her afraid. It was some seconds before she could trust herself to speak again, and then it was without preparation.

'Doctor, the answer is pre-paid. What am I to say?'

'Most answers are pre-paid, Mrs Avling.'

She sensed a double meaning which she could not grasp. He had reached the gate, and rested against its green-painted post, the rust-flakes from the metal rubbing off on his cassock. The churchyard was pebbled, interspersed with a few weeds which pushed up among the stones. The two now stood facing one another, though the Doctor seemed to find it easier to breathe with his chins sunk into his chest. She could see only the top of his head with its central strand of hair, his head which rose and fell with the movement of his lungs and hunched shoulders. The alcohol made him more than ordinarily distant; that, presumably, was what he wanted. She was not poetic in her own right, or the contrast between the tower and the fuddled wreck in its shadow would have moved her; but it came to her that there was a drama whose language she had not employed. The ritual of the Church, its intoned dogma and solemn cadences: there was a sound which must penetrate to him and awake him to his right nature. The priest leant with his back against the gate-post, the folds of his chin enveloping the button of his cassock, his breath still whistling up the passage from the lungs. Something in her wanted to spare him, but she crushed it promptly, for she had again found a voice. She would be tender, but she must be stern. With at first a hesitant confidence, then an onrush of enthusiasm, she felt her old manner come upon her, with a touch of theatrical *élan*.

'The sinner must be forgiven and welcomed back. You cannot ignore God, even if you ignore me.'

She was impressed by the dignity of it. There was no response for some seconds, and then the Doctor seemed to lift himself out of his torpor by a pull of his shoulders. His head came up, and the unprotected skull leant back against the flaking metal. The effects of his drinking were plain: behind thick rims his eye-sockets were raw and rheumy, the curve of his lenses magnifying the sore flesh. He put up a hand suddenly and she flinched, but he merely laid the palm on her bony shoulder and levered himself more erect. Perhaps the spirits had warmed him; his speech was slurred but soft.

'Old lady, it's not like that—at all.'

There was no way in; shame and mortification overcame her. The tears began to flow freely. He must see them, they were running down her cheek.

'But Christ commands us to forgive,' she cried desperately.

'She is what she has been.'

'What am I to say?' The water ran into her mouth, she felt it salt.

'To come into time, to forgive without taint of what time produces, to be pure as man never was . . .'

'But what am I to tell her?'

He stopped suddenly, and looked at her as if just made conscious of her presence. He ran his tongue over the thin blue lips, over the growth of his lower lip. Beneath the deliberate speech, increasing pain and desperate certainty.

'I ache within. I cannot forgive.' The alcohol seemed overwhelmed by deeper feeling, like oil on a tidal swell. Water was gathering in the corner of his red eye. She felt oddly glad and pitying.

'Tell me, tell me, dear Doctor, whatever am I to write?'

He walked on for some three yards, and she shuffled after. Unable to carry it further, he stopped again.

'We have both of us . . . lived too long with this. The deed is bound up in every fibre of me—woven into the thread of the world. The blemish cannot be picked out: it is part of the stuff . . . of which we are now made.'

He said no more, but walked towards the door in the bell tower leading to the vestry. She followed him like an awed animal, and could see that, although she didn't understand, his hand was trembling as he pushed up the latch. When the door was half-open, he turned, drew breath for a while, harshly, then spoke again, spacing his words between breaths.

'I forbid you . . . ever . . . to hold communication with that woman.'

He went in, hanging his stick on a hook in the wall, and closed the door behind him. Mrs Avling stood for a moment making herself presentable, and, pushing her handkerchief into her coat pocket, began to walk back to the Rectory.

CHAPTER
SIX

From the darkness of the nave came voices, which subsided as each became aware of a slithering of feet over the carpet of the chancel. In what little light penetrated from the east window past an overhanging altar canopy, it was possible to see a figure standing before where the cross must be. The window itself had once been coloured; but encrustations of soot on the exterior had so advanced from the leads of the design over the intervening glass that only occasionally did a crack in the centre of a panel flash the original red or blue. With a swish of sleeves against drapery the sacristan reached up and to the right, extending a long metal rod. He pointed it, steadied; and from the end puffed a single blue flame, which flared for a second and died away. Again the flame, and this time within its circle the end of a white candle, about the circumference of a man's wrist.

The congregation waited as the rod manoeuvred in the darkness. A third time the flame billowed out, and at last the wick caught. The blue had within it a core of white, which flickered as the blue failed, then steadied, staggered again and climbed: over the wick a dark arch, but above it a cone of light, reaching to the transparent point. All were absorbed in the fascination of flame: not the rumbustious fire of a domestic grate, crackling, spitting, racked by minor avalanches of red coal, but totally silent and motionless, except when infrequently it leant away before a sudden draught.

The sacristan turned his attention to a second tall candle, based in a highly-wrought stand to the left of the altar. With less difficulty this candle was ignited, and its light reached into the dark shadows behind the Service Book as it lay propped on its cushion upon the altar. Paten and chalice lost the sharp outline of their ornament, and became shapes of brilliant silver. A trickle of wax spilled from the pool beneath the flame of the last-lit candle and tumbled down its smooth shaft, only to freeze and solidify before reaching the base. The sacristan made a minor adjustment to the footing of the stand, straightened and moved silently to face the cross once more: a fair-haired youth, his white vestment like a high-collared bathrobe, drawn with a cord at the waist. As he inclined his head, the top of his neck showed raw and chafed. The ignitor, a slender length of chromium, in his hand, he shuffled down the altar steps and disappeared behind empty choir stalls.

The women snuffed the smell of molten wax as it reached them in the first two pews of the nave, leant down to adjust their kneeling-pads, or wondered up at vast roof-beams which the yellowish light revealed, ribs and timbers of a wooden man-o'-war inverted over them. Through a thickness of stone, a door banged back on its hinges and was pushed more softly to.

A ring of twisted iron on the door leading from the porch looped violently upon itself and rebounded from the oak. In response, the women in the second pew edged along, nudged those whose attention was wandering, and persuaded them to shift up to make room for the newcomer. But he, ignoring their invitation, stepped swiftly over the flagstones of the cross-aisle, and, after hesitating a moment, took a standing position behind the ranks of pews, up against a main pillar of the nave. From this vantage-point he peered into the darkness, first into that surrounding the circle of light cast from the altar, and then into the side aisles, evidently searching for some object. By this time his behaviour had attracted attention, and several of the women were turning their heads to snatch quick glances at him by the light from the porch door, which he had left open behind him. He was tall and thin, decently dressed in a dark suit, with a thick edge of shirt-cuff showing; but his face was half in shadow. Conscious that he was being looked at, he reached out with one finger extended, pulled back a prayer-book from a row of maroon and black books stacked along a ledge behind the last pew, picked it up, and holding it chin-high began to turn over the pages.

There was a muttered conversation; then a middle-aged woman gathered herself, rose and came clicking up the aisle towards him. While still ten yards away she smiled, holding the expression as her eyes travelled over his person: dark hair and heavy eyebrows, high cheek-bones with the resultant hollow eyes, lips that looked moist and very red, though probably enhanced by the pallor of his skin. She glanced at his perfectly kept hands and saw that they were white and fine, but the wrists sufficiently well-haired.

'If you would like to come down to the front, I'm sure that you would be able to hear and see everything much better.'

He looked at her over the book: unpleasantly enlarged eyes, their lids drooping at the outer corners, which made him look fatigued and somewhat hostile.

'Thank you. I am quite happy where I am.'

Her smile faded. The intruder began thumbing through the book again.

'You can't stand there all the time, you know.'

He looked up at her again and said wearily, 'If I am tired, I shall sit.'

Her friends in the front pews had turned to watch, wondering what kept her. She spoke a tone higher.

'Now it's perfectly clear from the board outside that the church is closed to sightseers during services. . . . We're just going to have Communion.'

'I am not a sightseer.'

She moderated her tone at once:

'Oh, I beg your pardon—then please come and sit with us. We don't generally have gentlemen at this celebration, the vicar provides it for the Women's Fellowship; but I'm sure you're very welcome.' A thought struck her. 'Or, if you prefer, there's plenty of other pews; but near the front, so we make a nice compact little group.' She smiled again and made as if to lead him off. But he stood his ground, frowning slightly at the altar frontal which had caught his eye, a deep purple on which was worked in silver thread the letters IHS in an intricate design.

'I shall have to tell the vicar you are here.'

'That would be most kind.'

'Are you going, or are you staying?'

He looked at her with some surprise.

'I shall stay.'

'Very well, then.' She walked swiftly across the stone floor to the door which he had left open, shut it, and pushed its mat closer to exclude the draught. Then, ignoring him, she marched back by a side aisle, bobbed to the high altar as she crossed the centre, and resumed her seat without speaking to her neighbours. Apparently unaware that he had caused any irritation, the visitor replaced the prayer-book and began examining the fabric of the building and its furnishings, which were slowly becoming clearer to him. When he noticed the disturbed faces turned back at him from time to time, he met them and their surroundings with an expression of austere distaste.

After some minutes, Dr Kemberton, swathed in voluminous white vestments, emerged from the shadows to the left of the pulpit and stumbled up the chancel steps towards the altar. The clergyman was wearing his favourite stole, one given to him by sympathetic pupils on his withdrawal from college seventeen years previous, and now so frayed that he normally reserved it for special feasts. As he took his position at the altar the congregation sank to its knees; those who had been staring back, embarrassed at being caught napping, hurriedly followed suit. Only the visitor remained standing; from his expression as he overlooked their bowed heads, it was clear that he thought they kneeled to the vested figure.

He could not know what help Dr Kemberton derived from his robes: in putting them on, he set aside his merely private emotions, taking upon himself the impersonal garment of the priest. The robing was a habitual prelude to a rite he had always celebrated, which the Church had dispensed in good times and bad for close on two thousand years, and this gave him strength to get through the prayers. The tradition must be carried on; and his consciousness of the weight he assumed supported him even for those physical actions which the service demanded.

He muttered his way through the Lord's Prayer, the Collect for Purity, the collects for the Queen and for the day, all of them in the same even monotone. His prayers were almost inaudible at the back of the church, but the visitor made no effort to catch their words, having already decided his attitude to the service. He withdrew into himself, and his face took on an expression of cold immobility, almost of torpor. The sacristan read the Epistle, but during the Gospel there was an awkward hiatus as the vicar lost his place and was forced to return to the beginning of a sentence. He stammered through the remaining phrases, to the distress of his congregation; but the stranger, though he registered what had happened, seemed unaffected, and when the women jumped up with evident relief to sing the Creed he returned into his self-absorption.

The vicar's singing voice was surer than his speaking; by the time it was necessary to come down from the altar to the steps of the chancel, he had regained control enough to read the notices without difficulty. The visitor lifted his head and stared at the priest with extreme concentration, as if lip-reading his trembling mouth. But though he gathered every particle of meaning, he seemed not to hear what he wanted; when Dr Kemberton had finished, and began fumbling for a further sheet among the pages of his book, the intruder stood irresolutely, on the point of leaving, and yet apparently unable to bring himself to do so.

The clergyman pulled a rough piece of paper from the back of the volume, placed it on the cover, and anchoring it with his thumb spoke to his congregation in almost his normal voice:

'Owing to a distressing . . . personal incident . . . I have been somewhat hampered in my preparation of a sermon. I have, however, been able to scribble a short b-bidding. In the place of a sermon, therefore, we shall sing the "Dies Irae", which you will find on the duplicated sheets in your pews; and afterwards I shall read from one of the Exhortations to be found on page two hundred and forty-six in the red prayer-books.' The women reached forward for some grubby pieces of card on the ledges in front of them, and one or two sighed and looked at their neighbours. The hymn was not a favourite, but had been written by a pupil of the vicar's; Dr Kemberton had admired it at the time, and, finding it amongst his notes, had introduced it to St Botolph's during the first Lent after his arrival. The plainsong melody for which the words were intended was played through on the organ manual, and, as the organist paused for Dr Kemberton to give his bidding, the congregation once again got to its feet. He waited till they were steady; then, holding his torn paper in one hand, he began to read from it, loudly and emphatically.

'Since this is the season of penitence and prayer, before the coming of our Lord . . . let us meditate upon that end. Let us think on things past, lodged now in the lying and fragmentary recollections of men; but wholly present to him for whom the past is as the future, and both as noonday. Let us look on them in the light that shall break upon them, in that great and terrible hour when things done shall be resurrected and known.'

His unexpected vigour took his congregation by surprise. As for the intruder, since Dr Kemberton spoke over the heads of his hearers, it seemed as if sense as well as sound were levelled directly at him. For a moment he wilted like a scolded child; then, recollecting himself, he faced to the vicar an expression of extreme obduracy. But control was achieved at a price: the tension in his facial muscles had so hollowed his cheeks that from the front he resembled less a child than a death's head with painted lips. That appearance was itself not long maintained; for when Dr Kemberton turned towards the altar and began chanting the first line of the hymn, the visitor's eyes took light, and he received its words with a pleasure that seemed to overwhelm any previous emotion.

The vicar's earlier drinking had improved his voice: it was tolerably in tune, deep, and the syllables clearly enunciated:

> 'Day of wrath, O day of judgement,
> All this earth to ashes rending,
> And the Judge of all descending.'

The women answered, with a sound at first thin and shrill, but gaining volume as each picked up confidence from her neighbour:

> 'Christ, the creature of our spurning,
> Christ, the author of our yearning,
> On our heads thy blood is burning.'

Dr Kemberton intoned again, the women responding antiphonally:

> 'Unexpected summons breaking!
> Christ, thou Child of our forsaking,
> Help our terrified awakening!'

> '—Taken in the act of nailing,
> By our hand the scourges flailing,
> All repentance unavailing.'

Again, the single, querulous voice:

> 'Who for us then intercedeth?
> Who for startled sinners pleadeth,
> When the Judge of all men bleedeth?'

But by this point the old man's energy was beginning to flag; his dwindling enthusiasm seemed to communicate itself to the visitor, who lapsed back into his previous torpor. In the final unison verse, organ and women's voices drowned out the vicar altogether:

> 'Lord, the lightning splits before thee;
> Christ, in anguish we implore thee,
> Crucified, spare those that tore thee.'

The hymn concluded, Dr Kemberton went to his stall, and from there mumbled the Exhortation. Towards the close, he turned, holding his prayer-book in front of him, and addressed the congregation more particularly:

'... *And because it is requisite, that no man should come to the Holy Communion, but with a full trust in God's mercy, and with a quiet conscience; therefore if there be any of you, who by this means cannot quiet his own conscience herein, but requireth further comfort or counsel, let him come to me, and open his grief; that by the ministry of God's holy word he may receive the benefit of absolution, together with ghostly counsel and advice, to the quieting of his conscience and avoiding of all scruple and doubtfulness.'*

He looked across the page to read from a strip of paper gummed in opposite, whose words had been composed by him some years ago to harmonize with the style of the Prayer Book:

'Nevertheless, since this exhortation . . . should in no way be held to detract from the validity and efficacy of p-public confession and absolution, I shall be available to hear private confessions *after* this service; and also after the services of Holy Communion at eight and twelve-fifteen on Sunday next.'

The women shifted uneasily at this suggestion; but it was clearly what the visitor had come to hear. A sudden flash of excitement brought two circles of colour to his cheekbones; as quickly, he was taken by a persistent trembling, so that he had to clatter across the stones the length of a pew and sit at the end of it to regain control over his muscles. The noise brought several heads round to look at him; and, reminded of his presence, they glanced back at intervals during the rest of the service to check on what he was doing. But he kept his head down, concentrating on keeping his limbs steady. The cold where he was sitting did not help his tremors to subside. He looked up once only, when Dr Kemberton raised paten and chalice in trembling hands, and, extending them to the congregation, proclaimed:

'The things of God . . . for the people of God.'

One after another, the women tiptoed to the altar rail, made their communion, and, on returning to their pews, bobbed toward the silver crucifix on the high altar, their heads uplifted toward it, with a peculiarly rapt expression. Nauseated, the visitor bent his head again, until the muttering ceased and there was a general exodus, those who passed him going by without comment.

Once the women were out, he unfolded and looked about him with renewed direction. Both candles had been capped and snuffed out; but by now the sun was pushing more light through the nave windows, coaxing glints of life amidst the decaying fabric from several brass memorial plaques. A whole sheet of metal let into the stone of the left-hand aisle led the visitor to discover beyond it a confessional box, snug against the wall and flanking a secondary altar. He went over to it, coldly overlooking its points.

Its design was in wood: catholic, with latitudinarian features. For the priest, there was a pygmy church porch about eight feet high, with a pointed arch topped by a Maltese cross. Its roof planks had been overlapped like slates, clinker fashion; and the Victorian cabinet-maker had foiled the arch, adding fleurs-de-lis at each cusp. Only his door smacked of the work-a-day: cut into three, its lower half on the lines of a stable or serving-hatch, and the upper divided again vertically, with a gap for peeking over the top, looking irresistibly like the swing doors on some Western saloon.

Tacked on to this hybrid but assertively ecclesiastic structure was a plain square box, roofed, and with its door space closed by a purple curtain. The contrast, and any distinction it implied, seemed rather to distress the stranger than to move any connoisseur's amusement. But barely giving himself time to register incongruities, he pushed back the curtain as far as its rod would allow, and left it bunched so as to let in as much light as possible. The interior was ampler than usual, and, in an attempt to deviate significantly from popish practice, a grille that communicated with the priest had been made larger, to allow of more man-to-man contact. As a further accommodation, there was a narrow seat along the wall, for any who had trouble in kneeling.

On the threshold the visitor hesitated, and seemed overwhelmed by a sense of futility in what he was trying to do. Several times within a few seconds, his expression veered between heavy depression and the stalest self-disgust. At length, he stepped inside to reach limply to the faldstool for a hornbook on which a card had been pasted, and the arrival of Dr Kemberton decided the issue for him: a swish of vestments, the stable door banging to, a heavy body slumped on to a bench, and then the sound of breath sucked through a skein of mucus. With sudden resolution, the visitor applied himself to the card he was holding.

> *I confess to God Almighty before the whole company of Heaven, and you, Father, that I have sinned in thought, word and deed through my fault. Especially have I sinned*

in these ways: . . . For these, and all my other sins which I cannot now remember I am truly sorry, firmly mean to do better, humbly ask pardon of God; and of you, Father, penance, advice, absolution.

The text had once been covered with plastic in imitation of an old horn sheet, but this had cracked and left only an edging of discoloured celluloid. As he read, the visitor pulled some remnants from under their retaining tacks; they shattered, and covered his hand with brown particles. Underneath was printed 'Mowbrays of Norwich'. The publisher's artist had tried to produce an illusion of illumination by interweaving red carnations and leaves of rue around each capital letter; but his greens were sapless, the blood-colour pale and lymphatic. But the visitor was offended in more than his aesthetic sense, for with a hasty movement he lifted the card to his eyes, slipped one hand round to support its back, and with a nail of the other scored a light indentation through the word 'Father' where it first occurred. There were several tiny tears of colour away from the white, but his obliteration was hardly detectable. With a surge of disgust, he tossed the hornbook back on to its faldstool. It failed to catch on the retaining lip, slipped over, and hit the flags with a clatter.

A purple curtain lining the grille on the priest's side was snatched back, and Dr Kemberton, like Punch in a booth, peered anxiously into that corner which the window cut from his view. The faldstool was empty, and the crossed ankles under the priest's nose suggested no very promising posture of penitence. Suspecting some mocking intrusion, he asked querulously:

'What is your name?'

The ankles withdrew from his field of vision. Dr Kemberton felt his question to have been improper, and modified it.

'—Your name in Christ, my child.'

There was no reply, perhaps because the visitor rejected any assumption of paternity.

'You wish to remain anonymous? Indeed, it is proper that you should.'

Again, a silence, whilst the visitor gathered himself.

'In the congregation of saints . . . you might call me Tribulation.'

There was no mockery, Dr Kemberton was prepared to vouch for it. But the priest was irritated by what he took to be a note of maudlin self-pity.

'I trust I shall have the opportunity,' he said. But his irony seemed not so much disregarded as unnoticed.

'Are the rites of the confessional sealed, as they are in the Roman Church?'

'As I observe them, they are.'

'What surety have I?'

'When I put on this stole'—Dr Kemberton gestured behind his lattice toward the purple silk at his neck—'from the moment of p-putting on to the moment of taking off, my lips are bound, and I may not speak to you again of the matter unless you first require me to do so.'

'And is this sealed by oath?'

'It is held to be assumed under the general vows of a priest.'

The visitor digested Dr Kemberton's customary reassurance for some seconds, then leant forward from the narrow bench on which he was sitting, keeping his cheek close to the partition.

'Then tell me, priest of Levi . . . what do you think of the sins of lust?'

Dr Kemberton tipped back his head and widened his grey eyes behind the spectacles, attempting to get his visitor into focus. He tried to recall which sect linked the established Church with the Levitic priesthood. *'Priest after the order of Melchizedek':* the basic contrast would come from Hebrews.

'They are very fashionable,' he said, after a suitable pause. 'Is it sins of lust you wish to confess, my child?'

The voice beyond the grille took on a hint on that high, manic resonance which Dr Kemberton associated unavoidably with certain Low Church preachers.

'Are you a vessel whole and acceptable for the word of grace?'

For a moment the priest was nonplussed, but then fell back on a half-forgotten ploy, assuming an air of self-consideration, and concertinaing his neck into his right shoulder.

'My hearing is at times—inadequate.'

He had gauged it accurately: the penitent was dislocated from his mood.

'You're a *fool,*' he exclaimed, half-rising to his feet with anger.

Dr Kemberton drew breath and settled back in his chair.

'"*He that calls his brother* Raca, *a fool, shall be in danger of hell-fire*"; and the place is *most* unsuitable.'

'It is also written *"You shall call no man 'Father'"*.'

Dr Kemberton decided to let be.

'Since I am here,' he said, 'I shall sit until I feel able to go back to the Rectory. If you have anything you want to say to me, I commonly take some minutes to recover my legs."

'But how can I know you are a fit recipient?'

'I am m-merely intermediary.'

The visitor dropped into a tone that coaxed, but with underlying urgency.

'Then tell me what you think of the lusts of the body.'

On the further side of the lattice, Dr Kemberton's profile sank into the shoulders of his surplice like a subsiding snowman. He reflected for some seconds, then, with a cough of irritation, said sullenly from amidst the white pleating:

'They have had their effect . . . on my most intimate family.'

But what was intended to warn off the intruder was received by him as a revelation that altered the whole nature of the interview. A touch of inspirational afflatus returned to his voice.

'Their power is not limited'—he moderated his tone to something more companionable—'but nor is it irremediable, whilst we remain in the flesh.'

The priest pulled down sufficient of his surplice from his shoulders to protect the exposed underside of his wrists, then asked drily:

'And what is your pr-prescription?'

'My prescription . . .'—he hesitated, but took up the word to lay some special emphasis on it—'my *prescription* is already taken. I ask only for endorsement.'

'So long as the regimen is rational and efficacious, I am agreeable.'

The penitent considered for some seconds, concluding softly:

'On those criteria, my mind is easy.'

'Then you have nothing to fear.'

But despite such prompting, and the unoccupied silence with which Dr Kemberton followed it, his visitor seemed to have difficulty in coming to the point. The priest became absorbed in an encroachment of icy cold from the flagstones, rising till it invaded the veins below his kneecaps. What felt like a heavy lorry, with a high-pitched sawing sound and a spurt of pulverized tarmac, ground away from the filling-station next door and trundled down Seshton Hill; while the flags were still vibrating, a clock in the west tower, as if jolted into action, jiggled its rods, whirred, and struck the quarter. Afraid of the silence building up again, the visitor launched in on his confession; yet his voice was surprisingly calm, even gentle.

'I have a friend—a friend of special value and importance—who has been seduced. After a long struggle, I pray that I find it possible to forgive . . .'

The priest broke in, with some agitation:

'Then you are *beyond* any help I can offer.'

The visitor checked, then whispered anxiously:

'Brother, I must ask you again if you are a taper *trimmed* for the approaching light.'

'If it is vouchsafed, I trust I shall recognize it.'

Once again, the visitor seemed impervious to any irony. Satisfied, he resumed.

'Then you must know that, with one's lover, love is a catalyst to forgiveness. —But as for the other, the prostitute, my instinct is to loathe and destroy.'

Dr Kemberton uncoiled, and with sudden sarcasm directed his words through the grille.

'"Prostitute" I generally reserve for the female of the species. If you mean "*gigolo*", my experience is that the concept is largely m-masculine fantasy. Where not simply a wishful attribution to the female of the purely appetitive . . .'—he tripped over the syllables and mastered them at the second attempt—'*a*ppetitive aspects of male desire, it survives as the last delusion of injured husbands. What evidence have you that their connection was merely . . . commercial?'

His inability to comprehend sparked a renewed impatience in the visitor.

'I *mean* a prostitute—if you need the word of scripture, a *whore*.'

The priest was conscious of a marked release of tension; he had been wholly under a misapprehension.

'Then you are . . . homosexual,' he said laconically.

It was as if he had struck into some underground hot-spring: his visitor leapt to his feet and threshed about the narrow confine of his cell, erupting in a great torrent and volume of words. Fearful lest his ears and brain had become too slow to latch on to what might be said, Dr Kemberton shouted above the gabble:

'Remember where you are! This is a place of p-prayer'—the spate slowed—'. . . of silence . . . calm . . . without calm, nothing can be done.'

'. . . It's like bacteria in culture—like blight on a jelly,' his visitor was saying, still waving his arms agitatedly and turning to and fro, but speaking slowly enough now for the priest to catch his words. He seemed to have lost his prophetic resonance. 'It extends over everything. Every choice, every preference, buy what you like—*sex*, they tell us, is the underlying bed-rock. Some of this I can tolerate: music, art—perhaps they *are* born in the glands—I'm not their protector. But you *are*: priests of the Established Church, you use these things, you've a professional interest, they work people up to your salvation. But you've said "maybe", "perhaps", when you ought to have shouted "false!", "untrue!".'

He paused, both to get breath and to allow an opportunity for excuses.

'We have shouted, often enough.'

'Oh yes, on piffling details—in defence of the parson's freehold, no doubt. But the major issues you have let go by.'

Dr Kemberton sighed, acknowledging a certain justice in the charge:

'You must remember that not many of us were intellectuals. We were bewildered and afraid: we lacked the competence to refute. It was one doctrine among many,' he said apologetically, 'even if it became dominant. We shouted with those who had possession of the ball.'

'You m-mumbled with those who gave dominion to the *balls*.'

Dr Kemberton was past being hurt by mimicry; but he was too stunned by the vulgarity to find words. The visitor continued, with the same nervous energy:

'I'm not impervious: my back winces at the ballet-poses struck behind me, the sniggers at a chance remark, the leer in my face that dares me to take it up—because it is now made impossible to believe in a friendship between men that isn't the wish to gratify an itch upon his body. I *detest* that feeling, I keep it out. One may love a man, for his beauty even, but for his innocence especially, and because he allows no entrance to corruption. — Can you, with the witness of your saints before you, believe that it is impossible to love without that word?'

'I do not say it is impossible; only there are few saints.'

The visitor lowered his voice.

'And yet our Lord himself stooped to honour that friendship by loving his disciple John.'

The priest sighed again and spoke with reluctance.

'Our Lord is, at all points, a difficult, a *dangerous* example to follow.' He added, to make amends for his previous carelessness: 'The word itself, an amalgam—a *conjoining*—of Greek and of Latin, is p-purely descriptive. It implies nothing about actions.'

The visitor answered with sick distaste:

'Even the *word* is unnatural coupling.'

Dr Kemberton made an extended effort to bring all his faculties to bear, and then asked with greater emphasis:

'If your love does *not* partake of this corruption . . . what in his desire offends you?'

The acuity of his question gave the penitent hope at last of an understanding listener. He calmed down somewhat and brought his face closer to the grille.

'I cannot bear that he should be part of a general, a *radical* vice. The apostle Paul, in the first chapter of Romans, writes of *"the invisible things of God, clearly seen, being perceived through the things that are made, even his everlasting power and divinity."'* The final flourish was recited with joyous intensity. 'But he also warns us against those *"who* exchanged *the glory of incorruptible God for the likeness and image of corruptible man, and of birds and beasts, and creeping things.* For this cause,"* says the apostle, *"God gave them up unto vile passions"*—not meaning, I think, that God *resigned* them, but that this was the inevitable result of their apostasy, unwilled by him except insofar as his nature must repel evil. —And *he* also found that his experience confirmed the truth of Scripture. But he has gone out of the way,' he cried. 'I'm not sure, even now, that I can get him back.'

The old priest warmed with unaccustomed pity, and astonished himself by regretting that the partition between them debarred any physical touch of sympathy.

'Young man, there comes a time . . . in some relationships . . . when we must be prepared to let go: when, paradoxically, the command that we "love our neighbour as ourself" means not greater self-sacrifice, but that we value ourselves enough *not* to follow them into Gehenna; where *"the worm dies not, and the fire is never quenched".'*

'Brother . . . too late. Remember that it was Cain, the murderer'—he seemed struck by some irony—'. . . who was *not* his brother's keeper.'

Dr Kemberton persisted with his advice.

'Young man, listen to your own texts. Cling to God, rather than to corruptible man. The scriptures mustn't be domesticated: if you attempt to trim and tie them up for your own use, they'll turn and rend you. You may call yourself "Tribulation" to satisfy an old priest who should have known better than to ask; but if you do *that*, your name will be tribulation, and your lot tribulation. You cannot hope to possess a fellow creature as you may hope to possess God—it is diabolic to try.' He raised a crooked forefinger, to stave off misunderstanding. 'No, I don't accuse you of perverted desires. But that hard text means that we must be prepared to withdraw from the pursuit of human comfort, give up all hope of companionship or understanding—and turn our faces to a God whose divinity and power *may* be manifest in his creation, but whose love is invisible; at most, an alleged promise, a doubtful possibility. If "by his works" shall ye know *him*, your text demands that we put our all on a bad risk—one who, whatever the treasures in store for us, confronts us now with only the comfort of a locked door.'

'But we had *passed* the lock; we had *seen* into the treasure-room,' he cried, holding on to the image obsessively. 'My key to the Kingdom has turned back: he refuses the lock himself, and denies *me* access!'

Dr Kemberton tried to soothe with generalities whose application would rub the sore only at one remove.

'The poet Wordsworth . . . like many another . . . spent a lifetime trying to recapture God in his created works; and found at the end that he was sifting sand.'

The comment was brushed aside, unreceived.

'As soon as the Spirit spoke to me of Paul's meaning, I knew that my love was holy.' He had raised with his nail a loose corner of varnish from the window ledge between them, and pulled back a long strip without noticing, until it broke off and curled around his palm. 'I recognized the source of that desire which scurried and fluttered behind my breastbone'—he scratched up another edge, and peeled back a further sliver—'. . . like a bird which is impelled by the homing device implanted in it by God, and cannot deviate till its need is extinguished and satisfied in the Eternal Sun itself. . . . We *knew* that to turn aside to bodily embracements would be to settle for a travel brochure, when we might have gone on to the Heavenly City. For the fading image, the paper crown, we received imperishable silver.' (The varnish refused to yield any further sacrifice.) 'I knew that, if I loved him, it was the Deity I loved in his image. —But he has smirched his face,' he cried. 'How can divinity be found in the brutish, the sensual? —*Changed*, in a moment, from God to Our Father of *Lies*.'

The priest responded with mournful severity.

'Only the heretic Blake . . . in the days of his naivety . . . saw Pity with a *human* face. He did not say that the same face is, alternately, a wolf or a vulture; or wears the sly, flitting smile of a fallen angel, testing out and mocking its own residual, unmerited attractions. No doubt that face reflects the distorted see-er; but its mask is also moulded by an endlessly ricocheting spirit within. It is painfully true: *"Put not your trust in princes, nor in any of the sons of men".*'

The sacred text abashed the listener: it was some seconds before he could set it aside.

'But the soul of man,' he insisted, 'accumulates power from every chance rub with his environment. God's energy is latent in his whole creation; it excites, *irritates* the spirit, a prickling tension, till it builds up sufficient charge to bridge the gap between itself and its negative counterpart, its cancelling Fruition.' His tone became harsher, embarrassment at his subject making him exaggeratedly strident. 'In carnal intercourse, man jumps that lightning into a path where there is *no* recipient. It spends itself in burnt earth. It is pissing against a wall.'

'Celibacy,' said Dr Kemberton wearily, 'is no infallible remedy for spiritual dryness.'

His tone brought the penitent to grip the ledge below the grille with one white hand, and to plead with his head almost up against the mesh.

'Then why is human love an ache *before* consummation, and nausea after?'

'Because of *sin*.' Again, the same exhaustion.

'Because to glut the soul's emptiness on copulation is to bloat it with stale bread.'

Dr Kemberton waved a hand across his face as if dispersing smoke; and outrage swept him irresistibly into that manic utterance he deplored in others.

'Because even there', he said, 'at our most God-like, the soul, damaged by mishandling from the w-womb, cannot entirely forget its injuries in communion with another, but to some extent enjoys *itself*, which is self-eating.'

'It is an *absurd* position in which to ape the Godhead.'

'God is no respecter of p-postures.'

'But he considers his elect'. A reverberation in the penitent's voice, communicated by pressure of a cheekbone, made the wooden panel buzz. 'And as the corn breeds not, but feeds men, beasts and the birds of the air, so we deny our seed its natural soil, retaining it unto the Lord, to grow up within us ears of wheat to his delight, bearing spiritual grain an *hundredfold*.'

Dr Kemberton pursed his lips and tugged on either end of his stole till he heard threads part at the back of his neck.

'Your Lord and mine,' he said, 'from a position of privilege, commands us to forgive. *"If your brother strike you on one cheek, turn to him the other"*.'

'But am I to turn my brother's face to meet another's blow?' The priest grunted in recognition of the point; but his visitor, fearing he was not making himself clear, fell into a renewed appeal. 'Imagine seeing one whom you love beyond value, enervated, sucked dry by some parasite, addicted to its toxins—made to depend on them, crave, need them, as a pig needs to scrape its bristles. It is madness to let such organisms live.'

Letting go of his stole, Dr Kemberton eased the furrows of his forehead up on to his scalp, and, dropping his hand slackly, left them to corrugate once more.

'Our Lord Christ . . . for reasons best known to himself, born free into this world . . . without load of hereditary perversion . . . beyond the circle of reverberation, out*side* that chain . . . *commands* us to forgive.'

Resistance made the visitor even more vehement. 'There are crimes of which society takes no cognizance—which infect not one person only but the whole body. Human law is the creation of men; it falls short of God's ordinance'—here his voice took on the same strident harshness—'and his elect are the lawgivers who are to make up the deficiency.'

Against this tide of emotional assault the old priest sounded weary and apologetic.

'If you will, I am only a needle in a record. I can but trace the groove laid down for me. However I may sympathize as a man, I have no authority'—his voice began to tremble—'no authority to endorse your feelings.'

The penitent pressed his argument, excited at signs of emotional involvement in his auditor.

'In war it is permitted to kill; and we are engaged in wars of heaven and hell.'

'I admit m–morality and the law don't skip together—but m–may we hope for justice on this earth?'

Encouraged by this plaintive question to believe that Dr Kemberton only needed persuasion, the visitor leant against the lattice-edge and whispered; but so hoarsely that it seemed his vocal cords were rigid in an effort to resist being used.

'Before I went, I made up my mind that I would execute justice, whatever the cost to my soul. I gave her the choice, either to leave him or to suffer; and she chose wrongly . . . and I executed judgement.'

Behind the metal mesh Dr Kemberton rolled a pink-rimmed eye, like a white rat in a trap, once only, before being immobilized in mindless horror. He tried to cling on to the fact that this must be the murderer of Lepage's mistress, and even rehearsed the concept over to goad himself into some fit reaction. But the external circumstance was submerged in blind panic and rage that those emotions which he had kept at bay for so long should present themselves incarnate. He groped around for his stick, his immediate urge being to beat them off physically. He thought of rushing to telephone from the vestry to get the offence removed, but was constrained by his physical limitations and the role he had taken on himself. The lunatic was protected by the rights of the confessional; by what devil-inspired intuition could he know what Kemberton had felt, had let himself momentarily lapse into, when he heard of the girl's death? Only once had he given way over the years to human weakness: he was agonized by the injustice of being thus linked. Hadn't he given her her freedom, when he might have saved his career, been revenged by holding on, subjecting her to a life which was openly false, instead of false underneath, only at root, disguised by social patching-over? There was surely no obligation to forgive without a word of repentance, of asking pardon? A single peccadillo linked him with this maniac. He was furious at the way the man had insinuated himself, not openly declaring himself till the last moment, but hinting, hooking sympathy, trapping him into betraying his weak underside. He comforted himself momentarily with the thought that there could be no reasonable parallel between the jealousies of perverted instinct and his own wrongs. But as he shied away from visualizing clearly the years of loneliness, rage rose further in him, so that he felt it like blood boiling in the arteries of his neck and bubbling at the lower lids of his eyes.

He forced himself to imagine hauling himself round, taking her back—and found instead how much he wanted to cut her away, hack the ties, as he'd read as a child of broken masts, gone overboard, cut adrift by hacking through the shrouds and stump with a hatchet. Cut away, blot her out. *'And she shall be blotted out from the Book of Life.'* The scriptural phrase echoed round his head and he tried it over silently on his tongue, in spite of his determination not to entertain it: *'and she shall be blotted out from the Book of Life.'*. . . 'The elect are the lawgivers who are to make up the deficiency.' She had condemned him to perpetual deadness, an endless burden of unfitness for the priestly office, when even this whore-killer had forgiven one, if not both. How could Hosea, lover of harlots, stomach her? Perhaps it was literary metaphor after all, only a preaching trick for characterizing faithless Israel in terms they could think of, the debauched wife. The cat's-urine stench of her sweat in heat nauseated him across a gap of seventeen years.

'Why . . . thinking as you do . . . have you come to *me*?'

'Because we of the fellowship, being in grace, have no rite of absolution. . . . Because I am not easy . . . because I have committed the fact.'

Dr Kemberton trembled, but was uncompromising.

'The fact of murder, unless repented of, is damnable.'

In a mixture of fear and excitement, the visitor brought his face to the grille.

'And I thought, even if this be wrong, damnable, when in that great and terrible hour, cast out from the elect, I stand with the least of his sinners crowding in at the door, he will come to me and say: "My son, stand forward, you who think yourself worthy of damnation, stand forward, for indeed you *are* worthy of damnation, and for that reason precious to me. What you did was not for yourself. I have said: *'Greater love hath no man than this, that a man lay down his life for his friend.'* And yet there *is* a greater, for you were prepared to undergo seclusion from my face; and for that reason are you saved. *'Friend, move higher up'*".' Tears started in his eyes. ' —I, the *least* of the brethren.'

But Dr Kemberton was already clawing himself upright, hauling on his wrists to supplement the frozen muscles in his calves; only his vestments, trembling like sheets in a wind, and one end of his stole with its frayed terminal cross, dangled at the penitent's nose. The priest made one last effort to preserve his role inviolate, beyond the limitations of human corruption.

'By the power of Christ vested in me, to loose and to bind— your sins I retain.' He looked down, to find that the intruder made no move or response; against the dark of his suiting his hands were livid, slim, obscenely delicate. Suddenly losing all control, Dr Kemberton roared down at him: 'Go *out* . . . hunted . . . accursed.'

Despite a persistent trembling in his tendons, the vicar supported himself with both hands on an inside strut of the priest's box, his fingers slipping on a plush coat of dust which layered its topside, but getting sufficient grip to keep him standing until his visitor had walked the length of the nave and left the church. Then, without taking rest, and leaving the edge of the door to crack back on his neglected stick, he climbed laboriously up to the high altar. His elbows felt its fringe of silver braid as he knelt heavily, arched and interlaced his fingers before him, taking care to keep them straight so as not to dirty his knuckles more than need be. Behind him his lower legs seemed extensions of dead flesh.

'I have taken the b-blood and the judgement on my own hands: together with the judgement, the blood, for they are inseparable.'

The crucifix to which he addressed his analysis was barely discernible. He bent his head on to his thumbs, and, to supplement his efforts with formal liturgy, reached out to where he knew the Service Book must be. But realizing the moment his eyes grew accustomed that his fingers left oily black prints on its margin, he pushed it away with a forearm protected by his white sleeve. For some minutes he strained to move some feeling in himself, but the hemp carpet was increasingly harsh to his knees, and he glanced uncomfortably round lest he were being overlooked. Eventually he lifted his head and said with quiet bitterness towards the hammer-beam roof:

'Old Artificer, you play very foul'.

Making the altar-frame creak under his weight, he pulled himself on to his feet, keeping his finger-ends off the cloth, then bowed formally to the cross and turned. Dry-cheeked, but almost the purple of his stole, and with a thumbprint of black over either eye, he walked down into the side-aisle to recover his stick. His hand came upon it as he felt about behind the door of the confessional box, but it eluded his grasp and slipped sideways on to the floor. Fortunately, it had fallen towards his seat, and by sitting and leaning forward he was able to reach its handle; but once the stick was recovered, the associations of the place were too disturbing for him to relax, and, despite apprehension that his wrist would not stand much strain, he made towards the vestry to wash and to disrobe.

CHAPTER SEVEN

Rain blended with, but did not obliterate a fringe of dog-dribble around the base of the galvanized-iron bus shelter. On a grey waste-bin, scribbled in black crayon, 'A. M. loves J.C.', and above it a heart, jagged, broken in two with great serrated edges, two sides of an indenture that would never fit. The school wall was half-undermined by colonies of martin-holes where kids had screwed pennies into its yellow brick. As Cathcut came level, a pair of hunched six-year-olds, forearms dug deep in navy raincoats and socks turned up over the knee, stared past him into the middle distance at a non-appearing bus, milk-teeth nipping their lower lips. Going home for lunch; their mothers must be off work. Round the school corner into Union Lane, Cathcut turned into the full drive of the storm.

Clinging droplets itched his left cheek, and water searched his parting where the thinning hair balded the scalp. He put out his hands in a waltz position, the left hand up to hold open the collar of his cape, the right arm crooked at the waist to keep the plastic off his body and carry rivulets of water away from his cassock. Plastic pregnant priest. Too much walking in composition soles had opened a split between the large toes of his leading foot. Under their yellow transparency the fingers at his nose looked like pre-packed chipolatas. He would have liked a cloak, but it was too ostentatious and expensive, more 'spiky' than he wanted; the cape was all-purpose, could be used on the bicycle, and didn't mark one off so much. Head down, looking through its open collar, it was possible to see the puddles. One, two, three, *one*, two, three, hold out your skirts! hesitate; reverse chassée. A neat back-step landed him in an unsuspected pool behind him. Never was any good at this.

He had detested dancing because of his parents' enthusiasm,

but had agreed to learn it at theological college, where it was taught as a social asset—optional, in case you had conscientious objections. Always having to infiltrate, pretend, evade. He'd heard that they ran a motor-servicing course at Fords now for missionaries; same principle: always recommend yourself as something different to what you are, talk God to a crinkle-cut over his sparking-plugs. 'Crinkle-cut' was hardly very liberal—where had he picked that up? He had spent his morning waltzing around, performing, helping a family to claim their rent rebate: mother at the fag-end of her twenties, three children under five, living in a kitchen and bed-sitter, no evidence of a man around—at least, he hadn't seen any shaving brush when he'd scrubbed ink off his hands in the kitchen sink, and he'd shrunk from asking direct, simply accepting what he was told for the rebate form, and leaving the signature for her to arrange. Social Christianity no doubt, the secular meaning of the gospel; but it was also evasion, getting a toe in the door and, as usual, funking any follow-up. There was always the hope that if you made yourself useful you would eventually come to matter, be taken seriously. Yet he felt faintly disgusted at buying his welcome, then refusing the fence. The glands ached both sides of his neck, and each nostril had a river of snivel. He snuffled into the wet plastic of his cape until its smell was too much, confident that in this downpour anything would be washed off before he had to face a meeting. He might almost have the glanders; here no one would even know what glanders were.

 A corporation bus lurched its nearside wheels into the gutter beside Cathcut, almost scraping him with its maroon overhang, and splashed yellowish, gritty water into the gape of his instep. As he put his weight on that shoe it flowed into the toe-cap, and when he wriggled his big toe against its neighbour there was a liquid-and-gravel lubricant. But the water took off the sting of the split. Skipping across the pavement out of the wash, he looked for a route number over the bus platform; but then decided that a few more yards wouldn't make much difference. Through a solitary, semi-circular wipe on the steamed windows of the top deck, he could see a hunched old fellow in a grey plastic mac, pulled tight across his shoulders, and a brown felt droop of a hat. He sucked on a pipe, his elbow propped on top of the seat in front, staring out over the rooftops. Chin and pipe pointed at the tall stacks of the generating station, which he appraised from behind a front of spectacles with little, tightened eyes. The rain was beating down effluent from the stacks. He responded with short, reflective puffs: 'Fuff, fuff—you blow filth at me, and I'll blow filth at you.' Vapour clung back at his mouth, nose, chin, then drifted away, and the window began to film over. The bus wallowed past.

How would you get at him? His age-group had been dragged over every flint in the road, all their yielding parts scraped out. They had smothered thought and feeling for fear of the boot, watched their personalities disintegrate into a repertoire of nods and bobs. And the dependants for whom they endured had, as often as not, died, or drifted away in search of work, which was as bad as dying, since there was no money to visit them, and the part you had in them dwindled or was displaced. If social history knew such privations, they were nothing Cathcut could match. He himself had never been out of work, he had not suffered moral oppression: the sour self-righteousness of employers who had tried to manage their tear-away machine by a manual which only fitted Ford, Mark One; and so had panicked, seeing squalor and unemployment in the easiest terms to hand, as marks of God's distaste, rather than brands which they themselves were inflicting. The resultant disease and dirt were further signs of the social pariah, those who 'didn't *want* work', even when there were two million pariahs. The victims themselves, ashamed of their faculties going to rot, felt that they must be in some way to blame; aside from a few non-conformist sects, they damned a Christianity that damned them, and retreated into kin-loyalty as their major standard.

There was a certain pride in having survived at all, coupled with pity for those who had gone soft, taken to drink, women, betting or religion. Cathcut remembered even his church-wardens' attitude to the pub-hanging dipso who persisted in coming in half-way through Sunday Matins, standing quite ignoring the congregation, head up, neck back into the loop of sisal that stood him as braces, singing maudlin hymns with tears in his already overflowing eyes. 'He's only doing time till they open.' They had wanted to keep him out, until Cathcut intervened: 'Even a drunk's psalm is music in the Divine ear.' — 'He must be tone-deaf.' Dipso aside, everything defeated Cathcut's naive notion that circumstances must eventually compel surrender to the Deity.

Old memories had not died, only calcified in the joints of the aged. There was the Church's role in the twenties and thirties, the seventy-year-old who'd pushed her locked knuckle-joints at him, one swollen arthritic fist, and refused even to let him in:

'What did you bastards do fer us in the Strike, come round now trying ter git yer toe in the door?—Lit'l poncey choirboys down from some vicar-factory up north, driving our 'orse trams with their fat arses propped on barbed wire ter stop us getting at 'em. I lost my first man of T.B. at twenty eight, 'is baby that I was carrying died of the same bug as killed '*im*—rotten with it when it was born; and when I went with two small kids and blood from pleurisy almost coming out of me ears, what did they tell me? "You're an able-bodied woman, you can work." Able-bodied *hell*. Where was the Church then? Done sweet f.a.'

'But the Salvation Army . . . ?'

'I don't say nothing against the Army. The Army's different. Or I *should* say, they *were*.' She shut the door.

That was all before Cathcut was born.

He stopped in a haberdasher's doorway to empty a shoe, resting his foot on the sill of a display window. The Army were across the road, running a converted hotel: 'THE EVERLASTING ARMS. Under Salvation Army management.' They'd left the inn-sign empty, just a swinging metal frame without a board. All the top windows of the hostel were flung open, their faded pink-check curtains blowing soddenly in the wind. The same brigadier as valued pure air had marshalled a team of down-and-outs into repainting the whole exterior brickwork pink, and all the woodwork a bright nursery-blue. To her 'great *joy*' (as she put it to Cathcut, her bonnet bounding with the passionate thrusts of her jaw against its strings) one of the inmates had been sufficiently fired to take on the letter-box as a regular thing. A gleaming sheet of brass witnessed to the permanence of his reclamation. The lower windows were boarded up to eye-level, but all along behind the centre of the sashes, on a narrow shelf which presumably once held Satan's own brew, was her collection of exotic cacti, each in its little individual clay pot.

The rain reduced to a drizzle and the brigadier appeared for a moment, one hand on the latch, spread-eagled against her open door, jollying along a gang of navvies who had taken shelter from the storm. They filed past her, obediently picked up their tools from the hostel wall, dried the handles on handkerchiefs, and stood looking at their waterlogged hole. The Electricity Board was replacing outdated cables, and they were having to go deep. One of the workmen, with a pink *Financial Times* over his head and tied in soggy flaps over each ear by a string, began to shovel at a great mound of gravel and sand that had spilled out too far into the road. The subsoil must be sand; that would explain the yellowness of the water in the gutters. A fawn retriever appeared from nowhere, sniffed over the wet heap dejectedly, edged its back legs part-way up the pile, and started to squat; the men roared. The shoveller pushed back his *Financial Times* from over his eyes, dropped his spade, and, bobbing down like a slip fielder with knees apart and hands at the ready, watched the emerging product. 'Cup it, Cowdrey!' cried one of his mates. 'Kick her off before she does it, fer God's sake,' pleaded another. But he leered round at his mates for connivance, and the foreman leaned back loftily on his shovel, belly out, thumb in his dungaree-strap, grinning toleration: 'Shit-minded bugger.' The bitch blinked long-suffering eyes, and like a milked cow patiently accepted the attentions to her rear end. Cathcut tipped his shoe, and a yellowish stream spattered on to the doorstep.

A click behind him, the shop bell ringing, and he panicked lest he be thought to have urinated. Hastily, he flourished his damp shoe to flick out a last imaginary drop, then shoe-horned it on with a pinched fore-finger. The doorbell kept ringing till the door shuddered back into its frame. He straightened and pulled back his cape from contact as a young girl pushed past him: spider-eyes, lashes mascara-ed on to a mask-like face, lacquered from top to toe. Her black handbag hung open, held by one strap, revealing Aladdin's cave, prospects of little gilt pins, pink ribbon on card, an emery board sticking up, and the flash of half a mirror peeping from an inside pocket. In some embarrassment she was fumbling, crackling a cellophane packet of stockings to get them into her bag. 'Black Witchery': fishnet, under a picture of slim, capering, tapering legs, suddenly crumpled. Cram them in—*snap*, decisively shut; *got* them, carry them off—lovely new legs. She teetered for a moment, toes jutting sharply over the step, pushing a powder-blotched nose enquiringly at the sky. Seen from behind, her short pleated skirt flared as though she had punched out a dustbin-lid to wear under it, and her thighs and calves struck Cathcut as sickeningly bulbous, liver-sausage limbs forced into a nylon skin. He traced with his eye the H of tendon and knee-crease. But not as lacquered as at first sight: there were brown gravy-spatters on both calves, and black hairs flattened in whorls under her stockings, like ferns pressed under glass. Shady Horsetail. Or Maidenhair?—let's hope so. It had stopped raining, so she left her umbrella hooked over her arm, and clicked firmly off to the left, high heels throwing her forward on to her toes, bottom jutting. 'Save us a bit off the joint, love!' A barrage of whistles greeted the lip-stick, the stockings, the black wig; Cathcut glimpsed a frightened eye rolled back at the witchery she had raised, and he registered a sudden, refreshing stab of pity. But she decided to run the gauntlet, nose in the air, clicking steadily till out of range; then she scuttled away, her bag of black power clamped tightly under one arm.

What was that behind him, out of the corner of his eye? Cathcut glanced down at a printed card propped among some reels of coloured cotton in the window: Victorian copperplate, with black, funereal edging: *'Haberdashers' Retail Association—our livelihood your satisfaction'*. No, not that—next to it. A flash of colour, red, white and blue. A Union Jack made into a lady's brief, stretched tight over a wire-framed rump; 'I'm backing Britain' in bold, patriotic lettering across the hollow buttocks. A loop of plastic-covered wire formed each thigh-space, caressed by a lace-fringe in darker blue. On the cream window-sill underneath, a hasty violent scribble in black crayon: 'And I'm *fucking* Britain!' He'd been standing right beside it, the navvies must have thought he was looking, and now there was only a sheet of glass between him and it: bottom to bottom, some solitary, Tyrolean boomps-a-daisy, bum-bouncing frolic. He blushed so hot that he thought the water on his cheeks must boil, and escaped into the street.

Ahead of him the black skirt swayed from side to side, as he watched mesmerized for each outward and upward flick to offer a glimpse of heavy thigh or a fringe of lace half-sunk in a buttock-crease. He caught himself at it, yet despairingly re-dedicated himself to the game. Swish, swash; swish, *flick*. Everything took on a new meaning here: drugs seemed acceptable, crime almost a righteous protest; what would elsewhere be lust was no more than a peck towards life through a hard shell of depression and isolation. Nevertheless, he eventually directed himself towards the window of Seshton Resale, pausing at a cardboard notice among the transistors: 'DANGER—electrified grille'. Why was it that music no longer reached him? Yet he had responded at the Youth Club, sufficiently engulfed in their flesh-pounding beat to be relieved momentarily from the pressure of his surroundings—until those surroundings had arraigned him for a volume of noise that he'd been too lost to restrict. He'd sided with his teenagers against local residents until the crisis was over, when he'd felt frightened and lost in another and less pleasant way. He could understand why they wrecked telephone booths: hadn't he himself felt an urge to put a brick through a plate-glass window in the High Street, 'Smarta Clothes', whose slim, arch-eyed, flawless dummies were an insult to life's pustules, to its cramped features and bent bones? As he pushed open a swing-door into the printing works, he glanced at himself in the glass. Raindrops clung to the fine hairs on his cheekbones. 'Rainwater's good for the complexion'—but he knew that twitching his eyebrows to flick off collected water had only deepened the lines on his forehead, and he flinched from looking again.

A bucket and mop lay abandoned on the concrete floor: the lunch-time buzzer must have gone. Between him and the stairs a well-known figure was poking his head through the door of Dispatch, where a light was still on.

'Did you use Poliphilus, like I told you?'

It was the father of the owner, recognizable by his khaki service mac, stained dark at the shoulders, and, as Cathcut came closer, a whiff of old man's damp—or was it just the odour of the mackintosh?

'Did you use Poliphilus like I told you?'

A grunt from inside, and the slap of several quires of paper dropped upon another.

'Get away with yer, yer nowt but a bag o' bones.' The works manager was an importation, and had a Yorkshireman's exaggerated accent off his home ground. 'If yer miss owt on yer lunch once more, we'll be able ter poke a finger through yer. Put yer through one o' yer lad's presses, print sum colour on yer. I shouldn't get across that Matron if I were you. I don't like t' look in her eyes.'

'P'raps she keeps her looks for someone else.' The old man popped his head the other side of the door to wink at whoever had come in; but he only managed to tremble one lid at Cathcut.

'Do what she likes, fer all I care.' The manager tore a corner of brown wrapping off a quarto-sized parcel, glanced inside and tossed it into a corner. 'Seckey an' Walder. —We had a right game of it, thanks ter you. Give me a fount wi' no fiddle-faddle, anyday. Wasn't till we got back first proof Sid found 'e'd buggered whole setting: s'got commas in roman *and* italic, and 'e'd jumbled the lot. Took composing room two full hours, with a box o' each an' a pair o' tweezers ter sort it owt.'

'But it looks nice: proper for the job.'

'Ay, it *looks* all right, I'll give yer that. But if yer don't want *your* lunch, I want *mine*; an' I can't go till I find where this order's got to.' He picked up another brown parcel, glanced at a printed specimen pasted on the outside, and, looking up, saw that he was still being watched. 'Thanking *you*,' he said, and pulled the door to.

A whole vocabulary was closed to Cathcut. How much did he know about the real concerns of these people? Not only was he an interloper; in the case of the old man he was even a dispossessor, for Cathcut had taken a flat on the top floor that had originally been fitted up for the owner's father, when the building of some sheds at the rear made space available. There the old printer could hear work going on and occasionally interfere; but when he stopped bothering about himself the family had reluctantly moved him to a home. The father was lingering over the staff notice-board, and Cathcut hoped to slip by. But his discreet tread on the staircase brought the door open.

'They don't want you poking around in Design.' Then, realizing his mistake: 'Oh, Mr Cathcut . . . been a chap here asking for you. Don't know what about. He may be up there now.' Glancing down the corridor, he spotted the old boy craning up at a notice. Age had shrunk him below comfortable reading-level.

'You still 'ere? You may be a gentleman o' leisure, but someone's still got ter cook your meals an' wash up after yer.'

The father quietly read one last notice, then, as Cathcut climbed the stairs, passed below him on the way out, interrupting his hamster-like chewing for a muttered '"Ow do?' but with face and bearing unreadable, as he might look at a moneyed ne'er-do-well. And Cathcut didn't do anything useful in their terms. Gentleman of leisure.

He had left his door unlocked, because he was half-expecting an electrician from Radio Rentals across the street to look at his record-player, so as to save him having to take it over—there was a general feeling that he shouldn't be exposed to effort. Standing in the open doorway, he caught a muttered flow of obscenities from the elder of a pair of men in white overalls, standing like albino vultures over his machine. The apprentice was young, red-faced and buck-toothed.

'. . . Ground 'is balls down to iron-filings.' The electrician dipped his finger down the turn-table socket, brought up a greasy amalgam, held up a red, podgy middle-finger towards the light to check that it was metallic fragments rather than dust; and then daubed a grit moustache under the inquisitive, over-long nose of the boy, who was peering down the spindle-shaft to look at the ball-race.

At Cathcut's cough and murmured greeting the lad started, flushed further down his neck, and inspected the spindle-shaft with a precisian's concentration. Half-embarrassed, his employer sang out the old naval warning: 'Pilot aboard!' He grinned his yellow teeth at Cathcut like a horse turned back from the trough, and watched sardonically as the priest pulled his cape from off his black cassock, hung it on a hook on the door, and after several misplacings positioned a newspaper and a sponge beneath it to catch any drips. 'Sheep in burial-rig,' he observed to his apprentice, who failed to laugh, or wasn't familiar with the expression. They went on tinkering.

Finding his room stuffy and rather high, Cathcut threw open a window, without thinking that he might give offence; and made matters worse by apparently breathing at it, though in fact he was staring glumly at the green slime and standing pools on the corrugated roofs of the sheds and in their gutters. Suddenly realizing that his action might be misinterpreted, he moved to tend the Rayburn, which had been installed for the old man. Hod in hand, he looked round dispiritedly on his hidey-hole: a barn of a place, still stamped by the personality of its previous owner, hardly a base for vital Christianity. Everything had an air of the temporary, the makeshift: his bookshelves were bare planks supported on bricks, all of them on forced loan from a nearby building site, Cathcut having been too shy to beg. A forgivable peccadillo, perhaps, since his stipend didn't run to tools for the job; but less excusable was his dwindling acquaintance with the contents of the shelves, unless this blight on his faculties was not his fault. Even his adaptations were becoming less inventive.

The umbrella was one inspiration, though. His sister had given it as a status symbol, but it must have been one of her bargain buys, for it had stood folded for so long that its silk-cover split at first opening. He had relished stripping off its spokes and converting it to practical use. He hooked open the Rayburn doors with its crook, then with a quick toss caught the warm handle and used the metal shaft to disturb the furnacite. Over the now glowing coals he scraped shiny snail-tracks in sooty black velvet on the back boiler. The soot flared like golden rain, and, falling on unburnt nuggets, lit up in little points of light, as he'd seen dark hillsides suddenly studded at nightfall when walking in South Wales. Nostalgically he repeated the effect, cutting with the umbrella point a listless, zigzag pattern; and then desisted, for fear he might weaken the boiler. There'd been a wretched case recently of a honeymoon couple shattered as they lay on their hearthrug, and the explosion attributed to an improperly fitted Rayburn, as his was. Its pipes led not vertically but diagonally through a rough hole in the partition plasterboard, to a copper tank fitted high on the wall of his kitchen area; a persistent, ominous farting and bubbling in the water-system was perhaps a consequence. He found himself frightened of dying in this dreary condition, and unprepared for joining the honeymooners in Kingdom Come.

Eventually recollecting the workers, he went over. 'It was good of you to come across. How's it going?'

The electrician straightened, and with a grubby, coarse-grained thumb gummed a stray forelock into his slab of black hair. 'Short answer is, it isn't. Don't know wot you bin up to, padre. Bin overplaying it?'

'I don't recollect having been "up to" anything.' Cathcut realized that his precise accent must sound like a correction. 'I haven't touched it for weeks.'

The electrician stuck a tongue in his red cheek, making the beard-stubble bristle, and mockingly appraised the priest, head on one side, eyeing his pale skin. 'No . . . I should say you 'adn't. . . . Dunno' 'ow you do wivout at the end of a long day, padre.'

The priest flushed. 'What seems to be wrong?'

'Naah, you tell *me*.' He pulled a red biro from his off-white coat, clicked it irritably, and, failing to retract the point till it was already halfway returned to his breast-pocket, added another line to the wadge of colour on his chest.

'Well, I'm not sure how far it's me and how far the machine. Before the turntable locked completely, it sounded rather harsh and discordant, that's about three weeks ago. But as I say, the fault may be as much in my ears. I haven't been too well of late.' Gratefully, Cathcut recalled a bit of technical jargon. 'There did seem to be some wow.'

'*Wow*, was there?' He raised an eyebrow to the lad. 'Git more than wow, you bugger up yer ballrace like that—pardon my French.' The apprentice silently hooked a circlet of metal off the spindle, and his employer lifted it from his screwdriver, cupping it in a sweat-lined palm for Cathcut to see. 'Take more'n a dab o' lubrication ter put *that* right.'

'I thought I must be getting poor reproduction. Its performance seemed to get steadily worse, so that some while ago I just gave up, I didn't seem to be getting anything out of it.' Cathcut, finding himself trying to grasp musical relations intellectually in a vacuum of sensuous experience, had, well before any mechanical failure, more or less abandoned the attempt as meaningless.

'Nah, hold it, padre, I didn't say that was all, did I? There's more causes of faulty reproduction than leafs on a tree. So your pleasure isn't wot it was?' He winked hugely at the lad. 'Point *one*,' and he clicked with his biro toward the gramophone cable, '*if* your apparatus isn't properly sheathed at entry-point, rubber or p.v.c., you get a loss of juice where you don't want it, into the system. . . . Here, come over here, padre, an' I'll let you in on a few trade secrets. —You AC or DC?' he asked, nodding at Cathcut's cassock.

'Both, I think.'

'Well, bully for you! When a customer comes in complaining of poor performance, there's a routine check. Is it insertion loss? —What you say, Sid? That wot they teach at the Tech.?'

'Yeah.' The lad seemed unwilling to be drawn in. 'Could be.'

'Or 'as 'is stylus bin bottoming too much? If that's negative, is 'is pickup satisfactory? Prefer a pickip wiv no side-thrust meself. —Side-thrust can be very disruptive, eh Sid?'

Sid, who had replaced the turntable and was using a stroboscope, merely brought Cathcut's standard lamp closer, and set his lips.

'Naah, if your stylus bobs abaht in the groove'—he demonstrated graphically with a finger in a palm—'*phut* goes yer reproduction agen. . . . Or I may suspect loose connections.' He rounded on the priest. 'Your terminals all right?' Cathcut was nonplussed.

'Why can't you bloody give over?' muttered the lad. His employer bent down, snatched out a two-pin plug and held it up triumphantly.

'Now *there's* a wopping crime: no third leg. Bare socket there.' And he started off round the room, humming to himself in a frenzy of irritable invention, pulling furniture away from the wall, while Cathcut tried to assure him that he intended going over to flat-pins as soon as practicable. '*Had a lit'l junction-box, nothing would it bear* . . .' Cathcut snatched up his spiritual diary as his table rolled by on its castors, and tucked the notebook out of sight. '—There you are! Might 'ave saved meself the trouble. Too many ahtlets off yer junction-box at the same time: you'll get an overload o' juice frew an' blow yer bloody fuse.'

Cathcut realized something was implied, but was too uncertain of the jargon to challenge. The only alternative was to maintain an apparently ignorant, unwavering glance; yet the more he feared letting down his gospel, the more his eyes crossed and blinked involuntarily.

'D'yer keep it on manual play?'

'I find it's easier to work.'

'You 'ave a point there.'

Cathcut asked a question, despite his rising colour. 'Is there anything I can do about interference?'

'Tried twiddling your knob anti-clockwise? Highly recommended by the trade, that is.'

'Is that good?'

He smirked. 'Some find it 'elps.'

By this time the lad had had enough. 'Where d'yer put the Philips, Bert?'

'Philips *wot*?'

'Philips screwdriver. Thought I'd 'ave a dek at the amplifier—if that's all right, Bert.'

'Under my arm!' Bert jerked his elbow upwards, mockingly exposing the arm-pit. He turned back to Cathcut; but the lad just stood there helplessly. '—Now don't act greener than you are. If you 'aven't got one, bloody well go over an' git one—beggin' your puddin ', padre. . . . Jaldi, jaldi, man!'

Cathcut made an excuse to accompany the apprentice downstairs, pretending that he expected a letter in the little wall-rack outside Dispatch.

'I was grateful you didn't join in that.'

The lad started, reddening even more.

'Why don't you go 'ome an' 'ave a shit, padre.'

'This *is* my home.'

"Ave a shit *any*way.'

The swing-door banged to behind him, juddered, and settled into alignment with its fellow.

There were only two items in Cathcut's mail, the first an advertising circular. Above the legend 'Levitate your spirits!' a winged whisky bottle with benignly smiling cap ascended heavenwards, to the rapture of a head-tilted crowd surrounding. The second item was an art postcard from a Cambridge friend still in his final year of research.

> *'Glad to hear from John that you're still slumming it. Must have its interesting side—but thought this might cheer you up. Still soldiering on under the auspices of Auntie State. Got to—the old goose stops laying next year. Toying with the idea of lecturing somewhere exotic. Bede sez advert. in Registry for job in Cairo—but prob. just like Brum. Yrs ever . . .*

The card was of a Blake design in the Fitzwilliam, the 'Angel of the Divine Presence clothing Adam and Eve with skins.' No such angel here. Cathcut felt immediately how much his religious emotion depended on trappings: on beautiful chapels, plainsong, the clear Cambridge intellect, a community of agreed importances. Here, St Botolph's choir each Sunday offered Chinese torture; and the home where Blake saw his visions they had just converted into a betting shop. Perhaps Cambridge merely clothed life in superficial decency; the clothes were unvalued here. Within a matter of weeks he had discovered how far the zest of university religion was a result of virtually excluding the physically decayed: the Cambridge Christ was a teen-age God, tied to an academic hearth, and didn't travel well. Looking again at the card, it struck him that Blake's colours were watery, the draughtsmanship poor; but on his return upstairs he screwed up the advertisement, threw it into his wastepaper bin, and resolutely propped his card on the top shelf of his improvised bookcase.

The squatting electrician got to his feet, clutching his back exaggeratedly.

'Hear that click?' Wiping a greasy finger on a mottled rag, he looked ruefully at the machine. 'Planned obsolescence, that's the trouble wiv both of us.' Cathcut half-opened his mouth to speak, but was prevented. '—Sorry, padre, that's not your cue.' He started replacing tools in his bag. 'Only one solution ter that— mend it wiv a new one.'

Cathcut drew breath, as though to jump a ditch.

'I want you to know I'm not oblivious to what's been going on. I don't resent it, but I'd like to know why you do it.'

The electrician arched his eyebrows and whistled the opening bars of *'For all the saints'*, as he slipped his smallest screwdriver into its retaining loop and zipped up his bag.

'Creeping Jesus! You love goin' in wiv both feet first, don't yer?' As Cathcut stood helplessly by, he secured the pickup arm, deftly coiled a length of lead to place it on the turntable and banged down the record-player lid, all the while singing coarsely to the tune of 'John Brown's Body':

> *'OH, 'e jumped wivout 'is parachute*
> *from forty thousand feet;*
> *'E jumped wivout 'is parachute*
> *from forty thousand feet;*
> *'E jumped wivout 'is parachute*
> *from forty thousand feet,*
> *When the petrol tank ran dry-I-I.*

> 'OH, they scraped 'im off the tarmac
> like a lump o' strawb'ry jam . . .'

With both thumbs he flicked the catches shut. Cluck. '—I'll 'ave it stripped down in the works, but it 'ud probably be cheaper in the long run to replace it. —Sorry, padre, I just can't stick vicars, something abaht them gets on my wick: p'raps it's all those long black nighties, makes me randy.' And in a raucous but plausible Somerset *cum* Cockney dialect he launched into a parody of a harvest hymn, as he humped Cathcut's player over to the door.

> 'Vurst the varmer sows 'is seed;
> Then the milkmaid starts ter breed;
> All is tightly gathered in,
> Lest the parson spy 'er zin;
> But wiv the vullness of the year
> The zwelling crops their 'eads uprear;
> AND the fruit let gently vall
> Plump in 'Arvest Vestiva-a-all!'

He put down the record-player. 'God in, fun out 's my motto.'

'But religion *is* fun,' Cathcut protested weakly.

'Sorry, padre, you're wasting your breath on me. I've slogged twenty years fer a bit off the cake, an' now I've got it, no holy Joe comes round telling me ter carve it up an' give it away. It's eat or be eaten down 'ere—an' if I go round taking down my pants for all an' sundry, who's goin' ter look after me wife an' kids?'

While Cathcut tried to sort this into some coherent case the electrician disappeared into the kitchen area. There was a clank from the hotwater pipe, and Cathcut watched a fleck of plasterboard float down from the hole in the partition. Bert came to the partition door, red hands dripping water.

'Got a bit o' tissue? Don't want ter wipe off grease on your towel. Sticks in the crevices wiv just soap.' Cathcut drew a Kleenex from a box by his bed.

'There's some detergent under the sink.'

'Oh, is there?' He went back. From the far side of the partition came a sucking sound of knuckles kneaded in wet palms. '"*By their fruits shall ye know them*"—that's one of Jesus's sayings, isn't it?' He appeared again in the doorway, found a clean side to his tissue, inspected it closely and wiped under either ear. Cathcut must have looked gratified. 'Oh yes, I was a Sunday-school boy, packed off regular after Sunday dinner, while Mum 'n Dad got workin' on me brothers an' sisters.... Only people I ever knew went to a padre in the airarm were either skivers, or shamming pi, so as ter git out of the glass'ouse. Padre smiled all over 'is silly chops—wonder they're such suckers fer all the greasers come oilin' round them.' He handed Cathcut a damp tissue. 'Now you can't get that aht of your system. —S'not your fault, it's the company you keep.' Cathcut silently dropped the tissue beside the torn-up circular in his wastebin.

'... Or take our family grocer—that is, if you can bear to. Pillar of the church, 'e is, does the boiler, goes round wiv the hat on Sundays, and the snobbiest bastard you ever did see: just another way of being a cut above the rest of us. I'm not saying 'e'd do yer down, but 'e's in it 'cause it keeps 'im in wiv the nobs. Always an ad. in the church magazine: "Mallinson—Comestibles".' He pulled some skin across his chin and looked sideways at his beard-growth in the mirror of Cathcut's dressing-table.

'"Rich man in 'is castle, poor man at 'is gate, Gawd made 'em 'igh and lowly, an' ordered their estate." —That still on the books?'

'Well . . . it *is* still in *Ancient and Modern*; but I think it's due to go at the next revision.'

'There you are! Opiate of the people. Respect your worsers. That's still as true as when Marx said it. Only use I've ever seen for religion is keepin' us under, an' causing quarrels. My mate's nephew did well for hisself, won 'imself an education, then got set on being a padre—not one o' your lot, I think. . . . Methodist, or somefink. Anyway, whenever 'e came home on vacation, you'd only to scratch yer balls ter send 'oly shudders up 'is spine. Naah that's not charity, is it? —You all right fer plugs an' adaptors while I'm 'ere?' Cathcut checked quickly, whilst trying to light on an approach.

'Jesus did also say *"No prophet is recognized in his own country"*.'

'Prophet! I've nothing against education, it's one of the things we 'ave ter thank a Labour government for after the war; but 'e was a regular bleeder to 'is Mum an' Dad. Come back to lift us out of the slough. Good luck to 'im; but I'm damned if 'e's telling *me* 'ow to keep my arse out of trouble. Any fool can be pi on a steady twelve hundred p.a.'

'I could use another round-pin adaptor.'

'Right.' He took out a pad and scribbled. 'Some of us 'ave to get our fingers dirty in this wicked world.'

Cathcut felt uncomfortable, and tried to explain his position:

'There's a move to put priests alongside workers on the factory floor. Sheffield started it, but it's catching on pretty widely. And being a Church which subscribes in some measure to the "priesthood of all believers", I think it likely that, some time, laymen will be authorized to conduct services.... You can do it as a lay reader *now*,' he added.

The electrician laughed uproariously. '*Christ*! What we pay the bugger for, if not ter be better'n the rest of us? You don't catch me leading any holy knees-bend . . . dumb as Jerry's code-books, all that chat to me. Only parson I ever 'ad any time for was old Keighley, two before Kemberton. Thorough Commie, 'e was: "A-bomb?" 'e'd say, "Better red than dead!", an' belt the ball up the field like a ruddy torpedo. —An' I'll tell you another thing,' he continued, fired by the recollection of a grievance. 'When my wife was in King's 'aving our first, the chaplain come round wanting ter know who'd take communion. An' as soon as 'e found she wasn't one of theirs, 'e dropped 'er like a hot potato.'

'That's a pity.'

'Pity? It's a bloody sin.'

'You wouldn't let me call on you?'

'Long as you don't ask me to go ter church, you can please yerself. Look at me.' He supported himself with one hand on Cathcut's shoulder in mock exhaustion, as Cathcut tried to bear up unflinchingly. 'Sunday's my day of rest. By the time I've got abreast of everything coming on the market these days, I 'aven't the energy ter screw a plug—let alone anything else.' He inspected Cathcut's Dresden complexion at short range. 'My daughter 'ud *love* you. Wife's as bad. Make cow-eyes at doctors an' anythink in a dog-collar.' He giggled at his clashing metaphors. ''Spose it's animal attraction: "Yes, dear vicar, no, dear vicar, up my fanny, dear vicar." —Know what I think, padre? I reckon all these 'assocks or cassocks or whatever are a kind of 'alfway-'ouse; know what I mean, *ambisextrous*. Soon as they're through with the gym-mistress stage, it eases the jump ter the dominant sex.'

Cathcut smiled wanly, but was angry enough to use a ploy from his theological college armoury.

'And what happens when you're dead?'

His opponent laughed contemptuously.

'When I get *really* tired of patching up the bits, I'll just gently fold up.' He slipped his horsy dentures into a hand, and tugged a single good tooth at Cathcut. 'Know what I want most of all, padre? To be bloody dead. It's more final 'n a fuck.'

When the electrician had gone Cathcut boiled up a tin of soup and, while it cooled, attempted, roll in one hand and pen in the other, to settle to a sermon. He was obsessed by the surgical swapping of organs; and though he did not believe in the man of all spare parts prophesied by his Sunday newspapers, a kind of 'ministry of all the talents' grafted together, his alarm was of a sharpness that only preaching would alleviate. *'Absurder'* and *'Sunday Crimes'* some college wit had christened them—could that be slipped in for light relief? To counteract his personal bias, Cathcut tried to empathize with a mother whose child would be, beyond hope, preserved; but in the abstract nothing came, and, as his mind slipped involuntarily to the dead girl, he shuddered to imagine segments of that waxy tissue incorporated into his own.

His scotch broth was grease-laden, and the chalk on his tongue seemed to absorb it as it slid by. With a middle finger he scraped from the back of his mouth towards his lower foreteeth, bit out a yellowish sediment from under his nail, and analysed it again with his tongue. All furred up: what he forced himself to absorb clogged him, he couldn't imagine, concentrate or connect. And as usual when this yawning panic that he might be no good attacked him, his shoulder and back muscles ached as if fire played along the tension-lines. What origin or what influence had cursed him with this Napoleonic urge to be superior? Dr Kemberton homilized gently on 'the martyrdom of mediocrity'— why should that cross be so impossible to accept? Laying down his spoon, Cathcut retrieved his spiritual diary from where he had tucked it under his counterpane, and flicked through it, wondering if there were sufficient material for something on such a theme. So rounded, ingenuous his hand had been at college; but now he felt a diary to be an unreal exercise, playacting. It implied an audience, another person or himself at a later date, for whom by words and the effort of writing he was imposing a false precision and coherence. Blankness now stood between him and the Deity: the top of his head was a blood-filled sponge, where every dart of prayer embedded itself, and lost its point in obstruction. Hoping to force devotion to flow, he tried to write, at the same time reproaching himself for noticing that his hand was more mature.

> *Lord, I am sick. I cannot even pray without watching myself. Unless you lift me out, crack open my hardened, recoiling heart . . . Lord, I am screaming inside in protest against you. Dear Lord, I do not want to be saved. I do not want to go on any longer. Lord, drag me screaming and kicking into salvation. Lord, I feel so sick. I have to*

go on, because the only alternative is sins which drug me for a while but leave me in the same condition. Help, Lord, or I sink. Lord, do you want me to go under?

He wept a little on reading it over, and felt refreshed.

When he was least prepared, there was an unmistakable tap at his door. He found that his cassock-sleeve unaccountably rejected water; and having fumbled in vain for a handkerchief, he met the emergency by dabbing an inside edge of his half-eaten roll beneath his eyes to soak up his tears. Brushing a damp crust-flake from his cheek, he got up—and let in Lepage. Lepage's gait was stiff, and Cathcut had an uncomfortable feeling that he had been sitting for some while on the concrete landing outside. He came into the room shielding his eyes from the glare of the standard lamp.

'Does the light hurt you?'

'It flickers.'

Cathcut felt that it didn't, but without comment picked up his lampshade from where the electrician's lad had discarded it, and replaced it over its bulb. Under cover of still blinkering one eye against the light, Lepage discreetly and methodically evaluated the details of the room; nervous of what they might be telling him, Cathcut toyed with the binding of a book that had thrust out of line on its shelf.

'What were they singing as I came up?'

Sudden pain, and the consciousness of blushing cheeks.

'—There was only one of them. There was very little tune for you to hear.'

Lepage stopped halfway through registering the titles on Cathcut's makeshift shelves.

'I don't hear tunes. There's a plate glass wall between them and me.'

The naked light bulb had exposed the freckles of Lepage's sallow, tightened skin as sharp as flecks on an eggshell; but trying now to read his face, Cathcut noticed that in browner, more subdued light the blemishes seemed softened into his complexion and altogether less disturbing.

'It's terrible when that happens,' he said softly, after some seconds' observation.

'One doesn't miss what one hasn't had.' Lepage resumed his examination of the shelves. The tone was dismissive, so that Cathcut was surprised he troubled with any further explanation. 'Music has always sounded to me like organized screaming. I can hear *geometrically* that the notes make patterns: but the patterns never link up in the heart. I can see that they should, out *there'*— and he pushed out with a hand towards the wall over the shelves—'like the lines of a triangle about to touch, make a perfect angle . . . but they never ring together.'

The thought of a world eternally without harmony dashed the priest beyond the point of moralizing. A numb oppression settled under his breastbone; and Lepage startled him by unexpectedly darting at the bottom shelf to pull out a volume of Renoir reproductions which Cathcut had bought in a spell of liberalism at college, when he was trying to mortify his puritan bent. Blushing, he watched helplessly as Lepage thumbed through.

'The only painter I've ever much cared for,' Lepage said, apparently searching among the plates and placing fingers between a couple to mark them for further attention. 'He catches the texture of flesh wonderfully . . . would always ask of a new chambermaid "Does her skin take the light?"'

Cathcut was gratified that they had a point of contact, even if he felt that he would never again enjoy Renoir so innocently. He caught himself involuntarily watching Lepage's downcast eyes for signs of excitement, and then reproached himself for being so crude, both humanly and psychologically.

'The body there looks somehow *curdled.'* With the same suddenness as Lepage had picked the book from the shelf, he turned it towards Cathcut, pinching it at its binding between thumb and forefinger so as to get the full spread of a double page.

Across the leaf sprawled Renoir's 'Nymph at the Spring', full length, lying on her left side with calves crossed, right hand stretched along hip and thigh, gazing out expectantly at the viewer. 'Circa 1882'. Lepage's equally intent, questioning scrutiny seemed to insinuate that a pose which Cathcut had always seen as challenging powers of draughtsmanship was no more than a sordid invitation, and her bare white flesh not nude but naked. Cathcut put aside the suspicion as a creation of his own anxiety; and yet yielded sufficiently to resolve that at the next jumble sale the Renoir would be slipped unobtrusively among the secondhand books.

'I doubt if the original was this *un-sunned,'* Lepage remarked, drawing attention again to the pallid flesh.

'There's a typically French story,' Cathcut said, half-smiling and stammering with embarrassment, 'that when asked about his source of inspiration he replied that he painted with his—er— *stem of life.'* No reaction from Lepage; he must be telling it badly.

'But the other version always seems to me more authentic, that some society lady was cooing around the old man when he was working: "M'sieur Renoir, how on *earth* do you manage?" — because he was crippled with arthritis by then, poor fellow, could barely hold a brush, as well as his eyes being weak—or was that Degas?—well, never mind. He replied: "Madame, I tie it to my *prick*."' Under Lepage's stare Cathcut faltered, feeling that, through trying to keep things at the level of undergraduate banter, he had been betrayed into an indecency. 'I suppose that's how history is made,' he concluded weakly.

Lepage eyed him with distaste and listlessly shut the book.

'He used to be my favourite painter; but now I find they have dead, doll's eyes.' The detective turned to replace the Renoir on its shelf.

'Every eye must seem dead for a while,' the priest whispered, ashamed at having been so tasteless; and taking Lepage gently by the elbow he tried to draw him to a chair. His touch seemed to trigger in Lepage a spasm of dry vomiting as he stooped. He shook off Cathcut's hand and felt for the wall in front, heaving his shoulders.

'Take no notice . . . it's purely nervous . . . *fatigue*,' he gasped, supporting himself in a squatting position with one hand on a shelf, and griping at his diaphragm with the other. Cathcut's Blake card fluttered down, over and over, till it reached the floor.

'Let me get you some milk, it'll cool your stomach.' Another attack of fruitless retching, as Cathcut hovered helplessly.

'Don't you think it's cold enough already? . . . It burns under here.' He rubbed his thumb several times over his sternum.

'Is there anything I can do?'

Lepage's muscles relaxed somewhat. Tentatively, he straightened up, lightly caressing his abdomen.

'I think . . . there might be one way of helping myself.'

Cathcut thought soberly of the amount of rooting over his past that Lepage would have to do.

'You know I'd do anything I can to help.'

There was a slight flicker of amusement, and Lepage frightened him by suddenly putting out a hand, as though agreeing to a pact. Nevertheless, Cathcut accepted it, whilst Lepage lowered himself gingerly into a chair.

'Thanks.'

'Your hand is *frozen*,' Cathcut said. Not bony or sadistic, as he had expected, but surprisingly limp and uncommunicative, with a disturbing suggestion of being controlled from some way back, like those wax or rubber hands which they had tucked in their sleeves as schoolboys, for a joke.

'Very little information has come in: she seems to have kept pretty close. . . . You know I shall have to go and talk to the family again?'

Cathcut blushed. 'I imagined you would.'

'You know me too well for me to pretend that it matters much to me to keep my job—though I'm sure you'd leap to my defence if I were pushed out'—he smiled unpleasantly—'but it matters in other ways . . . to finish this one.'

'I understand'—though Cathcut felt they were talking in slightly different senses, and that he was half-conspiring to understand Lepage in a sense congruent with his hopes, which Lepage was pandering to and mocking. 'I'll take you to the youth club this evening. Some of her old friends will be there—though she's been taken up elsewhere of late.' Cathcut looked suddenly dubious, and the police officer was immediately sensitive to it.

'I haven't much respect for the law, but in this instance its long-drawn-out processes seem infinitely more satisfying than any fit of violence.'

Cathcut tried to blot out disturbing innuendoes, concentrating on the virtual promise that was implied.

'You know I couldn't stand by and allow the law to be exceeded.'

Lepage smiled indulgently, touching his long nose on the tips of his arched fingers.

'I shall keep within the circle you draw for me.'

The priest doubted again if Lepage were not playing with him, but decided not to challenge, feeling that it was probably best for the moment to accept his actions and remarks at their face value, always bearing in mind that one could withdraw one's connivance at any point, and even threaten to do so, if necessary. Lepage sat for a while, in an interval of vacancy; then, appearing to activate his body by an effort of will, he sprang to his feet with a violence that made Cathcut apprehensive of another nervous attack.

'Come, *fisher of men.*'

He felt a shock of excitement and panic. 'Where to?'

Lepage smiled again at his nervousness, with a touch of affectionate contempt.

'*O ye of little faith.* . . . I have to interview the family; it would lend a certain *presence* if you were there, stop them getting out of hand.' Cathcut continued to hesitate. 'You *must* come: I can't manage without you.'

His admission released a surge of feeling in the priest. 'I'll come,' he said. The taut wires in his head slackened off, blissfully. Then a quick, childlike appeal. 'Don't let me down.'

'You'll need your cape,' Lepage said, looking towards the door where it hung. 'It's almost too cold for rain, but there's still a fine drizzle.'

Cathcut took from its hook the damp yellow plastic, still smelling of itself and of grit, pulled it over his head, and followed Lepage out.

CHAPTER EIGHT

Cathcut rang the door-bell and, as they waited, stole a glance at Lepage. His face was luminously pallid in a way that Cathcut had seen before only in new-born children or those about to die: the flesh had a milky, gelatinous look, semi-transparent, so that its tracery of veins showed through. Under his eyes the circles were so emphasized by the cold that he might almost have run round them with a sooty finger. At the grimness of his expression Cathcut felt suddenly afraid, anxious lest he were making some irreversible mistake: he knew he could trust Lepage's promise, and yet the underlying intention seemed unredeemed, undiverted.

The door was opened by a young girl of about eighteen. She recognized them immediately.

'Must it be today? Mother's near snapping-point already.'

To Cathcut's surprise she was quite prettily dressed. Perhaps her black slacks might be considered mourning, but above them she wore a white cotton blouse that cupped in tightly below her breasts and whose low top was pinked and scalloped. About her neck hung a small silver crucifix; and she had put on lipstick.

'I'm afraid it must. These things have to be done quickly.' He spoke kindly, for under the powder she was drawn with anxiety.

'But couldn't you just ask *me*? There's nothing mother knows that I don't know.'

'We have something we must discuss with all of you.'

'All right then, you. But not *him*;' and she nodded contemptuously towards Lepage, who so far had said nothing. But at this moment a broad, ungainly woman came running up the hall. Dressed in a brown printed dress with a yellow cardigan pulled over it, she had the same pointed chin and heavy eyebrows as her daughter, but was almost three times the bulk—her child, some thirty-five years on. There must have been a striking resemblance throughout the family: Cathcut glanced again at Lepage, but he seemed unmoved.

'Mother, you shouldn't run like that. You know what the doctor said about it.'

'Oh, I'm all right, darling.' She scratched a fringe of grey hair out of her eyes, and ran both hands down her broad flanks. 'Well, Janice, you might have asked them in; just so they don't think we never knew any manners.' She smiled at Cathcut with eyes that were puffy with crying. 'Won't you come in, sir, just to show we knows our manners?' The forced humour in her pretended illiteracy, the way she bit her lip after smiling, were very distressing. He found being called 'sir' unpleasant. 'You won't mind the kitchen, will you, sir? It's just that when we're on our own we find it more comfortable in the kitchen.' She led the way and Cathcut followed, giving place to the girl. Lepage came behind; when Cathcut turned to look back he was taking a scribbling pad from his pocket.

Within seconds they were seated in the kitchen, where a light was on, even though it was still mid-afternoon. The table was a dark brown, a good wood, but the surface ruined by white burn-marks, as if it was used for ironing. Cathcut's cape was silently taken from him and hung beside the boiler.

'You'll have some tea, won't you, sir? Steam is up, and it won't take a second.'

In spite of his refusal and her daughter's pleadings, tea was made; sighing, the daughter got down some cups and saucers from the dresser. Tea apparently included bread, butter and jam: the mother began cutting slices off a loaf, holding the bread against her bosom, and slicing horizontally towards her with a thin-bladed knife. Lepage put his notepad on the table in front of him. The mother suddenly dropped her knife with a cry, transferred the loaf to the other hand, and put her thumb to her mouth.

'Oh Mummy, you've cut yourself!'

'No, darling, I'm all right.'

She grabbed for the knife on the floor and began frantically carving at the loaf again, her face very red. A fair drop of blood showed.

'Mummy, *please* let me do it.'

'I'm all right, darling, really I am. It's just that I'm a bit overwrought;' and she looked reproachfully at the two men, tears welling in her eyes. Cathcut found himself genuinely sorry: it was not in any way a contrived or intellectually worked-up pity. He was glad at the ache under his breastbone; glad also that Lepage was brought into close contact with *this*. The daughter ran to grab the loaf, but her mother dodged her and, turning her back, continued hacking away.

'Well you might at least sit down to it.' In exasperation the girl pushed a chair at her and she sat down, legs wide apart, still working on the loaf in her lap.

'Mrs Driscoll, I can vouch for the fact that Inspector Lepage had no hand in your daughter's death. Indeed, he has, for that reason, a particular interest in finding out who was responsible.' He glanced nervously at Lepage, but the policeman sat on, tensely, without moving. The woman placed her half-cut loaf on the table and began scraping butter over the slices, head down, her eyes filled with tears.

'You're not the only boy-friend she's had,' she said suddenly, looking directly at Lepage, and scanning his face for a sign of jealousy; but she was disappointed. 'A much *younger* man . . . a Robert Evans.'

Lepage seemed to carve the name into his pad with his pen. The daughter continued with more pronounced malevolence and without her mother's touch of pride:

'In fact, she met him at a dance, a dance *you'd* taken her to.'

Lepage turned on her a terrible smile of contempt and hatred. But if Lepage had done that, even once, he could hardly hope to keep his part quiet. Lepage seemed to anticipate Cathcut's thoughts, for he broke his silence, turning towards him.

'We went separately, I introduced her to no one; and I did not even associate much with her—as you might guess from what seems to have happened.' Again he looked at the girl, who shrank away. Cathcut felt a wish to grasp her hand; or do anything that would reassure her that he was not a party to that scorn.

At this reminder of her elder daughter's life, the mother stretched out her arms on the table and, lowering her head on them, began to cry audibly. The younger daughter pushed her chair next to her mother, put her arm round her back, and, lifting her a little, brought her cheek against her own.

'Mummy, you've still got me,' she said gently.

'I've been so *betrayed*,' the woman cried.

Immediately, Cathcut saw the meaning of the lipstick, the pretty blouse, the necklace; he felt ashamed that for a moment he had wondered if the girl were going the same way as her sister. Over her mother's back she looked appealingly, as if begging them to leave; but the mother sat up, controlled her sobs, and enclosed her daughter's hand in her own.

'Isn't she a smasher, gentlemen? Just look at her, isn't she a darling?' she appealed to them excitedly.

Cathcut murmured something complimentary, watching at the same time the girl, who seemed quite bewildered by this new turn. She was indeed very attractive with her long, dark hair, pronounced nose, finely proportioned figure; but more attractive to him in her concern, in her pitiable anxiety. For a moment he felt that her mother played this over-strung child like a practised violinist; and though the result was sweet, he began to be angry at it. The woman continued her harangue, almost auctioneering her second child.

'And she hasn't a boy-friend yet, gentlemen, she's never even been kissed.' The girl blushed and looked wretchedly confused. 'Don't you think it's time she had a boy-friend, gentlemen?' She turned towards her. 'Darling, you *must* go out on your own and not bother yourself about me. I'm no company for you at my age. Look at me,' and she pulled at her unkempt grey hair; 'you want to be with people of your own age, not dragging around with me.'

'Oh mummy!' she cried, and hugged her close.

All this time Lepage had been staring at the girl's face, as if trying to see what her mother saw. His expression grew steadily more despairing. At length he broke in:

'What other acquaintances of your daughter can you name?'

The girl replied for her.

'You, and the other, are all we know of. We didn't see much of her after she left home.'

'And were you giving your daughter any support, financially, I mean?'

Again the girl answered, bitterly:

'You know very well we weren't.'

'And what about your father?'

Mrs Driscoll burst out into terrified pleading. 'Please, *please*, don't tell my husband anything of this, we haven't told him anything, not a word, not about you, I mean. And you, darling, don't mention that they've been here. All he knows is that she's left home and set up on her own. He gets so upset, you know, and then he's not really responsible for what he does or says. He's a good soul, but he feels differently about it, *would want to go to the police.*' Behind this last remark there was a veiled threat.

'So you don't want to tell them . . . about *me*?' Lepage spoke slowly, watching her face intently.

'No . . . no, you have a special reason to find out who did it.' And softening, she stretched a hand across the table and laid it gently on that of the man she thought to have loved her daughter. Lepage slid his hand from under, so that hers hit the table. He spoke again, watching her tear-blotched face.

'Because there'll be an inquiry, a coroner's inquest. And you will have to tell them about your daughter's friends. A pity, considering that probably no one knows but those here—and needless, too, seeing that I know *nothing* about the crime. Though I promise you—I shall.'

'When I think what they'll say about my girl, what I've heard said about other people's children. . . . It's not so much the neighbours, we don't have much to do with them . . . but there's no understanding on these things. And I have another child to think of. It's so *awful* for her.'

He put in quickly:

'Then it seems it would be best for all concerned if your *husband* represented you at the inquest.'

A silence followed as each interpreted this.

'And what about the other?' the daughter asked suddenly.

'If the inquest occurs before we make a charge, I will inform the coroner. I would prefer if his name were not mentioned in open court.'

The girl looked uneasy and turned to Cathcut.

'What is your advice, Mr Cathcut?'

Cathcut remembered Lepage's undertaking, and weighed the value to be placed on his word, together with the limitless opportunity of bringing him to face the consequences of his actions.

'I would do as he says.'

'Darling, you know all about these inquests and such, you're such a clever girl; memorize it all and explain it to me afterwards. I'll do what you say,' she said to Lepage, and waited as if expecting some expression of gratitude. Lepage sat looking into her face, tight-lipped. After staring at him a while she began crying softly.

'What made her do such a thing? Is it something I've done? I've tried to do my best, but I've gone wrong somewhere.' She shook her head, and the tears out of her eyes.

'Mummy, you mustn't keep blaming yourself.'

'Somehow I feel I'm to blame.'

'We are all liable to sin,' said Cathcut gently.

Greatly moved, she exclaimed fiercely at him:

'Oh, but that's not normal, that's not acquired, it's born in them, in the blood. It's low intelligence, they can't help themselves, poor things. —Came from her father's side, there's quite a few no-goods in *that* family. His father was always the same, unsure of himself, and all his brothers married beneath them: not bad women, mind, I'm not saying anything against them—but *not very bright.*' She emphasized this last as if the solution to all human wrongdoing were contained in it. There was an awkward silence. 'Oh dear, I do go on. Somehow I don't seem able to stop myself now.' She laid her head upon her hands again, and both men got to their feet, leaving their tea untouched; at once the daughter opened the hall door for them. Her mother looked up.

'No, darling, I'll go, please let me go, I'd be better for a gasp of fresh air, really I would.'

'It's cold out the front, mother.'

'I could put on another cardigan, look, I've got one here.' But she allowed herself to be settled back in her chair, and the door to be closed on her. At the front door the girl stopped, and brought herself to ask Lepage a question on her own account.

'I can't trouble mother with this. When will we be able to bury her body?' The courage of her asking, her tired, hollowed eyes, moved Cathcut even more. Lepage stiffened.

'When the post-mortem is completed, and the inquest opened. When permission is given, you will be told.' Lepage opened the door himself, and stepped out. Cathcut wanted to say something kindly, particularly as she had earlier asked his advice and must desperately need support. He stood with one foot on the doorstep and held out a hand. Was she so prettily dressed for her mother, or partly because she so much wanted affection?

'I'm afraid your mother must be rather a trial to you,' he said softly. She looked at him with sudden surprise and distress, ignoring his hand.

'*You* ought to know more about Christian charity, I should think.' He withdrew his hand and foot, and she shut the door. At once he felt ashamed; the remark was divisive, he had tried to insinuate a wedge between her and her mother. But he felt strongly enough to say, to himself rather than to Lepage:

'You know, she'll sacrifice herself to her mother.'

'Or do the other thing,' Lepage replied. There was no mistaking the bitter hostility in his tone, although Cathcut was convinced that the girl nauseated him rather than anything else. 'Or go the same way as her sister.'

Cathcut looked at the white face, now split by a smile that exposed a mouth of large yellow teeth and bloodless gums. Lepage was very acute, but there was no real humour: his amusement was stretched over a frame of despair and what looked like jealousy.

'You know, my pretty priest,' Lepage said, 'if you were, I'm not suggesting it is likely, but if you *were* to become interested in that girl... in a sense, it would make us brothers-in-law, would it not?'

CHAPTER NINE

They arranged to meet again that evening, outside the youth club. Lepage, as Cathcut had guessed he might, arrived some minutes early. Cathcut recognized him as he passed under a street light, ran, and caught up with him in the lobby. The semi-darkness and pounding beat within covered his breathlessness.

The hall was an abandoned scout hut, its lease reverting to the church as sponsoring authority when the troop caved in for lack of leaders—Cathcut had felt he hadn't the touch himself to keep it going. At intervals down the sides of the hall, wall-heaters cast a faint, reddish glow, and within the warm radius of each a group of youths or girls stood listlessly waiting, each group turned in on itself, segregated by inclination and expecting nothing in particular. Their inactivity irritated Cathcut, especially at a time when he wanted them to be vital. They cohered like rings of frog-spawn in a pond, none wanting to be born, afraid of breaking out of uniformity, of breaching the circle by showing any urge for life. Marriage, affairs, boyfriends were *breaking*—the others would mock, or ignore one glassily as an oddity.

'What are you? The Twilight people?' He jerked the cord of a light-switch nearest the door. 'Johnnie, can't you get some table-tennis going?' Johnnie was his brightest boy, and he knew by experience that it was better to work through *agents provocateurs*. Johnnie stimulated a little flurry of activity. A scuffed hardboard was produced from the men's toilet, bottle-green with white lines painted on it, and a rough deal table dragged out from the wall and under the light. 'Anyone got bats?' A general cry: 'Bats, bats.' One was pulled from under a form, its green-rubber covering peeling off one side. A ping-pong ball on a window-ledge proved to have a dent, and Johnnie went to the kitchen to steam it at the kettle. By the time he returned his group had melted away, no one could be found to play, and he was left by himself to listlessly bounce the repaired ball. Cathcut thought he ought to offer the support of a game, but was anxious to keep with Lepage. Behind him, someone switched off the light.

He piloted Lepage towards a woman with amazing blue hair under the neon light of the kitchen at the far end. Steering through the gloom, Cathcut was comforted by some minimal nods of greeting, but mostly they ignored him, swaying to the music and re-grouping, circlets of spawn disturbed by an eddy of current.

The record stopped as they came into the circle of light from the open door, and beyond the kitchen they heard the *flick-flock* of a badminton shuttlecock.

'Any tea in the pot, Mrs Temple?'

'John, Mr Cathcut's looked in,' she called through to the smaller hall. 'Think we might squeeze you one,' she said affably.

As they sipped tea another record was put on, turned up louder still, and a coloured disc activated before the spotlight. The increased volume, and the play of rapidly changing coloured lights across the dark surface of the pool, seemed to stir it up a little. One boy invaded another circle, and pulled out a giggling, bosomy girl. After some token dragging back, she consented, and they gyrated a few times, the groups watching with half an eye. By running on the spot and dragging his feet behind, the lad gave a passable imitation of holding his position on a moving escalator, his feet slipping away from under him. The girl giggled, snapping her fingers in time and flicking her elbows outward.

Lepage, by an effort of concentration, fastened on them a bone-dissecting stare. After a while they gave up, and returned to their respective groups.

'Do you want me to make an announcement?' Cathcut whispered.

No answer.

'. . . It's *your* speech, you'd better make it,' Mrs Temple was saying to her husband, a balding, middle-aged man, brilliant under the neon in white shorts and ankle socks, with blushing, over-heated knees.

'Look, I *hate* making complaints,' he protested to Cathcut in an undertone, conscious of a stranger present, 'but something *must* be done about this noise. We pay good money, and we can't hear ourselves *think*.' The clergyman and Lepage together seemed to make him feel a little undressed. 'Why don't they *do* something? You'd be better converting the heathen Chinese. . . . All this keeping them at school just makes them aimless drifters. You're supposed to be in charge, why don't you *organize* something?

When I was their age, I'd be running all over the place. Football one night, badminton the next—and I'm not so bad, even at my age,' he said, looking down self-consciously at his white, venous calves with their blue, projecting valves.

Cathcut made no reply, dispirited. He couldn't explain that the youth didn't seem inspired by any pleasure-principle of that kind, that he was weary of providing all impetus and energy.

'It's an age for standing around,' Mrs Temple said from the sink, in a tone of soothing maternal philosophy. She sponged flecks of detergent from her fleshy elbows. 'Why don't you go back to your game, John?'

'Sometimes,' he said at his wife's back as he passed, 'I wonder if we weren't better off in the war, killing one another, than all this standing around.'

Lepage had commandeered the spot and, arresting its disc of coloured transparencies, was idly directing the white beam to and fro over the audience. Cathcut could not make out if he was making some preliminary survey, or merely enjoying the dazzled, frightened faces that turned unseeingly toward the source of power. He seemed in no hurry to begin his interviews.

'Do you want more light?'

Lepage's attention was attracted by a group in one corner, their backs toward him, chuckling among themselves, engrossed. He turned the spotlight on them, and caught a fluttering kaleidoscope of cavorting legs, like an animated Shield of Man. The pictures turned livid purplish as the light caught the gleam of their bent, shiny surface. Lepage seemed irritated at the group's absorption and indifference to him. Leaving the spot to swing of its own accord, he came up slowly behind them, Cathcut reluctantly tagging after.

Reaching from behind, Lepage lifted out the nudes from among them and thumbed the magazine over, to muttered protests:—'You'll pay me five bob for that.' —'Thought you were above that kind of thing.' After a minute or two he paused, magazine in hand.

'Know anything about the Driscoll girl? . . . Know any of her friends?' The lads looked uneasy, shifting their feet, hoping that someone else would answer.

'Come off it, chief. None of us had anything to do with *that*. We like our crumpet *straight*.'

Lepage looked again at the pictures. Cathcut came nearer, in case of trouble.

'We never knew any of her friends, 'cos she thought she was

too good to be friends with us.' The bosomy, overdeveloped girl had joined the group, sensing something was up.

Lepage spread out a bevy of lovelies along the top of a wooden form. They waited while he contemplated, none daring to break away for fear of suspicion.

'When I look at my pillow,' Lepage said, 'it looks a clean, decent piece of cloth. But when I put my head down, go nearer, look into the weave, neither warp nor woof runs parallel, there are flecks and knobs on the strands. . . . Doesn't it worry you that, if you come close, they've got enlarged pores and broken veins? This'—he waved the paper—'is just optical illusion, a matter of distance.'

The lads listened apprehensively, looking at one another in bewilderment. Cathcut wanted to say that the perception of beauty depended on one's ability to appreciate—or is it to *construct?*—inherent form: that it could only be received by those who were harmonized, the intellectual parts quiescent. Only pattern could relate to pattern: harmony couldn't be perceived by discord. Without the initial experience, the sudden flash of inscape, the mind had nothing to work on; it couldn't understand why a chance arrangement and combination of molecules, viewed from a certain distance, in certain atmospheric conditions and accidents of light, should move joy in excess of evident, rational causes.

Only a harmonized mind could read the Divine handwriting. Music made no sense on its various levels unless intellectual and passionate faculties were properly ordered, the intellectual subordinate to the experiential. He had worked it out for himself, to cope with his own failing perceptions. But feeling that he was ceasing to be harmonized, he knew it only as a matter of faith, and felt sadly that he couldn't speak with conviction—and anyway, it seemed odd to be saying it about *this.*

'*Aaw*—*granted* they shave their fluffies, and the photo's retouched. . . . Come on, let's not get technical, chief. What's it matter, if it gets a raise?'

Lepage looked disgusted, and Cathcut tried to draw him away.

'Now, take the lady in question,' said the same lad, intoxicated by his own bravado, and propping his magazine back in its original position with an air of having gained his point. 'Fine feathers make a fine bird. D'yer mean ter tell me she didn't try to make the best of herself? All powder an' paint—regular doll on legs.' He made a shapely gesture with his hands.

'Stuck-up chicken,' said one of the girls sourly, joining the group and guessing from his words and gesture what they must be talking about.

'Wouldn't 'ave minded pulling some of the feathers off her.' He sniggered at his own wit. Cathcut winced at what Lepage must be suffering.

'Fer Christ's sake—not the *dead*.' One of the lad's companions held up a warning finger.

The bosomy girl, more acute, realized that he had got a bit above himself, and might be running into trouble.

'Ian Thorpe, all *your* sex is in your head.' She tossed her head contemptuously towards the opened magazine.

'Better'n what's on offer for real,' he returned, unabashed.

Cathcut hardly heard the answer; he was anxiously intent on Lepage's face as he surveyed the sprawling nudes. Lepage seemed deeply struck by one particular pose. Very white, with theatrical deliberation, he slipped a hand in his jacket and, drawing out his wallet, laid a further photograph down upon the magazine.

'Snap!'

It was a full-length study of the body, lying as found. The group looked down, backed away. 'You trying to turn my stomach?' muttered one. No one knew quite what to do.

'You shouldn't do that, it doesn't serve any purpose,' Cathcut whispered at last, tugging at his sleeve.

Quite unexpectedly, the lad Thorpe took Lepage's other elbow, saying in a very different tone, quiet but authoritative: 'Put it away, chief. Put it away,' nodding with his head towards the door. Instantaneously, almost instinctively, the whole group had formed itself into a wall between Lepage and the dead girl's sister, who had come unnoticed into the half-lit hall, and was standing on tip-toe, looking over heads. Lepage reclaimed his picture.

Cathcut felt mucky at what he had been looking at, unknowingly, in that pure presence. He attracted her attention to himself, pointing her to the light from the kitchen, and hoping fervently that Thorpe would quickly gather up his property behind him. As though to intensify the priest's shame, she had dressed completely in white, some gauzy substance too flimsy for a November evening; she had taken off her raincoat in the lobby and draped it over one arm. Cathcut knew it was all intended for him.

She pushed through to him directly, oblivious or indifferent to the stir her arrival had caused. Cathcut felt a sharp surge of relief, an aching longing for purity: an ache stimulated by those far-away, blue-grey eyes, whose distance seemed to promise endless search, aspiration without the corruption of bodily contact, the disappointment of fleshly satisfaction; the sharpness was akin to his recurrent longing for self-annihilation. She floated above all this vulgarity—he suddenly realized she was tall, stately as Solomon's palm tree: *'Turn away your eyes, for they disturb me . . . terrible as an army with banners.'*

'My beloved is like a gazelle'. . . . Under the eyes she was puffy, and the skin had pulled tight across the bony bridge of her nose from too much crying. Tripping up to him, she pushed a packet into his hand.

'You left this.' Warmed plastic. It was his cape, neatly rolled, now slightly scented; he had left it hanging by the boiler to dry. In her way of gently handing it over was an implied penitence for her previous asperity.

'You shouldn't have bothered.'

'Mother thought it would do me good to come out.'

'How is she?'

She shrugged her shoulders helplessly, then brightened a little.

'She thought we might come to a service on Sunday.'

'I'm glad.'

They stood for a moment, looking round.

'You know the police are here?' he said solicitously. She seemed so delicate, scented, fragile, standing within his protection as if belonging to him. He sensed a bottomless loneliness and restlessness in her, into which he could pour an ocean of concern and yet the need still remain, craving, unsatisfied. It made his spirit ache with longing: something so touchingly dependent that she would be frightened off and immeasurably damaged by the least severity.

'I know; I've seen him. . . . I shan't stay long. —Does he *have* to keep on bouncing that thing?' she asked irritably. Johnnie, Cathcut's favourite, was hovering just out of earshot, heavy with inept, unexpressed sympathy, still bouncing the ping-pong ball. 'He's always hanging around me, making cow-eyes.' She looked quickly at Cathcut, anxious lest she were forfeiting his approval. 'It's not my fault if there's something about him makes me feel a bit sick. I do wish he'd go away, especially *today*.' Cathcut felt suddenly irritated with him and was on the point of saying something, but was forestalled.

'Come on, Johnnie. I'll be your heart-throb for today.' The bosomy girl, realizing he was making himself a nuisance, had caught him by the elbow. But he pulled away and spun his back to her, still bouncing the ball, bending progressively lower, with great concentration patting faster and faster. Eventually he stubbed the ball on his palm, perhaps by design; it hit his heel and shot across the floor, lodging in Cathcut's trouser turn-up and then falling amidst their feet. With both of them trying to avoid trampling it and each other, the girl caught it under her instep, and retrieved it with a large dent.

'Oh Johnnie, I *am* sorry . . . somehow I don't seem able to help myself these days. Here . . . let me steam it out for you.'

'It's already been done; it won't work again,' he said sullenly.

But she rushed off to the kitchen, leaving Cathcut warm inside at her compassion, her generosity.

When she failed to return, Cathcut went into the kitchen. Mrs Temple was putting crockery into a wall cupboard.

'Your ball's there,' she said shortly, nodding to where it lay in a runnel of the stainless steel draining-board, perfect again in form.

'Where . . . where's Miss Driscoll?' he asked, with a throb of embarrassment.

'Gone out through the back door. I told her she ought to be at home with her mother.' A certain firmness in her tone made Cathcut regret once again that parish clergy couldn't avoid getting entangled in feminine jealousies. Janice had let herself be packed off without saying goodbye: he felt let down. But he put it down to her situation, the pressure she was under—and anyway, it was ridiculous to be making social demands at a time like this.

'Anyway, it's not company for *her* tonight.' Mrs Temple closed the cupboard door firmly.

Cathcut remembered Lepage.

In an agony of fear and guilt, he rushed back into the main hall and half-ran round its outskirts, jostling bodies and scanning faces. There was something about the Driscoll girl that called to the abyss inside him; he had allowed himself to be distracted, and now Lepage had slipped his leash and *he* would be responsible for anything that happened. Lepage was not in the hall, nor in any of the lobbies. Cathcut's desperation was evident: the faces in the darkness seemed to be mocking his frantic search.

'What's the matter? Lost your sweetheart, Cathy?' The overblown girl was calling to him. 'Lovely, isn't she, Cathy? Doesn't she make your heart *beat*?'—and she laid a hand on her over-ripe bosom. 'But you'll have to share her with Johnnie,' she said slyly, 'Johnnie's sweet on her too.'

'That man: the man I was with—where's he gone?'

'What you want to know for?' Her tone was insolent, he could have wrung her neck.

'Because I'm not interested.'

'What's it worth? Worth a kiss for old fatso?' She pushed her chest at him. Oh no! she too had aspirations; Cathcut was reduced almost to screaming at this latest complication. He checked round to see who had heard.

'Out in the passage, then.' They pushed through the crowd, in twin hastes of desire and despair.

Reaching out in the darkness, he kissed her with repulsion, his lips recoiling from her rubbery flesh, only too aware of the endless capital she'd make out of it. But perhaps they wouldn't believe her.

'It's only for what I know,' she said sadly.

'What *do* you know?' She was making the most of every moment.

'. . . I told him, try 'is own backyard . . . try Bob Evans.' A further jealousy struck her. 'Hey! . . . *You've* not been playing around with big sister too?'

'Evans? *What* Evans?'—though he panicked further at hearing that name from a second source.

'*You* know: Bob Evans . . . *Robert* Evans . . . "Robby the Bobby".'

There *had* been an Evans, an intense man in his twenties, whose chief ground for coming to the club seemed to be to distribute some tracts of dubious theological content; and of course, there *was* some connection with the police.

'What did you *say?*'

'That I'd seen *her*—the dead 'un—see *him* home most nights.'

Cathcut wanted to run, but wasn't sure where to run to.

'Where *is* home?' Each detail had to be dragged out of her.

'Hasn't got one. He lives in the station barracks.'

He'd be safe there . . . no danger for a while . . . there'd be nothing straightforward from Lepage. Cathcut relaxed at last. And his own punishment was mercifully averted, at least for a while. The girl's behaviour hadn't merited even a parting word, so he went out into the street in silence, intending to go home and think out his whole position in the light of developments.

CHAPTER TEN

'Now there stood by the cross of Jesus his mother, and his mother's sister, Mary the wife of Cleophas, and Mary Magdalene.

'When Jesus therefore saw his mother, and the disciple standing by, whom he loved, he saith unto his mother, Woman, behold thy son.'

'Then saith he to the disciple, Behold thy mother! And from that hour that disciple took her unto his own home.'

They sat in silence for a moment, savouring the reading.

'It's a pity that brother John died so young . . . and that John Senior was such a swine.'

Care made no response.

'I suppose you're working today?'

'I have leave till this fever subsides.'

She slapped the soiled dishes together under her son's nose, and took them to the kitchen.

'Our *Lord* was never ill.'

Care sat staring, his eyes watering. He was aware of her attempts to rile him, but they took place at a distance.

'. . . It's the things you do. You may think I don't know, but it's the things you do.' She banged the dishes about in the metal sink.

He leaned to the centre of the circular table and levered upright a heavy bookend by pulling with his fingertips on its upended base. It was a brass hand pressed down upon a black metal plate, the left hand of a matching pair which, when upright, supported on each side the black family Bible from which they had been reading.

'Stop *fiddling.*'

He put the two bookends together, so that the hands touched in a posture of supplication. With a sideways pass of his fingertips, he set the black table-centre spinning within its mahogany circumference. His mother returned from the kitchen, but ignored the gently turning hands.

'I made that book the centrepiece of my family. And I can but say it grieves me to see it displaced. It contains God's law for man, and I'll have no "inspiration", no *"tongue"*, that breaks from that centre.'

'The Spirit does not *break* Law,' he said wearily. 'It controls Law, governs its application to particular situations; but Spirit does *not* break Law.'

'"*Ye say ye have faith? Then let me see your* works*!*"' she cried, placing her palms on the table and leaning down to thrust her face into his.

They were interrupted by a long, hard ring at the front door-bell. It had a familiar, aggressive insistence which they both recognized.

'That's your friends from the Meeting.' She made it an accusation. 'They came last night, after you had gone to bed. I sent them away,' she said with satisfaction, then became suddenly suspicious. 'Why are they taking the morning off work, in the hope of finding you at home?'

'They know I have a fever.'

'I'll say you are in bed.' Her tone was suddenly wheedling, protective.

'You'll say that I will see them *here.*'

She came back with two men who belonged normally to different factions of the Meeting: Care was surprised to see them together. Brother Andrew he thought of as wholly good-natured, receptive to change; Brother Roberts had a mean, sardonic tone.

'It seems, Brother Care, you have a very persistent fever. . . . Have you asked the Meeting to lay on hands?'

'It comes and goes.'

'Ah yes! comes and goes . . . as does your other ailment.'

Care stiffened and waited. His mother gathered up the milk and the marmalade pot from before the visitors, checked that there was nothing on the chairs that might stain their dark suits, but left her family Bible defiantly open. Brother Roberts, by silence and by ignoring what was before him, managed to convey that this could not be expected to cut any ice; Brother Andrew, finding scripture at his elbow as he took his seat, looked over the passage they had been reading, and grinned round at them.

Brother Roberts kept accounts for a Water Board: he straightened his papers on the table before him and placed several biros meticulously beside them, like pipes waiting to be laid. Then he glanced up enquiringly at Mrs Care, who left the room. Brother Andrew waved affably after her.

Brother Roberts cleared his throat formally, before reading the complaint.

'On Sunday the 14th of November, during the free-prayer session of the Meeting, the irruption of a "tongue" was followed, not by prophetic *interpretation* (to which we had allowed ourselves to become accustomed), but by cursing and obscenities.' Brother Roberts ticked the item in his neatly written notes before reading the second.

'... On Sunday the 21st of November, a "tongue" from the same source was again followed by blasphemies and obscenities, from the same interpreter.' A further tick.

'... On Sunday the 28th of November, there was a repetition of these incidents, with the same speaker and interpreter as before.'

Brother Roberts eased his chair back from the table and hauled on a harshly knotted tie, as if anxious that nothing should infiltrate between his starched collar and a neck already raw. The biro between his right hand fingers stippled his chin.

Brother Andrew seemed almost to leap out of the confines of his suit. 'We represent *both* wings of the Meeting—insofar as the Meeting *can h*ave wings,' he said, looking anxiously across at Brother Roberts. They waited, tensely.

'We *must* have an explanation,' said Brother Andrew. 'Something we can take back to the Meeting. An explanation of some sort.' Brother Roberts controlled him with a look.

'When I speak the interpretation, I speak under inspiration. I have a moment of choice, either to rise to my feet or to remain seated; but from the moment that I accept the burden I am no longer master of what I say.'

Brother Roberts looked scandalized at such an admission. Brother Andrew pinched the edge of the table between thumb and forefinger.

'I am not the voice'—a twinge of pain crossed Care's face—'I am only *secondary*. But I have my inspiration too, which though subsequent to the voice is still a *gift*.'

'We *respect* the gift, we *respect* the gift,' cried Brother Andrew, extending his long neck in Care's direction, so that Care could see the oil extruded from his brow.

Brother Roberts pecked at his papers with his biro.

'The only *intelligible* voice the Meeting hears is *yours*. And *you* speak obscenities.'

Care blushed in excess of his fever:

'That is true only of the last three meetings. And I am confident that the source of infection has been isolated.'

'There has been a further, *extraordinary* meeting. I am empowered—Brother Andrew and I are empowered—to seek your withdrawal.'

'Temporarily,' assured Brother Andrew. 'Temporarily, till the matter is resolved.'

'It *is* resolved.'

They checked at something peculiar in his tone.

'That cannot be settled just on your assurance,' murmured Brother Roberts, leafing through his papers till he found the note he required. '. . . You say you have no recollection of what you utter?'

'I said it was peculiarly *difficult* to retain the interpretation. It requires practice and effort—which I am not always willing to make.'

Brother Roberts lifted an eyebrow at him. 'It might be a time when a little effort would isolate the truth.'

'Effort and passivity must be held in balance. Too much effort kills inspiration.'

Brother Roberts shrugged his shoulders in despair. For the moment he surrendered his spokesmanship to Brother Andrew.

'I have *faith* in the tongue,' said Brother Andrew, making little circles in the air with both his red hands. 'The first time I heard it, it cleaned the air for me, as if a vacuum cleaner had gone sucking all the little bits of dust out of it.' He drew a deep lungful, pushing his chest through his opened jacket with the motion of a breast-stroke swimmer. 'But that hasn't *changed*,' he said, 'it hasn't changed. And that *bothers* me.' They waited for him to make his point, but he seemed to think he had done so.

There was a scrabbling outside the door, and Care went out into the hall. He found his mother standing on a chair at the far side, scraping a fleck of paint from a window-light over the lounge door. It was just possible that from where she stood she could see through a corresponding light into the breakfast room; but he made no comment and returned to his visitors.

'I will accept a discerner,' he announced as he entered the room. 'It must come to a decision.'

'A discerner!' cried Brother Andrew, his face radiant as if he had glimpsed the vanguard of the Second Coming. Then a cloud intervened. 'But where are we to find a discerner?'

'To my sorrow, there has been no one in the Meeting empowered to discriminate tongues. We must seek outside. Other meetings have received the gifts.'

Brother Roberts distorted his biro into a right-angle and laid it around a corner of his note-pad.

'Authority from within the Meeting is bad enough. Self-appointed authority from *outside* is intolerable.'

Care smiled as though he had detected him in conscious untruth.

'But, brother, you know as well as I, from earliest days the Brotherhood has had leaders. And where leadership was least openly acknowledged, it was often at its most insidious.' He stretched to the centre of the table and set the bookends apart. 'He is the left hand, I am the right. Without a discerner, how are you to decide between us?'

Brother Roberts began to bluster.

'It is the *Meeting*,' he said, 'the *Meeting* that must decide. The Brotherhood has never had heads, no more than does this table.' He traced its circumference in the air with the point of a fresh biro.

'But till recently the meetings have not had the Spirit.' Care checked at Brother Andrew's pained look and corrected himself. 'At least, not in its most direct form. And the Spirit by its gifts creates differing functions, one of which is leadership.'

The telephone rang in the hall, and Care's mother showed her most panic-stricken face at the door. He jumped to his feet to prevent her from speaking.

'It's the Chief Constable,' she whispered, as he pushed her back towards the lounge. Deceived by her voluminous housecoat, he inadvertently pressed upon her bosom and shuddered at the contact.

'Mother, when will you learn that, if I take leave, I take leave.' He edged past her to the receiver.

'I hear you've left Lepage in charge.' The Chief Constable was at his most accusatory.

'Temporarily.'

'How temporary is *that*?'

'Till this fever subsides.'

'When I was your age, I came to work with a temperature of 103°.'

Care made no comment.

'—Half a hundred jobs are at stake in this. If we have to accept an amalgamation it's retirement or a step down for a round dozen of us. We need a success . . . particularly in this sort of thing, where the press always takes an interest.'

'The press knows as well as you or I that the murder of a prostitute is, as often as not, insoluble.'

'That won't keep them off us. I'll expect you today.'

Care put down the receiver sharply. He returned to find his visitors already on their feet. Brother Roberts had rolled his papers into a sceptre.

'We find your involvement with temporal authorities unfitting. It is not the practice of the Brotherhood to involve themselves in the world.' He looked sharply at Brother Andrew, inviting support.

'Hold hard,' said Brother Andrew, who was a leading figure in a Trades Council. 'Not all of us would go along with that.'

Care handed Brother Roberts a biro he had neglected upon the table.

'I have always taught that the room must be swept, before the arrival of our Guest.'

Brother Roberts sniffed indignantly and pocketed up the biro.

'We took opportunity during your absence to hold a brief discussion. We conclude that we must place your offer before the meeting. Till then, we ask you to withdraw.'

'Is *he* also excluded?' Care asked as they went out.

Brother Roberts paused on the threshold and looked at Care full-face. 'We are not unjust,' he said.

'*Both* of you. Both of you, till it is resolved,' added Brother Andrew, lest there should be any room for misunderstanding. He bobbed his way out.

Care returned to the breakfast table, sat, and idly picked up a folded paper napkin, fitting the longest side of the triangle into his back gums and tugging alternately on either protruding corner, so that it chafed several times across his furred tongue. The paper began to deteriorate into wet rolls in his mouth, and he desisted. His fever seemed to give him patches of hectic intensity and then leave him drained—or perhaps the patches of intensity *were* his fever. The departure of his guests left him ill-equipped to face his mother's onslaught.

He was in trouble, she insisted, he must share it with his

mother, though they had gone separate ways of late she was still his mother, she had a *right* to know, she found herself awake at nights for fear of the things he was getting into.

'I have to go to the station,' he said.

'It's those *men*,' she cried, 'because of those men. They have no conscience, no *law*.'

'It is not "those men".' He was well-aware of her ability to stir up a half-simulated panic, communicate it, and then take control. He smiled wryly. 'You yourself *wanted* me to work.'

The sudden fading of anxiety from her face showed that she knew she had forfeited the round. As quickly, she was off on another tack. He was dressed to go out, she would always insist on it for breakfast-time, but his hair was unkempt. She got into the hall before him, produced a hairbrush from nowhere, and in a second had hopped up on to her decorating chair and was standing, barring his path. There was no way his scalp could escape her ministrations. He suffered it for the sake of peace.

'Your hair has never been the same since I stopped washing it myself,' she said, drawing down a precise parting, and flicking up his forelock into a boyish quiff. He put up his hand to arrest the brush, resting his grip on her slackened wrist with a minimum of unwillingness.

'I feel so very sad, mother.... All that Baptist morality would never have set me free. I *had* to go on.'

He felt her arm stiffen. She pulled away and beat again at his scalp.

'The best kind of freedom, my son,' she said, 'is a good conscience.'

The housecoat smelt sweaty and imbued with cooking smells. He moved on up the hall, leaving her standing, her hairbrush poised. Before going out, he went into the lobby and scrubbed his hands again meticulously, wiping his face with the damp corner of a towel, but leaving his hair as she had set it.

'I shall be sleeping at the station till this is over,' he said to her as he emerged.

She staged a second catastrophe. 'You're *killing* me, springing this kind of thing on me, killing me by *inches*. How am I to explain it to Agnes when she arrives? ... Everything I've ever wanted for you you've killed. Whatever do you want to do *that* for? You almost killed me the day you were born. One of these days you'll be my death, my death.' She stopped in full-tilt, changing tone at the degree of resistance in his face. 'Why don't you say you'll *not* be my death?'

Care paused before answering.

'You seem so very certain that I *am*.'

Seeing the game was over for the present, she promptly adjusted her manner. 'I thank God,' she said, laying a hand on his arm, 'I thank my God that, however we are taken different ways of late, we can still share the scriptures together.' She pulled his head down toward her and kissed his cheek. 'Go where you have to.'

He brushed his cheek with his hand, like a child.

'Goodbye, mother.'

CHAPTER ELEVEN

Towards morning, after a disturbed night, Cathcut dreamed he was in the temple of Astarte. Music and décor were from Verdi's *Aida*, the Triumphal March. The long trumpets brayed, the people shouted: 'Hail, O Astarte, changeless in unending death!' The Guardians of the Shrine, shiny-naked, their members erect and high above their waists, filed down each side of the staircase, formed two lines, looked toward the black, opened doorway of the Temple. They rolled their hands over and over, as if applying oil to their erected parts, then pulled back their arms on either side, making a head-and-shoulders bow to the priestess, who now appeared in the doorway. The door was low, her stooped shoulders stuck between the jambs: she had three breasts, equidistant, pinned to a diagonal green sash tied athwart her chest like a drum-majorette. The teats jutted on the broad silk band as she breasted her way through the door, came down through the files to reach Cathcut. Behind her, clouds of black smoke billowed from the temple door, greasy as though from burning petroleum rags, flecked with fragments of burnt cloth or other matter. Queen Astarte came to a halt before Cathcut. Hands on his shoulders forced him to kneel, pushed his head forward to lick the circumference of her navel, salty and gritty. Plump belly-flesh pressed around his nose, his cheeks were moistened with belly-oil, natural or artificial. His head was pushed down harder, down into the navel which stretched itself around him, and he began gently turning as he dived through a channel of warm, dark flesh. The grip of the flesh seemed to hold and ease his aching shoulders, urging him gently round in the vortex. He knew that this was the opponent of Jehovah—they called him 'Jehovah', he noticed with surprise, and not 'Yahweh', as modern translators would have us think.

On awakening, he realized that his dream had given Astarte the face of Janice. He felt weak, spent. His body ached, but his veins seemed cleared, emptied, as if he had shed some heavy poison through the pores of his skin. He was covered in perspiration, and when he touched his chest and licked the finger, it was acrid, bitter. He wrestled for some while, to and fro, sifting over his recollections, trying to recall the dream and work out why it had associated Janice with the image of the Queen. He remembered the three breasts bouncing on their tightly drawn band, and felt sick. Trying to fathom it, the image led him to visualize Janice's own two breasts, decently horizontal to the line of her body; and then he felt ashamed for doing something it had not occurred to him to do before. He got up and drove his aching body through a few elementary exercises. Every time he pressed his arms backward and plumed his chest, he saw those three breasts jutting from their tightening sash.

The room was cold, but he barely noticed it. He sat in his pyjamas, trying to reason it out, stirring the coffee he had made for himself. The eddies reminded him of the all-embracing navel, the gently turning vortex. Aspects of the dream were obscene, and he felt vaguely responsible for them; but as a whole it had been cathartic—somehow it had got a lot out of his system. He comforted himself with the thought that one was not morally culpable for one's dreams, any more than for one's temptations: it was what one did with them that counted.

Nothing seemed to give him relief. The dream lodged in his memory like toffee in the base of a tin—each fragment adhered to the others and refused to yield its portion of meaning. He turned to read his Daily Office, but was overwhelmed with distaste: the dream seemed so much truer, more purifying. And yet their members had been erect as satyrs on a Roman cup—how could that be clean? He resolved to force a solution by ringing Janice: as it were, to drive out bad money with good. Instead, he got the mother.

'Oh, Mr Cathcut, how *kind*! ... Myself, I've been so distraught, I've hardly given the funeral a thought. But I *know* it's been troubling Janice a lot. ... Of course, we *must* bury her as our own.'

Somehow he found himself betrayed into undertaking a visit to the police-station, to enquire when the body might be released. And yet he himself had proposed it. The thought of serving Janice had been too much for him.

Only after he had dressed and got down into the street did he remember Lepage. His present mission offered a heaven-sent opportunity to keep an eye on him. Two such necessities coming together seemed so providential that he was carried through the remaining streets to the police-station with none of the usual rubs to the spirit.

But the station itself was a shock. Strange that he had not registered it till he had business there. They had pushed over a corner-block of Victorian terraces, and set this concrete fortress in the midst. The windows were small and high up, their sills on a slant, so that there was nowhere to rest a plant-pot or take a hand-hold. Everything seemed designed for defence. Two chutes in parallel let police cars into the bowels of the building and heaved them up on the further side. Between them a concrete ramp led to a first-floor entrance. Presumably the chutes had electronic barriers, that would only let in or out their own. He skipped hastily across the mouth of the IN-shute, listening for a car, and started up the ramp. It would be wise not to slip or to trail a hand unthinkingly, for the sharp, exposed stones of the aggregate might give one a nasty gash.

The entrance-passage was narrow and dark, like the Temple-mouth of his dream—but this time constriction was not pleasant. The ceiling slabs left him a bare six inches of breathing-room, and the walls pressed in, reviving the ache in his bones. He wondered how far police authorities calculated the impact of their arrangements. Ahead of him, above entrance doors of thickened glass, there was the hint of a grille that could be let down in the event of trouble.

Each sense-impression eroded the calm of his dream, drawing his mind to the surface by a succession of pinpricks. He tried consciously to fend off the assaultive orange carpet of the station foyer, its expanse made more extreme by the lowness of the ceiling. Only a Pakistani girl at the duty-sergeant's desk seemed able to withstand the neon lighting: he caught sight of his own hands, pocked with miniature craters all over their pallid skin. Her brown face rocked from side to side whilst he explained his errand, as if her head were rolling in a slippery saucer. All the senior officers were at the inquest, there was nothing she could do personally, but would he like to wait? He rather thought he *would*. She rocked her head affably once more and pointed him to one of the bucket chairs around the walls. But as he sank gratefully into its moulded plastic, some irregularity in the surface behind caught the sensitive patch at the base of his skull. It seemed that planks had been pushed into the wall while its concrete was setting, so as to leave an impression of wood-grain;

predictably, he had found himself a knot-hole. He shifted to another seat, and tried again to sink into his dream.

Only its general mood was now recoverable; but he drew sufficient support from it to be able to turn to an unfinished poem which had lain unattended in his pocket for several days. It seemed as good a way as any to rebut his surroundings. Smoothing out his pocket book, he mouthed over several alternative drafts, trying to divine which harmonized best with his present calm.

> *I went out to the desert*
> *They said you were there;*
> *I grated on locusts*
> *—they said you were there;*
> *In the taste of wild honey there to be found,*
> *Beyond the horizon,*
> *out of sound,*
> *In the bodies of women,*
> *or underground,*
> *Ready to meet me,*
> *Coming to greet me:*
> *They said you were there, they said you were there.*

The eighth line, in particular, had given him trouble: *'in the bodies of women'* seemed out of place in a devotional poem. But still within the ambit of his dream, he recalled how certain Tantric cults combined religious and sexual ecstasy; and he remembered the temptations of the Desert Fathers—it was not, after all, so inappropriate. Quite suddenly, in a rush of inspiration, he scribbled three more lines, without knowing how or why.

> *Bare the wood, cleave the stone;*
> *Split the shaft*
> *—and I am not there.*

He sat staring at the apparition, still in an ache of creation, not knowing what it meant. He could recognize a savage parody of the apocryphal Gospel of Thomas: *'Cleave the wood and I am there.'* But might he let it stand? He seemed to have completed his poem in a way that was quite unexpected.

The girl at the enquiry desk was like balm to the spirit: *'dark but comely'*, like Solomon's paramour. She noticed him looking at her and smiled shyly. His relationship with Janice had given him this aesthetic, non-sexual appreciation of women—which made it more odd that the dream should have linked Janice with Astarte.

His thoughts were disrupted by the arrival of Lepage and other senior officers, pursued by a gaggle of reporters. Lepage did not see him, but looked round desperately, searching for a way through the shouting. He pushed several times at the bodies surrounding him. Then with a sudden karate chop, he dislodged a hand that was clutching at the left arm of his raincoat, and broke into a curious shambling, skipping kind of run. Cathcut half got to his feet to intervene, but Lepage had disappeared down one of the concealed corridors that led from the vestibule.

The reporters gathered round the victim, somewhat abashed, and allowed themselves to be herded back by the outstretched arms of the duty-sergeant. There *would* be an opportunity, she said with embarrassment, nodding for evidence towards a long table that was being hastily set up in the foyer; a press conference had *definitely* been scheduled. Lepage's colleagues hovered about, hesitating whether to attempt a pacification; but on second thoughts they dispersed to their respective offices.

The injured photographer slumped into a chair alongside Cathcut, by a single easy movement unslinging his equipment with a clatter into the seat between them. He inspected his wrist for some seconds, testing the bone for bruises, then grinned ruefully at Cathcut. Still grinning, he leaned over his cameras to look at Cathcut's poem. Cathcut allowed him just as much reading-time as he could bear, then shut his notebook and returned it to an inner pocket. 'Classy,' said the photographer, 'definitely *classy*'.

Their attention was attracted by a murmur at the far end, and a gathering of legs on the mezzanine level—anything else was obscured by that absurdly low ceiling. Cathcut's photographer abandoned him to take up position. The legs intermingled, circled one another, regrouped, and filed down either side of the foyer steps to take their place at table. The twin files of officers were oddly reminiscent: Cathcut's dream nagged at the back of his mind like unfinished business.

Lepage's action had soured the whole meeting; but there was an atmosphere of suppressed tension that went beyond any immediate and obvious cause. The reporters were puzzled by it and made several little probing sallies, like hounds at fault. Their questioning was aggressive; but failing to start any hares, it petered out. The Chief Constable took command, fielding each query intended for his subordinates, turning accusations of negligence into appeals for public support. No, interviews with local prostitutes had turned up nothing. 'Unless there is greater co-operation from the public there will be no progress. I *appeal* to the public . . .' The television cameras whirred, and he expanded his chest toward them.

Lepage looked physically even more repellent under the neon, the brown discolorations of his shiny dome more distinct, his teeth a more unlovely yellow. He seemed subdued, as if in the presence of a superior, though it was some time before Cathcut could identify him —and only then because the Chief Constable was so assiduous in absorbing any questions directed that way. 'I have put Superintendent Care in charge of coordinating inquiries, and he assures me . . .' So Lepage had a superior. Cathcut determined to make his approach to *him*.

As soon as the Chief Constable had left, he went up to the table. Care remained seated, flicking particles of dust off his papers with a nervous, backward flip of his fingers. Lepage seemed provokingly indifferent to anything Cathcut might say, and made no attempt to head him off.

'I've come about disposing of the body.'

'What is that to *you*?'

'The family want to give her Christian burial.'

Care raised a quizzical eye.

'A common prostitute?' He got to his feet, shuffling his papers with hands that were strangely red. 'Mr Lepage, *Inspector* Lepage, has the details. Take it up with *him*.'

If Lepage was amused at Cathcut being fobbed off in his direction, he showed no sign of it. Only when they were halfway down the corridor leading to Lepage's room did he grunt once, perhaps in mirth, as if there might be some time-lapse between outside stimuli and their absorption. Otherwise, Lepage seemed tauter, and restless in a way that made Cathcut feel confident that he had not yet settled on Evans as a target.

His room was repulsively yellow, a bilious institution distemper. There was no plant, no coloured paperweight, only a single picture to relieve the bareness.

'Are you next-of-kin?'

The picture over Lepage's head was lascivious, but not in any straightforward way that Cathcut might object to: sepia breasts and spread hips of some fertility goddess, photographed by a Department of Antiquities.

'You know very well I'm not.'

Lepage pushed away a file in mock exasperation.

'But I can only deal with next-of-kin. Surely you could *approximate*? If not, a little ceremony would solder it up . . . if it *needs* soldering.' He leered meaningfully.

Cathcut was dumbfounded at such hostility: Lepage was doing more than merely amusing himself at Cathcut's expense. He felt provoked, and searched for a mode of retaliation.

'You know, you can't hang on to the body.'

This time, Lepage laughed outright.

'What do you think is for me in all those chopped *bits*?' His face was white with hatred.

Cathcut felt he had stumbled into broken glass. It had slipped his consciousness that Lepage would have to attend the post-mortem, sit in on the dismemberment of the corpse. But he was past being able to summon feelings of pity.

'I'll ring the father,' he said.

'Ring from here,' said Lepage, holding out the yellow receiver to him.

'There's a public phone in the lobby.'

'Ring from here.'

Cathcut backed away, scurried down the corridor, and pushed coins into a public phone.

As he had anticipated, Janice answered.

'Father isn't back from the inquest. I'll get him to ring when he comes in.'

He explained his plans for the funeral, that the body would be in church overnight, where relatives could look at it, that the laying-out of the body would be done by the undertaker.

'Mother will feel deprived,' she said tartly.

He neglected to say that the body might show signs of its evisceration. Instead, by the tone of his voice he tried to communicate that she was being protected, that everything was taken care of. She thanked him profusely. He went back to the office.

Lepage's smile made him feel guilty that he had so delicious an ache-at-heart. He knew to whom he had been talking.

'As soon as the father gives his consent, I will make over the body to you. . . . Doesn't it strike you as odd that I should be acting in this capacity?'

Cathcut avoided answering. Instead, he directed his attention to the picture, till its pendulous breasts caused him to look away.

'Wouldn't it be more proper to tell what you know? A word in the punctilious ear of Mr Care, and I could be re-assigned.'

Cathcut sat doggedly, feeling that that would be altogether too good, too easy. He wondered if Lepage's claw-marks would show up in any discrepancy between autopsy and doctor's report.

The phone rang. It was the girl's father. Lepage took note of his consent, but asked for a written document to be delivered at the station, for forwarding to the coroner. He held out the phone to Cathcut. 'Arrangements,' he said.

Cathcut made more of a meal of it than he would have done if Lepage had not been there. He described in great detail his plans for the lying-in, and this time mentioned the possibility of the corpse's disfigurement, as being a ground for relying on professional help. He felt more than a little uncomfortable at the grief-struck silence at the other end.

'Spare him,' said Lepage, infiltrating his fingers between the mouth-piece and Cathcut's chin, and blocking off his voice. Cathcut pushed his hand away.

'And the funeral, Mr Driscoll,' he said, 'the funeral is at ten a.m. *tomorrow*. *In* the church. The burial service, and then to the crematorium.'

Lepage's intervention had not been charitable, and was certainly not to spare his own feelings; Cathcut felt it was accusatory.

The two men sat facing each other across the desk. Lepage looked contemptuous.

'You like my picture?'

Cathcut blushed.

'I was wondering where it came from.'

'It was given me by my first instructor. He'd been in the Palestine Police in '47—thought it resembled my wife.'

The hair seemed to flow down from a central parting, ending in a roll-wave on either shoulder; it looked very modern.

'Does it?'

'Not any more.'

Lepage turned its wide hips to the wall and read from a printed paper pasted to the back.

> 'Terracotta. Syro-Phoenician. Date and provenance unknown. Ishtar, foremost amidst the Akkadian pantheon, retained her dominance through all the changes of Babylo-Assyrian religion. She was goddess of love and war, the first to taste those delights she inflicted upon others. All life depended on her; and if her favour was withdrawn, the bull

would not cover the cow, the ewes could not be joined to the ram. Her love was fatal to gods and men. In her presence the animals lost their native vigour. She made the lion amorous and trapped him in a pit; she subjugated the ox; and the horse, proud in battle, she destined to whip, halter and goad. Tammuz, God of the harvest, died through her embraces; and she sought him through the regions of the Underworld, stripping off her adornments at each of the seven gates, till at the seventh she let fall the robe that covered her nakedness.'

He smiled at Cathcut. 'They dig them out of the soil, all over Israel: little household insurances, in case their God let them down.'

'The funeral is at ten o'clock. As police-officer investigating the case, I rather think you should be there.'

Lepage ignored his challenge.

'This one has an inscription on the reverse, scratched in the clay. Syro-Phoenician, I presume. I got my friend to copy down a translation.' He read from some faded pen-markings at the top of the printed sheet.

'Hear us, O Ashtart, Queen of Heaven, thou that descended to Sheol, and charmed the shades with thine unending beauty.'

Cathcut tried to find an argument that would carry weight. 'The family would feel surer if you showed some concern.'

Lepage continued reading from the printed text:

'Her name and attributes remained the same throughout the West Semitic world: in Arabic Athar, in Moabite Ashtar-Chemosh, in Phoenician Ashtarath or Ashtareth, which the Hebrews transformed by false vocalization into Ashtoreth, substituting the vowels for the word "bōreth", meaning "shame". The Greek approximation to her name was Astarte.'

The name struck Cathcut like a thunderclap. It was not that he had been subconsciously evading the import of Lepage's inscription: he had simply not made the connection between his nightmare and these horrid little figurines. Nor had Lepage—of that he was certain; he was quite sure that his whole conversation had been fortuitous, that Lepage was merely exercising stale aggressive ploys on him, like a punch-drunk boxer. Anyway, the photograph, fuzzy with age, had plainly been with him for years. But that opened another appalling possibility: not that Lepage could in some occult way divine Cathcut's imaginings, but that he himself in sleep might somehow connect with Lepage's circumstances, his mental environment, the keepsakes that surrounded him. He dismissed the notion as fanciful. Yet he could but feel that, if only he had fathomed his dream, he would know better where he was—he would not be a prey to such absurd fantasies.

The mood of his dream had not entirely left him; if he could get by himself, he might be able to revive it. Lepage surprised him by expressing fatigue.

'All this has more than wearied me. I'll stretch out for a while.'

He took his telephone receiver off its rest, and turned toward a camp-bed set up in a corner of the office.

'Then I'll bid you goodbye. Sleep well.' Cathcut forbore mentioning the funeral again.

'And pleasant dreams?' asked Lepage, mocking his conventional solicitude. It was a mercy he couldn't know how appropriate his mock was.

For Cathcut's dream *had* been pleasant: the essence of it was somewhere *there*, in that fact. If he could feel his way again into its pleasantness, he might find the key. He dragged his feet along the corridor, nodded to the duty-sergeant in the foyer, then out of the building and toward the church, holding in imagination those widened hips, and feeling that all-embracing navel stretch around him.

CHAPTER TWELVE

After a day spent pondering one female mystery, Cathcut found himself in sole charge of another. At seven-ten that evening the undertaker's assistants departed, having endured a short 'Service for the Reception of a Body in Church', procured specially by Cathcut for the occasion. Being extraneous to the Book of Common Prayer, it clearly counted as overtime: the 'blacks' protested by giving back their most lack-lustre responses. He missed his verger's stentorian bleat; but Cathcut hadn't thought it right to take him from his evening soup and pâté, and had set up a trestle for the coffin himself, draping it tastefully with a soft crimson cloth. He robbed the high altar of its two tall free-standing candlesticks, positioning them on either side at the head of the chancel steps, to symbolize Hope and Resurrection. At the foot of the steps, immediately beneath where the tail of the coffin would lie, he had placed a prie-dieu, for anyone who felt moved to kneel. On it he put a large, gilt-edged Prayer Book, the presentation edition, open at the sentence *'I am the Resurrection and the Life.'*

Her family should have been there: he had made the timing of the reception almost excessively clear. It was not that he objected to being left alone with the body, even though it was visible; its coffin-lid had been laid to one side, till relatives could pay their last respects. It looked as he had been taught to believe, an empty husk, an untenanted tenement. But Janice at least might have been there—she could not have forgotten or misheard. He tested out his responses by giving the corpse a long, hard look. Its sheer immobility commanded respect. Death didn't overwhelm him with its finality, as he had been warned; on the contrary, he was fascinated at how all those fluid cross-currents, the electrical impulses, the interplay of chemical messengers, those endless transactions between cells, all that unceasing movement—twitches, throbs, nerve pulses, internal tides and rhythms—could simply freeze into an object. *That* wasn't her, it wasn't a person—'*Ichabod: the glory of the house has departed.*' She lay as lifeless as a pin-ball machine when there was no money in the slot—how those visits to down-town coffee bars had corrupted his imagination!

But—merciful heaven!—there was, after all, some point in their delay. Down in the nave, he spotted Dr Kemberton's appalling Advent hymn distributed all over the seats and back ledges of the first two pews. He rushed down the chancel steps and shuffled along a row, treading delicately to avoid displacing hassocks, and deftly slipping the printed cards from under their hymn-books on either side. '*Day of wrath, O Day of judgement*': what a comfort that would have been to mourners! He reproached himself for overlooking such a counterblast to all his careful preparations. Church décor was forbidding enough, with its '*Here lies the body . . .*' and '*Sacred to the memory of . . .*' gleaming or lowering from every wall, even assaulting your downcast eyes from the pavement beneath. Far worse to add the tone of a judgement-hall to that of a mausoleum. However you tried to dress up Mother Church in a natty suit and an Easter bonnet, she would whip out a death's-head from under her frowzy petticoats, and laugh at you. Not that he repudiated the spirit of her doctrine, just its judicial trappings. It seemed indecent to imagine the soul that had just departed being hauled up before some heavenly accounts-keeper, to tot up profit and loss. No doubt one's punishment was to *be* what one had become—but who was to say what she had become? The image of Judgement Day misled, both because it suggested a postponement of reckoning, and because it centred one's attention on acts, on things done. The publicans and harlots stormed heaven despite their acts. And a God who had imposed decay and corruption on all flesh would surely forgive much to those who had endured his gate of death.

He was interrupted, while consigning Dr Kemberton's hymn-sheets one by one to the church boiler, by the advent of Janice and her mother. He buttoned the remaining copies of 'Dies Irae' into his cassock-front and, with one thumb in his belt, supported them in his bosom.

'Oh, Mr Cathcut . . . *would* you oblige me by holding these?' She pushed a large bunch of chrysanthemums into his arms, so that he doubted if his arm-pressure was adequate to hold both them and the concealed hymn-sheets together. He let his belly go slack, in the hope of arresting 'Dies Irae' at the waist.

Mrs Driscoll unloaded an assortment of glass bowls and vases, a pair of red-painted kitchen scissors and a small roll of chicken wire from her black leather bag, scattering them over the chancel steps.

'Excuse us if we set up our little workshop,' she smiled. '. . . *So* sorry to be late—we got rather held up.' With deft fingers she separated out the white chrysanthemums in Cathcut's bunch, retaining their stems in her fat right fist, and then lifting them out with one quick yank, to the imminent danger of 'Dies Irae'.

Cathcut pressed hard on the remaining flowers.

'Don't *crush* those stems,' she objected, 'they'll drop quicker. —Hold *those*!' she commanded Janice, pushing the bouquet she had culled into her hand.

Cathcut and the girl stood side by side at the chancel steps, both clutching their respective posies, white and yellow. Still no word of apology about the service. He looked reproachfully across at her, but she stood staring ahead at the pots and vases, as if to say there was nothing to be ashamed of. She looked rather sulky and resentful, as though his expectation was unreasonable, as if the whole performance had been *his* affair. She made him feel like someone who had prepared a party for a friend, been left to eat the cake by himself, and then been judged self-indulgent for doing so.

'Hope' and 'Resurrection' would not do: the candles must be moved back from their guardianship on either side of the corpse, so as to give a softer light. Mrs Driscoll hauled herself up into the chancel, and rolled and twisted each candlestick on its base, like a tree in a tub, till she had them where she wanted. Cathcut stood helpless, still clutching his flowers, and expecting 'Dies Irae' at any moment to slip down on to the chancel steps. Wax from the tilted candles spattered over her black tweed coat, solidifying immediately in grey, semi-transparent streaks; but she remained as oblivious to that as to the body itself. It was astonishing; he had anticipated a collapse. Instead, she treated the corpse like a recalcitrant patient that was unfit for visitors. She lifted its head, slipped out a small velvet pad put there by the undertaker, and substituted a white lace pillow. Supporting the weight of the head in one ample red hand, she plumped up the pillow till it fluffed out nicely, then let the head settle back into it.

'If you want a job done well, do it yourself,' she observed, gazing at the improved effect.

She arranged the girl's hair about her face, tweaking a curl or two on to forehead and cheek, but gathering her long tresses in at the neck, so as to leave plenty of pillow visible. Then, on impulse, she reached into her bag, pulled out a wide lace frill and held it around the head like a bonnet; but after reflection, she concluded that it didn't suit.

Cathcut looked appealingly at Janice, who took no part, but seemed determined to resist the implication that anything might be wrong; he began to wonder if he was being over-sensitive. He knew these people liked a 'good do' at a funeral: only a few decades back it would have been straw in the street, black plumes and black velvet caparisons for the horses. But her mother seemed to be positively enjoying herself—where was yesterday's weeping, her grief-struck collapse? Perhaps all this activity was a distraction? That would be the kindliest view.

Mrs Driscoll held up a limp white hand.

'Look at those nails,' she protested. 'You'd think he'd at least have run round them with a pair of nail scissors.'

'Nails grow after death,' said Cathcut, feeling his arrangements called in question.

'I *beg* your pardon?' She looked at him as if he had said something impertinent.

'Nails grow after death.'

She decided to ignore him, and began brushing the high-necked dress that clothed the corpse with a small travelling clothes brush, pausing at intervals to pick fluff off the nap.

'I'm half prepared to bet he hasn't used those clean under-things I sent him.'

Cathcut was terrified lest she start prying under the skirt.

'They do, you know,' she said, noticing Cathcut's horror. 'Anything you can't see they keep for themselves.'

'He's hardly likely to want a woman's slip, Mother.'

She laughed a cynical little laugh. '*I* know *them*. Anything new. He'd give it to someone in his family. I've dealt with them before—you've no idea.'

Janice shrugged her shoulders and gave up the discussion.

On the point of checking, her mother was distracted by a

distant cough. She raised her head and listened, brush poised.
'Janice, if that's one of ours, run and tell them we're not quite ready yet. Ask them to wait a moment.'
Janice affected to be at a loss, waving her bunch of chrysanthemums helplessly. Mrs Driscoll rushed down the chancel steps, snatched the flowers from her and, with a playful slap on her rear, urged her toward the porch. She then hastily bunched the flowers with their heads level and snipped several times across their stems, spattering the top of Cathcut's prie-dieu with a green salad of chopped and oozing bits.
Cathcut determined that 'Dies Irae' must take its chance. He laid his own bouquet along a pew, and retrieved the Prayer Book from under a mantle of leaves and stems. Despite every care in wiping its surface, he left a thin brownish smear, as though a caterpillar had excreted across the page.
'I'm sure you won't mind helping me,' said Mrs Driscoll. She put into his hand a cut-glass vase containing a core of chicken wire. On closer inspection, it was imitation cut-glass, for its bevels were too rounded to have been cut by a tool. He stood by helplessly, as she commandeered a small table normally used for the elements before communion and placed it on the left side of the body, where Cathcut's candle had been. Before he had settled on some alternative to suggest, she took the vase from him and sent him to fetch water. When he returned, the vase was in position, and she was threading chrysanthemum stems into chicken wire so that the blooms splayed out in a circle. He poured water for her over their stems. Through glass facets it all looked a distorted tangle, as if saplings had sprouted through a wire fence.
'A bit of ivy 'll cover that,' she said, winding a strand of variegated creeper from base to top, and sealing each end to the back of the glass with a sliver of cellotape.
With equal speed she retrieved Cathcut's abandoned flowers, sheared off their heads and half an inch of stalk, and dotted them at intervals around a glass posy-ring. Then with one sweep of her sleeve she brushed the green salad off the prie-dieu and into her opened bag; but her circlet of yellow flowers slid on the canted desk-top, slopping water till drips ran from either end of its retaining lip.
'Can that go?' she said to Cathcut.
It would have to: he felt ashamed to say that someone might want to pray there. He compromised by moving the prie-dieu sideways and to the right, so that a worshipper would face across

the aisle. A round-topped stand from a side chapel proved much more satisfactory, and better suited the proportions of the bowl.

Janice returned, with a drab, elderly woman.

'It's only Auntie Edie,' she said, in justification of having admitted her.

Aunt Edie clasped her hands across her belly and bobbed to Cathcut several times.

'This is Mr Cathcut, Edie. He's been so kind to Janice in all this.'

'He's been kind to *all* of us, mother,' said Janice pointedly.

Mrs Driscoll ignored her correction and, having checked round, retrieved a chrysanthemum stalk from the chancel steps.

Edie was ushered up to the coffin.

'Wait!' cried Mrs Driscoll, and from her seemingly inexhaustible bag, shedding fresh snippets of chrysanthemum, produced a further flower in a cellophane wrapper. She joined the corpse's hands across its breast, and between its pale fingers inserted a single, red hot-house rose, barely out of the bud.

Edie looked on approvingly.

'She always *was* a lovely child,' she said. Then, conscious of Cathcut's presence, she made one or two perfunctory dabs at her forehead and chest, trying ineptly to sign herself with the cross as she genuflected towards the coffin.

The body was beginning to smell. Mrs Driscoll stood four-square to receive her dues, legs apart, her nose pointing up towards the altar canopy, her purple head-scarf lapping her black coat. Edie came behind her and squeezed a broad elbow through the cloth.

'My dear, I *do* feel for you.'

They stood side by side, looking towards the high altar.

After some moments, Mrs Driscoll hauled a substantial length of silver chain from her pocket, followed eventually by a large hunter watch. Its case had already sprung open.

'Have you the right time, Edie? I can't afford to have mine repaired.'

Rather apologetically, Edie presented a neat lady's wrist-watch, and guardedly brought it alongside the hunter. Their times coincided.

'Good heavens!' cried Mrs Driscoll, 'John and Ethel will be on that eight o'clock train, and no one there to meet them. —Edie,' she said, her head buzzing with arrangements at the sight of her scattered equipment, 'I've put you and Sidney in the box-room, on a mattress. I *knew* you wouldn't mind. John and Ethel have come *such* a long way, I thought they ought to have the bed.'

'Where'll *you* sleep?'

'Oh, don't you worry yourself about *us*. —Under the dining-table, I suppose, like we did that Christmas!' She laughed at the recollection.

Another thought struck her.

'Mr Cathcut, *would* you be so kind as to call on my husband and bring him here? I want him to see her as she is. Something to remember her by.' She smiled, and a tear tipped over her lower lid. 'He hasn't anyone of his own sex; he needs the company of another man.'

From this Cathcut divined that she wanted Mr Driscoll's viewing over with before her visitors arrived; but he was glad to be of use.

'I can't leave the church unattended,' he said, hoping that Janice would volunteer to watch by her sister. But Janice seemed as anxious as anyone to be part of the welcome for John and Ethel.

'You can pull the door to,' advised Mrs Driscoll, 'so it looks as if it was locked. You'll only be gone two minutes.'

She stuffed her unused materials in her bag and made for the door, with Edie half a yard behind. Janice at least stopped for a word.

'Thank you,' she said, turning full-face to Cathcut and holding out her hand. 'Thank you for everything.'

He was astonished at how she was dressed. Like her mother, she had kitted herself out in total mourning: a black pleated skirt and a dark, close-fitting jacket, both of which emphasized her slim waist. Her stockings were black lisle; but now he saw, under her light and somewhat transparent celanese blouse, the ominous shadow of a black bra. It quite spoilt the pleasure of holding her slim fingers.

As he ushered her out of the darkened church, leaving just those twin candles on either side of the coffin, he was reminded of her sister. Could the sister be the source of such tricks, imitated unconsciously or unthinkingly? He worried over it, all the way to collect their father. It had looked so obviously an exercise in allure, of the crudest and most unsophisticated kind, that it must surely be accidental. Perhaps that was the only garment she had clean that day. At the worst, she might have some crazily naive notion of harmonious dressing. He preferred the naivety-solution: for Janice didn't just give an impression of innocence, she totally convinced you of her child-like *unformedness*, as if she had somehow remained below the age-threshold when such dressing would become significant.

Her father was full of indiscriminate anger, darting his red eyes here and there like a bull seeking occasion to charge. He had thrown aside his shirt-collar, and there was a print of verdigris under his Adam's apple where the stud had irked him.

'What did she send *you* for?' he asked, looking at Cathcut's cassock. Then some recollection surfaced amidst his rage. 'Oh— you must be Janice's young man.'

It didn't seem a time to deny it, however hurtful she had been. Janice; Janus, the 'god who faced two ways': her name might even be related. But if there was some deceit in accepting the role offered, at least it allowed him to help.

'They want you to view the body,' he said. 'I'll take you there.'

Mr Driscoll glared at him as if he were a traitor.

'You can do it alone,' Cathcut assured him. 'They've gone to meet a train.'

The old man accepted the viewing itself as a matter of course. He wrapped a scarf around his neck to conceal his undress.

' —Not *that* one—my *tweed*!' he shouted, as Cathcut tried to sort him out a coat. Then, as though recognizing that the young man was, after all, not quite family, he added 'You know, all this has been *terrible* for us.'

It was a shock to hear the mother's accents coming through. Much as her husband might resent her, his dealings with the outside world seemed reduced to parroting her phrases. Cathcut preferred his anger. They walked up Seshton Hill in silence.

It was one of those nights that serve as a critique of human behaviour. The wind that tightened the pores on Cathcut's cheeks had scoured the lower atmosphere of every trace of smog. There was little traffic about. The whole sky was a dark but translucent blue, through which the stars broke as points of unadulterated light. Their stillness was that of the dead girl, and of the candle-flames beside her. In the face of those myriads of dispassionate onlookers, Cathcut felt his own actions the least inadequate, even if fussy and over-anxious—his own actions, and the silence of the man beside him. He was sorry when they reached the church.

His regret became acute when he pressed on the porch door whilst fumbling in shadow for its latch, and it yielded to his touch. He hadn't locked it, in case by some chance Janice or one of her relatives returned before him; but he distinctly remembered turning that iron ring till the bar on the inside had slotted into its catch. Nevertheless, the interior was still in darkness; perhaps the latch hadn't dropped fully, and a freak wind had blown it open. He piloted Mr Driscoll down two steps and along a cross-aisle, listening through their footfalls for any hint of movement. The candles still stood guard in the chancel: anyone who had slipped in for a little thieving would have suffered a salutary shock. It seemed natural, as they turned into the main aisle and up toward the chancel steps, to put an arm across Mr Driscoll's bulky shoulders; and the old man suffered the gesture without resistance.

Once in the chancel, Cathcut's worst fears were confirmed. The coffin-lid, which he remembered replacing, just as clearly as he recalled closing the church door, was again laid to one side. He switched on some overhead lights, causing Mr Driscoll to screw up his eyes and shield them with a hand; but there was no one save themselves in the sanctuary, and no scuffling from the rest of the building. He left the father alone to cope as best he could, and sat down in a choir-stall.

What troubled him most was that one part of his mind had anticipated this, from the moment he had agreed to leave the church unattended. And yet he had still not locked the door. Was that a calculated risk, or had he been tempting Providence, giving opportunities?

Mr Driscoll disturbed him by his restlessness. He scanned the contents of the coffin only briefly, then padded up to the high altar, and stood looking up at its valance. After a while he walked back, barely glancing at the box as he passed, and sat himself down in a front pew of the nave, staring silently at a brass lectern. His silence seemed, after all, a more appropriate response than kneeling. But he hadn't been settled more than a few minutes when he got to his feet again.

'I'd better go,' he said. 'I can see myself home.'

Cathcut looked surprised.

'I can't *feel* anything,' her father said, groping for explanations. 'There isn't a moment that isn't taken up with knowing there's someone out there who did *this*. He's stopped me caring for my own flesh and blood.' Only his last phrase sounded the least like an echo.

'It's being taken care of,' said Cathcut, feeling acutely dishonest. But at least he had avoided any claptrap about forgiveness.

The moment Mr Driscoll had gone, he fetched a censer from the vestry, to cover his actions in case of interruption. The body gave off an odour like overripe oranges: perhaps the undertaker had scattered scent, knowing she was to be on display. When his censer was pushing fumes through every hole, Cathcut censed her body top and toe, and then peered down over the lip of the coffin. As he thought, a great wad of hair had been cut from behind one ear, down near the nape of the neck, leaving her scalp bristly and leprous. It wasn't an injury you could imagine an autopsy making or an undertaker leaving unconcealed.

He transferred the censer to his left hand, spilling great clouds of incense over her feet, and trailed his right fingers across the pillow, prepared to release his grip at any resistance. But as he had suspected, a single severed lock came away in his hand. Tucking it round the little finger that held the censer, he felt for some waste paper in his pockets, remembered 'Dies Irae', and slid out a sheet from his bosom. Into it he dropped the curl, folding the paper around it with one hand, and screwing it up very tightly. Then, with a shudder that ran right down his leg, he put the paper through a slit in his cassock into a trouser pocket, for later disposal. He couldn't bring himself to rearrange her hair, but he did check the lace of the pillow lest any strand of cut hair were still clinging to it. He hoped to avoid an outcry from her mother.

Cathcut felt guilty at his challenge, which Lepage had thus answered. But if it *was* an answer, where were the signs? In hope rather than expectation, he checked about for bibles laid open, hymn-books at an appropriate verse, some obvious token— though he doubted if Lepage had the knowledge required. The coffin-lid pushed to one side was evidence of surprise, but it was not flamboyant enough to be itself a gesture. He should not have neglected his post: he suddenly realized that he felt it would not be beyond Lepage to have answered all this chocolate-box frippery by scalping the head of the corpse to a half-inch bristle. It would be a gesture parallel to slapping down a photo of her body alongside those naked pictures.

But Lepage—and surely it must be he—had cut a wad of hair from where it would be least visible, for some indeterminate purpose of his own. He wouldn't be taking a memento, for there was nothing sentimental about Lepage—and if he were seeking some remembrance, why this great fistful of hair? The quantity also ruled out some sentimental relative, unless Mrs Driscoll had cut souvenirs for general distribution. But that was too bizarre, even for her; and he hadn't seen her kitchen scissors wielded anywhere near the corpse. Had Lepage become so much an obsession that Cathcut thought immediately of him, without considering other alternatives? Could the other one—Evans— have wanted a keepsake? But the funeral had been arranged so hastily, by telegram and telephone, that only closest relatives would know that her body lay for inspection in church overnight—they, and Lepage, who knew all the arrangements because of Cathcut's foolish dare, because the priest had been frightened by him, and had wanted to sting.

He shuddered to think of Lepage lifting the girl's head to make his cut. It must have been an exercise in bravado, a testing of how much he could stand. That made it no worse than Lepage's initial attack on the corpse; in some sense it showed a gain in self-control, however perverse. Cathcut had not reported the first mutilation, so why should he feel a duty to respond to the second? Fortunately, the maiming had been so discreet that he would not have to offer an explanation. And, thank God, he had brought himself to remove that hair, so with good luck the mother would discover nothing. A reference to Dr Kemberton now would be bound to entail a reference to the police, with the undoing of all that he had tried to achieve. That might not be a bad thing; but he would need time to be sure of it. He should offer up such a decision in prayer, before acting to collapse his whole edifice. Providence might not want Lepage to evade reality and duck all consequences. To act now would be to set in motion an uncontrollable process, to forgo his power of direction, without taking time to discover what right action in such circumstances might be. He decided there would be less harm, for the moment, in treating what had happened as a pastoral matter between Lepage and himself.

CHAPTER THIRTEEN

In the interval between sleep and full consciousness, Dr Kemberton was hit by panic: the incipient cataract in his right eye had worsened markedly overnight. His bedroom presented its usual soft haze; but a large segment of it was now obscured. He twitched first the left eye-lid shut, then the right, confirming that the obstruction was limited to the retina of his right eye. But the white blear had shifted somewhat to the periphery of his vision after the second twitch. He half-closed that eye, and guardedly wiped his eye-ball between the lashes with a corner of his bed-sheet. The sheet came up moist, and milky-yellow. His obstruction had only been a discharge of mucus, presumably dragged over the iris as he fluttered his eye-lids out of sleep. He reproached himself for his lack of control: such failures in self-assessment made stoicism unnecessarily difficult.

He fumbled for his stick on the back of his bed-side chair, and thumped its toe into the lino. 'Avling!' he roared—no point in courteous prefixes to a shout. 'Avling!' he shouted again, beating the floor. Mrs Avling surprised him by coming in immediately, carrying a jug of cold water which she placed by his wash-basin; she must have been waiting on his call, sitting at the head of the stairs. He hooked his spectacles over his ears, tugged the sheet up to his chin, and watched her. She unloaded a fresh towel from her arm on to the wash-stand, then lovingly folded his face-flannel and draped it over the basin-rim. Some lingering pleasure about her movements suggested that she was recalling the moment when she had used that same flannel and that very basin to wash his feet. A sudden cold snap had so stiffened his hip- and knee-joints that he had judged it only rational to ask her for help—even if it would be at the cost of giving her 'anticipations'. It was a fitting reward for all her faithful service that she should be permitted, eventually, to make a babe out of him; but she would get her reward slowly, bit by bit, and only as it became necessary.

She was back again, this time with his clothes. He watched attentively, just to assure himself that she observed due form and ceremony: first, the long, low table, two feet from his bed; then his socks laid out upon it, properly separated, and not rolled up together in a ball. Beside them, his long woollen underpants, discreetly tucked away under his vest—*her* refinement, that one, not his. Next, his shirt, and beside it his black stock, with a fresh dog-collar clipped on to it, and his studs already fitted. Newly polished shoes were slipped under the table, their heels towards his bed. Finally came the coat-hanger with his jacket, waistcoat, and (over the bar) his pin-stripe trousers, all of which she hung on a stout hook which had been double-screwed into his bedroom door. As ever, she measured with her eyes the distance between that door and his bed, looking appealingly. And, as ever, he waved her objection aside:

'When a man loses control of his trousers, Mrs Avling, he begins to lose direction of his soul.'

He was making rather too many of these ponderous, slightly *risqué* jokes at her expense of late. But at least it got rid of her, leaving him free for the first engagement of his day.

He pushed a right leg down to the floor, untucking sheet and blankets. Then, by pressing hard on his stick and thrusting against the mattress with his left arm, he levered himself into a sitting position, swinging his left leg out to join the other. The next movement was the only purely unpleasant one in the whole exercise: he pulled his night-shirt over his head, which not only left him sitting on his bed like a great, naked William pear, but exposed every portion of his body at once to the bite of December cold. Pyjamas would have been less all-or-nothing, giving opportunity for sectional exposure; but pyjamas would have added a further round of problems, and they presented more of an obstacle if one was taken short in the night.

He reached hastily for his underpants, got his toes into them, hauled them up to bunch under his thighs, and, by rolling first on to his left side and then to his right, hitched them up over each buttock as it lifted off the bed. By wriggling his toes and pulling on the cloth he got both feet through to the floor; but he had to bend down painfully and experience that fearful dizzy sensation, so as to ease out a ruck around his left calf. When the dizziness passed, he allowed himself to put on vest and shirt, as a respite before the next major task. Then, taking one sock, he leant back, resting neck and shoulders against the window-ledge on the left side of his bed, bent his left knee (the joint so *painful!*—it felt bruised under the knee-cap), gritted his teeth as he increased the flexion on the joint, till with a quick snatch he pulled on his sock in one single movement and lay back, panting. He took his right sock from where he had left it beside him on the bed, and tried to repeat the operation; but the sock twisted itself into a knot and had to be unravelled before he could dart his foot into it. His stock and collar furnished another respite. Then the *pièce de résistance*, the finale, his trousers. He pushed on the bed with his left hand, thrust down with his stick, and, by leaning his weight over its shaft, got himself on to his feet, and hobbled across to his suit where it hung on the door. His joints were painfully stiff in the early morning.

It would, of course, have been simpler to have pulled on his trousers in the same way as he had pulled on his underpants. But he told himself that to wriggle worsted in that way under his backside would produce innumerable wrinkles, particularly if it were still damp from Mrs Avling's ironing; and besides, he would be certain to pick up a mass of fluff from his blankets. In reality, he enjoyed the contest. By tugging on the waist-band of his trousers he got them through their hanger, and held them hip-high, with their turn-ups just brushing the floor. For a moment he trusted himself to his own unaided legs, while he grasped his cane midway down its stem and hooked its handle securely over the top of the door. Hauling on the stick afforded relief to his aching leg-muscles in proportion to the exertions of his arm; and it gave him greater security than the door-hook, which on a previous occasion had broken away under his hand. He was now ready for the next manoeuvre.

With a shake of the waist-band and a deft circling movement, he got the seat of his trousers to belly out, exposing both leg-holes. Then, standing on one leg and pulling hard on his stick, he painfully raised his left knee until his foot could get into the appropriate leg-hole. With his toe turned up to catch the cloth, he slid his hand along the waist-band to his braces, which Mrs Avling had attached but left abnormally long, in obedience to instructions. He hitched the left support over his shoulder, and let it settle into his collar-bone. From there on, it was comparatively easy to reach down and bunch the left trouser-leg up on to his limb, rather like feeding material over a curtain-rod. As soon as his foot appeared at the nether end he put it to ground, breathless and conscious of the vein bulging at the side of his temple, but otherwise triumphant. He rested on both feet for some seconds, his trousers hanging in folds below his left thigh and the right leg flapping loose on the floor, whilst he gathered strength for the climax to the action.

The final act required him to transfer his stick to the other hand, again engage the top of the door with it, pull hard, and lift his right knee outwards and somewhat higher, till he got the foot over the waist-band of his suspended trousers. He held the waistband out and down with his right hand, and had almost touched his corporation with his knee, when he remembered the events of Tuesday's confessional. Immediately, he put his foot down, standing on his trouser-leg, and putting such strain on the left brace that it cut painfully into the loose skin between his neck and shoulder. A dozen times yesterday the same recollection had ruined his austerer pleasures, distracting him in the performance of some delicate physical manoeuvre, or abstracting him from a devotional exercise. He hopped and staggered back to his bed with the aid of his stick, holding up his left side below the waist, and dragging his unfilled trouser-leg along the floor after him, extracting it with difficulty from between the legs of his bedside table and chair. Fortunately, the woman was so obsessive a cleaner and polisher of lino that the floor was unlikely to be dirty—though his trousers could hardly take any more shine than they had derived already from her constant ironing and pressing. He sat on the bed, angry with himself for having retreated in such disorder.

He was determined not to have another day ruined in its stoic lines, in its austere if attenuated beauty. Whatever was done to him, it should never be said that he had deviated one inch from his vocation, from his sacred duty. Like Bruce's spider, he would pick himself up after each humiliating defeat and again address himself to the task. He rolled over on to his left side, crooked the right knee till he could slip it into his trouser-leg, and wriggled the garment up under his buttocks. It might not be his preferred method, but today the cloth would have to suffer.

He felt hag-ridden by this memory, invaded. The guilt at having momentarily given way to feelings of vengeance was now slight: some allowance must be made for human frailty, and he was beyond the vanity of seeking perfection. His unease was nothing that self-confession, self-absolution could not allay. No action of his had ever carried those feelings of wrath into performance—it needed no confessor to point out that obvious distinction between himself and his visitor. Nevertheless, he would not conceal or cloak his offence before the Almighty. He would make reparation, or seek out some appropriate penance. He got to his feet again, hobbled across to the door, and pulled on waistcoat and jacket. Only the body might be masked, he told himself—not the soul.

What demanded exorcism, the release of expression to another, was a choking sense of bitterness—so bitter that he could taste it, like bile slipping up past his oesophagus. He was bitter at the trick that had been played on him, at a device designed to expose a weakness which he had never attempted to deny—as though he were arguing with a contestant who would never admit the ground where the real dispute between them lay, but needed to point out to him his human limitations, as if they were some justification for what had been done to him. 'Old Artificer', delighting to catch you in grammatical solecisms, when you were reproaching him for fraud. He was angry with himself for having given the shred of an excuse to his opponent; almost every waking thought was devoted to giving no ground for complaint. Such bitterness demanded to be expressed—but to *whom*?

The confessional was sacrosanct, and no action of his should ever allow scope to the accusation that he had betrayed his priestly trust. Let the betrayals be all one-sided. He could not take the risk that his comments might lead to the apprehension of the murderer; and he was experienced enough to know that, once a man starts talking, he cannot easily predict the boundary at which he will stop. Somehow his auditor must himself be bound—another priest, like himself under the seal of the confessional. Immediately, his thoughts turned to Cathcut. *There* was the source of the irritation he had felt with that young man ever since his arrival: Mr Cathcut, with his fair hair and fairer complexion, so perfectly represented the God with whom he had to deal. Dr Kemberton pulled on his shoes, made himself dizzy again by tying his laces, splashed cold water in his face to revive him, and set off in search of his curate.

The obvious place to look was in church, for it was about the time when, if no other duties intervened, they met together to say their Daily Office in public. He found Cathcut in the chancel, hollow-eyed and looking as though he hadn't slept all night, sitting beside a coffin. Some extravagant penance, the priest thought: meditating on the facts of mortality and undermining his health. If something was wanted in that line, couldn't he himself furnish the young man with almost daily food for thought?

'Whose body is it?' he asked.

'The Driscoll girl,' Cathcut replied, looking as uncomfortable as a cat caught watching at a bird-bath. 'Her funeral is at ten.'

'I don't recall giving permission for that body to lie in church overnight.'

Cathcut blushed.

'It's so commonly received a custom now, I didn't think it necessary to bother you.'

'Please *do* b-bother me in future.'

Of course, there wouldn't be a future for that particular offence. Mr Cathcut, or rather Mr Cathcut as the servant of his master, had contrived to bring into church a memento of Dr Kemberton's recent shortcoming, in case he were backsliding or trying to argue his way out—or, at the least, the insinuation was that he might need such a reminder. Cathcut's fault was to be such a willing accomplice; he had *deserved* to hear his confession.

He bundled him into the confessional box despite his protests, hung one of his own stoles about his neck, and went himself to the penitent's section, falling heavily to his knees at the faldstool. Cathcut looked doubtfully at him through the grille.

'Young man, you know the rules of the confessional?'

Cathcut dutifully repeated 'the formula:

'When I put on this stole, from the moment of putting on to the moment of taking off, my lips are sealed, and I may not even speak to you again of what you tell me, unless you first request me to do so.'

'I am myself m-minimally m-modifying those rules,' Dr Kemberton said, lest Cathcut try to wriggle out by citing his own instructions against him. 'I admit my procedure is somewhat unorthodox . . . but since the purpose for which the rules were devised is preserved, I can see no ground for objection.' He glared at Cathcut in case he wanted to object; but the young man seemed to have no stomach for disagreement.

'The person responsible for *that*'—Dr Kemberton inclined his head in the direction of the chancel—'came to me in the confessional on Tuesday morning.'

'May I know his name?' cried Cathcut, in great excitement. '. . . Under the seal of confession,' he added, obviously ashamed at so ill-disciplined a curiosity.

'Of *course* you may not. —And I do not concede that the person was either of the m-masculine or of the feminine gender. The incident only has relevance insofar as it relates to my own confession. Are you ready?'

Cathcut bowed his head submissively, twitching at his stole, though it was perfectly in place.

'If you have composed yourself, I will begin.' Dr Kemberton paused for a moment, then read from the hornbook at a great gabble, inserting only one new phrase:

> 'I confess to God Almighty before the whole company of Heaven, and to you . . . that I have sinned in thought, word and deed through my fault. Especially have I sinned in these ways through . . . fantasies of vengeance. For these, and all my other sins which I cannot now remember I am truly sorry, firmly mean to do better, humbly ask pardon of God; and of you . . . penance, advice, absolution.'

Cathcut seemed at a loss.

'Seek more details,' prompted Dr Kemberton.

'Tell me more,' said Cathcut obediently. 'What *were* these fantasies of vengeance?'

'You know my m-matrimonial circumstances?'

Cathcut blushed once again. 'I *had* heard . . . rumours.'

'There is no occasion for rumours. My former wife abandoned me some seventeen years ago, suddenly and inexplicably. Soon after came a letter, forwarded through her solicitors (who were, incidentally, also *my* solicitors), implying that she was living in great comfort of body and soul with another man, and asking that I furnish her with a divorce, on evidence supplied. I furnished it.' He looked quickly at Cathcut, who took it as his cue.

'Does that trouble you?'

'Not a whit. I turned the other cheek, gave no ground for complaint. I am simply angry with myself that, when the death of this girl was announced, I fell for a moment into a foolish superstition . . . into believing that there is in this world a punishment for infidelity, for injuries inflicted. It was childish of me, and I regret it.' The young man looked as if one cloud, at least, had been lifted from his horizon.

'But do you *repent* of your feelings?' asked Cathcut, greatly daring.

'I repudiate my feelings, and confess that, in rejoicing at her death, I took both the blood and the judgement on my own hands. —You need not point out,' he said sharply to Cathcut, 'that I did not carry my vengeful feelings into any direct action. It is enough that they were there.'

Cathcut seemed non-plussed, like a schoolboy forestalled in the act of playing a wrong stroke.

'The priest should now demand that the penitent . . . make any reparation within his power,' said Dr Kemberton.

'Can you make reparation? —In an appropriate form?' asked Cathcut.

'I have a God-sent opportunity.' The priest smiled ironically. 'Her lover—I will not call him her husband—died last month. She seeks a home. I will give her that home.'

'But do you forgive her *in your heart*?' said Cathcut, looking appalled. At least the young man had *some* backbone, he would fight.

'I have confessed my sin, and sought absolution. I will make reparation, I will do penance. What happens in my heart is no longer my affair.'

'But have you sought for grace to forgive?' enquired Cathcut. This was better: the fellow was showing some spirit.

'Oh, I've sued for grace,' said Dr Kemberton. 'At morning, at evening and at noonday, I've wearied heaven with my prayers.' He brought his face closer to the grille, gripping the top of the faldstool with both hands. 'But what reparation can he make *me* for the corruption of my nature?' He tapped his breast-bone with a crooked forefinger. 'I've become sour and mean, shrunken in my sympathies, because I wait for my vindication. And if I cease to wait for vindication, I cease to hope for a God who vindicates himself. And that would be a lack of faith,' he said bitterly.

'But what kind of vindication do you *want*?' cried Cathcut.

'He has injured me in the roots of my being, provided me no means of healing. Who will love this remnant of flesh? Will he now presume to judge me? I have searched my behaviour, and when I am being most honest with myself, there is nothing for which I can say "I was to blame". I have been humiliated, defamed in my profession, exposed to public scorn. I have not sought revenge. But I thought, for one foolish moment, that I might have vindication—and it is for *that* he presumes to arraign my conscience. He has tormented me beyond measure. If a man enter into judgement with his God, how may he secure the Lord's acquittal? If I do not hold him to blame, I betray myself. It would be easier if I could say "God is not unjust, because he is not *there*." But I have this foolish sensitivity, Mr Cathcut—I *know* he is there; I *know* he is unjust.'

'Despite everything,' said Cathcut, 'try to believe that he does love.' It sounded contemptibly lame. This young man wouldn't make even a worldly success of the profession.

'What is there in his vaunted grace,' asked Dr Kemberton, 'to assure me I have love? I'm a mean, decaying old man. What is there to be loved in *me*? She did not find me lovable. Is *that* lovable?—he pulled at his several chins—'Or *that* ?'—he held up two trembling hands—'Or *that*?'—and he spread one eye wide with his fingers, exposing a red rim, and an eyeball crazed with broken veins. 'Do *you* love me?' he asked Cathcut, turning the knife. The young man at least had the honesty not to attempt a lie.

'I'm not sure that I *can* absolve you,' said Cathcut guardedly.

Dr Kemberton shook with passion.

'I will *have* my absolution,' he roared. 'I have followed the forms, I will make reparation, there is no ground on which you could deny me. I will take her back, in the hope that even the Deity has a sense of shame.'

'But how can I absolve someone who will not absolve God?' Cathcut asked.

Dr Kemberton looked at him with new respect. He paused for some seconds.

'Young man,' he said, 'he doesn't deserve it. He hasn't the power to undo what he has permitted. If he feels anything, it must surely be fruitless remorse. —Now give me my due.'

'I believe you *have* been faithful, according to your lights,' said Cathcut.

'I *know* I have been faithful. Only he has not kept faith with me.'

'I *will* absolve you,' said Cathcut gently, 'if you will consent to wait.'

The old man's voice began to tremble.

'I have waited,' he said, '"*till my heart has become . . . as a w—wine-skin in the smoke.*"'

'Nevertheless,' replied Cathcut, under inspiration, 'wait, because it would be better that he be as in your dreams than as you believe him to be.'

He had hit on the weak spot in his armour, that sentimental streak which he despised. Dr Kemberton wept, copiously and long, cursing himself that old age brought any emotion so near to the surface. Correctly interpreting his tears, Cathcut pronounced the form of the absolution over him.

CHAPTER FOURTEEN

'*Heaviness may endure for a night,*' murmured Cathcut, his eyes easing with tears of gratitude: '*but joy cometh in the morning.*' Throughout the night he had watched beside the coffin, sore that he had been able to convince no one else of the necessity, and guilty that only he knew how real the necessity was. 'It 'ud have been by itself in a funeral parlour' was Janice's parting shot, before leaving with her family. So he had sat out the night alone, with his mind like stale porridge: not porridge left to go cold, but simmering quietly by itself, with a heavy yellowish crust through which little *pets de nonne*, mere thought-farts of doubtful quality, pushed up when you least expected them—most of them inconsequential, but some of them pretty sour. *Thwunck*—that one had been especially unpleasant: the notion that he had not taken the death seriously in itself, so that this vigil was no more than he deserved. He let his mind go lumpish, resisting what might bubble through. *Thunk—thibble—thunk*, welling up from the same crater: the thought that he had used this murder for his own ends, slapping on the label 'providential dispensation', never conceiving that he might have a vengeful streak, till Dr Kemberton had revealed his own. Several times he tried to move his mind to prayer, but only succeeded in stirring up a string of unwelcome recollections: Lepage tearing at the corpse of his mistress, Lepage slipping his leash at the youth club, Lepage with a whole fistful of the girl's hair—all of them reminders that Cathcut's controlled experiment was not so controlled after all. They disturbed his concentration, and left him with a sense of self-disgust.

And then, like the stirring-in of syrup, thinning his mind to a liquid sweetness, had come Dr Kemberton's confession. It was evidence of a divine pre-echo to all he had been trying to do: some wise physician had used this same terrible event as barium, illuminating the hidden cancer, till even Dr Kemberton had faced his need for the surgeon's knife. The same force was at work on Lepage: however he might twist and turn, he was 'the deed's creature', the inevitable product of his actions, of his undeniable human nature, and of this unlooked-for catastrophe. In Middleton's play, the devil-figure had used such a revelation to draw Beatrice-Joanna to a greater damnation; here, Cathcut would stand like an angel over the narrow way, pointing Lepage to an alternative to despair, a way out of the trap he had willed himself into. A surrender to divine direction let one out of that endless chain of action and counter-action, where the past created the present, where action determined character, and character conditioned deeds.

But if Lepage had somehow acted against his own nature, or was running counter to the grain of the world in which he found himself, then he couldn't be that threat to belief, to everything that a Christian stood for, which Cathcut had imagined. His own intervention was, to a degree, unnecessary: the correcting process would have worked without him. Anyway, a large part of what he had hoped for in keeping silent had been achieved. Lepage had been brought to face the body, the autopsy (so it seemed), the destruction of everything he had set his hopes on. He hadn't been able to shrug off the consequences of his actions, or to elude the grief of the family and his own vengeful feelings. He was showing signs of strain, physical and (on the evidence of this last action) mental. The experiment had almost run its course. It wouldn't be safe to let things go on beyond the discovery of a suspect; it was time to take the pot off the boil.

'Can I put the lid on for you now, sir?' said a voice beside him.

Cathcut started, entirely misunderstanding.

'Time to batten down hatches, eh?' The undertaker's assistant jerked a thumb toward the coffin-lid, which Cathcut had laid over the body before commencing his vigil.

'—Ah yes! If you please,' said Cathcut, smiling wryly: it was more than time to shut Pandora's box. He discovered guiltily that he could not at present recall the girl's first name. But she had given her all—'Pandora' would do very well.

'It'll cost, y'know,' said the assistant.

Cathcut looked puzzled.

'Parlour to here last night'—he leant across the coffin-lid, holding a brass screw between thumb and forefinger, and screwed it down with a heavy, black, brass-bound screwdriver. 'Then out here again for this little trip'—a second screw went home just as smoothly—'and back again in three quarters of an hour for the big do. It'll cost all right,' he said, with deft flickings of the wrist. 'Way above the standard rate. Boss thought you ought to know. —Not that *we* see much of it,' he insisted, completing the final turn.

'I'm sure it'll be all right,' Cathcut assured him. It hadn't occurred to him that his arrangements might run the family into extra expense. It was acutely embarrassing. He resolved to explain it to Janice at the first opportunity. But before anything, he must confront Lepage.

Both intentions were thwarted by Lepage arriving early for the funeral, in company with the girl's family. Cathcut couldn't make out whether he had met them at the door, or had had the face to pick them up at their home. Mrs Driscoll held a black handkerchief to her lips beneath her veil, as though taken with nausea; but Janice chatted amicably enough to Lepage, ignoring her mother's objections. Where was her previous contempt? Or had her charity allowed Lepage a status, arising out of their common grief? It was more than Cathcut could fathom. Lepage, at any rate, was slyly sheltering behind the family, obviously aware that, if Cathcut had discovered anything, he could hardly speak out in front of them, or even take Lepage aside without making an evident palaver, letting on that he had something not suitable for relatives' ears.

Before Cathcut could pull on his surplice and get down from the chancel to greet the mourners, the undertaker cut in, halting them in a cross-aisle, murmuring to Mrs Driscoll in discreet tones, pointing out where it was customary to sit, ascertaining which of the family required to be pall-bearers, holding the coffin in miniature, as it were, between his pink, over-scrubbed hands, assigning bearers with a forefinger to either side of it, front and back, with little steering movements indicating where care must be taken over steps and carpets, where there was a tight corner from main aisle round toward the porch—and in every turn, he presented his humped, shiny-black back to Cathcut, its ample curve saying clearly enough 'Keep out: this is business for professionals. The magic-words come *later*.' From the edge of the group, Lepage seemed amused at Cathcut's frustration—or was he simply imagining it?

Cathcut felt resentful at Janice's insensitivity to her mother's objections; in this instance, at least, the old woman showed a greater sense of decorum. How could Janice bear *any* contact with that hideous man? Perhaps her innocence not only protected her, but also gave her no means to understand? He noticed her change of dress: today the white blouse had become lace, making even more obvious the black bra underneath. Was it yesterday's garment? —Or had she an inexhaustible supply? He felt violently jealous that Lepage should be so near; he had to get her away from that polluting gaze.

He called her out, after murmuring his condolences to Mama.

'Can't you tell me *here*?' she exclaimed, looking archly at Lepage. 'There's surely no need to go into a corner.'

'I *must* speak to you alone.'

She shrugged her shoulders, looking again at Lepage, as though they were both sharing some joke at his expense. What had Lepage taken opportunity to tell her? It was as if she implied that Cathcut had an interest in her which amused them both. Or was she, as Lepage had once suggested, the reincarnation of her sister, and now competing, seeing what she could do on her own account? He felt his suspicion unworthy—but what had Lepage found opportunity to say?

His conference attracted the attention he wanted to avoid. Lepage leered, as though implying that Cathcut's only interest was to get closer to those black-cupped breasts. As he led Janice into a side-aisle, he could see her mother nudging the most-favoured relative, and almost heard her satisfied whisper: 'Janice's young man.' He made his explanations as matter-of-fact as possible.

'We're not *made* of money,' Janice observed.

She fixed him with her grey-blue eyes. He felt he had been slapped in the face.

'I could help out,' he said, thinking that his position would surely allow him to get credit from the undertaker, and pay it out of his stipend over several months. 'I'd be *glad* to help,' he said again.

'Allow us *some* pride,' she exclaimed. He felt violently fended off, embarrassed at having presumed a relationship which he couldn't rely on. Why was she being so hurtful? She continued to look into his eyes, as though searching out his guilty thoughts wherever they might be hiding.

'It's that man, isn't it?' she said, nodding over her shoulder at Lepage. 'All this lying in church over night'—her voice had a contemptuous edge—'it's all been done because of him. Because you wanted to make him face up to my sister.'

She wouldn't let his gaze drop, challenging him to come up with an excuse. More than anything, her contemptuous tone cut like a knife. How could he say that it was done, basically, because he loved her, because he had wanted to take the responsibility off her, to arrange everything in the best, the most productively Christian way for all concerned? If she didn't know that already, if a malicious innuendo from Lepage could have turned her whole attitude against him . . . a pit of loneliness opened beneath him. He felt his most hesitant movements toward a human contact had been crudely, vulgarly betrayed.

'It's your mother saying that, isn't it?' he accused her, clutching at a straw, praying that she would say 'No, it isn't, it came from Lepage'—and then, however, schoolboyish it might seem, he would have a chance to say they were rivals, she mustn't presume everything Lepage said was gospel.

'My mother can make up her own mind—and so can I,' she snapped.

There was absolutely no hope of getting the record straight. How could she put any faith in that man, even be attracted to him, when for all she knew he might be trying to pull off just the same trick as with her sister? And yet—what was it that attracted Cathcut himself to Lepage? Perhaps she, like her sister, felt the lure of his defiant depravity, the charm of self-destruction?

'I'm going to start the service,' he said with dignity, 'and I hope, in the course of it, that you'll realize how unjust you've been.' She turned on her heel and went back to her family. Cathcut got the impression that she toyed with the idea of putting Lepage among the intimate mourners, but decided not to provoke her mother too far. Lepage sat himself on the edge of the left-hand aisle across from her, and the two exchanged smiles.

Cathcut brought the next misery on himself by his retreat. Janice opened the prayer-book in front of her, and with a helpless shrug showed it to her mother. Mrs Driscoll brushed aside her veil, peered, and then raised her eyes heavenwards, as if to say 'What can one expect in this corrupted age?' Lepage saw the problem, even before Cathcut from his place of eminence had realized anything was wrong: a gather containing the Burial Service had dropped from its binding. Quick as a flash, Lepage slipped to the back, found a more perfect copy, walked down the aisle fluttering its pages to find the right place, and with a little nod of his head and a humorous click of his heels handed it to Janice. Mrs Driscoll glowered; but Janice accepted it sweetly. Lepage stood looking at her, just too long for decency; she blushed and turned away, on the pretence of checking her page with her mother.

'I know that my Redeemer liveth,' Cathcut proclaimed from the chancel, 'and that he shall stand at the latter day upon the earth. And though after my skin worms destroy this body, yet in my flesh shall I see God: whom I shall see for myself, and mine eyes shall behold, and not another.'

Lepage returned to his place and stood staring ahead.

Was it by chance that Cathcut had selected that second Sentence from among the three provided? He resolved to keep the rest of the service unsullied by his personal concerns. But its material defeated him. Psalm 90 was innocuous enough, though Janice kept glancing sidelong at Lepage, who ignored her. In the Epistle, however, it would have violated all sense to have kept a certain emphasis from his voice.

'. . . what advantageth it me, if the dead rise not? Let us eat and drink, for to-morrow we die. Be not deceived: evil communications corrupt good manners. Awake to righteousness, and sin not; for some have not the knowledge of God. I speak this to your shame . . .'

Janice was looking desperately at Lepage, who seemed to take pleasure in snubbing her. Mrs Driscoll tugged imperiously at her sleeve, pointing out that she had slipped back more than a page in her perusal of the service.

Cathcut mouthed through the lesson to its end, but his thoughts were now irretrievably in the world before him. 'Evil communications corrupt . . . ' Perhaps Janice also was the 'deed's creature', a victim of what had been done to her, and not to be held accountable for the oddities of her behaviour. He had seen how her mother manipulated her feelings; maybe the girl knew no better way. There was a great void caused by lovelessness and exploitation. She grabbed at attention from any source, however repugnant it might ultimately be to her. Only a knowledge of God could fill that hollow, or crack her out of her accustomed mould.

They sang Crimond's setting of the Twenty-Third Psalm, thinly and raggedly, as the bearers came up into the chancel and made themselves ready. At a finger-snap from the undertaker, who led the procession as majordomo, the coffin was lifted shoulder-high. Two of his assistants took the head, the foot being supported by Mr Driscoll and the most-favoured relative. Cathcut edged along after them, intoning 'Man that is born of a woman hath but a short time to live . . .'

But one of the undertaker's assistants was a clear six inches shorter than his fellow; as they negotiated the chancel steps the coffin took an alarming lurch down towards the left-hand side. Cathcut expected any minute to hear a skull crack within the coffin-head. As swiftly as before, Lepage left his place, crossed deferentially before the majordomo, whispered in the ear of his underling, and within seconds had taken the bearer's place at the left hand side of the coffin. He looked back at Cathcut as he eased the body on to his shoulder, wild-eyed at thus defying the decencies. As the procession moved off again, there was about his bearing something insolent and triumphant.

Mrs Driscoll seemed positively to gobble on her handkerchief; but Janice bowed her head as they passed, as though she approved of, or at least assented to Lepage's gesture. The cortège halted again before that awkward turn toward the south porch, as Cathcut, omitting the Prayer of Committal, took them through the Kyries, the Pater Noster, the Prayer, Collect and Grace.

The mourners remained kneeling, heads bowed, whilst the coffin was loaded up outside. On his return, the girl's father pumped Lepage's hand, as though the police officer were both a family friend and a potential avenger. Cathcut was sickened to see how Lepage played up to him, returning a firm grip, a straight eye, and a manly pat to the shoulder. He was taking advantage of Mr Driscoll's gullibility to act out the part of distressed admirer, for the benefit of Janice and her mother. It was more than time for Cathcut to forget about sparing their feelings; he broke up the charade by demanding to speak with Lepage alone. He failed even to apologize for a delay.

Lepage walked away and sat in a front pew of the nave, staring ahead at the draped trestle that had borne the coffin. His latest act of will seemed to have left him quite spent. Cathcut followed him down the aisle and stood at his elbow. The priest glanced round to make sure her relatives had all moved off toward the porch.

'What game are you playing?'

'I'm not aware of playing *any* game. I wish play were possible for me.'

'The body was interfered with last night. In church.'

Lepage turned on him an eye that was both weary and all-seeing.

'Have you reported it?'

Cathcut realized that he had declared his intentions, perhaps even his motives, to Lepage, simply by doing nothing. He felt stymied.

'Not as yet,' he said.

'Then, if you have taken no action,' said Lepage in a passionless voice, 'and presuming the interference was minor, it might be kinder to the family to let matters rest. —Though that is advice strictly off-the-record,' he added.

Cathcut was certain Lepage was responsible, but he could detect no sign to confirm it.

'Aren't you angry?' he asked.

'Yes.'

'At the interference?'

'At much more than that.' Lepage lapsed into silence.

'At having lost your titillation?' enquired Cathcut again, made spiteful by Lepage's recent antics. He hardly cared how far he provoked him.

'Not a titillation, little priest. A lust of the spirit. I'm angry at losing that.'

'You've tried to revive it with Miss Driscoll.'

'Miss Driscoll?' Lepage waved her aside with a gesture of contempt. 'She's an empty, flibberty-gibbert little husk. She has features in common . . . externals. . . . She doesn't take my soul.'

Cathcut was too frightened to be indignant, even on Janice's behalf.

'Why do you *want* it taken?' he asked—though he half-knew the answer.

'Because it's a burden to me. It makes me conscious.'

'Isn't that a blessing?'

'No,' he said with finality, as though instructing a child. '. . . Enjoy it, Cathcut: she's wanting her pound of flesh.'

'Miss Janice?'

'No, not Miss Janice. *She* doesn't know *what* she wants.'

'Who then?'

Lepage waved a finger over his shoulder towards the church door.

'That.'

'That has no claim on you. Death ends all such claims.'

'Then why are you so pleased about it?'

'Isn't it time to give up?' Cathcut pleaded. 'Time to declare an interest?'

'What interest?' said Lepage limply. '—Unless you call Robert Evans an interest?'

'You've arrested him!' cried Cathcut in alarm, fighting down a ridiculous image of Lepage, in the privacy of a police station, coldly and silently force-feeding Evans with the girl's hair.

'Oh no. We don't arrest our own kind. Not till there's *extreme* provocation. No, no, we're just pulling him in for a little discreet questioning.'

'But he isn't guilty!' cried Cathcut. '—I'm sure he's not guilty,' he added quickly, conscious that Lepage had begun to take an interest, and wondering why he was so certain that Dr Kemberton's visitor could not have been Robert Evans.

'I really must give my condolences to Miss Driscoll and her family,' Lepage said, half-rising to his feet.

Cathcut pushed down hard on his shoulder.

'Dr Kemberton—my superior—' he said abruptly, 'had a visitor last Tuesday. I know no name, no details. But he gave me to understand he heard a confession to the murder.'

For once Lepage seemed taken by surprise. He considered the information for a length of time.

'. . . I seem condemned to lose myself in distractions,' he said at last. 'You had better keep Miss Driscoll.' There was something humiliating about his resignation. Cathcut felt that Lepage had known all along that his attempt to break out by a willed passion for the dead girl's sister would be a failure.

'You'll have difficulty,' Cathcut said anxiously, 'since it was told him under the seal of the confessional. Traditionally, the priest may not even give a hint. But if you allow me to accompany you, another priest may be able to allay his scruples—for the sake of a greater good.'

'I'm quite experienced at applying moral pressure,' said Lepage.

'But it must be pressure of the right kind,' Cathcut insisted. 'Arguments such as only a priest could manage. Otherwise he'll shut up like a clam.'

For answer Lepage got to his feet, walked back to Mrs Driscoll where she was surrounded by a knot of relatives at the door, and seized her black-gloved hand. He leaned forward, as though to murmur his sympathies. She drew back sharply, leaving her glove in his hand, suddenly taken with a choking sensation, gasping, unable to get breath. Her face went quite puce, and she sat down in a convenient chair, still unable to heave-in enough air. John, the most-favoured relative, compelled them all to stand back and give her room; but Aunt Edie darted forward to lay her veil back over her hat as though afraid she might suck it into her open mouth. She was handed a glass of water, but coughed over it. Janice looked reproachfully at Cathcut, who had run to fetch the water. 'Palpitations!' her mother cried, 'It's my palpitations!', rolling as she sat, and rubbing her chest between her heavy breasts. It did really seem that she might be on the point of a heart attack. Her husband snapped out of his abstraction. 'Maud! Maudie!' he shouted, kneeling in front of her broad-spread thighs and slapping her cheeks, unhelpfully and quite painfully. She caught his hand, and put it down. 'For God's sake, stop *that*,' she said. '—I *do* beg your pardon,' she gasped to Cathcut, at the same time taking the hand with which Janice had been massaging her back, and patting it within her own.

'Mr Cathcut . . . I can't go on . . . I'd like to, but I can't. *Would* you look after my Janice, see her through, so that we give her sister a proper send-off? I'll have to go home, my Albert 'll have to take me home. It's all been too much for me,' she said, laying one hand on her still-heaving bosom, and dabbing at her eye with the black handkerchief.

Everyone hesitated, in case she were not quite certain of her decision.

'Miss Driscoll would welcome the support,' Lepage said.

Cathcut was caught: there was no way he could refuse such an appeal. Nor was it entirely unpleasant to receive Mrs Driscoll's accolade, even if it might later backfire with Janice. But he was in terror lest Lepage again get out of hand.

'It *would* help me,' said Janice, slipping her hand through his arm, and looking up with her most tender, trusting smile. 'Surely you were planning to go anyway?'

So he was, despite there being a duty-priest at the crematorium—but he hadn't known he would have to keep an eye on Lepage. The 'blacks' had come back into the church and were waiting with ill-disguised impatience.

'Don't move on that business without me,' he said to Lepage, triumphant at least that he had Janice securely under his protection, but wondering if Lepage had ever in fact wanted her.

Lepage seemed to nod his assent.

Ill at ease, Cathcut led Janice out into the cold. They walked round to the north gate, and took their position as chief mourners in the first car after the hearse. The coffin on which Cathcut had lavished his night-watches was barely visible beneath its forest of chrysanthemums. Their own driver kept a reverent brakingdistance behind, never veering out of line by more than a foot, anticipating where traffic might cause the hearse to slow, or those rarer stretches where it was possible to pick up time; so that the distance between the two hardly varied. The corpse seemed to draw its train after it by an invisible thread. Cathcut reflected wryly that, for once, he was as much the 'deed's creature' as any of them, unavoidably a prisoner of circumstance, at least for the moment. He prayed fervently that the interval might not prove crucial.

CHAPTER FIFTEEN

Lepage rang the Rectory bell.
'I have an interview with the rector.'
'Vicar,' said Mrs Avling.
'I have an interview with the vicar.'
'That is *inconceivable*,' boomed Mrs Avling. 'Dr Kemberton holds his interviews between the hours of five and seven on Wednesday evenings.'
'Is he always so invariable?'
'There is a daily beauty in his life. He is *entirely* governed by ordinance.'
'If not by eternal decree,' said Lepage. Mrs Avling tangled her eyebrows at him. It seemed that to lack an appointment meant total disqualification.
'But he appears to be free,' Lepage said again, nodding to where Dr Kemberton was clearly visible, writing at a bureau positioned in the bow-window of his dining-room.
'He is engaged in a family communication of *peculiar* delicacy,' said Mrs Avling, glancing toward Dr Kemberton herself, with the air of a matron who observes some recalcitrant schoolboy buckling down to his homework.
Behind the glass, Dr Kemberton was seen to screw the paper on which he had been writing into a tight ball, squeezing it in his fist with convulsive spasms, before tossing it into a basket. He took a further sheet, and began writing again.
'His way is *beset* with thorns,' observed Mrs Avling, by way of explanation.
'It will be thornier yet,' said Lepage, taking an identity card from his breast pocket, 'if he doesn't answer a few questions. I am a police officer, investigating a murder.'
Mrs Avling's pleated lips opened into a withered O; but despite several gnawings with her fore-teeth on empty air, she failed to

find words with which to defend her employer. Lepage pushed past her and made straight for the dining-room door. 'In the *drawing*-room, I *beg* you,' came a strangled voice behind him. But it was too late.

Dr Kemberton turned his head like a long-eared owl, red-eyed and startled. He seemed to be trying to recall if he had made an appointment—but the inappropriate room, and the inconceivable hour, made that unlikely. There was an empty cup on the bureau in front of him, and to one side of his pad a water glass and a small bottle, as if he had just been taking medicine.

'I write here after m-morning coffee,' he mumbled, waving a hand over the cup. 'P-personal . . . *business* matters. These regency bays give excellent light, at all times of the year.'

'Lepage,' said Lepage. 'Police officer.' He flourished his identity card again.

'Ah!' exclaimed the old man, slipping his pill-bottle into a coat pocket. He shuffled his papers for some seconds, till his brain threw up the information he wanted. 'Mr Lepage,' he said conclusively, putting his letter very firmly under his blotter, but placing it deliberately, without subterfuge. Lepage let it appear that he had noticed.

'I need to talk to you about the Driscoll girl,' he said.

'You have come from her funeral?'

'After a detour—yes.'

Dr Kemberton indicated a chair beside his bureau.

'Thank you, Mrs Avling,' he said aloud, waving a hand in her direction, with general benediction for this departure from routine. She acquiesced reluctantly, and withdrew. The priest knit his knuckles on the writing-top and leaned over them to look into Lepage's face.

'Though as a priest it was my duty to reprove you . . . as a man, I am deeply sorry.'

Lepage stared into the filaments of his irises, which pulsed behind their lenses like tiny grey sea-anemones.

'Neither your reproof nor your sorrow concern me.'

'But you *must* accept human comfort.'

'*You* have the only comfort I require.'

Dr Kemberton sat back in his chair, as though in anticipation of what was coming.

'How so?'

'A confession to her murder was made to you last Tuesday.'

'So.' The priest deliberated for a while. 'It seems God's little soldier has let him down.'

'Soldier?'

'Only Mr Cathcut could have told you *that*.'

'Mr Cathcut sacrificed a lesser to a greater good. I hope you will do the same.'

'Mr Cathcut broke an oath,' said Dr Kemberton angrily. 'An implied *oath*.'

'I thought God's representatives might allow themselves a little liberty with the rules.' Lepage fiddled with the edge of the blotter before looking up.

'Not those who have been tempered by tribulation . . . by the fires of adversity.' The priest's face set impassively. 'Canon law forbids any breach of the seal of confession . . . on pain of irregularity.'

Lepage considered him for a moment, casting about for some way in.

'*You* seem to have had the rules burnt into you.'

'Rule', the priest responded, linking his hands again on the bureau in front of him, 'is the guide-rope that enables me to move from point to point in my day.'

'Yet you don't seem to do it with *love*,' said Lepage, with a glance that took in the priest's crumpled pin-stripe, his cream walls, and his dark, comfortless furniture.

'Does the schoolboy love the rod?' asked Dr Kemberton sharply.

'No,' Lepage said, watching his face. 'But he might be kissing it to spite his schoolmaster. "—Look at *me*, sir, how *good* I am."'

'Who *are* you?' asked the old man in fear, turning in his chair to face him. 'What are my motives to *you*?'

'If you like,' said Lepage, flicking at the water glass with the back of his nail, 'I am one of God's assayers. Testing if you ring true. . . .' He put the glass down again, positioning it with particular attention over the blotter. '—But you know very well who I am. I was the girl's lover. As police officer engaged on the case, I hope to be her avenger.'

'That is not *right*,' protested Dr Kemberton. 'It is quite improper.'

'It isn't *right*', responded Lepage, 'that you protect her killer, for motives that have more to do with spiting God than with the sanctity of the confessional.'

Dr Kemberton waved his mottled hand in protest, then put it to his forehead as if struck with sudden pain, grinding his thumb over the prominent vein on the left side of his temple and rocking it as though to interrupt the blood flow. Lepage jumped to his feet and leaned over the old man, placing both his hands on the bureau.

'I've checked on the situation. Cross, *Evidence*, second edition. There is no basis in English law for a priest's privilege. I could cite you to court and *compel* you to answer.' Dr Kemberton hunched over, silent and absorbed in his pain. 'What has your God done for *you*?' said Lepage again, with a gesture that took in the old man's body from top to toe. 'Do you make your rules to punish him for *that*? You're fat, short-winded'—he leant forward to speak almost into the priest's ear, who sat grinding at both sides of his head with clenched fists—'your wrists *shake*, your hair is a narrow bootlace across your skull—do you love him for *that*?'

Dr Kemberton struggled to his feet, seized his water glass from in front of Lepage, but then replaced it hastily over his blotter and staggered over to the sideboard, where he poured himself a fresh glass, spilling water over his wrist and on to the tray.

'I'm an old man,' he said, standing red-faced, and interspersing sips of water with gasps for air. 'In p-poor health,' he said, feeling for the back of a dining chair with one hand, pulling it out clumsily and lowering himself into it. 'Why do you assault me like this?' He held his glass in his right hand, and, leaning his left elbow on the table, parted his eyebrows with a forefinger, as though to ease the veins between.

'Because you're a *fraud*,' said Lepage. 'Your principles are not principles kept for their own sake. No one keeps principles for their own sake. It's for what you can *do* with them. In this case, you can prove to God he is unjust: by following the code, by being more merciful than the Ever-Merciful.' He watched intently the priest's reaction.

'The rules of the confessional were established for a reason,' said Dr Kemberton. 'Otherwise, no man would trust the burden of his conscience to another. I have no responsibility to the secular arm. My only responsibility is to the state of a man's soul.'

'Ah yes,' said Lepage, standing at the bay window, as if his attention had been drawn by something in the street. 'Fine words. If *only* they were true. But what do you care about the state of a man's soul? Your interest is to fulfil your contract to the letter, so as to shame your God into declaring a dividend. You're working for a pay-out.'

'Anyone who works for *that*', said Dr Kemberton, 'will toil till Judgement Day and beyond.'

'Be judge *yourself*,' urged Lepage earnestly, turning from the window to try a new tack. 'Step out of the rules for once. Why should he escape on a technicality? Show yourself juster than God.'

'Show myself juster than God?' echoed Dr Kemberton in a bemused, befuddled tone, as though in a state of semi-intoxication. Then he pulled himself together. '—But how can it be just to help a lecher to avenge his loss?'

Lepage checked. 'I, like you,' he said slowly, 'have a job that must be done, with or without my inclination.'

'But you have assured me that no one works from principle.' Dr Kemberton leant back in his dining chair, smiling with satisfaction at his riposte.

'You can bring me to face what I have done. You can prove to me that I can't just take my pleasure and run.'

'So that you can wreak havoc on some unfortunate wretch?' Lepage eyed him intently. He moved again towards the bureau.

'If I exceed the bounds'—he laughed—'you can shame God again. You can pull down judgement on my head. —But since we are agreed that no one acts from principle—'

'—No man acts from principle *alone*,' corrected Dr Kemberton. 'Human motives are unavoidably . . . many-stranded.'

'If they *are* so many-stranded—then I ask myself why you are protecting this man.' Lepage lifted the water glass and set it to one side.

Dr Kemberton got to his feet.

'I am nearly seventy years of age,' he said. 'I have high blood pressure, with the concomitant fatigue. If I am to meet the calls on my time and energies, I find that I must restrict my parish interviews to no more than fifteen minutes.'

'This is not an interview; it is a police inquiry. You are protecting a criminal. And I ask myself why. Could he be a member of your flock?'

'I will answer no questions,' said Dr Kemberton, still standing his ground.

Lepage slowly set the green blotter itself to one side, picked up Dr Kemberton's half-finished letter, and with an insolent smile began reading it where he stood. '*I am unwilling to use your adopted name,*' it began, '*and reluctant to accord you my own. . . .*' He looked at Dr Kemberton over the paper. 'I think you are protecting him because you identify with him.'

Dr Kemberton supported himself by one hand on the dining table.

'I gave no indication of sex.'

'But you wouldn't identify with a *woman*.' He waved the uncompleted sheet at him.

Dr Kemberton remained stubbornly silent.

'You are protecting him, because he has done what you would have liked to do, and dare not.'

Dr Kemberton stood stock-still for nigh on thirty seconds, and then broke.

'My will has *never*—for one *moment*—consented to any act of vengeance,' he roared.

'But it has consented to be an accessory after the fact.'

'No!' cried Dr Kemberton. He again fell silent.

'How . . .' ventured Lepage again in a soft voice, 'how *can* your God bless you when you shelter such things in your heart?'

Dr Kemberton began to tremble. He sought the security of the chair.

'Perhaps,' said Lepage again, 'if you could push this one thing from you, the heavens would open, and the rain *pour* down. Perhaps you would sprout hair on your head, and *"your youth"*—how does it go?—*"be renewed as an eagle's"*.'

Dr Kemberton considered for some seconds with head bowed. When he looked up, the lower part of his lenses was distorted by water.

'I *will* tell you,' he said, 'but not for any hope of reward, or because my anger is stirred against my God. *"Shall the dust dispute with him that made it?"* I will tell you as a token that I *utterly* repudiate those feelings of vengeance I have cherished for so long. When one's only fellow-feeling is with a murderer, it is time to break.'

'To break your rule?'

'I will accept the lesser guilt, to be purged of the greater.'

'It may, after all, be for his good.'

Dr Kemberton looked him between the eyes.

'Not at your hands, Mr Lepage. As soon as I have given you the information you want . . . I shall immediately inform your superiors of your involvement.'

'That would publicize your breach of trust,' said Lepage.

'I will take the shame, to be free of my burden.'

Lepage shrugged his shoulders and resumed his seat beside the bureau. He placed his notepad before him.

'Let us have what you know.'

Dr Kemberton rose unsteadily from where he had sunk and moved back to his writing chair, taking Lepage's hand to lower himself, but retaining it in both his own.

'His name is Tribulation,' the priest confided in a thick accent, scanning Lepage's face for approval like a maudlin drunk. His breath was a compound of coffee, alcohol and some medicament.

'That is not a name.'

'A pseudonym. A *nom de guerre*.' He clasped Lepage's forearm tighter. 'He's a warrior in some fanatic sect.'

'Christian?' Lepage asked, drawing his arm free.

'Nominally. By their own estimate.'

Lepage delayed before asking the next question.

'And his motives?'

Dr Kemberton looked at him, and hesitated. 'He was afraid . . . he was under the apprehension . . . that the young lady . . . was inveigling his lover.' He hesitated yet further. 'His *male* lover.'

Again, he put his hand over Lepage's. This time, Lepage let it remain.

'A jealous homosexual,' he said, after a long pause, staring in front of him. 'With religious delusions.' The sheer banality of it seemed to overwhelm him.

They sat for some moments with linked hands.

'And his appearance?' Lepage asked at length, liberating his writing hand. 'Description?'

'Youngish. Young hands, young voice. Hands very fine and white. *Nastily* white, despite being well-haired . . .'

'Is that all?'

'The grille prevents a clearer view.'

'Can you give me nothing more?'

'He was not a *practising* homosexual, I think. . . . I *beg* you to believe', the priest said with animation, 'that, however m–mistaken he might be . . . he killed in protection of an ideal. If that can in *any* way m-mitigate his guilt . . . in your eyes, and the law's . . .' He exhaled a distillation of coffee over Lepage.

'Killing on principle,' Lepage said, 'is something for *judges* to believe in. He *may* be lucky; or he may not.' He again stared into space, alternatively gripping and releasing his pencil. '. . . Is that all?'

'I have tried,' the priest pleaded. 'I have *squeezed* my recollection.' He kneaded his forehead, as if it were putty in which a further lump might be discovered.

'Do you feel purged?' Lepage asked.

The priest laughed a curious, high-toned laugh, and fixed on him a roguish, conspiratorial eye.

'Yes, I do,' he giggled. 'I do.'

'Then help me to purge myself.'
The conspiratorial look faded.
'How so?'
'Don't inform on me.'
Dr Kemberton ceased kneading.
'Why ever not?'
'I have a debt to pay. . . . Don't leave me trapped.'
Dr Kemberton brought his hands together in a prayerful posture.
'Whatever makes you think you can escape her?'
'I might try.'
'Once the bond is made,' the priest said, reaching grimly for another sheet of paper, 'whether formally or informally . . . it can never entirely be broken. "*So long as ye both shall live*".'
'She doesn't live.'
'But she does. In the cells and cellars of your memory. Traces that will light up at every slight reminder. They lie in wait.'
'I can erase them. I can *will* them into oblivion.'
'And have part of your head that you can't visit? Pray for a brainstorm, my son,' said Dr Kemberton, pressing Lepage's forearm once more, but with what seemed a somewhat malicious pinch. 'Pray for a sudden, obliterating stroke. That way you will remember nothing. —And now, if you will excuse me, I must write to my erring wife.'
'I will sit here in case you recall something further.'
'I fear that I shall. And so will you.'
He wrote laboriously for some minutes, making light, a-rhythmic scratches with his pen, whilst Lepage lapsed into torpor, staring at the pen-shaft as it twitched, scrabbled and shook. Dr Kemberton stopped mid-way, again clutching his head with his hand, and pressing with his palm over the temple. Lepage snapped back to consciousness.
'Are you all right?'
The priest managed something approaching a smile. 'Of course,' he said, still holding his head with one hand, but beating time irregularly in the air with his outstretched pen, in accompaniment to his words. '*Birth*pangs. "*They that* wait *upon the Lord shall re*new *their strength. I shall* rise *up as an* eagle. *I shall* run, *and not be* faint".'
He attacked his notepaper furiously, writing at great speed with much spattering of ink, and dashing tears from under his spectacle-rims with his left hand as he wrote. After completing a further line, he dropped his pen, and pushed inky fingers into

the hollows above each cheekbone, dislodging his spectacles on to his forehead.

'I feel quite ill,' he said. 'Call the woman.' He hooked his wastebasket out from under the bureau with his foot and leaned over the crumpled papers, retching fruitlessly.

Lepage roused himself from his stupor, walked to the door, and called Mrs Avling from where she was smearing polish over the leather top of a hall table.

'He feels unwell. Bring a bowl.' Mrs Avling ran in, still holding her polish-tin in her hand, seized an empty fruit bowl from the sideboard, and pushed it under the priest's nose. She took off his spectacles, laying them on the bureau out of harm's way, but then backed off, as if afraid she had offended. Dr Kemberton motioned her to come closer. She stood beside him, polish held out of sight but carefully level, and inclined stiffly over him, like a gantry-crane assuming a load.

'Your hour has come, Mrs Avling,' he said, looking up myopically from the bowl, and speaking as if from a mouth filled with toffee. 'I must wane . . . and you must wax.'

Mrs Avling looked doubtfully at her tin, unsure as to what was required.

'For heaven's sake, woman!' he cried. 'I need a doctor. Ring Hudson. My whole right side has gone dead.'

Mrs Avling rushed to the telephone in the hall. 'The Doctor! A stroke!' she hallooed into the mouthpiece, in a tone that would have pierced the furthest row of the gallery. Fortunately, her accent was unmistakable. 'Dr Hudson is out on call, Mrs Avling,' said the receptionist at the other end. 'But his partner, Dr Williams, is still holding his surgery. I'm sure he'll come as soon as possible.' She had to be content with that.

'The doctor is out,' she announced on returning to the room. 'They are sending his boy.'

Together, Lepage and Mrs Avling removed the vicar's collar and stock, and eased him out of his jacket. Mrs Avling fell to massaging the limp right arm.

'I may have pins-and-needles,' the priest said drunkenly, 'but I can still feel you rucking my skin. It is most unpleasant.'

She desisted, and they stood helplessly, unsure what else to do.

Dr Williams was boyish but forty; with the wry affability of one who plugs leaky dams, in the certain knowledge that they must sometime collapse. A few well-chosen questions established the how, where and when of the attack.

'And what brought this on?' he asked.

'He was forced to receive a visitor in the dining-room,' said Mrs Avling, her glare leaving no doubt as to the focus of blame.

'I had questions to ask', said Lepage, 'in the course of police inquiries. Though he was not directly involved, they caused him some pain.'

Dr Williams began a routine examination, not scamping anything, but paying particular attention to the priest's blood-pressure, which he took at either arm. He consulted a card.

'Did you take your tablets this morning?'

Dr Kemberton nodded heavily.

'In good spirits?'

Dr Kemberton cocked an eye at him, then gave Mrs Avling a sidelong glance over his shoulder. 'In good spirits,' he confirmed.

'I want you to lift that right arm, as high as you can get it.'

Dr Kemberton raised his writing arm very slowly, elbow on the bureau, letting his hand go slack and watching it all the way, till his forearm came vertical and the hand hung limply from the wrist. 'Like an eagle,' he said thickly, rocking his outstretched hand from side to side like a bird in flight. 'It shall rise up as an eagle.' He darted the agitated hand to and fro and from side to side, like a bird of prey hovering. The whole arm went into an uncontrollable spasm from the shoulder downwards, a muscle on the inner forearm at the elbow standing out like steel cable. His eyes bulged, and he seemed to be staring past his animated claw at some bemusing apparition in the street. The right side of his face began to twitch, his lips making little putting-sounds as they clapped together.

The doctor leaned forward and smoothed the right cheek with a caress, laying his palm flat to suppress the spasm. 'Open.' He squeezed both cheeks between thumb and forefinger, as if trying to retrieve an object from the mouth of a child. Dr Kemberton's jaw sagged, saliva spilling over his lower lip, filling the folds of his chins, and hanging from the lowest in a clear, silvery thread. A set of false teeth dropped into the physician's hand; he gave them to Mrs Avling, who committed them to a glass of water.

'Can you swallow?' Dr Kemberton nodded, and they saw his Adam's apple lift hesitantly, and fall. 'Then I want you to take those, and get them down with a good drink.' He put out a hand, and Mrs Avling pushed a fresh glass of water into it. 'They'll control those spasms.'

'What does he mean about eagles?' he asked over his shoulder, while he assisted the priest to drink. 'Does he watch birds? Does he *keep* birds?' Mrs Avling stiffened, and looked scandalized.

'It's a scrap of conversation,' Lepage said grimly. 'A passing remark. It doesn't signify.'

The physician opened his hand suddenly and silently, two inches from the priest's right cheek-bone. Dr Kemberton continued staring.

'There's no sight in the right eye.'

Mrs Avling sobbed. A similar flick on the left side caused the old man to blink, and then to focus on the physician's face with a look of alarm.

'It's hemianopia,' Williams said quickly. 'One-sided blindness. It may well be temporary.'

Mrs Avling put her damp handkerchief from her cheek to her mouth, and followed with wide eyes this improbably youthful magician, whose word of power could turn blindness into a passing affliction.

The terms began to pile up, as the doctor realized her need. 'Hemiparesis, bordering on hemiplegia,' he ventured; and Mrs Avling brightened visibly for both. 'But I'm inclined to doubt infarction, or any embolism, despite the relative suddenness of the attack. —Ah, you understand Greek, do you, old chap?' he said, noticing that Dr Kemberton had raised his head sharply on the first word. 'Hemi-par-*es*is,' he said distinctly into his ear. 'Weakness on one side. Lean on the left arm, and we'll soon have you lying flat.'

He began squinting into the unseeing eye with the aid of a tiny light. 'I'd suspect papilloedema, probably bi-lateral, with haemorrhages and exudates . . .' Mrs Avling nodded, mouthing each word. 'There *may* be some cerebral lesion, but given the history and that *extravagant* diastolic reading'—he began coiling the squeeze pump and tube with which he had taken the priest's blood-pressure—'I'm inclined to take a risk. Let the hospital sort out the details.' The instruments went back into his case. He produced a large syringe, and a solution. Dr Kemberton lay back in his chair, turned on his left side, increasingly drowsy, and breathing quickly and noisily like a man struggling in a nightmare. Mrs Avling tucked a cushion under his head, to take off the hard edge of the chair-back. The doctor rolled up Dr Kemberton's left shirt-sleeve, and selected a prominent dark vein on the fleshy part of his forearm. 'Now if I'm right,' he said into his ear '—do you hear me?—if I'm *right*, the effects should be quite miraculous. I'm giving you three hundred milligrams in solution, and you'll feel it going in—*fast*.' He depressed the syringe at speed, the liquid in its container rapidly dwindling to nothing. 'Keep that bowl handy,' he said to Mrs Avling. 'It may make him want to vomit.'

Mrs Avling seized the bowl, placed it on the old man's chest, and, cradling his head in her right arm from behind, lifted his chins and dropped them over the rim of the bowl.

'Hospital?' she said, turning back with her eyes wide in panic, and restored to voice at the thought of her treasure being taken from her.

'The pressure will take some hours to go down. And the hospital must monitor that blood-pressure till we've got it right. I also want them to check for anything else. But if I'm correct,' he said comfortingly, 'you'll have him back in a couple of days.'

'Will he be able to answer questions?' asked Lepage.

Mrs Avling abandoned the bowl, which remained tucked at an angle under Dr Kemberton's chin, and advanced on her enemy.

'A man has hemiplegia,' she cried, bearing down on him, 'hemiparesis, and hemi-amamopia . . . and *you* require *questions?*'

'Your questions,' said Williams, looking severe for once, 'if not the underlying cause, were probably a contributory factor. I suggest you lay off for a while. —Have you a car here?'

'Only an old Ford. Too small to manoeuvre him in.'

The doctor turned to Mrs Avling. 'Fetch pillows,' he said. 'And plenty of blankets. I'll take him in the back of my shooting-brake. There's foam-rubber on the floor, and we'll get him to hospital twice as quick as any ambulance.'

'I'll ride with you,' Lepage said quickly.

The doctor looked at him with suspicion. 'If you do, you'll hold his head, and ensure that his airway is kept free. And any problems with the breathing, I want to *know*. —Otherwise, his housekeeper can do it.'

Lepage moved over to Dr Kemberton, who by this time seemed in a semi-coma, and assumed a position to lift him. The priest looked very flushed. The two men lugged the heavy body out into the hall, down the steps and into the back of the brake, where Mrs Avling busied herself easing-in cushions and propping pillows. Lepage climbed in beside the priest, and, sitting braced against the front seat with his legs outstretched, cushioned the old man's head on the inside of his thigh. Mrs Avling opened her mouth in protest.

'Gather up anything he might want: glasses . . . pyjamas and little personal effects. Watch and shaving tackle. Toiletries—that sort of thing. You'll probably find we are still in Emergency. If not, ask there, and they'll direct you to a ward.' Mrs Avling submitted, out of respect for the doctor's skill in matching words to things.

In gathering up pencil and paper for Dr Kemberton's emergency pack, she came across his letter. She felt that circumstances entitled her to read it: it was, after all, her hour.

'*Emma*'—the name was heavily underlined—'I am old and bewildered, I may not be able to understand. But if you will accept such limitations, limitations which are not of my making, I will welcome you back.'

Underneath, in large letters, with thick, impetuous downstrokes, spattered with ink and stuck all over with thumb-prints, he had written:

'*Return, return, O Shulammite, return, return, that we may look upon thee.*'

She puzzled over 'Shulammite', turning the paper several ways to catch the light; and then screwed it up, as being more than the erstwhile Mrs Kemberton had deserved. Instead, she telegrammed from the post office, taking the woman's address from a now redundant envelope: '*The Doctor has had a stroke. They have taken him to hospital. Come immediately. Avling. Mrs.*'

CHAPTER SIXTEEN

Cathcut maintained his aloofness all the way to the crematorium, even when Janice stubbed her toe against a flagstone on entering, bit her lip to suppress a sob, and her eyes filled with tears. He refused an invitation from the officiant to take over the committal, or at least to participate in it; yet he refrained from making support for Janice his excuse. When the coffin and its catafalque sunk through the floor to subdued electrical whirrings, when the space it had occupied was somehow filled with a dull bronze, tomb-like lid, on which a thick, chunky cross stood out in low relief, even then he denied himself the opportunity to squeeze her arm, or to put his own arm protectively round her. She faced the hideous red brick of the building, the perfunctory mouthings of its duty-priest, the timed and orderly disposal system that tried to present itself as a gateway to eternity, all the subterranean clankings, and an odour of burnt rosewood and heavy animal fat blown in at the door—all this she faced in the front row of the pews, standing quite alone. Her relatives, he knew, would register his coolness, and that would make it more painful to her. But what could he do?

Anything else would have been an unhealthy collusion: a tacit agreement to wipe out her recent behaviour as if it had not been. After the committal, he toyed with the idea of staying behind to receive her sister's ashes, then invading their funeral junketings an hour later with his offering in his hand; but he decided that that would be too extreme. Instead, he compromised by handing Janice first into the car home, then packing in Aunt Edie as a meagre wedge between them—a drawn sword, in every sense.

Janice endured it till they were on the point of descending Seshton Hill. But as the tower of the Minster came into view below, she grasped her midriff, spreading her fingers broadly over her tight abdomen. 'Driver!' she cried, striking him urgently between the shoulder-blades with three gloved fingers of the other hand. 'Driver! Stop the car!' Without waiting, she wound down a window at furious rate and stuck head and shoulders through it, her hair flying and spreading, mouth wide open and teeth hung out to dry in the icy slip-stream. The car glided to a vacant corner, and stopped. In a rush she scrambled past Aunt Edie and over Cathcut to the near-side door, pressing on his knees and trampling his toes. She stumbled up the kerb to lean on a convenient lamp-post, and retched several times; but then fell to breathing deeply and holding it, like a runner recovering from a race, with a little white lace handkerchief held delicately to her lips.

'Poor child,' said Aunt Edie, her wrists still crossed in her lap. 'Every time her mother took her to Southend, she was sick over the back-seat of the coach. It's the excitement. That, and the movement.' She looked expectantly at Cathcut.

He relented so far as to get out of the car and walk over to where she was standing. Under her funereal face-mask, she did look a most convincing green. With her long, sharp nose, and an excess of powder broken into crumbling lines each side of her mouth by her grimacing, he wondered why he had ever thought her pretty.

The second car drew in behind them, and Uncle John wound down his window.

'You in trouble?'

Their own driver leaned across to the kerb-side window, and called:

'I can't wait here long, miss. I'll be done for obstructing the corner.'

'Go on, go *on*,' she cried, waving them forward with several thrusts of an underarm action. 'I'm just a little sick. He'll walk me home.' She glanced at Cathcut from under her eyebrows. 'It's only a yard or two. The air'll do me good.'

'Oh. —Oh yes, right-o!' Uncle John had seen the point. He wound up his window again, and Cathcut saw him exchange a few smiling words with his wife. The cars moved off, leaving the priest stranded and angry.

'I'm not sorry to have a break from them,' Janice said, glancing at him again to assess his mood.

They must be an almost intolerable burden, all together, Cathcut thought; he wondered if he were not being over-hard on her. If he *never* relented, how could she ever learn better ways?

She fell to trembling violently: deep, persistent shiverings that were too spasmic to be simulated.

'You've caught a chill.'

She put up the points of her jacket collar, and held them pinched together under her chin. 'It's my own fault. I came without any breakfast.'

'Why ever did you do *that*?' He sounded exasperated. Then he recollected. 'Oh, I'm sorry. I'm being stupid.'

She laughed wryly at herself. 'No, it's not that. I was quite capable of eating breakfast. I was just afraid of getting fat.'

He looked at her frail, trembling figure, shaking within a jacket that now looked a size too large.

'But you're *not* fat.'

'I know. But sometimes I get anxious. If you'd got a family like mine, you'd get anxious. We run to lard.' She might have turned his ill-temper against him; instead, she had chosen to tell the truth.

'Would a cup of coffee put on weight?'

'No. . . . But the nearest coffee-bar is half a mile. I'm not sure I can make it.'

'There's my flat just round the corner.'

'I wasn't asking for *that*,' she said quickly.

'I know you weren't. But you need somewhere to get warm and put something down you.'

'But wouldn't it make for complications?'

'Complications?'

She looked at the ground and would have blushed, if she had had the blood to summon. 'Well, you know. . . . Clergymen. People are just *waiting* to gossip.'

He was grateful to her for mentioning it; but somehow it made it more incumbent on him to defy convention. 'You can't let other people run your life—especially if you're in the Church.' He was on the point of adding that they'd only be there a few minutes, but stopped himself because the implication seemed indecent.

He placed his arm round her for warmth, and they walked along with her bony little shoulder pressed so firmly into his pectoral muscle that it began to hurt. The pain and the easy, gentle scent of her hair merged into a bitter-sweet intoxication. How shapely her knees looked, pushing out alternately from under the pleats of her black skirt—they at least were not skinny. It must be some extra fat on the lower thigh that made their contours so unlike a man's. Her black lisle stockings had today become a smooth, tight-stretched nylon tan. He remembered her other transformation of costume and flushed with excitement, staring ahead into the middle distance to prevent himself looking down at her blouse and breasts. He continued holding her till they had passed the door of Dispatch, and only let go when they were on the stairs to his flat; he felt quite sorry that there had been no one to register his defiance.

His room hardly put forth a converting power; instead, it spoke too clearly of the state he had let himself slip into. A packet of Jacob's cream crackers lay unsealed on the table, and next to it a shiny, yellowed square-inch of cheese, both abandoned when he had rushed to prepare for the reception of her sister's body in church the night before.

She smiled at his embarrassment. 'My mother would say you needed a woman's touch.'

So he might, Cathcut thought—but not that particular woman's. He led Janice across the chilly linoleum to his assortment of properties crowded up against the further wall, and handed her into his settee. She bounced up again as if on springs.

'It's *icy*!' she cried, looking over her shoulder ruefully at the black vinyl. She moved closer to the stove, plucking at her black skirt with both hands, wriggling and fluffing out her layers of lace petticoat like some black-and-white bantam ruffling its down against the cold. Then she laughed, flicking her skirt away behind. 'It's frozen me through to me nothings!' Cathcut registered more than a hint of her mother's false plebeian.

He crouched over the Rayburn to hide his colour, and agitated a handle on its right side, rattling spent coals through into the tray and sending up ash within the stove in white clouds that clung like snow behind its mica windows and seeped through the doors to settle as a fine grey dust. But he was rewarded by a red glow within. He decided not to choke it with further fuel.

'It's very efficient, once it gets going,' he said, opening wide the draught-control. With one hand he brushed a fleck off her skirt as she stood there. He took his umbrella-stick from where it hung on a pipe, tossed it over so as to catch the stem, and, squatting down, loosened a catch with its wooden handle and hooked open the Rayburn doors. Heat came out at him. Inside, a crust of black furnacite hung apparently unsupported over a fiery, incandescent vault. He tossed the umbrella again, catching it by its handle like a skilled drum-major and then attacked the overhanging cliff with its shaft, forcing the coals down into the fiery gulf. The shaft broke from its handle.

Janice laughed. 'Why don't you get yourself a proper poker?'

He felt cut, misunderstood. 'I like to make do.'
She looked round at the bare room. 'I can see *that*.' The fresh coals began to flame, and she backed away. 'If you leave the doors open like that, I'll get chilblains. It's already making my knees blush. You men forget that there's only a layer of stocking between us and the outside world.'

He glanced back at her reddening knees, chestnut-red under her tan nylons, and submissively shut both doors. But as he crouched, flounces of white lace swept by him at eye-level, held down by her sober black skirt: underneath, he saw, she went to a funeral dressed as though for a party.

'Can I make the coffee for us?' She had already started for the partition-door, divining where the kitchen must be.

'No, thank you. *You're* supposed to be ill.'

'Not as ill as this room makes me. . . . Would you mind if I did something about it?'

'Please yourself,' he said, and retired to the kitchen. From there he heard furniture being banged about, and was on the point of sallying forth to ask that his gramophone records be respected—but restrained himself and concentrated on getting coffee essence into his cups rather than on to their saucers.

When he returned, his settee had been shoved out to the right at an angle of ninety degrees to the hearth, and was balanced on the other side by his single armchair. The small table that had held his record-player was midway between them, and likely to peel its veneer in the heat from the stove. He couldn't help feeling that Janice had no flair for interior design.

'It *is* efficient,' she cried, almost knocking the coffee-tray out of his hands once, as she leapt up to throw off her jacket and fling it over the back of his settee; and then again a second time, when she plumped herself down into the cushions, stretching her stockinged feet luxuriously towards the radius of the stove. She lay back, letting her tight tummy spread a little, and waved a lacy arm languorously over her handiwork. 'What d'you think?'

He drew the table towards them and set down his tray. 'This table is convenient. Sugar?'

They sat side by side on the settee, sipping coffee demurely together, as if they were playing at 'Mothers and Fathers'. That was it: *playing*. Cathcut's kitchen-dreams of coming home to her after a long, gruelling day, of their shared companionship in the faith, of all that delicate femininity waiting to salve his sore aesthetic sense—it all seemed an indecent fantasy. Marriage wouldn't make those well-divided breasts or that trim waist into a licensed pleasure. And he knew why: he could never stir her to any reciprocal desire—it would all be one-sided. That screwed up his passion to a devouring anguish. Touched, she would always be untouched. Her coquetry was so entrancing because it could never be carnal: no one would ever scale those hills of snow. He remembered that he hadn't eaten for sixteen hours or more, and wondered whether to chew on a biscuit to calm his stomach; but he couldn't bear to dull the intensity of his longing.

True to form, she eluded his preoccupation as soon as instinct made her aware of it. She jumped up, and with a jerky, ungainly motion slipped across the lino in stockinged feet towards his bookshelves.

'Even books can be made to brighten a place up,' she said, squatting down before them.

He looked helplessly, hopelessly, at her long, slim back and her tumbling hair. 'Show me.'

She set her hands about eighteen inches apart and plunged them into his shelves, bringing down whole blocks of books on to the floor. In a short while she had imposed a new order, pushing all the black bindings to one side, and sorting the rest according to the colour of their spines. About her busy-ness was something of her mother's tyrannical bustle. 'How do the colours of the spectrum go? I can never remember.'

He walked over and took a volume of *Chambers' Encyclopedia* from the drabbest pile, flicking through its pages till he found the place. 'Red, orange, yellow; yellow-green, green; blue-green, blue, violet.' He shut the book, and returned it reluctantly to its heap. 'Books do have a use, you know.'

'I know *that*. Look.'

A rainbow-glory was appearing on every shelf, with the black bindings, of which there were plenty, serving as a foil each side to set it off. She slipped in a few half-tones at intervals, so as to keep her bars of colour roughly parallel, right down to the floor.

'What do you make of it?'

'Spectacular. Quite extraordinary.'

She sat back on her heels, admiring what she had done, oblivious to any hint of irony. But perhaps his failure to comment further, alerted her.

'—Are those your records? May I look at them?' She must have known already what they were, since she had moved his record-stand on to the floor when she commandeered the little table. She sat on a small hearth-rug that Cathcut had shifted to one side away from the ash, her weight on one hip and buttock, her feet

tucked up under her with knees and ankles just visible, rising like a swan from out of a circle of black pleated skirt. She scattered the records evenly around its circumference, twisting her slim waist to inspect the sleeve of each. '. . . Debussy. I could listen to Debussy for *hours*.'
'Could you? It's not one I play much. For me, it doesn't progress.'
'Who *wants* to progress? It's like dreaming for ever.' She twisted again to inspect another sleeve, her black shiny tresses parting to fall each side of her face, and exposing the delicate wisps of her hairline where it met the nape of her neck. She tossed her hair back, and it fell again to her shoulders.
How long would he have, he asked himself. How long before those neat eyebrows burgeoned, before hairs pushed through that pointed chin, or the pores enlarged into pocks? Would he mind when her flanks thickened, when her jowl and belly hung in folds of fat? How could he *not* mind? But perhaps by that time he would have become more stable, ready to support her through the long years of decrepitude. He felt guilty even for speculating, aware that in this longing to freeze the present moment was something forbidden, corrupt. But its sharpness made all other longings insipid: how could he turn his back on divinity?
'Where's your record-player?'
'In dock. At the menders.'
'Never mind.' She giggled. 'I've brought my own.' She stepped daintily out of her circumference of records, and came round to where she had left her handbag beside the coffee-cups. Its black, imitation crocodile-skin bulged with unaccustomed weight. From it she plucked a large plastic heart, almost natural size, but coloured a repellent flesh-pink. 'Mummy gave me this, just before the service. I suppose she thought it would cheer me up.' She displayed a transfer stuck over one ventricle, of a boy and girl in Tyrolean costume linking hands and kissing. 'Look!' On the other side was a loop of pink petersham ribbon, so that an affectionate child might hang the organ round its neck. From the point depended a second, miniature heart, which Janice yanked vigorously till it seemed to come away in her hand. But it was still attached to the mother by a long, umbilical cord. The moment she let go, the string began to be reabsorbed into the belly of the larger vessel, which all the while played 'The Waltz of the Flowers'. As soon as the little heart had been hauled back into place and had touched the greater, all music stopped.
Cathcut must have looked appalled.

'Don't you like it?'

'It—it's a pretty tune.'

Janice sat with the music-box in her lap, staring miserably ahead. The box looked like some newly delivered embryo. 'Isn't she *odd*? It's more like a present for a babe.'

Cathcut could find nothing to say, and contented himself with gathering up his records.

She turned to him with wide, appealing eyes. 'Do you think she'll *ever* let me go?'

Cathcut felt a pang that reached to the pit of his longing, widening it into a devouring gulf. He rushed over to where she was sitting, threw an arm round her, and with the other hand picked the heart out of her lap, his blood racing and his loins stirring because in so doing he had inadvertently brushed her thigh. Her hair tickled his cheek and neck. Encircling her with both arms, he held up the musical box in front of her face with one hand, and with the other yanked its cord. 'Watch.'

The heart sang tinklingly, melodiously, until the last remnant of cord had disappeared, and the little pink bobble was tight against its mother.

His own heart beat even more wildly at what he was going to say. 'Every time that little one breaks away, the mother sings sweetly until she's hauled it back. And then—caput, finished—the music stops.' He let the box hang from its ribbon, then dropped it on the table, but still kept his arms round her. 'And that, my dear, is what happens to you, every time you try and break away. Either singing, or fussing, or some other kind of blackmail. The only way to stay independent is to stop your ears, and cut the cord.'

Panic came into Janice's eyes; she struggled like a caught dove. 'Let me go! Stop *mauling* me!' He only pressed her tighter, linking his hands, squeezing the soft flesh of her upper arm, trying to press into her a sense of his concern. Her face began to blacken, her eyes to hollow perceptibly as he watched. Darting her head down, she nipped his right wrist with her delicate little teeth. The internal shock was greater than the pain of the bite; he let her go.

'*Look* what you've made me do! You brought it on yourself. If I'm held like that I can't get my breath.' Her complexion had become dark and muddy.

'I wasn't restricting your breathing.'

'All right. . . . —But you choke me with the horrid things you say. *Poor* Mummy.' Her eyes began to water as she gathered her toy and bag. 'After all she's been through. And today of all days.'

She struggled unaided into her jacket, and searched round for her gloves.
Cathcut found them for her, on a shelf under the coffee-table. He stood gazing down at her as she pulled on her shoes, his arms folded, all his judgemental powers returning. She avoided looking at him. Because he was aware of the depth of his failure, he wanted to perish gloriously.
'The problem is, you *like* the kind of corrupting attention she gives. —Because she never holds you responsible.'
'She's *often* blaming me,' she said sullenly, her hair concealing her face, pulling back at her second shoe till she could slip her heel into it.
'But not for the things you *ought* to be blamed for.'
She tossed back her head, and got up to go. 'Only *you* want to blame me.'
'Only I *care*.'
'Rubbish!' she cried, 'absolute *rubbish*! You've only known me two minutes. How can that compare with a life-time of looking-after? I'd better go where my *real* friends are.'
'It *isn't* rubbish,' he said firmly, trying to catch her eye as he opened the door for her. She rushed past him and down the steps.
'Don't bother to see me home. I've recovered,' she said from the lower landing.
'I *hope* so,' he called, leaning over to watch her thin wrist with its silver filigree bracelet as she trailed it down the banister of the flight immediately beneath him. Then he returned to his lonely room and shut the door.
He determined to remove every trace of her occupation. After washing his coffee-cups, and chipping lipstick with his nail from the rim of one, he turned his attention to the books. In their rainbow-spread, they came close to Dr Kemberton's spontaneous disorder. He squatted for some seconds in front of her arrangement, just so that its passing should not be unmarked; and then doggedly re-sorted the volumes by subject and function, restoring them to a rational order. The exercise had about it the austere pleasure of maths, or of some monastic office.
He was a little less certain over the furniture, and looked for ways to combine her dispositions with his own. It was perhaps an improvement to set his settee at an angle to the fire; but not so stark an angle. At one end you would be cooked, at the other frozen. He lugged its further extremity inwards, butting his record-table aside with his rear. Something black stuck up between the cushions. He tugged, and discovered a flimsy lace

glove, one of the pair he had handed to Janice. While pulling on her shoes, she had pushed it down a crack in the upholstery. Not a toe, then, left in the door, but a glove—in case the wind changed, or her allies re-aligned themselves, and she wanted a reason to come back. What calculation in the midst of passion!— Perhaps he had not offended as deeply as he thought. Perhaps there might still be hope. He put the glove to his lips, but was overcome by a synthetic scent of lily-of-the-valley—something bitter, spirituous yet fatty in the perfume-base. In a fit of revulsion, he pulled open the doors of his Rayburn, burning his fingertips, and tossed the glove on to the live coals.

It shrivelled instantly, giving off a heavy black fume that recalled the matter-laden smoke from Astarte's temple in his dream. Within seconds, all remnants had been carried up in little fragments of white ash, leaving the coals pure and glowing, as if they were a crematorium furnace from which the body had been purged away.

His action filled him with elation. If she asked for it back, he could say truthfully that it was not there. If she thought he was keeping it, that would be *her* folly. He felt light-headed, joyful, like a runner who has burst the band of pain that constricted his chest, and knows that in the vigour of second-wind he will outdistance the field and get alone to the tape. Only one thing still clogged him: the recollection that he had betrayed a confidence.

There was nothing else for it: he must make a clean breast to Dr Kemberton. It would anyway be necessary to alert him to the danger from Lepage. But more than that, Cathcut must confess his double motive: both the panic over Evans and, more compelling, more blameworthy, his fear lest Lepage win influence over Miss Driscoll. The old man might not understand; but he would have to absolve.

He went at scout's-pace down Seshton Hill, and met Mrs Avling lugging a suitcase down the Rectory steps.

'You're surely not *leaving*?' he exclaimed.

'My master calls me,' said Mrs Avling, in a tone that had waited sixteen years to be heard.

She hardly looked to be dying: if anything, she seemed invigorated. Cathcut frowned in puzzlement.

'—He has been badgered by some man, and became quite ill. They have him at present in the hospital.'

'A stroke?'

'A stroke,' she confirmed.

'Will he live?'

'Yes. But he will need constant care,' she added, with ominous satisfaction.

Dr Kemberton was the first clear victim of his obsession with Lepage. If Cathcut had not told, he would not have left the old man exposed. For the first time, he felt an inexpiable guilt. Nothing could undo the events of those few minutes when he had amused himself with Janice. While he was evading one trap, another was engulfing him. It would not do even to alert Superintendent Care: for if Lepage had got any information before the vicar's collapse, taking him off the case would only leave him freer to wreak havoc. Dr Kemberton could not, and Lepage would not, divulge anything that had been said. Nothing could compel Lepage; and he had only to deny that he had learned anything. Cathcut now had a moral duty to confront the policeman; but he would be in a stronger position if he had some idea of what Dr Kemberton had let slip. He decided to haunt the hospital, out of respect and concern for his superior; but with a remnant of hope that something might yet be saved.

CHAPTER SEVENTEEN

Every interview that Care conducted seemed to increase the intensity of his fever. At the conclusion of each he dragged himself across to Conference Room One, which had been requisitioned as his Murder Incident Room, held a cold flannel to his aching wrists and elbows, and then scrubbed his hands at a little wash-basin in the corner, till cracks appeared in the soft-webbed skin between his fingers. He had noticed on many occasions before, in himself and in his colleagues, how the mere hearing of a confession would operate to coarsen the spirit of the hearer; but this time he seemed to have no defences, the tide of prurient recollection threatened to engulf him. His fever had weakened his control, so that the incidents he heard took on a hallucinatory quality, would persist in playing themselves out in his head, with bizarre and repellent elaborations, long after his informant had left the room. Only the bite of carbolic soap cauterized his soul; it was absurd to make the splits in his hands so raw, yet he looked forward to each new washing as a purgation.

It was better, nevertheless, that nothing be shed on to paper; and to encourage potential witnesses to come forward, the Chief Constable had promised on his behalf that every degrading episode would die in the telling, with only relevant facts recorded, and no means of identification save a name ticked from a list. But the details of how each informant had spent his Sunday night lodged and fermented in the policeman's memory. In desperation, before cleansing himself yet again and reluctantly picking up another confessee from the bench outside his door, he allowed himself a psalm, one for each interview, reading from the black Bible kept open on his desk. By 8.45 on Friday morning, after a rush of callers on their way to work, he had got through to Psalm 53: *'The fool hath said in his heart, There is no God. Corrupt are they, and have done abominable iniquity: there is none that doeth good.'* Some of the verses steadied his imagination; but others were too judgemental to ease the corroding sadness he felt as each caller slipped into a familiar routine: first, the inaudible muttering, then conspiratorial winks and shiftings in the seat, till the facts came tumbling out in a flash of lubricious defiance. *'Oh that I had wings like a dove!'* Care recited with the author of Psalm 55, *'for then would I fly away, and be at rest. Lo, then would I wander far off, and remain in the wilderness. . . . Destroy, O Lord, and divide their tongues: for I have seen violence and strife in the city.'*

The next verses cut to the quick of his recollection: to his entrapment in the 'tongue' and in its defiling interpretation. There was the root-cause of his weakness. Yet he could only clear his name at the cost of what he held most dear:

> *'For it was not an enemy that reproached me; then I could have borne it: neither was it he that hated me that did magnify himself against me; then I would have hid myself from him: But it was thou, a man mine equal, my guide, and mine acquaintance. We took sweet counsel together, and walked unto the house of God in company.'*

The words so fitted his condition that he was moved to tears. There was a tap at his door: a detective-sergeant with a stack of papers.

'Happy days!' He looked at Care full-face, then tactfully averted his gaze. 'A selection from this morning's mail. Six letters claiming the honour of having topped a Tom; another seven saying the villain ought to be congratulated.' He laid the items on the desk in three piles, carefully distant from Care's Bible. 'We've left the ones addressed to you personally for you to open. —Oh, and there's twenty-four questionnaires from last night's haul that Phipps thought merited a follow-up; if you'd just glance through, and let us have an order of priority.' He looked at Care's watering eyes. 'You sure you ought to be here?' He pushed across a clipboard for his superior to sign.

'Why wasn't that house closed?' Care asked wearily.

'The girls worked from their separate rooms, and never doubled-up. There wasn't a thing we could do to touch them— or the landlord.' He left quickly, his bonhomie punctured.

At the top of Care's personal pile was a yellow envelope addressed in a printed hand that his mother reserved normally for notes to the milkman. The message inside was also printed in capitals, as though she had felt some necessity to command his attention: 'AUNT AGNES HAS ASKED TO SEE YOU. CAN YOU CALL IN? MOTHER.' The message read innocuously enough; but its paper was scented, and in the top right-hand corner was a spattering of small blue flowers with yellow eyes—no doubt, they were intended for forget-me-nots.

Sick at heart, and with his fever rising in his cheeks, he forced himself to peruse the questionnaire—answers as to whereabouts on the night of the girl's death. Halfway through a dreary pile of forms, he caught sight of another yellow envelope, under a manila packet that looked to contain a counsel's brief. When he pulled it out, it was also addressed to him in capitals; and like the first, it had been delivered by hand. His wrists shaking with anger, he ripped open its flap; and saw a single lock of dark, mouse-like hair, tied with a meagre blue ribbon. He shook it violently on to his open Bible, and a quarter sheet of yellow paper fell out also. 'IN CASE YOU HAD FORGOTTEN' was printed on it in red biro. His wrath at this latest ploy took him in much the same way as his interpretation of the 'tongue': he felt involuntary jerks and twitches start in his larynx, while pinpricks of electrical current played over his elbows and the top side of his forearms, just as they did when he was about to rise in the meeting and give voice. For a moment he panicked lest his resentment should somehow trigger that other, malign utterance; but then reflected that in every case it had needed the impetus of the 'tongue', to which he gave only the interpretation. But he sat gripping each side of his desk till he got control; and then, without pausing either to wash or to read his Bible further, and with his remaining confiders left to an extended wait, he went down to the basement, took out a car from the pool, and drove home at reckless speed to confront his mother.

His mother was sitting to breakfast in solitary state.

'Mother, why do you *do* this to me? I would have come without *this*.' He tipped out the hair with its ribbon on to her mahogany table. His mother looked at it askance, then returned to scanning at arm's length the height and depth of her paper, which she had folded long-wise so as to expose two columns of print only. He brought their family Bible from its place between the supporting hands, found the chapter where they had left off reading two days earlier, and laid it beside her greasy but empty plate. The pink net she had stretched over her curlers seemed to shed an aura of bacon smells and stale toast. His mother glanced with a flat, fishy eye at the opened page of scripture, then returned to her paper. Why had she let herself deteriorate so far in the brief interval of his absence?

'Your aunt is still sleeping. I shall take her her breakfast at ten.'

'It's your turn to read,' he wheedled gently, edging the Bible towards her hand.

'Not with *that* thing on the table.'

'But that's no more than what's under the pink cloud on your head.' He smiled to cover his teasing.

'How *dare* you!' cried his mother, laying down the long columns of her paper at last. 'How *dare* you compare my morning coiffure . . . to the hairs of unrighteousness!'

Care looked astonished.

'—That's some fancy-woman,' she went on, 'some empty-headed, flibberty-gibbert creature that you've tangled with for a night of love—and now she's trying to remind you of your obligations. I've seen it coming, I've seen it coming a *mile* off; but I never thought it would sink to this.'

He brought the quarter-sheet closer, under her nose, watching her face intently. But her lips and jaw had set in that familiar, self-righteous rigidity. 'You mean you *didn't* write this?'

'You needn't put it under my nose. You forget I'm long-sighted. *Very* long-sighted.'

'This *isn't* your ribbon? *Not* your hair?'

'Would *I* do such a thing?'

Care took refuge in silence. His mother rose to her full height, and began ceremoniously to collect her dishes.

'I should have known it when you took to sleeping at the station. But I was naive; I thought that, for all that you've gone funny ways of late, you wouldn't throw off your mother's training so easily. To think that you once studied for the ministry. *"How are the mighty fallen!"'* She made her quotation a sneer.

He felt the layers of accusation stack round him like unwashed dishes, so that if he didn't break out soon, he would never get from under them.

'Mother,' he said, tugging at her housecoat, whilst she endeavoured to whisk it free as she carried her crocks before her. 'I'm going to do what I'm always most reluctant to do: I *swear* on this

Bible'—and he stretched his hand over the gospel text—'that I have *never* had any improper relationship with a woman.'

At the oath his mother relented, laying her dishes again on the table. 'You wouldn't lie to me, son? Not to your own mother? You swear by God's honour?'

'Mother, I've already taken an oath on the Bible—on the record of our Lord's crucifixion itself.'

'But by God's honour, son. God will never forgive anyone who takes his honour in vain.'

'God's glory and honour are not to be touched by anything I, or anyone else, can say.'

'But for your mother, son. So I can be sure I believe you. By God's honour.'

He deliberated at length, painfully.

'All right. For you, if for no one else. I swear. By God's honour.'

But to utter the words at all humbled and humiliated him.

At so complete a victory her face relaxed, and her blue eyes showed an affectionate twinkle.

'Perhaps I'll wake your Auntie up after all.'

'Not now,' he said. 'This *thing* requires my attention.' He slipped the lock of hair and its message back into their envelope, and returned them to his pocket.

She seized him by both his shoulders, looking intently into his eyes. By experience, she knew he would tell her nothing about his work.

'Don't forget, my son—"*Be ye* pure, *even as I am pure*".'

He drew her head towards him with both hands, and kissed her forehead on the soft lines beneath her curlers. 'You want a purity beyond what flesh and blood can supply, mother. Something out of this world altogether.'

'But make the attempt,' she pleaded, laying both hands on his sleeve. 'Sleep at home tonight.'

He gently lifted her fingers from his arm; but he felt himself irretrievably hurt.

'On my mattress at the station, or here—what does it matter? What difference could it make?'

'If it makes no difference, you can give me the pleasure of your company.' She pursed her lips with determination. 'I like you under my eye.'

'You could watch me every hour of the day, and find nothing to oblige you.' At his reproach, her eyes took on that slightly frantic look.

'I know what I know,' she murmured darkly, as if that were

quite sufficient to justify all his failure to please. Then a thought struck her.

'It couldn't . . . '—she hesitated, but gathered force with her suspicion—'it *couldn't* be that Robert of yours?'

'His hair is black. Blacker than mine.' But he found himself angry again at having slipped into defending himself. 'What are you suggesting?'

'Oh nothing,' she said, a melodious note creeping into her voice. 'It's just that he *is* a little *odd*, isn't he?' She smiled innocently.

'No odder than I am. I suppose you call that odd?'

She continued smiling. 'Not particularly, dear. Just a *normal* oddness. Nothing out of the ordinary.' She patted his hand. 'It happens all the time.'

'*Nothing* has "happened".' To cut short the exchange, he picked up his car keys, tossed them into the air, and caught them. 'I'll be in late, tonight.'

Not troubling to reply, she hummed to herself sweetly as she took her dishes to the kitchen.

When he returned to the station, the bench-full outside his door had thinned noticeably. He dismissed those who still persisted, and retreated inside, turning the key to discourage callers. His fever had moderated somewhat, but had left him spent and depressed.

He sat for a while looking at the paper which had accompanied the lock of hair, holding it against the light to read its watermark, then staring at its red lettering, trying to isolate some identifying feature amidst the stark sansserif. He chose to ignore a tentative tap at his door.

There was a second, more definite knock, and the door handle turned fruitlessly.

'Who's there? What do you want?'

'Detective-Constable Evans, sir. I'd be grateful if you could spare me a minute.'

Care leapt to open the door, his heart bounding in a great surge of hope. He tried to conceal his pleasure; but once inside, Evans stood awkwardly, as if even his presence there had compromised him.

'Take a chair.' Care motioned towards the place where his informants sat to disburden. Whatever the breach between them, Evans still paid him the compliment of imitative dressing: the same dark, formal suit, the same strictly-drawn parting—though Evans' suiting picked up a blue-black tone in his hair, and the azure of his tie was surpassed only by his astounding eyes. Were it not for those eyes, the resemblance would have been too close for Care to have risked furthering the boy's career, lest he be thought to cosset a near relative. As it was, his selection had provoked comment.

'I didn't send for you,' Care said. 'I thought it would be taking unfair advantage.'

His explanation met with no response.

'. . . Robert, let me at least lay hands on you and pray for your health.'

Evans looked up at him sullenly. '*I* will, if you will allow *me* to do the same.'

'Robert,' Care insisted, 'one of us is very sick. Let us try to find out *who*, before it goes before the Meeting.'

'That is what I was saying.'

Care stood to one side of his desk, shuffling papers in a file. 'Robert, your name appears as an associate of that girl in at least two reports of interviews. Your prints must be all over her room.'

Evans looked at him again with his blue, reproachful eyes. 'That may be so. But I didn't kill her. I, of all people, had least reason to do it.'

'Why so?' Care laid his hand gently on the boy's arm. He reminded him so sharply of himself ten years ago: the same rawness at the squalors of the profession he had embarked on; the same high cheekbones and full, somewhat over-blown lips. But everything about him was finer: his frame more delicate and composed, his skin whiter, without that bluish jowl. And because of his co-ordination, a more consummate athlete than he could ever be. 'Why do you say that?'

'Because I loved her.'

Care withdrew his hand, feeling a rush of pain. It was as if the spirit of his mother took control. 'How could *you*, sealed by Christ for his elect, tangle with such a woman? A common *whore*.' He moved angrily to the other side of his desk and sat down.

'She *wasn't*,' Evans burst out, provoked to defiance. 'That's what you say, that's what's implied in all the jokes out there'—he tossed his head in the direction of the Murder Room—'but it isn't *true*. She *despised* herself. All right, she was kept by some man she was too ashamed to tell me about—but she *wasn't* on the game.'

'Robert, such relationships block the soul from God. God and the Ashtoreth cannot dwell in the same temple.'

'I don't say that of *you*. Some strange things live in *you*, without invalidating your faith.'

Care flinched, but summoned all his charity. 'Brother, the whole body suffers with the pollution of one member. If your toe touches acid, your mouth cries out.'

'But not what *you* cry—not *my* mouth.' He sounded petulant, but his eyes were wet, as though he were maligning his idol.

Care sat silent, recalling with fear how his throat had begun to move on reception of his mother's message—but not his mother's: the message of someone else. A notion came to him, and he clutched at it.

'Did you have a love-token—a keepsake—from this girl?' He slid the hair out of its envelope, its strands held together by the thin blue ribbon. 'Did you send me a reminder? A last vestige of your obsession?'

The young man looked at his superior full-face, his blue eyes like those of a hurt child. 'I know you love *me*,' he said reproachfully. 'I've never called it an "obsession".' He took from his pocket another yellow envelope, tipped out a second lock of hair, and placed it beside its fellow. 'This was addressed to me this morning. Slipped into the outside box after last night's collection, and before the 8 a.m. check. It's not been through the mails. There's no way it could have come from *her*. Not directly.' He looked with silent misery at the relics between them.

Care took time to think. 'Who else among us . . . has had billets-doux?'

'No one I know of. I haven't asked anyone, but I've listened. —Surely they would have told you?'

'So we've been specially chosen.' Care picked up both locks and weighed them on the back of his hand, fingers outstretched, in an assessing, judicial manner that made the lad wince. 'Most probably it's one of her hangers-on, who thinks we're making slow progress. But why *you*? —Unless he knows of your connection?' He tipped the hairs again on to a sheet of paper.

The boy flushed angrily. 'I told you, she *had* no hangers-on. And there *was* no connection. If I'd done what you think I've done, she'd have put me in the same category as the others, I'd have lost her for ever.'

'Better that, than that you *both* be lost.' He darted out a hand to seize Evans' wrist where it rested on the desk, unsettling the strands of hair with the speed of his movement. He lifted the forearm from the table, and stretched the delicate fingers towards him with a caressing motion of his other hand.

'Robert, not only are your prints all over that room, they'll remain on a file at Scotland Yard until they are identified or the case closed.' He made as if to pull the outstretched fingers down into an inked block on his desk, but then relented. '. . . Yet if I take your prints so as to eliminate them and destroy the record, I'll have to inform the Chief Constable, and there'll be a major scandal within the force.' He checked himself in mid-flow, aware that there had come into his voice more than an echo of his mother when attempting to stir a panic. He reverted to his prime consideration.

'Robert, this corruption lies either in you, or me. Let us decide it between us, before it goes to the judgement of the Spirit.'

Evans put his hands in his lap, doggedly refusing to budge. 'I'm weary to the *core*,' he said. 'Let it go to judgement.' But the pain of his double loss seemed to overwhelm him.

Lepage put his head round the door. '—I'm sorry. I didn't mean to disturb a tête-à-tête.' But it was hardly an apology.

Care flushed. 'This is not a private matter. Detective-Constable Evans was an associate of the dead girl.'

Evans opened his mouth to protest, but then pursed his lips and bowed his head.

'I know,' Lepage said, pushing the door to behind him, and looking hard at the young man. '*I* gathered the information.' He waited for some reaction.

'Fortunately for him, he has a cast-iron alibi. He was at a religious meeting.' Evans looked up with surprise.

Lepage propped a large plastic bag in a corner beside the door. 'Witnesses?'

'Plenty,' said the lad, and again sank his head. 'I can't help feeling,' he insisted, nodding from side to side whilst still looking at the surface of the desk, 'that if we knew who'd sent that hair, we'd have our man. Perhaps whoever kept her? The one she wouldn't talk about?'

'Hair?' Lepage appeared at a loss.

'Detective-Constable Evans and I have both received portions of the girl's hair through the post this morning.'

'How do you know that it came from . . .'—Lepage pinched the loose skin of his throat with a throttling motion—'. . . our *customer*?'

Care caught Evans' eye. 'We were of the opinion that it came from one of *her* customers—trying to stimulate a little action.'

Lepage scanned his flushed face.

Evans seemed furious at being dragged into his superior's assumptions. 'It's *her* hair all right. Same colour, same texture. If you must, you can get Forensic to check it out. They're bound to have taken a sample.'

Lepage turned to him. 'At what church should we enquire? — To check *you* out? Methodist? Anglican? Catholic?'

Care attempted to intervene. 'Enquiries had better be discreet. It's an awkward time. The Chief Constable won't want one of his officers mixed up with a whore. The God-fearing public doesn't understand it.'

'There can't be too many of *them*,' Lepage said, glancing across at Care's opened Bible.

'Take my prints,' Evans burst out impetuously, stretching out the fingers of both hands, while Lepage observed them closely. 'Eliminate them. I want him *found*.'

'Or *her*,' said Lepage, looking at them both. 'Why not a jealous wife?' He lugged his plastic bag from the corner, hoisted it on to a corner of Care's desk, and from it dealt a succession of smaller bags, each containing a labelled garment. 'These came back from Forensic.' He turned to Evans. '—You don't embarrass easily?' The young man shook his head. 'In my young days we used to call it "Pantie Patrol".' He began pulling articles out of their wrappers and shedding them over the expanse of the desk-top, covering files, pens, letter-trays, even the text of scripture. 'The negligé she was wearing at the time, items of underclothing, "whore's drawers"'—he waved a garment under Evans' nose— 'anything distinctive, or bought elsewhere than Marks and Sparks. Someone's needed to go round every lingerie shop in a five-mile radius, dress shops, ladies' outfitters, not forgetting the little corner-shop haberdasher. Use a trade directory, take a picture of your friend. Check if they remember any of these being bought, and who bought them. —*That* we've already identified.' He hastily abstracted a synthetic chiffon scarf from the pile, all the while watching Evans' expression. The lad seemed more grieved than abashed. 'Of course, you may recognize some of them *yourself*,' Lepage added slyly. 'In which case, there'll be one less to check.'

Care shifted the tail of a blouse from off his Bible. 'Isn't that a job for one of the uniformed girls? They get better results. I don't want my CID officers wasted on that kind of work.' He looked with distaste at the array of garments.

'I'd *like* to do it,' Evans said defiantly. 'I *owe* it to her. —And I never bought her anything. It wasn't that kind of relationship.'

'I'm glad to hear it.' Lepage handed him the empty bag. 'The God-fearers will be pleased.'

There was a double tap at Care's door. When Lepage opened it, it was the Pakistani sergeant from the enquiry desk.

'I'm *profoundly* sorry, sir.' She bobbed round Lepage to address Care. 'I've a gentleman with me. He insisted on my bringing him to you personally. He wouldn't wait for me to ring through.' She was aware that she should not have acquiesced, that her superiors would think her feminine and remiss.

'I tend to regard the telephone as a product of this latter age,' said Brother Roberts as he came through the doorway. 'Like television and wireless. Despite their uses.' He checked and stared at the scattered garments, seeming to regard them as confirmation of his worst suspicions—the raiment of Anti-Christ. Care and Evans jumped awkwardly to their feet.

'—I didn't hope to find our David and Jonathan together,' Roberts said to Lepage, grinning unpleasantly. 'The two pillars of our society,' he confided. 'Founts of the Spirit. The twin tablets of the Law.' He seemed oblivious to the possibility that he might be interrupting a meeting. He turned on the other two, assuming the posture of a bailiff delivering a writ. '—I've come about our little problem. A summons from the saints meeting at Glaston Street. You will present yourselves before an Assembly of Con–science, at ten o'clock tomorrow, in the house of meeting. At *your* request'—he nodded in mock obeisance to Care—'a discerner has been brought from Birmingham. *Birmingham*,' he said again to Lepage, lifting his eyes heavenward. '*Can any good thing come out of* Birmingham?'

'Discerner?' Lepage queried.

'One of our pillars is *cracked*,' said Brother Roberts. 'Shaky at the foundations. A soiled tablet . . . a broken reed.' He made a little nibbling motion with his foreteeth over his lower lip after each sally, like a hamster cleaning itself. 'But we don't know *which*, do we, gentlemen? So we need a discerner to help us.' His sniff indicated that he expected little assistance from *that* quarter. He eyed the garments before him.

'This is not a bazaar,' Care explained. 'These are items in a police inquiry.'

Brother Roberts smiled indulgently, looking him in the face and nodding slightly, as though inviting him to confess a depravity well-known to them both. I'm always willing to give a man rope, his expression seemed to say—he'll be sure to hang himself. '—You've had a loss.' He turned suddenly to Evans, plucking with thumb and forefinger at a black crêpe armband that blended so well with Evans' suiting that, till then, his colleagues had not noticed it. 'Sorry to see that. Somebody close?' 'It's for the lady who owned these, I believe,' said Lepage, waving a hand over the clothes. 'A token of mourning.'

Evans blushed scarlet.

'You'd better pick up *those*, and be on your way.' Care pushed the garments in the boy's direction, his manner grim and unyielding. Evans began to slip each item into its protective bag, looking at his superior with his blue eyes, reproachful that he should have taken so mean an advantage before Roberts.

'I'll be on my way too,' smiled Brother Roberts. '—But perhaps I'll forgo my share of the finery.' His teeth went into a positive ecstasy of nibbling. 'Tomorrow then—prompt at ten.'

Care retrieved the remnants of hair from his desk, returning them to their respective envelopes, along with the accompanying messages. He handed both packets to Lepage. 'You'd better have the paper checked for prints.'

Lepage inspected him full-face. Care's eyelids drooped at the corners, a pained look as though his fever was giving him a sore head. 'People don't make mistakes like that these days—too many detective films.'

They stepped across to the Murder Room, and Lepage stood by, whilst Care scrubbed his hands at the sink.

'I'm sorry your Meeting is in difficulties.'

Care paused in his washing whilst a phone rang in one of the cubicles on the far wall, till he was sure it would be answered. He made no comment.

'. . . Have I your permission to extend the inquiry?' Lepage studied the fine skin of his superior's neck.

Care splashed water on his raw cheeks, and shook his head to clear his eyes and eyebrows. He seemed entirely preoccupied with his pain.

'. . . There's nothing from the *modus operandi* files, and oddly, nothing like it in England, Wales or Scotland during the last six months, except one in Lanarkshire—and they've got *him*.'

Care straightened up from the sink and stood looking at him, his eyes still misty, his fever obviously rising. He felt for a towel.

'. . . The questionnaire's been taken to every male within a three-mile radius. We ought now to go up to six. Porson's got it all set up. Can we *do* that?'

'Do what you think is necessary.' It was evident that Care wanted to rest.

'Is that *carte blanche*?'

Care stood wincing slightly as he dabbed the coarse towelling into the cracks between his fingers. '*Carte blanche.*' He threw the soiled towel into a discard-bin.

'Without reference back?'

'Just keep me posted, for form's sake.'

'Oh, I'll be sure to keep you in touch,' Lepage promised. He watched his superior out of the room, heard him cross the passage, enter, and lock his office door behind him.

CHAPTER EIGHTEEN

Cathcut was waiting in the vestibule to Ward 'G' of Seshton General Hospital—'G', he suspected, was unacknowledged code for 'Geriatric'. But Cathcut wasn't sitting in the actual hospital: he was riding the roller-coaster of panic, a dizzying, plunging and soaring switch-back of fear. The hospital was as distant as that blue December day outside the ward windows; as crisp, as chilly, and as unrelated. He tried to reason things through, to hold himself to a straight, logical line; but found he was being wrenched round suddenly in a U-turn, his stomach muscles clutched into a knot with resisting the sideways thrust, then pitching down with the bile thrown up into the back of his throat, as if wheels thundered over steel sleepers in a roaring crescendo of sound—'The Bishop, the Bishop, the Bishop, WHAT will the Bishop say?'—down into the open mouth below, the flapping, white, triangular, bunting-like teeth, the black maw, oblivion, annihilation; not just condemnation to a perpetual curacy in this hole for ever, but defrocking, expulsion, the wrath of God, the outer darkness. Then out into the light again and up on high, swept round in a broad arc, with a consciousness of cool, calm people passing you by, like diminutive manikins and toy cars seen from the roller-coaster, all moving by their own free-will, oblivious to the terror enclosed up there on the circuit: nurses scurrying by in a protective cloud of starch and disinfectant, safety pins hanging from their prim apron fronts, but the pins dangling for all the world like bobbles on the breasts of some nightclub dancer.

Anything for a cessation of pain, of terror. Why not throw oneself off, anticipate destruction by the one willed act of which you were still capable?—Seduce, if necessary force Janice, commit oneself to the Queen of Nothingness, roll in a sloth of self-destroying indulgence till they chose to come for you. He tried to pray, to cling to a text—*'Lo, I am with you always, even to the end.'* But that was as little comfort as the handrail before you on the Big Dipper: a guarantee against being thrown off only so long as your fingers had strength to hold on, and you could withstand the cramp in your palms.

His panic began to mount further, step by step, in steady increments: Dr Kemberton might have to resign through ill-health, Dr Kemberton might well not want him, Dr Kemberton would surely die. He rose, oh so slowly, up a precipitous slope, confronting a wall of steel, with the terror and temptation of making a backwards somersault into nothing; with the knowledge that the cranking and straining as you get to the top, even if there is no sudden snap to send you careering backward, will only end in pitching you over the hump into another terrifying swoop: Lepage on the loose, Lepage with information no one could wrestle from him, engineering inflictions, horrors, till they caught up with him too late, and then Cathcut would be seen at the root of it, Cathcut would be held to blame, guilty before God and man. A jerking turn, then down again, familiar territory, like the reiterated sequence of a nightmare, trundle, trundle, gathering speed—'The Bishop, the Bishop; a betrayal of priestly trust.' As the train rushed down it shuddered to a sudden halt and Cathcut got off, staggering, blinking in the darkness, not sure if this was annihilation or reprieve. It was Lepage who by his unexpected appearance had pulled off the trick of halting the terror-train for him. Cathcut hovered between gratitude and fear of another round. He looked at the policeman across the vestibule, conscious of bruised diaphragm muscles, trembling nerves along both arms, a stab of pain between his aching shoulders, a pressure of unreleased wind at the top of his stomach, dry mouth, chapped lips, his scalp itching and scaling. Could all that happen on a ten-minute ride? Lepage said nothing, but picked up a magazine from a pile on the chair beside him.

He had on his lap a large brown paper bag, crumpled, but containing some substantial, irregularly shaped object. Surely he could not be bringing grapes? Or even an assortment of fruit? That would be too much—Cathcut felt the wheels start to move again under him.

'You're surely not going to question him further?'
Lepage looked up from his magazine. 'I doubt if he knows much more than he's told me already.'
Cathcut felt a steel hand clutch the bruises on either side of his bottom ribs. 'Then why are you here?'
Lepage abandoned his reading entirely, setting it to one side. 'I'm not quite so devoid of conscience as you might think.' He rolled the top of his paper bag over tightly, compacting the parcel in his lap. At one point, a tiny segment of brass like four finger-ends broke through its paper covering. 'I once put a poor, dear old teacher behind bars for interfering with schoolchildren, and I wept as he went down—particularly as his pupils hadn't been entirely guiltless.'

'Give it up,' Cathcut pleaded. 'You say there's nothing in it for you.'

He laughed shortly. 'Oh, I'm not enamoured of my own solution; I don't expect so much in the way of release as I once did. —But I have a kind of curiosity to see things through.'

Cathcut decided to stake everything on one desperate throw: after all, given Lepage's present mood, the moment might never again be so propitious.

'If it isn't improper', he began guardedly, '. . . to spread it yet further . . . *what* did Dr Kemberton tell you?'

Lepage looked sad and weary, like an old tom whom it no longer amuses to see the mice jump.

'One of the classic tales: an ageing queen, jealous because his lover takes a more normal turn. Or rather, a *youngish* queen— young voice, with fine, white hands. And a member of some fanatic sect, giving themselves prophetic names: "Tribulation"— I suppose, from the sorrows before the Last Days. It's quite a narrow field: there shouldn't be too much difficulty. —But it all seems somehow irrelevant, as though she'd been knocked over by a passing car.'

Cathcut was astounded to have got so much from him in one go. Even if Lepage cut loose, provided Cathcut kept with him now when he saw Dr Kemberton, there would still be enough information to bring him down.

'It *is* irrelevant,' he said. '—To *your* problem.'
Lepage looked at him narrowly. 'You think I have a problem?'
'I *know* you have a problem.' But he provoked none of the rage he expected.

'So I have. But a problem without solutions.'
They were silenced by a flurry of activity behind the glass

doors leading into Ward 'G', both of them succumbing to a sense that personal concerns, however insistent, were improper in such a place; that they might even, by their irrelevant murmurings, have triggered off some crisis. Curtains were being pulled hastily around a bed half-way down the ward, a little staff-nurse who held a leading-curtain jumping into the air at intervals with the material still in her hand, so as to clear runners where they had bunched and jammed on their curtain-rail. A bottom-end of two oxygen cylinders and two black wheels of a supporting trolley stuck out indiscreetly from underneath the curtain, rather spoiling everyone's attempt to give an impression of an unscheduled blanket bath. So did the number of bodies whose back or buttocks pushed out through that olive-grey shrouding. A house surgeon came running, checked himself as he passed through the doors from their vestibule, but walked swiftly down between beds and disappeared behind the screen. After a while, a profound silence and stillness spread over the ward, seeping out to the visitors. Ward lights were dimmed, and curtains pulled round other beds. The shapeless lumps within each, who previously had lain locked in solitary enclaves of pain, stirred at the swish of runners, as if they recognized a passage of dark wings over them. Cathcut found himself taken with a hysterical giggling, fiercely suppressed, as shrouds were drawn progressively the length of the ward: 'Curtains for you—*and* you—*and* you.' His earlier panic seemed to have exposed a vein of cruel gallows-humour in him. Some seven or eight minutes elapsed, and then a trolley appeared from behind the first bed to be screened, pushed by two hospital orderlies. On it was a draped corpse. Cathcut noticed with relief, as they negotiated it through the doors held open by a pair of nurses and took it off to a service-lift, that its shape was long and lean, not the domed heap he imagined Dr Kemberton would be. Anyway, he had been told that his superior had a private room at the far end. One of the door-keepers, a young probationer distinguishable by her blue-and-white striped dress, rushed by them with a red and blubbery face, the puppy-fat on her legs and above each elbow wobbling with her haste. 'Poor biddy,' said her companion, an altogether trimmer staff-nurse in darker blue, with a black, tightly drawn belt. She addressed her comments to Cathcut as a fellow-professional. 'Every time they lose one, they take it personally. They always feel as if they've been to blame.'

Cathcut smiled knowingly, flattered by her confidence, conscious of Lepage eyeing him from across the way.

'But she'll lose it,' he said. '—Get hardened to it in time.' His staff-nurse seemed disappointed in him. 'Not if she's at all like *me*.' He could see now that her eyes were themselves a little red and moist at the corners. He cursed himself for falling so readily into the cynical clichés of his society: he had been justly reproved—and by an ordinary, merely secular working-girl.

'You're not *really* a believer,' Lepage observed when she was gone. '—Not much faith in the milk of human kindness.'

The ward settled back to normal, waiting for its next visitation.

'. . . Nonetheless, it wouldn't be my taste to die here,' Lepage said again, echoing Cathcut's thought.

'But you're not averse to putting someone *else* to die here,' Cathcut replied bitterly.

'Fortunately for my conscience, he won't die.'

'But he might have done.' Cathcut hesitated for some seconds before driving home his last knife. '*There* is one solution to your problem'—he waved in the direction of the departed corpse—'the *final* solution.' He felt absurdly pleased at his macabre allusion.

The staff-nurse interrupted them as if they were schoolboys bickering. 'I've managed to have a word with the doctor who's looking after him. You can see him now. —Together, I think; but mind, no more than ten minutes.' She looked at Lepage. '—And nothing upsetting.'

'He rang me,' Lepage said.

Dr Kemberton was enthroned amidst his hand-maidens: semi-prone, propped upon pillows, with Mrs Avling standing at his bed-head, tall and arms akimbo, hands resting on her bony flanks, like the female eunuch of his modest harem. She observed with lofty condescension the ministrations of a lesser handmaid, who proffered a saucer and feeder-cup to the ailing man. His disabilities seemed to have released in him an extraordinary hilarity.

'Ah,' he cried, observing the pair of them at his door, and brushing aside his feeding-cup with a gracious gesture of the left and unaffected hand. 'The twin keepers of my conscience: Gog and M-Magog, *terrible* giants—terrible accusers.' They had returned to him his teeth. He affected with the same hand to cover his spectacles and shield himself from the appalling presence. His raised elbow and forearm trembled somewhat, but he could maintain them in position. He peeked round the fingers, chuckling. 'But I have my defender, you see. My Rose of Sharon.' He nodded towards the sad little woman beside him, who leant forward anxiously to pat his pillows and settle him into them. 'Curate,' said Mrs Avling, bending forward stiffly to act as king's remembrancer, and pointing at Cathcut with one forefinger for the benefit of Mrs Kemberton. 'And . . .'—but she could find no word to describe Lepage. The two men stood on the near side of the bed, whilst Dr Kemberton with a great show of wrist-flexing and prestidigitation fumbled for Lepage's hand with his right, tugged the fingers closer to him, and, refusing to relinquish them, proceeded to use them as an exercise-pad or squeezing-ball. Fortunately, his grip was not as yet very strong; but Lepage tolerated the action far longer than Cathcut would have imagined.

Mrs Avling relaxed her stance so as to hiss into the policeman's ear: 'See what destruction you have wrought.' She returned to her former posture.

Mrs Kemberton drew Cathcut to the window, a little out of earshot of the sick man. Once again Cathcut's expectations were defeated: the ex-wife was no painted Jezebel, nor was there any sign that she had ever been so. The attempt itself might have proved ridiculous, for she was short and dumpy, with her hair divided by a central parting into two wads of white, slightly yellowed and uncarded wool, in which you might expect the burs still to be sticking. Her upper forehead had retained a pink, school-girl smoothness, but at the cost of piling the stretched skin in folds and wrinkles over her eyebrows, making her look an apt consort for Cro-Magnon Man.

'When he's not so high, he's been worrying about the Sunday services. I think he'd be off and out to do them if they'd let him.'

'Tell him, when he thinks of it again, that I'll have them all under control. —In the way that he would wish.' As he might wish *now*, Cathcut thought: with a touch more *hilaritas* than usual.

Mrs Kemberton had somehow anticipated the mood of the occasion by wearing not black or navy, but a woollen coat of rich brown, with a little violet voile scarf, which in its attempt to be pretty in the midst of decay seemed not tarty but courageous. Contrary to expectation, Cathcut found himself liking Mrs Kemberton. She looked sadly towards the bed. Lepage seemed actively to be encouraging the clergyman to exercise himself upon his fingers; and from their expressions, nothing but pleasantness passed between them. Anyway, Mrs Avling stood ready to bring down the scimitar on anything improper.

'I know it's ridiculous to feel responsible for him being like this; I know it would have happened anyway. But you see,' Mrs Kemberton said in a rush, water standing in her eyes, 'uprightness like that *shrivels* one's life.' Cathcut had a sudden vision of the clergyman's shrunken, scelerotic heart, purple under a pale pink skin, but all over black spots and strings.

'If you want a penance,' he murmured, glancing in Mrs Avling's direction, 'let *her* stay. She's built her life round him. She's got nothing else.' —Except her books, he thought to himself; and *he* is her only hope for linking them to reality. It seemed to be tacitly assumed between them that Mrs Kemberton would be resuming her former duties.

'I know.' She nodded. 'Anyway, this will be more than one person can cope with.'

There was an awkward silence, which Cathcut attempted to fill. 'I'm glad you've come.'

She looked up anxiously into his face. 'Did you think I wouldn't?' As quickly, she turned to look out of the window. 'I suppose I forfeited my right to be thought well of, seventeen years ago.'

He hastened to repair the damage. 'You were only a name to us,' he said. It had been on the tip of his tongue to say 'a reputation', but he pulled back at the last minute. It was clear she wanted to disburden further.

'It's no fun,' she confided bitterly, 'being an occasion for sin; or'—she fished for the term across a gap of seventeen years—'a *remedium p-peccatorum*. I don't know what you teach them in church, or whether it's what they do as young boys—but every time they approach us they feel it's a failure or a defiance, anti-God. And so it *is*—for *them*,' she said emphatically. 'That's the tragedy. We stand in for some dark god we know nothing about. They're not wrong about it: they're destroying themselves, and God's world in the process. It's some form of protest: a scream against the conditions of existence, perhaps. —Don't *you* feel aggressive towards women, young man?' She pulled Cathcut closer by tugging on his cassock-front.

Only if they're old and ugly, Cathcut thought—but how can you say that, especially when you are looking down that length of pink scalp between its wads of white hair? He thought of Janice's perfected form and longed to lose himself in it, away from all this pain. 'I'm not married,' he said to extricate himself. 'It's out of my experience.'

She looked knowing. 'If that were *true*, we might have a better chance. It's what they've tasted before they come near us—*any* of us. It turns their brains. Even while we're beautiful,' she went on, as though responding to his unvoiced thought, which he found disturbing, 'even then they're in two minds. One half wants to freeze us as we are, not a hair or dimple out of place. Yet at the same time, even as they're making love to us, another part of them wants to destroy us, corrupt us into something that no longer torments them. —Do you understand what I mean?'

Cathcut felt he had happened inadvertently on some wise woman: some untutored folk-leech with a craft older than Christianity or his science, who had lanced a deep-seated boil in his spirit, letting its dark poison drain into his system to be counteracted and dispersed. He turned to the window, not this time to evade her but to absorb the crisp blue air, to let the light heal his opened and cleansed wound. The cold reflected from the glass soothed his itchy scalp and crystallized his thought. He felt in tune, under inspiration.

'I think you err in just one respect,' he said. '—In making the longing and the destructiveness *simultaneous*. The one *precedes* the other, just by a fraction. So it's not the beauty they're destroying, though it may seem so. It's the pain, the longing it gives rise to.'

She took his hand, turning him away from his window like a dancer to face again the current situation. 'There,' she said. 'I knew so. You *do* understand.'

The league of amity between Lepage and Dr Kemberton had broken down, as signalled by Mrs Avling's percussive drumming with her long bony fingers on either hip-bone. Lepage had resumed control of his hand, and was rolling the crumpled part of his paper bag round its base and tucking it under his arm, as if ready to depart. He looked more than usually dark-eyed.

'I do not *insist*,' Dr Kemberton was saying, '—indeed, I *cannot* insist; and m-mercifully, my disabilities have released me from m-many responsibilities—many things.' He patted the hand of Mrs Kemberton, who had resumed her place beside him. 'But it remains my opinion . . . that to use public office . . . to pursue a private vendetta . . . is *improper*.' A facial muscle commenced twitching from the corner of his lip to his left eye, triggered perhaps by such an excess of plosives.

Lepage looked uncomfortably at the twitching nerve, but persisted.

'I find the pursuit a distraction,' he said grimly. 'I shall be sorry when it is over.'

Dr Kemberton put his uninjured hand to his face, and

attempted to still the moving flesh. The spasm pushed Lepage to comment further.

'Revenge', he said, in angry disregard of the company, 'is like rape. As my customers report it. More fun in the thinking than in the performance. —But you may rest assured, I shall do nothing that exceeds the law.' He made as if to leave.

But his assurance did nothing to quell the vibrating muscle. They waited while Dr Kemberton struggled with it, saw the panic rise in his eyes and sweat ooze amidst the pink folds and purple veins of his forehead. Eventually Mrs Avling could stand it no longer and pushed an alarm-bell.

The staff-nurse was mercifully prompt. 'Don't worry. It looks more alarming than it is. *Not* your old trouble,' she emphasized to Dr Kemberton, mouthing her words as if to a deaf foreign tourist. 'A side-effect of your injections.' She tapped his upper arm to remind him. 'Sometimes they make you twitch, sometimes a bit sweaty and mucky'—she removed his spectacles and dabbed a tissue over his forehead, then firmly took his left hand from his face, and, turning it over beside the other, cleansed the palms of both. 'Sometimes you'll feel sick. Do you feel sick *now*?' she asked abruptly. Dr Kemberton shook his head: a helpless child who had at least not disgraced himself that far. 'Time for a turn then, I think,' she said, deftly manipulating a turning-sheet under his shoulders and buttocks till he was tipped on to his left side. She moved several pillows from under his head, positioned his legs, and placed a stainless-steel, kidney-shaped basin on the bed by his nose. As if by conditioned reflex Dr Kemberton began to breathe deeply, looking out past the bowl with frightened, myopic eyes. She spoke to the company, who had drawn back to give her room. 'We have to keep the injections going till the tablets take over; and sometimes that type makes them a bit twitchy and panicky. *Good*'—she turned back to her charge—'*Feel* those tummy-muscles working. And now, *cough*. Cough again.' Dr Kemberton coughed, with an audible moving of mucus, but no product. 'Keep at it,' she instructed. 'Now I must see to my other babies.'

Lepage stepped forward and looked down at the stricken man as though he were some great grey seal, stranded panting and defenceless on an open beach. Cathcut moved to protect his superior, but was halted by Lepage drawing his present from its paper bag.

'I've brought you a gift,' the policeman said. 'Flowers didn't seem quite appropriate. But this'—he looked at the object in his hand—'I saw it in the window of a second-hand shop.'

On the bed, beside the steel dish and within the old man's field of vision, he placed a miniature eagle in gleaming brass, polished, and standing with wings spread, much as you might find it on a church lectern—but of diminutive size.

'Second-hand goods!' Mrs Avling snorted. The rest made no comment.

Dr Kemberton seized on the gift, clutching it to him with his uninjured hand, and rolling half-way on to his back once more. His eyes filled with tears.

'A foolish thing to give a sick man,' Mrs Avling said again in her cruellest stage-whisper.

'He doesn't seem to think so,' Cathcut responded, watching the clergyman, who was cradling the bird in his bosom with his left hand, whilst testing the returning sensation in his right by pressing its sharp copper beak into his palm. He looked up at his erstwhile accuser and smiled, but could say nothing. He returned to playing with the bird. His womenfolk untucked the end of his top-sheet and straightened his legs, which had become crossed in the turn.

'That was a moving present,' Cathcut said to Lepage as they left the ward, touched both by the gesture itself and by what he saw as evidence of an unsuspected good taste. 'Did it mean something?'

Lepage stopped in his tracks. He seemed quite inexplicably angry. 'If *you* don't know, who *can*?' He continued with his onward rush.

Cathcut felt that he must somehow have passed over a major distress-signal. He rushed after, with the lifeboat.

'It's a symbol of hope,' he ventured. 'Is that it?' He tried again. 'Or is it one of the gospel-writers? St John has an eagle for his sign.'

Lepage pushed a button to call the lift, and stood facing him, feet apart, alternately rocking backward on his heels, and then forward on to his toes, keeping him under police observation. Cathcut coloured, feeling he had made a fool of himself.

'Then you will have noted', Lepage said, 'that my symbol is much diminished.' He stepped into the lift.

The cabin lurched downward before being pulled up short, leaving their stomachs hanging in mid-air, and Cathcut hoping that it would snap its cable and plunge them both to the concrete below, mangling them together in a tangle of wires, pulleys, matchwood and limbs at the foot of the lift-shaft, like Holmes and

Moriarty locked in a death-grip. Anything to put an end to this contest. Janice was lost to him, so why should a merciful God not cry curtains to them both?

The doors pulled back for a gaggle of young nurses, fresh-faced and round-bottomed, going off duty. Cathcut had a compulsive urge to disgrace himself finally by seizing on a plump posterior, drawing it to him, and sinking his clerical teeth into a nape of flaxen hair under its starched cap. But he did nothing, only following them longingly with his eyes as they preceded him from the lift, threw their capes round them, and then trotted down the corridor to the main exit. Lepage didn't take opportunity to mock his barely-disguised interest; perhaps Cathcut had seen the beginnings of a change of heart?

'You made Dr Kemberton a promise,' he observed, as they walked side by side down the polished corridor. 'First to me; now to him.' Lepage neither confirmed nor denied it. Cathcut could stand it no longer. 'Surely your gift shows, plain as a pike-staff, that you care what he thinks?'

Lepage stopped on the hospital's outer steps. He too was not without his signs of stress: Cathcut could see a scabbing of the flesh on the curl-overs of either ear, and behind, in the narrow fringe of hair that gave him the look of a renegade monk, were large flakes of scurf. The nostrils of his long, crooked nose also showed raw and red, as if he had taken to repeated nervous snuffling and pulling at it.

'When I was a boy,' Lepage said, 'I used to go to Saturday morning pictures. And I learned something, even from the westerns. The fast-gun is always longing for the day when he will meet someone faster on the draw than himself. To give up being invincible. I *want* to run up slap against a brick-wall. It's only a pity'—he gestured with his thumb in the direction of Ward 'G'— 'that *that* one crumbled.'

'He didn't crumble. He was kicked.'

Lepage opened his great hooded eyes at him. If the whites had yellowed, the irises were a rich, vivid brown. 'If you could show me one way of being other than I am—other than *you* are—I'd take it.'

It was the most that Cathcut had ever got from him. Despite the brutal insult, he felt there was still hope. Perhaps they might run on for just a little longer?

'The only way I know,' he said, pausing for greater effect, 'is the way of love.'

Lepage smiled and shook his head at him. 'Keep clear of Miss

Driscoll,' he advised, still smiling. 'She won't be good for you. You're a baby in this life, and she has all the tricks of her race. Whether another man could manage her I don't know. But you're not the one.'

'I won't get the chance,' Cathcut replied sullenly. 'She doesn't like me.'

He tried to tell himself that Lepage was only trying to warn him off for his own advantage; but, surprisingly, that seemed too mean an interpretation to be entertained. Similarly, it seemed untenable that Lepage could be faking a loss of interest in revenge. He wished fervently that English had preserved the Greek distinction between words for religious and for erotic love. They walked to the crossroads in silence, then went their separate ways: Cathcut to read evensong at his church, and Lepage to the offices of the secular power.

CHAPTER NINETEEN

Care sat facing a double rank of rattan chairs: twelve high-backed thrones for such apostles and elders as at the Second Coming shall sit in judgement over the twelve tribes of Israel. A sister on one end of the second row leaned forward to catch the eye of her fellows and cue in the first line of a hymn. 'Le-et . . .' she sang, breaking the word over two notes, then pausing expectantly. 'Le-et' echoed her companions, and launched into their invocation, rocking gently from side to side with glazed or half-closed eyes, to a bounding, enthusiastic beat:

> *'Le-et . . . all your lamps be bright,*
> *As the Bridegroom comes in sight,*
> *With new light, with new light;*
> *For in Pentecostal flame,*
> *And the blessings of His Name,*
> *Our Jesus comes again*
> *With new light.'*

The chorus went still more swingingly, even gathering to it some male voices on its way:

> *'With new light, with new light,*
> *Put your terrors all to flight, with new light.*
> *You are standing in His sight,*
> *So let all your lamps be bright,*
> *With new light, with new light!'*

Care roused himself to defy them.
'I will accept the judgement of the Spirit,' he said emphatically. 'But not the judgement of women.'

The second rank of thrones stirred uneasily, and a single soprano voice continued the hymn as though in answer, joined first by her associates, then by one or two of the men in front:

> 'Male and female, brides are we,
> As the Spirit sets us free,
> With new light, with new light.
> Child or parent, black or white,
> In our wedding garments bright,
> We are equal in His sight,
> With new light.'

'Despite your so-called "light",' Care insisted again, 'the Spirit commands through the Apostle Paul that women keep silent in all the churches.'

'Who made you judge over us?' asked the soprano cheekily, looking to her father for approval. 'This is the *new* dispensation.' Her father owned the building in which they met.

Care looked sadly at the vacant chair beside him. It, and an armchair for the Discerner, remained empty.

'I elect to be tried alone,' he said again. 'In the presence of the Discerner.'

'But since the Discerner has not arrived,' intervened the girl's father, 'I must ask you to remain silent. Till this present matter is resolved, you have no voice in this Meeting.' In the power-vacuum created by Care and Evans' disgrace, a residual authority had fallen to him as landlord to the saints.

'Any voice I have had,' Care said, 'has been at the prompting of the Spirit. *"What the Lord has given, the Lord has taken away."* Without the Spirit, I would be as sounding brass.'

'Not sounding brass,' the girl replied quickly. 'More like a lavatory cistern.'

No one laughed at her joke; but no one repudiated it either. A doorbell rang below.

'My dear,' said her father, 'would you be so kind as to act as our doorkeeper?'

She bounded downstairs and opened the street door to a balding, middle-aged man with a bent nose and stained service mackintosh, over whom, in the intensity of her triumph, she poured her displaced fervour.

'You must be the Discerner!' she cried ecstatically, showing him a rank of beautifully clean but overlarge teeth.

He looked at her somewhat more coldly than she could have

wished: at her straight, shiny hair cut to the form of a helmet, her black helmet-fringe and dark ear-pieces curling forward to protect each cheek; at the pencil of black hair on her upper lip that followed the curve of her headpiece above, at the leaf-green jumper over large, overdeveloped yet passionless breasts; at her haunted, hunted, hyperthyroid eyes; and at a nose already sharp, that in a year or two would become a mere finger of bone and gristle.

'The saints meeting in Glaston Street?' asked Lepage.

She nodded, her confidence ebbing away under his scrutiny.

'I wandered up and down like the spirit in waterless places,' said Lepage, 'till I heard singing. Then I knew it must be the place.'

'Did you like it?' she asked anxiously. Lepage looked at the brown, stained, embossed wallpaper of the hall. He seemed puzzled. '—My hymn, I mean. I wrote it myself.'

'Ah. Did you now?' He examined her yet more closely, having already picked up her desperate longing for approbation.

'I'm quite clever, really. I could have gone to university. I had a place, but they wouldn't let me take it up.'

'And why was that?' Lepage paused with one hand on the stair-rail, and a foot on the bottom tread.

'Oh, *you* know. The Meeting. Taking degrees from worldly institutions, an' all that. *You* know. At least Brother Care wasn't behind *that* one. Even if he's behind most things.'

'Is he though?' commented Lepage. 'But doesn't his police-work get in the way? Surely *that's* a worldly institution?'

'Oh, he can talk his way round anything. Him and that *boy*,' she added, with an extra touch of contempt. 'He didn't like the doctrine of my hymn. Said it belonged more to the coming age.' She passed an open thumb and forefinger down her face, changing to a more sober mien and a lugubrious tone. '"Not the age we are called to live in".'

'Doctrine?'

'Oh, you know. "*Male and female*" . . . "*equal in His sight.*" *He* likes to keep us down.'

'Does he now?' said Lepage. He let himself appear to deliberate, and then to take a decision of some moment. '—Is there somewhere we could talk privately? Before going up?'

She fell in immediately. 'Oh yes, there is. Father doesn't encourage deliveries on the old sabbath. Here. Wait.' She fumbled in her pocket for a key, and hastily let them in by a side door into the store-room of a ground floor shop. Beyond a further door, they could hear voices, and a till ringing. She locked the door behind them for greater security; but then pulled down her plaid skirt over her somewhat inflated belly, stretching it tight across solid thighs. Affecting to be more at ease than she was, she stretched one hand along a shelf of tinned soups in boxes, with the other edged her helmet-fringe up off her brows, and faced him expectantly. Lepage seemed amused.

'I have to decide between two men,' he said.

She scanned his face for any hint that she might venture a comment. 'I know.'

Lepage raised both eyebrows at her, enticingly.

'—But if you ask me, there's no question. Everyone knows that an interpreter doesn't reproduce *exactly* what the "tongue" says.'

'Interpreter?'

'You're trying to test me, aren't you?' She smiled at him coquettishly. 'The interpretation's just as much an inspiration as the other, only we can understand it. So *I* say, something nasty has got into Brother Care.'

'And not into Mr Evans?'

'Oh *him*! He's only a dumb doggie, except when the "tongue" takes him. And even then, afterwards, he waits on the interpretation for his cue, and just echoes his master's voice.'

'So you'd say he's unusually bound to Mr Care?'

'Bound!' she exclaimed, laughing. 'More liked *married*. Some of us naughty ones'—she leaned forward confidentially to push her nose into Lepage's face—call them "Mr and Mrs Care".' She giggled: two sharp little noises, stifled in a snort.

He looked at her with a rising tide of revulsion, which even his rational empiricism could not suppress.

'It must be hard to be so ugly,' he said.

She went scarlet, brushed past him to the door, yanked out her key, released herself and fled upstairs.

Lepage followed at his own pace. In the upper room she had already taken her position on the second row, sitting staring ahead, a handkerchief concealed in her left fist. She was surreptitiously wiping each eye in turn when she thought it might pass unnoticed. He observed the rows of wooden benches, the bare, ash-grey floor, sash windows down either side, a double rank of assessors, and Care motionless in his chair, his back toward him. As if he were a mere spectator, Lepage found himself a corner of a bench nearest the door, and at furthest remove from the proceedings.

'"*Friend, move higher up,*"' called the girl's father, motioning to him from a central throne. 'There is a place prepared for you.' He extended a hand royally in the direction of the armchair before them. Lepage came up past the rows of benches and sat himself in it, facing side-on to the vacant chair, and beyond it, to Care in profile. His superior still looked resolutely ahead.

'I am a police officer investigating a murder,' Lepage announced. 'And there are people in this room whom I would like to question.'

The girl bit hard on the handkerchief in her hand, to prevent an exclamation. The Assembly as a whole seemed quite nonplussed by this sudden reversal of its role. Some appeared ready to vacate their thrones at once; others waited on the grocer in their midst, who failed them completely; a few, out of habit, and because he was also a policeman, looked to Care for guidance.

'If you are a police officer,' said Care after a pause, in an even tone that betrayed nothing of any professional acquaintance, 'then you must know that it is an offence to disrupt divine service.'

'No board outside. No times of service,' said Lepage stolidly. 'I doubt if you're covered by the Act.'

The Assembly were like sheep without a shepherd; or nestlings confronted by an unexpected cuckoo. Whatever might have been their backsliding, Care took pity on them.

'Though I hold our brother responsible in this present business,' he said to them, 'I am convinced he had nothing to do with any matter in which the police might be concerned. All that is required is that some of you bear witness to his presence at our gospel meeting last Sunday night.'

'I don't know how you can be so sure,' said Evans from the door, in his clear, high-pitched voice. 'Seeing you weren't there yourself.'

Lepage looked from one man to the other, then back again, trying to gauge what had led the lad to reject the proffered exoneration, and why he might be attempting to implicate his friend.

'I've an old fellow downstairs who needs help,' said Evans again. 'Roberts 'uz done his wrist getting him here, and can't lift him.' A tall, gaunt man jumped to his feet with suspicious alacrity, anxious to escape this embarrassment and follow Evans downstairs.

After much stumbling of feet on uncarpeted stair-treads, they reappeared, bearing on their linked hands a man of improbably advanced years, who by the white stick which hung from the elbow that he had hooked round Evans' neck was at least partially blind. It seemed most reasonable to assess him in terms of what he *had* been: a foot that caught and was dragged over backwards, painfully, as they crossed the threshold (though he made no complaint) suggested that he had once been abnormally tall—his bearers with an effort hoisted him higher, to avoid a second accident. The tufts of white hair over each pointed ear, and also his long straight beard, all had a faint gingery hue, that might have been a reminder of previously auburn locks, but might equally well have been a sport of hair-follicles asked to perform well beyond their natural life. Since he made no move to disengage himself, his supporters carried him like an African chieftain the length of the meeting-room and deposited him reverently in his armchair, which Lepage had hastily vacated. Evans accepted the place pointed out to him, rubbing his neck where the stick had pressed into it. The old man settled a tartan travelling-rug about his shoulders, a useful supplement to the natty but thin grey worsted coat that covered him only to one half of his abnormally long thighs. He stretched both legs before him slowly and tentatively, the light grey material of his trousers hanging so as to reveal a variable ridge of bone from thigh to ankle, as if there might be no flesh or muscle there at all. He smiled at an audience which he could sense, if not see.

'I trust you'll note where I am.' He laid his white stick lengthways from above his knee to between his extended feet. He smiled again, sharing his self-mockery with his unseen friends. 'People tend to find me something of an obstruction.' His voice was so fresh and melodious that it silenced them more than his extraordinary antiquity, or the presence of Lepage. Brother Roberts, who was bringing up the rear with a walking-frame in his uninjured hand, positioned it to the right of the Discerner, and placed the old man's hand upon it. He then took his seat at the right hand of the grocer as secretary to their commission, drawing a notebook from an inside breast pocket. A whole clump of biros sprouted from his wounded hand, like darts waiting to be thrown. He selected one dart, and inscribed a heading on his pad. Only then did he notice Lepage, who had taken himself to a nearby bench.

'The Assembly of Conscience meets behind closed doors.' He sniffed; and seemed to recall where he had seen Lepage before. 'Nor is a brother permitted an advocate, unless by express permission of the saints.' He sniffed again peremptorily, in a manner that required an immediate withdrawal.

'I am hardly an advocate,' said Lepage.

The grocer whispered to Brother Roberts, who became progressively more pinched and sombre.

'If you would care to wait downstairs, officer,' he said eventually, in a changed and obsequious tone, 'in the ground floor shop, which will be warm, I give you my personal guarantee that no one will leave this meeting until you have had the chance to speak to them. Just as soon as we have completed our business.'

Lepage concentrated his attention on the backs of his two suspects.

'You must know, sir,' said Roberts, this time respectful but not obsequious, 'that we will be within our rights to evict you.'

The Discerner's stick fell through his legs and hit the floor, either by accident or to command attention.

'Be at peace, my children,' came the melodious voice. 'After all, what we say in private must be proclaimed from the housetops. I see no reason why the gentleman shouldn't stay. Indeed, I think he would agree with me that it is very appropriate that he should.' He turned sightlessly in Lepage's direction, awaiting an answer.

Lepage's face for the first time registered pain. It was evident that it would not be possible to avoid a reply. 'I stay for professional reasons,' he said quietly, after a pause. The Discerner turned back, but as though delicacy alone led him to accept that explanation.

Brother Roberts was clearly torn between an instinct for secrecy and the lure of at least one uncommitted onlooker on whom to exercise his powers. Desire for a fit audience won out, and he discreetly consulted a few scribbled notes on the reverse of his pad; but with a degree of concealment that suggested a wholly spontaneous performance was the true mark of grace.

'Brothers and sisters'—he sniffed—'beloved brethren in Christ; fellow-heirs with me of the promises of God to those who remain faithful, even to the end . . . the scriptures warn us in many places how *"the Devil, like a roaring lion, walketh about, seeking whom he may devour"*, 1 Peter 5.8.' He looked mournfully at the two likely carcasses before him. 'We know also that *"false prophets shall arise and deceive many"*, Matthew 24.11; even that *"false messiahs shall come, able, if that were possible, to lead even the elect astray"*, verse 24 of the same'—he looked more pointedly at Care. 'And especially, in these latter days, are we exhorted to watch, *"lest the wolf leap over by a side-wall into the sheep-fold, and devour the flock."* He sniffed vigorously, and laying a fresh white handkerchief over his palm, tweaked his nose from side to side to absorb the current droplet and ease out whatever might be accumulating to interrupt his further flow.

'"Watch, therefore,"' he continued, stuffing the handkerchief into his trouser pocket, '"for ye know not at what hour the thief will come"*, Matthew 24, 42-4. —Would that we had obeyed the injunction of the Apostle John, when he enjoined his brethren to "*test the spirits, whether they be of God*"! For what has manifested itself among us is plainly not of God.' He paused to look again at the two culprits before him: Evans returned his gaze, but Care seemed bowed with a great weight of grief. 'These our young brethren'—he brought a note of tenderness into his voice—'are not to be judged after the holiness of their ways: for we well know that the Devil is able to use in the flesh those who are otherwise lambs without blemish, perfect in their walk before God. But what has come to pass amongst us'—he drew breath for his peroration—'has caused the Adversary to reproach the way of the Lord; it has brought dissension and dishonour to the household of faith. This assembly of labouring brethren is summoned . . . to satisfy the conscience of the saints'—he sneaked a glance at his pad—'and to vindicate the holiness of God's house.'

The Discerner let loose a gargantuan sigh: so immense, it seemed improbable it could have been accommodated in so spare a frame. Brother Roberts chose to take it as a request for recognition.

'We are fortunate to have our beloved brother from Birmingham'—he nodded in the Discerner's direction—'who will assist us in our endeavours to know the mind of the Lord. It may be that we shall clear one or other of our brothers of that wherewith he is charged; but let us, at the least, exert ourselves to sift out Satan from our midst.'

'But there is nothing demonic *here*,' interposed the Discerner, in his sweet, reasonable tone. 'Nothing at all.' With one hand on his frame, he got to his feet without assistance. 'I would like,' he said, as if he had come to a decision that relegated all that had gone before to an irrelevance, 'to place my hands on the head of each of the young men in turn.' With the gaunt man leaping up to support one elbow, the Discerner edged towards Evans, and leaned down heavily with both hands on his skull, looking towards the assessors to address them, but directing his words some inches above their heads. Evans bore up well under the pressure, though his neck muscles became very apparent. 'Your representative who was so kind as to meet me at the station informed me very fully of the *facts*.' It was not so much the Discerner's tone as the way he leaned slightly on the final word that implied that he had heard a great deal more which he thought it wise to set aside. 'Demonic possession is very rare among baptized Christians,' he went on, as if he were a surgeon lecturing students over the head of a patient, all the while manipulating Evans' skull, then passing a hand gently over the features of his face. '*Real* possession I see in about two percent of all my cases.' Keeping one hand on the boy's head, he slid the other affectionately down his smooth cheek, round the chin and up the other side, then pressed it firmly over the moulding of his lips.

'I would have thought your name was John?' he asked smilingly. 'John: *"the disciple whom Jesus loved"*.'

Evans shook his head under the hands, vigorously. Feeling the movement, the Discerner wagged his own head in amused self-reproof. 'Strange,' he said, though not apparently much disconcerted by his error, 'I must be becoming fanciful. But I could have sworn it was John.' He was standing without support; and as if to concentrate a flagging attention he closed his sightless eyes, leaving his hands on the boy's head. Most of the onlookers shut their eyes also, half out of habit, half out of respect, despite their curiosity to see what was going on. Only Brother Roberts sat baleful and unblinking, letting a drip form on his nose.

'And now,' the Discerner said, 'our other friend.' He reached out in the air, feeling for where Care sat with his face stern, his eyes fixed on infinity. The gaunt assistant took the old man's wrists and outstretched hands, themselves a lecture in anatomical structure, and placed them on Care's thick, dark hair. Immediately, the hands seemed to recoil about half an inch. The Discerner pushed his right hand down on Care's skull, spreading the fingers wide; but slipping the left between the chair-back and Care's neck, he ran it firmly yet gently up and down his spine, stretching the vertebrae.

'Relax,' he said softly. 'Remember that the Spirit is a spirit of tenderness, of love, and of truth. *"The bruised reed he shall not break." "As a father pitieth his children, so the Lord pitieth them that fear him"*.'

Still standing, but under no obvious strain, the Discerner again put both hands, the right over the left, on the crown of Care's head, and waited silently, meditating, or perhaps praying, but with no detectable movement of his lips. Lepage observed Care's examination with the same weary attention he had given to

Evans's; yet seemed to hold the whole performance in contempt. Meanwhile, the Discerner's features were remarkably transformed: his nose became more aquiline, his nostrils more elegantly flared; the skin of his face, which before had appeared grey and crêpe-like, now smoothed, glowed on each cheek, and all the stringy facial muscles and lax tissue seemed to tauten and compose momentarily into some pre-existent pattern of harmony and serenity. The effect lasted only a minute or two, and then the old man collapsed and had to be helped to his chair; but thereafter Lepage watched him with marked respect, as if the episode had been profoundly disturbing.

'Does either the "tongue" or the interpretation lead to forgetfulness—amnesia?' asked the Discerner, lolling back, his overlong legs outstretched, his voice croaking with weariness. He pinched his left thumb between first and second fingers, marking off his question.

'Neither,' replied Care, answering for both of them. '—Though I am rarely able to recall the content of the interpretation itself.'

'No loss of consciousness?' Again, the bony mnemonic: his thumb transferred to between second and third fingers.

'None.'

The Discerner moved his thumb into its third and final position. 'And does anything in this so-called interpretation speak to the abuse of a brother or sister?'

Care hesitated; Evans was too pained to answer.

'No one in particular; but all of us in general.' The girl had jumped in to fill the gap. 'Every woman in this Meeting is insulted. . . . And God too,' she added as an afterthought.

'Blasphemy *and* obscenity,' confirmed Brother Roberts, with the lugubriousness of a judge anticipating a hanging verdict on at least two counts.

The Discerner further stretched himself in his chair, easing the tendons around his Adam's apple with his bony fingers. His throat was like the neck of a plucked chicken, even to the wisps of white feather still clinging to his red bosom; he had slipped open the top button of his shirt to aid his breathing.

'And the interpretation of this "tongue" comes always to the same person?'

They craned forward to catch his words. Three or four people answered together.

'Yes, yes. Invariably. Always the same person.'

'Such *anger*—and *pain*,' said the Discerner, shutting his eyelids, contorting his face, and pushing with one hand over the other into his midriff. 'More than human nature should be asked to bear.' He did not seem to be commenting on the Assembly.

'This pain,' asked Lepage, '—where *is* it?'

The Discerner acknowledged the voice behind him by a slight sideways inclination of his head, but otherwise went on with his complaint. 'Such anger and pain,' he moaned again, pinching at the loose skin between his brows.

'My dear brother,' urged Brother Roberts in a tone less than affectionate, 'we *beg* you to discriminate. Exercise your gift.'

'Such pain,' complained the Discerner once more, whilst the Assembly of Conscience raised eyebrows at one another and hummed with exasperation.

Care left his chair, knelt beside the old man, and taking both his bony hands, drew them to his own head. 'Discern, father,' he said. 'Lift this weight from us.'

'"*You shall call no man 'Father'*",' Brother Roberts reminded him severely.

'Discern, father,' Care repeated, softly, pleadingly, ignoring the comment, holding the limp fingers in place on his dark hair.

'I begin to see something, very clearly,' said the old man. The Assembly leaned forward on the very edge of their chairs to hear him. Everyone felt this would be the crucial moment. The Discerner thoughtfully fretted a few strands of Care's hair between his fingers. 'I never put a name to what I see, but I suggest a picture. Something for you to take or leave, as the Spirit moves you. If it is not for you, will mean nothing. If it *is* for you, you may receive it as a word of knowledge that the Spirit gives, or push it away—that is the nature of pictures.'

'Yes, yes. We understand,' they urged eagerly.

He laid his fingers out flat along Care's head. 'I see a tunnel, very dark, but with light at either end. There is a road, with two footways. High up, on the left hand side, half-way through the tunnel, a young boy has been crucified. He is nailed through his hands and his feet, to the rock of the tunnel-wall. But he feels very little pain: only joy that, as people pass through the tunnel, they will look up and see him suffering. Before, he suffered in silence; now everyone will know what he feels and be compelled to pity him.' He screwed up his face. 'Aged about eleven, I think. Crucified by the cruel Japanese—because he would not renounce the faith. He knows he will die; but that is preferable to people not knowing his pain.' He contorted his face yet further; and taking his left hand from Care's head, began to knead his own features. 'Not a *real* picture, I think; but something the boy daydreams about. Very often. Retreats to, when the pain gets too intense.' He lifted his sightless eyes toward the twin ranks of assessors. 'Does anyone here recognize that boy?'

They shifted awkwardly; looked at their feet; shook their heads.

'*I* know him,' Evans said. 'But only in a kind of dream myself.' His eyes were moist.

There were two dark circles on the ash-grey wood where Care knelt, head bowed. As they watched, further tears hit the floor and spread, absorbed quickly by the dusty surface. He kept his head down.

'Between the "tongue" and the interpretation,' asked Lepage, '*who* is at fault?'

The Discerner rounded on him. 'You are an honest man,' he said sharply, 'but honest with the eyes of the blind. You touch only surfaces, and try to deduce the relation between them. Such blindness *"darkens counsel, by knowledge without understanding".'*

Lepage refused to be baulked. 'They brought you here to answer that question.'

The Discerner shook his hand in the air irritably, as if chattered to when listening for a far-off note. 'Such *pain,*' he complained again. 'The pain underlies *everything.* Without the pain, none of this would have happened.'

'*What* has happened?'

'Nothing that it would profit you to know,' replied the Discerner even more sharply.

'Let *me* be the judge of that,' said Lepage. 'After all, *"the truth shall make me free".'*

'Ridiculous! Absurd!' exploded Brother Roberts. 'Our time in this Assembly is being *wasted.*'

The Discerner turned his sightless eyes on him with an air of distaste. The hands linked over his cavernous midriff began to tremble. '*Petty* little man—little man in a hurry. Unless you cut to the root, you will never understand how the branch grows.'

'I can see the fruit,' said Brother Roberts, counter-punching with a text from scripture. '*"By their fruits shall ye know them."* And *I* tell *you,* the fruit is *rotten.*'

The Discerner sighed as if wearied by more than one lifetime of human weakness. 'He who opens himself to the Spirit opens himself to many things beside.'

'But not unless he lets them *in,*' riposted Brother Roberts triumphantly, and looked to his audience for approval. One or two nodded agreement from their thrones.

'Father,' pleaded Care again, lifting his head where he knelt. His cheeks were now dry, but his eyes glittered. '—Father, both of us have had the Spirit. He as the voice, I as the interpretation. Decide. Decide between us.'

'Yes, decide,' echoed Roberts. '*He* wants it, *we* want it. At least make a distinction between them and justify your rail-fare here. It doesn't have to be right.'

The Discerner was nettled at last. 'I have *never* asked for more than unavoidable expenses. I *never* take fees.' He shook his head violently, as though to dislodge the notion. 'As for your present problem'—he pushed Care's head away with one hand—'it's obvious where the trouble lies. In the interpreter. An interpreter only interprets what the "tongue" means for *him*. He never reproduces its exact terms.' He shrunk into his chair resentfully, in the attitude of one who, on a point of honour, had been lured into betraying a trust. The power had gone out of him.

Care continued kneeling for some seconds, then got stiffly to his feet, his face pale and mask-like, his full lips bloodless. 'Then I beg leave of this Meeting . . . for a time apart, in which to purge myself.'

The girl began softly singing another verse of 'New Light'. The Discerner endured it for a moment, then threw out his hands to his helpers. The gaunt man and another seized him under his armpits, lifted him up like a scarecrow, and began carrying him from the room. His stick rattled along the bench-ends and struck the door-jamb as they took him through. With his tartan rug up round his ears, the Discerner looked as miserable as Pilate after his handwashing. Evans ran after them with the old man's walking-frame, anxious for a respite.

'You won't forget you have to return, brother?' called Roberts officiously, eyeing Lepage with a lap-dog obsequiousness. He turned again to Care after Evans had left the room. '—And now for your request. My advice'—he paused for effect, nibbling on his lower lip and clicking his biro ecstatically—'is that the request be denied, and that this Assembly report at once to the Meeting.'

'I move,' said the grocer's daughter, raising a schoolgirl-hand, 'that the Meeting be advised that Brother Care cannot satisfy the conscience of the saints'—she looked along her row, gauging support for that first move—'and further, that the Meeting be advised to withdraw itself from him.'

Care, who had remained on his feet whilst his request was pending, drew himself to his full height. 'The conduct of this Meeting,' he said, 'has been given over to fanged *Jezebels*.' He had patches of colour under either eye. Without waiting for a vote, he walked past empty benches and out.

'You see, brethren—and sisters,' observed Brother Roberts, nodding pleasantly in the direction of the grocer's daughter, 'Satan is being foiled in his attempts to have it all his own way with us. He tosses about and foams *"like a wild bull in a net"*. — Is Miss Curtin's motion agreed?'

They looked at one another.

'*Nem. con.*,' said a voice.

'Thank you, Jesus!' exclaimed the girl softly, head bowed. She began to sing again, swaying mildly, her wrists primly crossed, her eyes shut tight. The female assessors, and not a few of the men, joined her in her singing.

Lepage left in disgust, following Care downstairs, all notion of interviews abandoned. Care was still in the hall, finding his way barred by Evans.

'Keep away from me, Robert,' Lepage heard him say. 'Keep away. For your own good. For your soul's health.'

The sentiments of 'New Light' echoed down the stairs, this time with an ornamental descent over the chorus-line. Evans drew himself flat against the wall, and Care rushed past him, out into the street. After nodding to Evans, Lepage followed his superior for some yards; but then desisted until such time as he could consider more carefully how to make his final approach.

CHAPTER TWENTY

All that morning whilst Cathcut sat to compose his three different sermons, all due for completion by 8 a.m. on Sunday, the 'Pirates' were in command: accompanying him as he stole *'with cat-like tread'* into the kitchen to make himself a reviving cup of coffee; conducting whole comic-opera choruses and semi-choruses inside his head as he settled to it again, pen in hand, mind cluttered and unreformed. However much he tried to stop, even to the extent that he exerted himself to try, words, phrases, whole tunes to a song kept echoing in his brain; he caught himself humming and then murmuring again, and bit his tongue between his front teeth to still it, painfully. Nothing he could hit on for a sermon carried conviction or sparked any life—no inspiration for those who are *'going to meet their fate, in a highly nervous state'*. *'To their fate'. 'Nervous state'*. But *what* fate, and why in so nervous a condition? He was even quite excited at having the whole conduct of tomorrow's services to himself. —*'Go, ye heroes, go to glory, go to glory and the gra-a-a-ave . . .'* What had started this infliction? He hadn't heard *The Pirates* for years, never sung a line of it, on stage or off. So it must be some trivial, chance connection that had set the whole piece a-jangling in his head. And then—*'Tan-tan-tara, Tantara'*: Janice knocking at his own front door—*'And to us it's evident, these attentions are well meant.' '—Evident.' '—Are well meant.' '—Evident.' . . .'—Are well meant. . . .'* The chorus dwindled to a silence as he spotted the suitcase in her right hand.

'I've had the most awful row with mother,' she gasped, wide-eyed and desperate, her bosom heaving within her flimsy blouse at the exertion of having lugged her case up several flights of stairs. She looked anxiously round the landing and back downstairs, fearful of being overheard. 'I *know* it's a risk . . . but could I stay here just one night? —Or just part of a day, till I can find somewhere to live? . . . Only it's Saturday, and . . .' Her voice trailed away, her eyes filled with tears. So vulnerable, so appealing; but he seemed slow to catch on. She stimulated him with a little, passionate outburst: 'I just couldn't stand it a moment longer.'

'*Though to us it's evident, these attentions are well meant, evident, are well meant* . . .'

Cathcut cut across the choruses in his head. 'You can't stay here, under any circumstances,' he said. Every finger fled its keys, each reed slipped from the mouth, the bows came to rest, the baton dropped. The silence was exquisite.

She snatched at the handle of her case; yet the weight seemed to drag it from her hand. She stood there helpless.

Not taken in for a moment, he nevertheless decided on a temporary relaxation. 'At least, tell me what happened,' he said, motioning her across the threshold. The case suddenly became more manageable, and she slipped it within the door, before collapsing in a chair.

The band began again: '*Perhaps it would be wise, not to carp or criticize.* . . .' In an altogether softer tone, he asked:

'What was it all about?'

She hesitated for a moment, as though not wanting to hurt.

'About us. About my coming here.'

Cathcut began to be a little heated. 'But she herself *asked* me to look after you.'

'I know. But she said it didn't include taking me to your flat.' She gave him a quick little glance, whilst holding a handkerchief under one eye. 'She called me a *slut*.' She put the cloth delicately to her mouth and bit on it, very prettily, to stop her lip from trembling.

Cathcut felt confused, outmanoeuvred, needing time apart to recollect the exact sequence of events. Then he saw that she was black under one eye.

'She must have hit you!' he exclaimed.

She burst out into silvery, slightly hysterical laughter. 'You don't know much about girls, do you?' she giggled. 'It's only my mascara. It's been running. I've had a cry.' Recovering, she looked about. 'Can I go to your bathroom? Behind that partition in your kitchen, isn't it?'

He nodded, and she skipped off to the kitchen, leaving him

angry with himself at his ignorance—or rather, at his inability to apply even ordinary, common-or-garden knowledge to his dealings with her. There was a great and prolonged sloshing of water from behind the partition, almost as though she had taken the liberty to bathe rather than merely to wash her face. Eventually she reappeared, her eyelids scrubbed pink and naked, her blouse-sleeves turned back to the elbow, and in one red hand a pair of his clerical-grey trousers, tightly wrung, and smelling of a mixture of diluted urine and detergent. In her other hand, held up between thumb and forefinger, was a single wet lock of hair.

'I saw your trousers dumped in the bath and washed them out for you. And look what I found in the pocket, wrapped in a wet piece of paper. No wonder you've no time for lady friends!'

He felt violated, as if she had been rummaging through his private parts.

'It's my housekeeping,' he said. 'Just a bit of rubbish I picked up off the church floor.' The lie was near enough to pass.

'Oh go *on*,' she cried. 'Pull the other one. Since when have people taken to cutting their hair in church? And such a pretty one. It's a keepsake.'

'I wouldn't call it pretty. If it wasn't wet, it 'ud be quite mousy-coloured. But that's not the point. I have no "lady friends".'

'Not even me?' she asked quickly, smiling in his face. She waited for a response, but got nothing; then shook out the legs of his trousers with a sharp crack. 'Then I shouldn't be doing *this*.' She hung them over the back of a chair before the fire, where they started to contribute to the occasion an unlovely steam. 'Anyway, I'll leave it there for you,' she concluded, curling the lock round one corner-knob of Cathcut's record-table, where it settled about the wood like a wig on its mould.

He made his trousers the excuse to be alone, sending her to his bathroom to hang them over a line above the bath. 'O Lord,' he prayed, 'I'm like a child in a mine-field. Show me what way to go.' Then he dried up. He called to mind the collect for that week, trying to adapt it to his need: *'Almighty God, give us grace that we may cast away the works of darkness and put on the armour of light, now in the time of this mortal life in which thy Son Jesus Christ came to visit us in great humility . . .'* Pity it was only a visit. Before he had had any time to find himself, Janice was back.

'I'm surprised to find you're so old-fashioned,' she observed. 'I thought you were rather daring, bringing me here the first time.'

He felt the strongest compulsion against explaining himself, a marked disinclination to cast pearls before swine.

'This isn't the way to do it,' he insisted calmly and soberly, catching her eye, even though she was trying to evade him. 'You're only running away, giving her a lever against you, and against me. There'd be nothing in it for both of us but blackmail and innuendo for ever. I'm not prepared to accept you on those terms.'

'They're the only terms you'll get,' she said shortly.

'Then if those *are* the only terms, so be it. But the right way is to go back, face her down, tell her you forgive her, if necessary, but that you have a right to make your own decisions, be responsible for yourself, that what you do is your own affair. Only then can you be free.'

'Free!' she exploded scornfully, tossing her head. '*You* try it! I'm as free as a puppet on a string.'

'But only because you won't cut the cord.'

She looked at him hatefully. '*You* compromise *me*, and expect *me* to do the fighting! What kind of a man is that?'

'A man who knows enough not to fight your own battles for you.'

She checked at that, eyeing him warily, on the point of releasing some further barb, but half-respectful of the quality of his opposition.

'Perhaps you're right,' she said suddenly, letting her resentment go like a petal in the wind.

He was taken with a violent, choking elation, his heart so leaping as almost to obstruct his breathing. 'I *love* you,' he said. 'I'd do anything to prize you away from your mother. But in the proper way. In a way that sets you free to come to me independently, not with me as some counterweight, and you in the centre being pulled either way, depending on who tugs harder. And I'm not going to be something you can throw into your scale, as it suits you. Because *you* are at the centre of it, you know. You pretend to be just the beam, all innocent and swayed according to who puts on most pressure. But really you hold the balance, and you're playing off one side against the other.' He had dared so much in his fervour, he wondered if he had lost everything.

She had listened all the while, apparently only half-attending, looking over his shoulder in the direction of the left-hand window, as if waiting for him to finish his twelve-times table. But then she surprised him again.

'I know.' She laid both hands on his arm, arresting his attention. '*Listen* to me.' She tugged on his arm, hugging it to her. 'So far as I *can* care for anyone, I care for you. But I'm *naturally* wicked, and I'm frightened to be any different. I don't know if I *could* stop.' There was a tone, and a sadness in those blue-grey eyes, that was not pretence. 'I've been corrupted since the day I was born,' she said bitterly, curling her lip in self-scorn. 'And I can't just blame mother. You didn't know my elder sister. She had the same treats, the same win-you-overs: but she wouldn't play along. Everything was thrown back. I was always the good one. But if they bought her a dress she didn't want, she wouldn't spoil it by accident, she would just refuse to wear it, she'd give it away, sell it even, *anything*. And finally she left home—in the only way she could.'

'So you don't blame her?'

'I wish I'd had the guts to do the same.'

'Even with that man?'

'*Any* man would have been better than *that*.'

Cathcut began to see a pattern. 'So your coming to me was a repetition of your sister?'

'No it wasn't,' she corrected, shaking tears of shame from her eyes. 'I *knew* you were a decent man. That you'd feel obliged to marry me. I'm not as good as my sister. Or as brave.' She paused. 'But I wish I was as dead as she is.'

Salves, palliatives, soothing words: Cathcut knew he must withhold them all. 'What will you do?'

'Go back, as you suggest—without much hope that I can do what you want of me.'

'*I* don't want it,' he rejoined quickly, anxious lest she should already be starting to slide away. 'Or if I do, I want it for *you*. — Or to be even more precise'—he felt the occasion demanded the most scrupulous exactitude—'I want it for *both* of us.'

'I think you're talking of an "us" that can only exist in the land of dreams,' she said gently. 'I don't think I'm capable of it.'

'With Christ *"all things are possible"*,' he reminded her, with genuine fervour.

'Ah yes, my dear.' She turned to him with a first recognizable softness in her eyes. 'I'm sure that's true for you.' Her voice began to tremble. 'But some of us he doesn't visit very often.'

Still he withheld any comfort.

'I think he visits me in you,' she said again. 'That's why I—mother—can't leave you alone. How do you like *that*?'

'Not at all,' he said swiftly, repressing a sense of alarm.

'Don't worry.' She laughed wryly. 'We don't follow you to worship you. We'd just drag you down to our level; and when we'd got you there, we'd so despise you we'd torment you till you

lost any memory of what you once were. That's the kind we are.'
He put to death any twinge of an impulse to object.

'Ah well.' She sighed, and lifted the suitcase again. 'It's back to the trenches, I suppose.'

He held himself to the reflection that, if she had managed to carry her case all the way here, she was just as capable of taking it home again.

'I'll have to come down and open the double doors for you. It's after one, and they'll have locked and bolted them.'

'Thank you.' A coquettish twinkle came back into her eye. 'Thank you, *Lord*.'

He let his face register his displeasure. They walked in silence downstairs, and she stood waiting whilst he unbarred the doors.

'Aren't you embarrassed at people seeing me go out like this?' she asked teasingly. 'I could leave the case for you to bring round later.'

'No,' he replied shortly. Then he permitted himself to laugh also. 'Your mother might *eat* me.'

'Pretty gristly, all that moral fibre,' she chuckled, jumping up on both sets of toes to peck him on his cheek. Then she was gone.

He went upstairs with a twin sadness: aware, as she was, of the unlikelihood of her being able, unaided, to make a break with her mother; but more painfully aware that his gospel condemned him to hope foolishly, beyond reason, and against natural cynicism, that she might pull it off. It would have been less painful to have made a clean break himself. As it was, he hovered between mere experience and what seemed the fantasies of faith, unable to betray either to the other.

The lock of hair round the knob on his record-table felt like an accusation. Had it been mere forgetfulness? Or had he kept it as a relic, unwilling to part with his only surviving memento, if not of her, at least of someone close to her in every sense—and in more ways than at present he cared to visualize? He decided that for once he was probably being too hard on himself; but he took the lock to the kitchen sink, held it over a lighted match, and watched the sizzled strands drop and reform themselves against the wet sides of the sink, before he washed every trace down the plug-hole.

His action enhanced his sense of a cold, clear, attenuated austerity: that thin but distinct exhilaration one feels after having chucked a drug—tobacco, alcohol, sex, even over-eating—before dryness and emptiness invade, and the symptoms of withdrawal start to bite.

The stench of burnt hair led him to throw open a window; and then to seek what fresh air he could in the street below, intending to wander aimlessly whilst he mulled over his sermons. As he passed through the swing-doors, he staggered and struck a shoulder against one edge, smiling to find himself reeling like a child taking its first steps. That was it—like a child—he had thrown away his crutches—no wonder he had that sense of exhilaration: and there was the theme for his sermons. '. . . *Forsaking what lies behind, and reaching out to that which is before, let us run the race that is set before us, and win the crown of everlasting joy.*' Letting go would be so much easier with any clear sense of there being something in front: a child would only totter if it could see a rail to get to. But what he had done was beyond reason. And yet nothing could have suppressed the gut-reaction that it would have been quite wrong to let her stay—not contrary to some code of rules: more like knowing that one further drink will set your whole system awry. Perhaps nobody took the leap of faith until they were pushed.

Six or seven streets took him, without thinking, to the police station. Immediately, he knew what he must do. There was one further crutch that he had *not* thrown away. The longing not to be alone; the necessity of having someone agree with you – that was part of his interest in Janice; it was the root-cause of his obsession with Lepage. Harder to leave that man alone than to give up hoping that the girl might somehow break rightly with her mother and return to him. 'Lord,' the disciples had said, 'we have toiled all night and caught nothing; but if you absolutely *insist*—out go the nets again.' But they had *caught* their miraculous draught of fishes; no one had asked them to cut their trawl loose and watch it float away down the tide. Come, fisher of men.

'I need to speak to Superintendent Care,' he told the girl at the desk. 'Urgently, in connection with the recent murder.'

The station was like a mausoleum. She saw him looking round as she waited for an answer from the switchboard, and smiled her brown smile. 'It's Seshton,' she confided, full of gossipy, innocent indiscretion. 'They are playing at home. You know what these men are. Every uniformed officer is on crowd-control; and half the CID are finding they have the most urgent business that way.'

He walked along deserted corridors, not able even to hear his own footfalls, pausing for a moment to glance in at the door of the Communications Room, where one man was receiving telephone messages and passing them on scraps of paper to another at a wireless console, who leaned forward each time to transmit instructions to his unseen actors. When they looked up, Cathcut walked on.

Superintendent Care was a long time answering his door. Even when the lock shot back there was a second delay, and the sound of moving furniture. Presumably, he was re-arranging files.

It was clear the superintendent was not well. The skin of his hands had tightened as though in consequence of some inner stress: shrunken yet dry, white and corrugated on the back of each hand, it had torn into little red cracks at the intersections between the fingers. His wrists had a nervous, exhausted tremor; and the same strain was reflected in his face, where the skin was again tightly drawn, cracking around the eye-sockets and in the corners of his mouth, and the lips sore and split. He looked utterly exhausted; yet his eyes glittered with nervous excitement, and his hair seemed to have sprung up wildly overnight, like cress sprouting on a strip of flannel. The open Bible on the policeman's desk gave Cathcut very little comfort.

'You have something for me,' Care said, smoothing a piece of paper before him with both hands in a way that opened the raw cracks between his fingers, excruciatingly. *'Please*, don't do that,' Cathcut wanted to say. 'There's no need to stretch them so painfully.'

'I've been suppressing information,' he blurted out. 'About the murder. About the involvement of one of your underlings. Inspector Lepage. Not that he had anything to do with her death, I'm prepared to swear to it. Nothing about him gives me that feel.' He couldn't stop himself seeing, as Care gripped his pen, how some clear matter exuded from the cracks between his knuckles. 'But he had an affair with the girl before. And I wanted him to face the consequences, what he'd got himself into. That's why I didn't come before.' Care only gripped his pen tighter.

'—He shouldn't be *on* the case, should he?' Cathcut appealed, suddenly fearing that he had made a fool of himself, that Lepage's involvement was already known and approved of.

'We wouldn't normally use someone with that degree of personal interest,' Care said. It seemed a dry, official reassurance, one hundred miles from what the man was actually thinking.

'I've done wrong,' Cathcut began again, addressing the open Bible, which at least seemed capable of receiving a confession. 'I couldn't bear for him to be the way he was. It threatened me. So I suppressed information.'

The book received his words, but remained black and impassive.

'And there's the hair,' Cathcut added in desperation, still smelling the burnt fragments in his nostrils. 'Someone got into the church, between the autopsy and the funeral, and cut off a segment of the girl's hair.'

'An admirer,' Care responded at last. 'One of her hangers-on.' Cathcut took a big breath. 'I don't think so. I think it was your Lepage.'

Care flared his nostrils in disgust. 'Not mine.' He brushed a hand across his paper. 'I'm not responsible for the men I have to work with.'

He stared reflectively at the priest's dog-collar, so that Cathcut snatched at it in case it had unexpectedly gone awry.

'What grounds do I have to believe you?'

Of all responses, it had never occurred to Cathcut that he might not be believed. His mouth dropped open. The fellow's whole arm was shaking, as though the possibility of one of his force being slandered had put him into a towering passion.

'What grounds do I have to believe you?' Care asked again, his eyes glittering. 'Not ninety per cent sure, not ninety-nine per cent sure, but one hundred—enough for me to act?' His face was like parchment, his whole upper body trembling. 'I get information from every imaginable source. How can I judge . . . if what I hear is *true*?'

'But—' Cathcut spluttered, his mind trying to latch on to the problem, 'but you can't *expect* that kind of certainty. It's a matter of trust.' He thought suddenly of the Communications Room: a message given, a message written down, passed to a second, transmitted again to unseen persons who would act on it—every stage a matter of trust, a judgement that others had not misrepresented, misheard, or deliberately deceived.

'You see,' said Care, his face drawn into lines, like crumpled paper stretched again under tension. The tremors subsided. 'Every action a matter of trust.' He seemed to have access to Cathcut's train of thought. 'How do we do it? If we added it up rationally, calculated probabilities, we'd never reach a certainty where we could act. Perhaps it's little signals, subliminal messages, the angle of a head, the cast of an eye, that gives us a gut-reaction we feel we can work on. But it's all on a base of trust.'

Cathcut looked at the open book, hoping it might be some bond between them.

'Perhaps the Spirit gives us guidance,' he ventured.

Care doubled up, as if he had been struck a blow in the midriff and was about to vomit.

'And if the Spirit deceives us?' he gasped, looking up whilst still angled over the desk, with wild eyes and sprouting hair.

Cathcut was completely thrown, conscious of a strain in the central point between his brows, and aware of an answering pressure in the veins on Care's forehead and over each eye. The policeman ran his fingers down either side of his nose, as though in pain, then probed and massaged the glands under his neck. Cathcut hoped he would not put that question again.

'Do you think,' Care insisted, phrasing his query with deliberate emphasis, 'that God . . . if prayed to repeatedly, *incessantly* . . . could let one become the leader . . . in a dance of *fools*?'

Gut-reaction or not, Cathcut knew he was on the edge of a pit: body-language, subliminal signals or whatever—they were shouting 'beware!'

'I don't know,' he replied. 'I can't say.'

Care took his forearm within both trembling hands, so that the tremors communicated themselves right down to Cathcut's midriff.

'And nor can I,' Care said, leaning forward and holding him with those 'mad Mahdi' eyes. 'Nor can I.'

'I've done what I came to do,' Cathcut said, wrapping a little cloak of dignity about him, trying by the tone of his voice to set a distance between them. 'I take it that I may go now? I'm sorry not to have spoken up earlier.'

'Oh yes.' Care released his arm. 'No point in holding you further.' He glanced again at Cathcut's dog-collar, then at the Bible between them. 'Go your ways, brother. In the peace of uncertainty. *That* will prevent you from acting.'

Cathcut was moved to protest.

'But I *must* act.'

'I know.' Care got to his feet, about to open the door. 'So long as you remember that to act at all is to act *wrong*.'

'That I will *not* believe,' Cathcut almost shouted, making toward the proffered bolt-hole. 'Never, never, *never*.'

'Think of your past actions,' said the voice behind him, with slow, insidious, overstrung insistence. 'Go over all of them. Of which of them could you say with certainty, "I was right—events have proved it"?'

Cathcut felt his forehead knot even tighter, a radical panic clutch at his heart.

'No,' he said in a small voice, looking inward at a kaleidoscope of activity as it passed before him, shaking his head from side to side. 'No. Not one.'

'And nor can I,' said the voice again.

'That is why we need God's forgiveness,' Cathcut burst out, turning to him. 'Always, every hour of the day. Not so much for what we've consciously done wrong, but for *"our own unwitting sins"*.'

Care looked at him very curiously.

'Perhaps that is why we need to forgive *him*.'

'I must go now,' Cathcut pleaded. 'I have sermons to write, things to be got ready for tomorrow.'

'That's all right,' Care said, as though releasing him. 'Go now. But remember, we can never do right. Not one minute of the day.'

'I don't care,' Cathcut almost shouted again. 'I shall *do*. I shall *act*. I shall *bear* my mistakes.'

'Good.' Care put a hand on his back. 'That is what it means to be one of the elect.'

'I don't *like* that doctrine,' Cathcut protested, twitching his shoulder as he went through the doorway. 'St Paul in old age, when the mental arteries had hardened, trying to put God's foreknowledge into a rational system. I never *have*.'

'But you haven't chosen it,' Care said finally. 'You have been chosen.' He shut the door on him.

CHAPTER TWENTY-ONE

In the half-light of early dawn, as the tenor bell of St Botolph's tolled for first communion, Lepage pressed the doorbell of the Driscoll home. Janice answered it, in a voluminous yellow negligé; but so puffy and red about the eyes that he wondered she could see out at all.

'It's a week—or almost—since we found your sister. I thought you'd like a report on progress.'

She snuffed the morning air, peering up into his face, clutching the ruched nylon high about her neck. Behind her, in the hallway she was trying to screen with her body, stood a large leather suitcase, still unpacked.

'I think I'll be able soon to make an arrest.'

She moved to block the doorway more fully, and flounces of night-attire pushed their warm odours towards him. 'What are you here for? You don't have to ask our permission.'

Since he last saw her, she had cut back her hair by at least half a length—quite recently, for tiny wisps still stuck in the tissue of her nightdress and negligé. Beyond her elfin locks, at the far end of the hall, he saw a similar if greyer and more bloated head, peek anxiously round the kitchen door. It was withdrawn, and a chat-show on the radio turned abruptly to religious music. *'Libera me,'* boomed the BBC's best Sunday voice, unctious and fruity. 'From Fauré's *matchless* Requiem. At the request of Mr R. Emmanuel, of Basingstoke. "Set me free, Lord Jesu Christ, from pains of endless death."' Janice swept down the hall, and, jamming the kitchen door shut with a butt of her hip, closed off the sound.

'Go on and do it,' she said imperiously on her return. 'Make an arrest. You don't have to wait on us.'

'Come with me,' he pleaded, one foot in the door. 'Same terms as your sister. A flat of your own, and I pay the bills till you've set yourself up. —Till you can get a job and stand on your own two feet. Give it a try.'

She blew air sharply through her nose, tossing her head contemptuously.

'And meanwhile, I lie flat on my back? For *you*?'

He shrugged his shoulders, but not without a touch of embarrassment. 'On the same terms as your sister.'

She looked up again into his face, screwing her eyes yet tighter, then tilting her head to one side as though to catch aspects of his expression she could not take in at first glance. 'Why are you doing this? You know it wouldn't work. . . . Are you frightened, or something?'

He looked grim, but did not answer.

'Go and get on with it. Make an arrest. Pay her what you owe. Then perhaps you won't feel so bad.'

'There's no way I *can* pay it,' he said quietly.

She softened a little at that, looking at him with a pity he almost welcomed.

'I'm not my sister,' she said. 'It wouldn't work. You know it wouldn't.'

'We could give it a try. At the least, you'd get your freedom.'

'As a stand-in for the dead? I'd rather be dead myself.'

'We could try,' he persisted.

The kitchen door burst open, and her mother came running up the hall—a mass of blubber shuddering under its restraints. Halfway, she checked, turned one ponderous hip towards Lepage, and reaching up under her skirt on the protected side, eased out a stocking-suspender that in her haste she had trapped between her corset and the soft flesh of her thigh. Then she continued her rush.

'Out!' she cried, hacking at Lepage's foot in her carpet slippers, which struck like clubs wrapped in felt. 'Out! —And *you*'—she turned on her daughter with withering scorn—'*Cover* yourself!'

'I can't come with you,' Janice said defiantly across her mother.

'Why ever not?' He looked down contemptuously at the rucked skirt over her mother's broad flank.

'Because I owe something to that young man. He believes that there's something in me that I don't believe-in myself. I ought at least to try.'

Mrs Driscoll scanned both faces, her eyes welling with tears; then decided on strategic retreat.

'Sentiment,' said Lepage. 'A bit of priestly twaddle. He won't get you free of *that*.' He nodded to where Mrs Driscoll had settled herself on the leather case, which bulged under her as she sat sobbing convulsively, head in hands.

'Mother, pull yourself together,' said the daughter sharply. 'You're not playing at funerals now.' This shaft was greeted with a howl, then further sobbing. The case bowed ominously.

'Rather than this, I wish the ground 'ud opened and swallowed me *up*,' her mother moaned, rocking to and fro.

Both locks burst simultaneously, with the crack of two starting-pistols. The case opened its mouth like an engulfing maw, and Mrs Driscoll sank stern-first into a froth of petticoats and undergarments, things such as no gentleman should see displayed, especially on a Sunday.

Lepage looked down on her as she heaved helplessly, knees up, exposing her pink, knee-length drawers under their band of constricting elastic, and rolling on her back from side to side. The case-edges fractured under her.

'She's ensured you won't be going away for a while.'

'I wasn't anyway.'

'She's made certain you don't.'

'I know what I am. And I know what she is. But someone has asked me to be different. And at least I'm going to try.'

He looked into her puffy face.

'You're sentencing me,' he said.

'No, I'm not.' She knelt down suddenly and rooted about in the remains of her case, feeling under coats and dresses and beneath her mother's body, ignoring the clutching hand and the pleading eyes. 'I'm sending you out to battle. Like a knight with his lady's favour—here you are.' She produced a maroon bra, yanking its elastic free. 'Here's something my sister passed on to me when I was getting a big girl. Tie it to your lance, or something.'

Mrs Driscoll began to gurgle and foam; and by rolling violently to one side finally up-ended the case and scattered the contents over herself. She got maroon-faced to her hands and knees, and knelt there, gasping.

'I shouldn't have wasted my time,' Lepage said. He struck the garment from the girl's hand and pulled the door to against them, leaving them together.

He decided to leave his car and walk to his destination. Halfway up Seshton Hill, he succumbed to an urge to turn in at St Botolph's—to look, he told himself, at the young man who had defeated him—even if in a contest that had never really been. He slipped in with all his professional furtiveness, and got to the back of the nave without disturbing for a moment the tiny band of worshippers up in the chancel. Cathcut read to them, spoke to them, moved about distributing the elements as they knelt in the choir stalls, in tones that seldom reached Lepage as more than an unintelligible murmur. One part of him wanted to break into that circle of light, to disrupt it by an unsympathetic presence; a better part preferred to grieve in the shadows at the distance between them, as symbolized by those thirty wooden pews.

Their communion over, the worshippers left in twos and threes, while Cathcut consumed the remaining fragments of wafer one by one and raised the cup to his lips. He covered paten and chalice with a fine linen cloth, took them up in both hands and was about to leave. Lepage felt the strongest unwillingness to let him go: he went to a stoup beside the porch that he had noticed on coming in and began to wash his hands, noisily slopping water.

Cathcut turned on a nave-light, came down from the chancel, and stood there watching, paten and chalice in hand.

'I'm trying if it works. Holy water, isn't it? *"Wash ye, make ye clean".*'

'The intention is everything.'

'God knows, the *intention* is there.' The moment he spoke, he was seized by a violent fit of sobbing, so intense that he sat on the end of a bench to control himself. But despite Cathcut's presence—perhaps even because of it—he didn't want to stop: every sob was a relief from intolerable tension.

After a while, he registered that the priest made no response—almost as if he had taken a vow of silence.

'Shouldn't you want to confess me, or something?' he asked, lifting his head from his hands, cocking one eye at him.

'It's not my place to interfere. I've meddled long enough.'

'Good heavens, man, have you passed some kind of self-denying ordinance? I've got to make an arrest.'

'Make it.'

'But I'm tired of simply destroying. I want help.'

Cathcut looked back at the high altar. 'You may have noticed our altar cross: it's Venetian, a rather fine silver-gilt. Over there, at the back'—he nodded toward the west wall—'is a wooden one we carry in processions.' He paused. 'Those who refuse the silver, get stuck with the wood.'

'Is that your help?'

'Possibly. They both have a potential to lead *somewhere*.' He looked Lepage in the face—almost, it seemed to the policeman, for the first time. 'I should have remembered a play we read at university: "Y'are the deed's creature; y'are no more now"—I ought to have waited, and let you be.'

'You can't escape involvement.'

'I've managed to make myself withdraw.'

He turned his back and carried his vessels into the vestry. A hollow metallic clang announced their return to the church safe. The lights went out in chancel and nave, controlled by a master-switch. No one came back to extinguish the candles.

After leaving St Botolph's, Lepage made a long, weary climb up the remaining quarter-mile of Seshton Hill, turning left when almost over its brow into a street of substantial Victorian houses where Care had his home. As he came within Care's garden-gate and looked toward the front door, it seemed that the base of the right door-post had been stained a dark, vivid crimson—a splash the colour of fresh blood, as if with some hope that the Angel of Death might be persuaded to pass over. Only when he had mastered his inclination to turn heel and go did he realize that the sprinkle of colour was a spray of scarlet roses, still in bud, darkening round the edge of each petal with a brownish pencil-line, but not sufficiently withered to have been exposed to an all-night frost. The cone of pink tissue that covered their stems was likewise damp but not soggy, despite there being droplets of mist or dew on the blooms. Placed, therefore, some half hour or so before his arrival—but by whom, and for what reason thus neglected?

Care's mother recognized him immediately.

'What do you want? He's not here.' Her belligerence might have been the reaction of any woman whose man is liable to be called out on a Sunday; but Lepage felt it had more to do with the roses at her feet.

She consulted a hall clock. 'He was here half an hour ago. Like as not, he'll be at his Meeting.'

Lepage looked at the roses, but did not move.

'D'you know where that is?'

He nodded.

'I might have guessed. I suppose you're all in it together.' She began to close the door.

'Not me,' said Lepage. 'Not me.' She paused a moment, scanning him through the remaining gap. '. . . He was at home last night, then?'

Her body locked as if her vertebrae had been pulled by a string tightened from the base of her spine.

'I only asked'—he smiled reassuringly—'because, as far as I can gather, he wasn't at the station last night.'

She looked him between the eyes, searching for any hint of an insinuation.

There was a long pause.

'If you're wondering about the roses,' she said suddenly, following his glance, 'he brought them for me.'

'I couldn't imagine otherwise,' he smiled again, nodding courteously, his voice like honey. '—Is there anything I could take for him? He'll have his razor, I expect. But a fresh face-flannel? These cases can keep one away from home quite a while.'

She checked his face once more.

'I imagine he's got all he wants,' she said bitterly.

'Pyjamas perhaps?' He urged again, so gently, so considerately. 'Service blankets can be a bit rough on the poor old skin, and he's not one to sleep in his shirt.'

She looked again at the brown, somewhat stupid eyes, so devoid of any hidden depth.

'I suppose I could find him some fresh night-things.'

'Oh—and any letters,' he called after her. 'Saturday's mail?' The string through her vertebrae took another twist. Her shoulders arched and stiffened.

'There,' she said on her return, showing him a familiar yellow envelope before wrapping it in a set of striped flannel pyjamas. 'Tell him his mother sent it.'

Lepage rearranged her foldings respectfully, and tucked the bundle under one arm.

'He must have taken his pills with him last time.'

'Pills?'

She offered no further elucidation. He looked down with even greater puzzlement at the wilting roses in their pink wrapper. 'He must be very fond of you, your son. Hot-house, or flown in from somewhere, I'd guess, and not exactly sixpence a dozen. They really ought to be in the warm. They're not bred for our December weather.'

'The pills are for his fever. To help him sleep.'

'Ah yes.' He picked up the bouquet and laid it in her arms, across her bosom. 'I imagine he'll be sleeping well enough in a day or two. These things don't normally last too long.'

She sniffed the heads of the roses lingeringly, trying to tease out a scent from their closed buds.

'Glaston Street, I believe?' Lepage queried, from halfway down to the gate.

She threw her bundle from her on to the concrete of the garden path, then dried her hands by running them down each hip-pocket of her housecoat.

'I won't be *bought*,' she called after him, with terrible firmness. 'Do you hear that? Tell him, I won't be *bought*.'

When the door had closed and he had turned a corner, Lepage checked within his parcel, and noted with satisfaction that the yellow envelope had been steamed open and then re-sealed. Some tears in the flap of the envelope, though gummed down again, gave her away.

At Glaston Street, people were standing on street corners, in doorways, even at upper windows, letting the morning damp into their rooms and on to the tinsel of early Christmas decorations. All were gazing toward the door of the Meeting, as if some loud altercation had just taken place. High above the knot of disputants around the door was a tall, tapered pole, standing like the rallying-point for some lost cause. When Lepage came nearer, he saw that it had a claw at its upper end, and was no more than the implement used for raising and lowering shop-awnings. But the awning itself was flush against the wall, only detectable by a scalloped edging under the line of the first-floor windows. 'MURGATROYD—GENERAL STORES: PROVISIONS FOR EVERYTHING' read the sign beneath it.

Evans held the pole, barring the doorway to Care. On each side of him were prim, dark-suited men, to each of whom he attempted in turn to give the pole. But they seemed to have no hands, and he was left holding it, awkwardly, half-heartedly.

'They won't let me let you in,' he was explaining to Care. 'I'm not a free agent.'

'Take hold of freedom. Let the Spirit move you.'

'Oh *no*!' Evans cried. 'I couldn't bear any more of *that*!'

'"Be not faithless, but believing,"' Care proclaimed loudly.

The pole waved to and fro, as though to mark the movements of Evans' mind.

'... Don't you see? They're trying to pit us against each other.'

'They've already *done* that. We're full of holes already.'

'Only if we let Satan deceive us.'

'Oh no,' said Evans, looking at Care full-face with his amazing blue eyes. 'The holes are *real*.' He grasped his pole with both hands, and it assumed a rock-like steadiness.

'At least agree to speak for me before the Meeting.'

Evans hung his head, leant it against the shaft. A tear ran down its oiled surface, taking the colour of linseed as it ran.

'I can't,' he mumbled, covering his whole grip with water. 'I don't *believe*.'

Everyone became very still.

'Police officer,' Lepage said sharply, flapping his identity card, and pushing through from the back of the small crowd. 'Obstructing the footway. Disturbance of the peace.'

Evans looked from one supporter to another, pleading with them to take Care in.

'Let the world take it out of our hands for once, laddie,' said the gaunt man Lepage had seen at the Assembly of Conscience. 'It 'ud be better for everyone.'

They persuaded Evans to duck the claw of his pole under the lintel, and even helped to lift its further end. The pole once within doors, the black suits followed, and the door shut behind them. Two or three bystanders dispersed, and Care and Lepage were left alone.

'Your office, or mine?' Lepage asked, waving back with a hand those who still hung out of windows.

'Mine.'

They walked in silence through streets of terrace houses toward the station.

'Nobody wants either of us,' Lepage said, as they traversed the long corridor to Care's office. 'We two should stick together.'

Care made no comment, but preceded him into the room, took his accustomed chair at his desk, and sat staring into space supporting his chin on his hand, and with his elbow pressed into a pile of disregarded papers. His eyelids had ceased to droop, but his eyes focused on a painful middle-distance well beyond the confines of the walls, making little scanning movements as if to clarify some point of detail that had become obscure. He frowned slightly, and for a moment seemed on the point of weeping. A lock clicking-to from the inside roused him to scan his desk anxiously, agitatedly, looking for a prop. Lepage took the chair immediately in front, where Care's interviewees had sat to confess.

'You had a passion like mine,' Lepage began. '—Obsessive, irrational—and you killed to protect it. We should stick together. For me too nothing else mattered. And you injured me by taking it away. Everything that made life worth living to me you took away. So I can understand why you did it.'

Care reached for his Bible, and began reading aloud:

'The transgression of the wicked saith within my heart, that there is no fear of God before his eyes. For he flattereth himself in his own eyes,

until his iniquity be found to be hateful. *The words of his mouth are iniquity and deceit: he hath left off to be wise, and to do good.'*

'An obsession,' Lepage said again. 'Irrational, overpowering. I know.'

Care turned over a page, rubbing it between thumb and forefinger in case two leaves had adhered. '. . . *Thou shalt make them drink of the river of thy pleasures. For with thee is the fountain of life: in thy light shall we see light.'*

'"*Like the deaf adder that stops its ear,"'* Lepage interjected, *"and will not heed the voice of the charmer."'*

Care looked at him for the first time, halting his reading. He pressed with his thumb into the opened binding till its spine cracked, watching Lepage's face.

'I didn't know'—his eyes looked strained and hurt—'I didn't know you were a Bible-man.'

'Sunday-School, scripture lessons. It's hard to avoid. Perhaps you'll condescend to talk to a "Bible-man".'

Care opened his mouth to speak, then ran his thumb along his lips as though to clear them.

'Tell me about *that,'* Lepage said, interpreting the gesture.

'. . . I'm lonely,' he ventured again, since there was no response. 'Cut off from my obsession. I'll never feel like that again. Every pretty face will be just that. Or remind me of *her.* . . . And you'll be lonely too. He won't even allow you near him when he finds out. Or when he even suspects. Which he's bound to do soon, if he doesn't already. No letters, no prison-visits. . . . So we might as well stick together, and share our pain.'

Care made no reply.

'. . . Silence itself is a form of confession,' Lepage insisted. 'So you can take *that* as read. You haven't denied what I say. So why not push it out and get shot of it?'

'. . . You mustn't think I'm angry,' he continued. 'There's a side of me that's quite glad to be rid of my obsession. So you mustn't feel I'm resentful.'

'. . . Good heavens, man,' he burst out, jumping to his feet and leaning across to shout down Care's ear, yet conscious of himself building his irritation into a passion. 'Do you think you can murder a girl to protect your frigging lust, and get away with it?'

Care pushed the book from him and hung his head. 'I'd object to your language,' he said quietly, 'if I had any ground from which to do so.'

'That's *right,'* Lepage cried again. 'You've got a mind like a running sewer on the subject of women, and when you put yourself in a trance, it takes you over. Of course you've no ground. No more than you had to kill my girl.' The possessive on his lips sounded forced and unnatural. He noted that Care showed no reaction.

'I am not answerable to the Ashtoreth,' the policeman said. 'Nor to those who commit adultery with her on the high places.'

'Oh, Ashtoreth,' Lepage cried again. 'I know all *about* Ashtoreth. The Semitic goddess of sex, isn't she? All right then, the Ashtoreth. I'm a man of religion too, after my fashion.'

'Not *my* religion,' said Care.

'Little boys, little girls,' Lepage observed, settling back again into his chair. 'Same obsession, different twist.'

'I know the city to which I am called,' Care insisted.

Lepage shifted uneasily.

'I know the means by which I am called.'

Lepage shifted again.

'"Who shall lay anything to the charge of God's elect?"'

'Killing,' mused Lepage, recalling Dr Kemberton's comment with contempt. '"Killing on principle." "To protect an ideal."' He laughed, provokingly.

But Care could not be brought either to confirm or to reject the accusation.

'. . . Do you deny that we're birds of a feather? A couple of obsessives?'

Care eyed him, but then continued reading, silently.

'. . . There's nothing I can do to touch you, is there? You don't even have to pull rank on me, tell me to be silent, send me away. If I say anything outside of this room, I proclaim myself a lunatic. No witnesses, all your training used to avoid anything that might incriminate you. The perfect crime. —Except that your guilt led you to talk to an unreliable old man.'

He thought he saw Care's fingers tighten on the top corner of either page.

'—Not of course that he can testify as to which of you he saw. You're too much alike, you and your shadow. But that won't trouble *me*. If I don't have you, I'll have him. Either way, it'll *hurt*.'

'There isn't enough to convict him.'

'Not to convict, perhaps. But enough to do him harm. He might even have to leave the force.'

'He must pay something for his service to the Ashtoreth.'

It seemed probable that the superintendent had been walking all night, while his roses rested in a sink of the Murder Room, waiting to set their seal on his deliberations. Cracks at the corners of his mouth and eyes had healed over, leaving a brownish-yellow crust; his hair was flattened by the morning damp, but not before he had thought to comb it. His chin was newly shaven. In all, he looked spruce and pulled-together, despite successive rejections.

'Confess,' Lepage pleaded. 'Do it of your own free will. Don't make me break you.'

Care continued to treat him as an intruder on devotion. '*I am distressed for thee, my brother Jonathan,*' he read from a marked place a third of the way through his book. '*Very pleasant hast thou been unto me: thy love to me was wonderful, passing the love of women. How are the mighty fallen, and the weapons of war perished!*'

'I don't think he *had* fallen,' Lepage interrupted. '—Which means everything you did to her—to me—was built on a lie.'

Care smiled, and even shook his head in mild reproof.

'The Spirit doesn't lie.'

'The Spirit doesn't speak blasphemies. Or obscenities. At least—so your friends tell me.'

Care appeared quite unruffled: he interlaced his fingers over the scabbed splits in his hands, and leaned across them, smiling benignly like any well-intentioned psychiatrist. 'No doubt there are some inconsistencies in my behaviour, the cause of which time will reveal. But what are we to say to *your* inconsistency? A middle-aged man, experienced in the world, believing only what he sees, yet confessing to an "obsession"—"irrational, overpowering". Isn't *that* a contradiction?'

'A sexual itch,' Lepage protested, feeling uncomfortably that this was a re-run of some half-forgotten conversation. 'It doesn't signify.'

'If it were that, it wouldn't centre on an individual. Any passing whore would do.' Care leaned across the desk to hold Lepage with his eyes—eyes that were full, brown and compelling. 'It's both worse—and better.'

The voice was that of an elder brother, promising that a favourite toy could be mended, with no crack showing; that the recalcitrant sum would come out; that the impossible, half-heard tune might assemble itself from a cacophony of notes, and strike the heart. If only one would wait and listen. Lepage told himself that it was good to keep a suspect talking.

'The great goddess has you in thrall,' Care went on. '"La Belle Dame sans Merci". Promising a salve for unappeasable longing. The salve of eternal death.'

Lepage allowed himself a moment's indulgence. 'I want a

death *beyond* death. The death of the spirit.'

'—And yet she won't let you die. She keeps you in a kind of half-life, neither living nor dying. However demented your surrender, she returns you to life. To its meanness and squalor. Until you rush to her again. And her priestesses,' Care insisted, '—those unfortunate women that trigger your longing—them you despise. It's *her* you want, through all her manifestations. As soon as they've served their turn, you toss them aside. This last one you despise as much as you did the others.'

'I hate her,' Lepage admitted. 'Only my body grieves.'

Care nodded. 'Because she breaks your isolation—that pure and perfect independence from all considerations and claims, where you shut yourself in enjoyment of your dream. If Ashtoreth, Queen of Heaven, will receive you, everything else is redundant.'

'You seem to know me pretty well,' Lepage said. '. . . Do you also know that I want to be free?'

'"*The Lord has looked down from the height of his holiness,*"' the policeman intoned, without consulting his text, '"*from heaven he has looked upon the earth: to hear the groaning of the prisoner, to deliver those condemned to die.*"' He leant across and took Lepage's right hand, holding it between his injured palms, pleading with his wide eyes. '"Now *is the appointed time.* Now *is the acceptable hour*"'.

'I'm playing with you,' Lepage warned. 'I won't let you go.'

'"*We have escaped like a bird from the snare of the fowler,*"' Care recited again, with greater intensity. '"*The snare is broken, and we have gone free.*"'

'If I were to accept your freedom,' Lepage said, 'I'd need to know where it leads.'

'To a postponement,' Care urged, caressing his hand. 'To an acceptance that your longing can never be satisfied. Not in this life.'

'I *can't* wait.'

'And to a recognition'—Care began to speak cautiously, tentatively, still appealing with his eyes—'that you are a dependant creature, made with a longing and necessity, to which truth and beauty are the spur . . . but which God alone can satisfy.'

Lepage felt his skin wither, the blood withdraw from his pores, his mouth set in that tight line that so repelled his associates. 'I don't *deny* your God,' he said. 'I simply value my independence.' He disengaged his hand.

'What kind of independence is it,' Care asked, 'that rejects one slavery for the sake of another?'

'Don't forget,' Lepage warned him, 'it was you that cut me off. Perhaps for ever. You've seen men deprived of their drug. I don't forgive.'

'There is *real* nourishment,' Care urged. 'Besides the drug.'

Lepage felt a sour fever rise and spread through his veins; he knew his breath was foul, but did not restrain it. 'I'm sick of longing. I'd rather die. My only fear is that I might long for ever.'

'"Stay me with flagons, comfort me with apples,"' Care recited softly, '"for I am sick with love."'

'If you touch me on the raw,' Lepage said, 'I shall destroy you.'

His superior shook his head over him and sighed. 'I think you are one of those who must kill God before you can know him.'

Lepage laid his bundle on the desk beside him. The superintendent glanced at it, without appearing to recognize the garments as his own.

'Confess,' Lepage begged again. 'And let me leave you in your illusions. If I can let you be, there'll still be a corner of me that hopes you had something I didn't understand. Don't make me break you.' He felt his face crinkling under the stress. 'I'm weary of being always right, in the most sordid of explanations.'

'If you know something to my discredit,' Care said firmly, 'you must tell me. *"The Spirit of Truth shall lead me into all truth."*'

Lepage looked at his calm features, the fine eyes, the welldivided hair, his high, austere cheekbones, and the facial disfigurements that seemed to heal by the minute.

'Your "spirit" is a lie,' he said. 'Everything you've been and done has a commonplace explanation. As common as dirt. As for your "voice", I can produce it at will.'

Care spread his hands wide, like a Christ in Majesty. '*"Put me to the proof. Try my mind and my heart. Look well lest there be any way of wickedness in me."*'

Lepage dismissed a last vestige of compunction.

'You *are* what you've been,' he said contemptuously. 'The boy his mother made. Only now I can provoke your "tongue" without any heavenly intervention. That makes *me* the puppet-master.'

He pushed his bundle across, snagging a thread on a sliver of wood, so that it lay doubled and stretched across the desk between them. Lepage snapped it with a tug.

'Open.'

Care unfolded the legs and sleeves of his garments, cautiously, as though he expected a bomb inside. Instead, there was a further yellow envelope, lying on the breast pocket of his pyjama jacket.

He looked up and laughed, his nostrils curling.

'She asked me to tell you she sent it.'

His smile faded.

'She didn't like your present,' Lepage insisted. '"A *naughty* boy, away from home all night."'

'Walking,' Care protested, his colour rising. 'Clearing my mind.'

Lepage simulated a characteristic harshness of tone.

'"Tell him," she said, "tell him, I won't be *bought*."'

Care stiffened. His wrists began to tremble.

'"A *wicked* boy. Deceiving his mother with the girls." —Only, *we* know,' Lepage said, 'that women are abhorrent to you. That's why you took your love to a man.'

'It *was* love,' Care insisted. '"*I have run the race. I have kept the faith.*"'

'I don't doubt it. Only your "spirit" led you into a betrayal. Of him, of her. It got you into something no roses will put right. *Nothing* will buy her now.'

The trembling spread to the whole of Care's body.

'I put your roses into her hand. But she threw them to the ground. —Look,' he said, picking up the envelope, slitting it open with one finger, and pushing it under Care's nose. 'Take it. *Smell* it.' He plucked the lock of hair from inside and rubbed it into Care's palm, pressing the strands between his clenched fingers. 'Perhaps it's not what you think. —Mousy hair; *mother's* hair. I put your roses in her hand, but she threw them to the ground. "Tell him," she said, "tell him I won't be *bought*." I don't think you killed any *girl*. You killed your mother.'

Care half-rose to his feet, attempting to shake the lock from his hand; but it adhered to the congealed matter between his fingers, and curled round his middle digit. He flicked once, twice, then sent it flying across the room, as he gripped both sides of his desk, his arms shaking, and the heavy wood beginning to move.

'Speak, damn you, speak!' Lepage shouted.

For a moment, he feared he had misjudged. Then Care slowly put his head backward, threshed it from side to side, mouth working, teeth grinding, the promontory of his Adam's apple making little spasmic jerks, up and down. Tears flowed down both cheeks. He howled once, wolf-like and protracted, then fell to babbling, not obscenities this time or anything intelligible, but injured whimperings, grunts, snarls, the pre-language of animal hatred, noises like a child crying, yet all broken up by the machine-gun juddering of his jaw and lips.

A sharp knock at the door arrested the fit before it had fully run its course. Care stopped abruptly, mouth open, still shaking, saliva running from the corner of his mouth, over his chin and down the left side of his neck. He felt a wet corner of his shirt-collar, then pushed at the underside of his chin several times with the fingers of the same hand, listening. He seemed half-dazed; and when his name was called, he sat down, eyes staring, and began absent-mindedly probing the tendons of his wrist with the other thumb. His pupils were dilated, his breath very short. Lepage observed him for a moment, and then risked opening the door a crack.

'Is everything all right?' Evans asked. He had a piece of paper in his hand.

'He's been taken ill.'

Evans pushed into the room, and Lepage locked the door again behind him. They stood watching as Care turned away, dabbed at his split mouth with a pure white handkerchief, then held the cloth to the light to inspect a yellowish stain.

'What happened?'

'I had an attack, Robert,' Care said faintly, his back towards them. '*Without* your "tongue".'

Evans stood irresolutely, unsure what to do with his message.

Lepage nudged him into a corner. 'This didn't happen just like that,' he murmured, looking the youth hard in the face. '—What have you got?'

'Something from his Meeting.' He offered it to Lepage without hesitation.

Addressed on the outside and folded once, the note was brutally short:

Dated this Lord's Day, 5 December, 1965
On the advice of its Assembly of Conscience, this Meeting has determined to withdraw itself from you, as being a vessel of dishonour and an abomination. This decision will be communicated to the Metropolitan Meeting. Any attempt in future to force yourself into the Upper Room will be treated as an invasion of private property.

Signed: E. Roberts
T. Dexter
for the Brotherhood meeting
at Glaston Street.

Lepage sighed and returned it. 'Can it wait?'

Evans nodded, and pocketed the paper. Care seemed once more to have relapsed into stupor, staring ahead like a puzzled somnabulist. A few minutes had sufficed to mark the years between the two men: Care's skin had lost its tight, boyish sheen, and had crumpled into lines about his mouth and eyes, and all across his forehead. He looked very white, and shivered despite the warmth of the room. Unsure what to do for the best, Evans busied himself with patting the patient's hands with his handkerchief, and in clearing the saliva from his chin and neck.

'Should we call a doctor?' He seemed hesitant, as though aware that an interruption might be inopportune.

'I'm feeling weary,' Lepage said. 'I need some air. Keep him here, and keep with him. Aspirins are as much as anyone can do. If he wants any meals, have them brought from the canteen. No alcohol. There's water across the way'—he took the door key from his pocket and replaced it in the lock—'or Mrs Throsby's tea, if he can face it. If not, boil a kettle. Put some paper and writing implements in front of him. Let him write down all he wants. If anyone interrupts, tell them you're in conference. And stay *with* him.'

He shut the door behind him, and waited till he heard it lock; then walked swiftly along corridors, across the vestibule, down the main ramp, out into a December day, zigzagged through several streets of crowded terraces, turned sharp left down Seshton Hill, down like water seeking its lowest point, past the church, through a shopping centre, by a side-road over the railway bridge, till his further progress was blocked by the grey, torpid current of Seshton Reach. The river moved wearily round an easy bend, any ripples made sluggish by oil slicks and chemical effluent, past abandoned wharfs and warehouses whose corrugated-iron sides and roofs were rusted into patches that showed a grey light behind. There was no vegetation above the water-line, only a vivid, orange-brown stain, as though rust had run off the decayed machinery on the quays and coloured the runnels, the drains, and those points where rainwater entered the stream. A froth of chemical or detergent had scudded across the current and piled up around the footings of a substantial warehouse; but it showed no sign of loosening the pervasive scum-line, save some yellow discoloration in the foam itself.

Traffic noise from an iron bridge a hundred yards to the right led him to take the left-hand tow-path, picking his way across steel cables and along the sleepers of a light railway from which the rails had been removed. The stream beside him smelt like stagnant water; but his senses were too dulled to find it very offensive. He slipped on some loose ballast and stubbed his toe against a rusted chair in one sleeper, but felt it less than the blows of Mrs Driscoll's feet.

'I can't get her off,' he said to himself, thinking of the elder daughter, noticing how sluggishly his words came from his tongue. 'Every move I make pulls me in further.'

Ahead of him, a pair of gulls, flown inland from a storm at sea, shifted on their separate bollards, turned sideways to watch him as he passed between them, and eyed him with a lustrous, alien eye. He decided to walk until his depression lifted, or his strength failed him.

CHAPTER TWENTY-TWO

Evans secured Care's door from the inside, but left the key in its lock.
'I don't see what good it'll do just sitting here,' he said. 'You're not fit to work. Let me take you home.'
Care sat with one elbow on his desk, his thumb propping his chin, gazing out along the ridge of his knuckles as though they were some fascinating foreground, and the wall behind just a distant and diffuse backdrop.
'. . . I've found some skin-salve. "*For stings, bites and mild abrasions.*" Let me put it on those hands.' Evans rubbed some ointment from a first-aid kit into the cracks between Care's fingers; Care suffered it, but otherwise paid him no attention.
'. . . Here, wakey, wakey!' The lad snapped his thumb and second finger several times before Care's face, then passed his palm across the eyes, laughing awkwardly. 'You'll need to get your overcoat on, before I can get you to the car.'
He took Care's black crombie and his scarf from a peg, laid the coat about his shoulders and wound the tartan several times round his neck; but Care sat on, letting his coat-tails trail on the floor.
'. . . There's plenty more Meetings where they came from. I wouldn't take on so.'
A telephone rang on Care's desk, and Evans answered for him: a lass from the canteen, whom Lepage had told in passing that they might want something. Evans recalled his mother's panacea.
'. . . Squeeze some fresh oranges into a glass, add boiling water, and stir in as much brown sugar as it will take. Oh, and give us a couple of aspirins, if anyone's got some. —No, he *doesn't* want cordial. If he did, he'd have asked.' He must have sounded

unduly sharp: when the glass came up, it was set in the midst of a large plate, surrounded by six orange skins, and even the pips presented for evidence.

The fresh acid of the fruit, together with the tang of the sugar, seemed to revive Care's attention. He ignored the aspirins, but pulled at an orange-skin with his foreteeth, until juice flowed on to his hand, causing him to suck the joints and shake them ruefully. Looking for something on which to dry his fingers, he noticed the paper in front of him; he picked up a sheet and used it, crumpled it into a basket, then took a fountain-pen and began scratching at the surface of the next sheet. Within minutes he had built up a substantial doodle, leaning over to black-in certain portions with extreme attention, and seeming to derive great relief from the care he lavished on its detail. Further doodles developed from the main drawing, extending and reaching down to the foot of the page.

Evans humoured him for a while, then walked up, and with his feet tangled in Care's overcoat, looked over his shoulder.

The drawing was in black-and-white, a hard outline with no shading, childish yet vigorous. A bathing beauty sat on an upholstered throne, wearing a one-piece swimsuit with a sash across it. In one hand she held an orb, in the other a sceptre which projected across her bosom and nestled into her collar-bone. Her crown was a circumference of triangular spires, each topped with what looked like a large pearl; and under it her hair hung down each side in long, corkscrew ringlets that almost reached her shoulders. On either side of her stood twin halberdiers, both in wide-brimmed Spanish helmets. Along her naked thighs lay a massive book, closed, and bound with metal bands. A Nubian slave knelt before her, in a kind of short schoolboy tunic that showed his black legs. His head and upper trunk leaned across a block, but everything below heart-level was wrapped in a continuous chain, wound round many times to bind his hands to his side, but extending right down his legs and attached to a great black ball at his feet. A long, two-handed sword was raised above him. In the next sketch the scene was repeated, save that the prisoner's head had been lopped off, showing a section through the neck, and the base of the severed skull. There was no blood, but a tiny circle within the larger circumferences marked the place of the cut vertebrae.

Successive smaller cartoons continued the stages of the action, the executioner's sword shearing each time like a bacon-slicer, right down to the first circle of chain. In a third picture the shoulders had gone, in a fourth the upper chest, and in the last the blade had cut through to the vital organs. In section, you could see two circles for his lungs, and between them a dark, exposed heart. Still there was no blood. The executioner wore a black, helmet-like mask which obscured everything but nose and mouth; but behind the eye-slit was a large white eye with extended lashes, full-on, as in an Egyptian painting, though the face was in profile. The executioner's tunic with its strips of armour might have indicated either sex; but from the shape of her thighs she was female. Evans detected a marked resemblance to Miss Curtin.

'She's a bitch, that one,' he observed, pointing to the figure. 'She hates men, because they won't look at her.'

Care stiffened, and seemed displeased. 'I got what I deserved.' Setting his doodles aside, he took a further sheet of paper and began to write at great speed, covering the paper in a neat, minuscule hand, with almost no corrections or erasures.

Evans resigned himself to a long wait, settling himself on a high-backed chair in a corner of the room, stretching out his legs, looking at his scuffed shoes, and reaching down at intervals to flick off a speck of gravel. Care glanced up at him from time to time, as though to refresh his memory.

'It's no good your writing,' Evans commented after some minutes. 'They're not going to let you back. They never do, that lot, once they've got someone out. I think I'll leave them myself.'

'We were mistaken,' Care said sadly. 'Or perhaps we deceived ourselves.'

'Not me,' Evans objected, wiping his toe-cap with a handkerchief. 'I never thought they were much cop.'

After a further half-hour or so, Care gathered his sheets together, folded them lengthwise twice, and tucked them inside the cover of his Bible.

'If you're well enough to write *that* much,' Evans said, 'you're well enough to write reports.' He got up as if to go.

Care gathered up a set of keys, scribbled a brief note, pushing it into an envelope, then took a full bottle of tablets from a drawer and slipped them into his jacket pocket.

'Robert, I want you to come with me. But before we go out, I'd like it if you'd consent to read to me.' He retrieved his writings from his Bible, turned to an Old Testament passage and pushed it across, his finger marking the verse. Evans sighed and looked reluctant. 'Please do this for me. I won't trouble you again.'

Evans took the volume and looked the passage over, as if still determining whether to oblige. He sighed again, sat down and started to read, though with a childish degree of hesitation, and not much expression.

> 'And Elijah said unto him, Tarry, I pray thee, here; for the Lord hath sent me to Jordan. And he said, As the Lord liveth, and as thy soul liveth, I will not leave thee. And they two went on.
> 'And fifty men of the sons of the prophets went, and stood to view far off: and they two stood by Jordan.
> 'And Elijah took his mantle, and wrapped it together, and smote the waters, and they were divided hither and thither, so that they two went over on dry ground.
> 'And it came to pass, when they were gone over, that Elijah said unto Elisha, Ask what I shall do for thee, before I be taken away from thee. And Elisha said, I pray thee, let a double portion of thy spirit be upon me.
> 'And he said, Thou hast asked a hard thing: nevertheless, if thou see me when I am taken from thee, it shall be so unto thee; but if not, it shall not be so.
> 'And it came to pass, as they still went on, and talked, that, behold, there appeared a chariot of fire, and horses of fire, and parted them both asunder; and Elijah went up by a whirlwind into heaven.
> 'And Elisha saw it, and he cried, My father, my father, the chariot of Israel, and the horsemen thereof. And he saw him no more: and he took hold of his own clothes, and rent them in two pieces.'

Evans looked up, noticing Care's rapt expression. '—Do you want me to go on?'

'No,' Care said, his face still shining, having lost for a moment the marks of weariness. 'That will be enough. Now I want you to meet someone.' He pulled his overcoat round him, slipped his arms into its sleeves, and moved over to unlock his door. He had tucked his packet back inside his Bible, and held the cover closed with one hand.

Evans looked doubtful. 'Are you well enough to go out? I don't want you keeling over on me.'

'Thank you. I'm better than I've been for some time.'

The boy shrugged, and followed his superior into the corridor.

They traced much the same route as Lepage had taken earlier, till they came out on the brow of Seshton Hill. A pale afternoon sun was catching the roofs of terraces in the valley, making their wet slates glisten and the windows shine. Care looked out on a fine rain beating down the smoke-haze, at a band of yellow light on the horizon, and at a covering of low, heavy cloud.

'"*Ah, Jerusalem, Jerusalem,*"' he murmured over the cramped streets. '"*How often would I have gathered you to me as a hen gathers her chickens, and you would not.*"' He turned to Evans and smiled gently. 'I thought I was going to "*throw fire on the earth*". Now *you* must be Elijah.'

The lad looked at him to see if he were still feverish; then began to bluster. 'Be realistic,' he urged. 'Everything I had I got from you. The "tongue", the messages—you gave them all their meaning. Without that, I'm nothing. Or almost nothing.'

Care soothed him. 'You aren't yet strong enough, Robert. You need further instruction. That's why I'm handing you over. But you will do better than I. "*When you come to yourself, strengthen your brethren*".'

'What "brethren" do I have?' He screwed up his face in exasperation, and looked suddenly very boyish. 'I don't *have* any brethren. Certainly not *that* lot.'

'It'll become clear in time,' Care promised. He started to walk down the hill, with Evans tagging after.

At St Botolph's, Care turned in across the gravel and made for the south door. 'He should be here,' he announced.

Instead, they found a tousle-haired girl, sitting alone in the darkened church with her back towards them, looking up at the high altar. About the aisles there was a faint smell of candle-grease and stale incense.

'I'm looking for the curate—Mr Cathcut,' Care murmured in her ear, touching her on the elbow. 'Do you know where he is?'

Janice turned full-face to look at them.

Care was taken with a persistent trembling, so violent that it seemed he might collapse and complete his fit. He stumbled back into a pew two rows behind her, and sat with his head between his hands, shaking.

'What's the matter?' she asked. 'Did *I* do that?'

'No, no,' Evans assured her. 'I told my friend he shouldn't come out. He's not well, and he comes over faint. But he's obsessed with meeting this fellow, what's his name—Cathcut. Do you know if he's coming back?'

'If he was, I wouldn't be here.' She brushed her curls off her forehead with the back of her wrist. 'My sister was killed last week. Her funeral was in this church. I'm just sitting here, thinking. —But you'd know, anyway,' she said, recognizing

Evans for the first time, a shadow of alarm crossing her face.

He peered down at her, trying to imagine her with eye make-up and flowing hair. 'I'm sorry,' he said, grasping her hand and holding it in both his own. 'We're doing all we can. I'm *very* sorry.' She turned resolutely away, and stared toward the east window. 'Do you . . . could you tell me where to find him? If I don't humour that one'—he nodded in Care's direction—'he'll *never* rest.'

'He'll be taking communion to the sick. And to the old vicar. You'd best wait for him outside his flat. He's sure to go back there sometime.' She gave him a few simple directives for getting to Cathcut's apartment; but before she was done rehearsing them, Care had stumbled out of the building.

'I have to leave you, Robert,' he said as they climbed Seshton Hill together. 'I want you to take this paper and give it to Mr Cathcut.'

'What good will it be to *him*?' Evans protested. 'He's not one of us. —Anyway, I was told to stay with you.'

'He will understand.' He re-cast his sentence. 'Only *he* will understand.'

'Just as well,' the youth exclaimed. 'I'm blowed if *I* do.' They continued in silence through a maze of streets, arriving by a side-road almost opposite Cathcut's printing-works.

'This is where we part,' Care said. 'Take my paper'—he proffered the folded sheets—'and give it into Mr Cathcut's hands. Personally. And tell him I sent you.'

Evans became quite dogged. 'I have my orders,' he insisted. 'I'm not to let you go. I must stay with you.'

'But I order you to deliver my paper. As your senior officer. Wait over there'—he pointed to the double doors—'and stay till he comes.'

Evans's blue eyes flashed with the consciousness of manhood. 'You're not well enough to be alone. You're probably not even responsible. How would I feel if you walked under a bus?' Then a solution occurred to him. 'Let me at least see you back to your mother's.'

Care turned very white. 'I *must* go, Robert. Read that, and you'll see why I must. Read what you've got in your hand.'

Evans unfolded the sheets and turned them over, inspecting their blank backs as if some clue might be concealed on the reverse side. Then, reluctantly, he started to read from the beginning, shielding the surface with his body from a light drizzle; page after page, putting each sheet to the back with increasing speed, his face puckering, his eyes hot and moist. At the last page he broke down altogether, sinking his backside to the wet pavement, leaning against a wall with his head back, and howled tumultuously. 'You've been *spying* on me!' he shouted through his tears, his mouth working. 'Get off! Get off with you to the river, and *drown* yourself!' He shut his eyes so as not to see Care going, and must have blacked out altogether. When he came to, he found the man he had to wait for, standing over him.

'Are you all right?' Cathcut was asking. 'You've not been drinking, have you? Are you on drugs?'

'Read it,' Evans cried, pushing the tear-blotched writings up at him.

'Later,' the clergyman said. 'Let's get you into the warm first.'

'For Chrissake, *read* it,' Evans shouted. 'Read what he's *done*.' He staggered to his feet, pushed the papers into Cathcut's hands, broke from his embrace, and rushed off into the rain.

It seemed hopeless to try and go after him, especially in a cassock. Cathcut unlocked the swing-doors and made his way upstairs, having first, from force of habit, checked his mail-rack, even though it was still the weekend. Once inside his flat, he drew up his standard lamp to an armchair and settled to read what he had been given, half expecting to find it some kerfuffle about nothing.

CHAPTER TWENTY-THREE

'If you had looked into his eyes,' it read, 'you would have understood it all, everything that I took on myself, that later happened to me. The eyes were of a piece with the "tongue": the clear, bell-like sound seemed to clean the air, the eyes had such an unsmutted blue that you felt everything that passed through them must be clarified, perfected by their agency. Perhaps he didn't look out on our world at all. He was everything I wanted for myself: pure, beautiful, unstained. He wasn't clawed inside, like me; there were no voices telling him everything he did was flawed, inadequate. There was no tension anywhere in his body—everything beautifully moulded, the body a perfect expression of his spirit, without any war between the two—you could tell it in his every movement. I suppose he wasn't very clever—it seemed insignificant as against the voice. If he had that, he had everything. The first time I heard it, there was no disputing—every syllable was reality, there *could* be no deception, you felt any deception in the room would be struck dumb or wither away. I did what I could never conceive of myself doing, when it stopped I rose to my feet, threw back my head—and it was like a river of words pouring over the rim of my teeth. I felt like an overfilled pitcher that had been tilted, there was a volume of words passing through the channel of my throat. I watched my body from above, as it were, somewhere in the top of my skull, but that was only the intellectual part of me, conscious of speech taking place outside itself, trying to listen in, but hearing only the words. But I was *in* the words: the real me, behind my breast-bone, seemed to ripen, burst out of its scars like ripening fruit. My whole body was warm, with pleasant thrills of electricity playing over the surface of my skin, and every muscle rejoicing in the singular power that reconciled them perfectly with their function, like a harp in tune. Later, I learned to allow my mind just sufficient activity to retain something of what was said, but others were always in the position of having benefited more, and I relied on *him* (for his "voice" was not such as to leave any after-effects) to recall the message in the interpretation.

'The Meeting responded very well—there was an authenticity in the "voice" that would have been hard to dispute. Only when the messages were clearly advising courses of action was there any difficulty, for those who had long-established positions as elders of the Meeting felt that their advice carried less weight, even might be set aside. This was especially so when the "voice" advocated social action, for the Brotherhood has tended to avoid involvement in the world. Nevertheless, we jointly became (as it were) leaders of the Meeting, he as the voice of the Spirit, I as the Spirit's servant, interpreting what was said. Under the guidance of the Spirit we began to evangelize, and to lay hands on the sick—but no one else got a "tongue", and anyway it would have been hard to match the purity of that first voice. All went well, until that first terrible occasion, when, though the "tongue" seemed as usual, my body as I rose to interpret was heavy, racked, at odds with itself. I couldn't *hear* what was said, but I hardly needed the hurt, astonished faces to know that something was wrong. For the first time when I sat down, I felt weary, my muscles aching as if after indulgence in alcohol. The muscles under my chin felt stretched, torn. Even as I sat down, I caught his eye—and detected for the first time an imperfection in that limpid blue—or rather, the blue was not touched, but the whites had yellowed, a liverish tinge that was most unlike him.

'Even before I knew what had been said—for the Brotherhood are too decorous to come out with it easily, and Robert could not be persuaded to tell me—I sensed that something about him had changed. His face was humanized—you couldn't say in any sense that it had become ugly—but it had lost some of its unworldly beauty. He noticed more about his immediate surroundings and seemed amused by them. He appeared disenchanted with me, his laughter soured by a touch of cynicism. What was particularly painful was that he seemed unhesitatingly to hold me to blame. Not that he reproached me, but there was the unquestioned presumption that if corruption was entering into our communications it was making its inroad through *me*. When I met members of the Meeting during the next week I assumed such a possibility for the sake of unbiased inquiry, and to encourage them to let me know (though in general, not specific terms) what the content of the interpretation had been—but it irked me that *he* did not accord me the same benefit of the doubt. I was puzzled that we had not lost more of our grip on the Meeting than we had, given how ready they were to see Satan under every bush: I suppose the genuineness of those first revelations made them unwilling to let them go so easily. However, when the same thing happened again, I knew they could not be held for long. I was half-hoping there would be no "tongue" the next Sunday, but it came as if on time, and I rose to my feet determined to bring things to a test. Nothing I could hear in the tongue itself suggested anything might be wrong; but try as I would, when the interpretation took me I could not hold on to anything in it. The effort distracted me from watching the brethren; but when I sat down, some were holding their head in their hands, others even groaned aloud. I felt feverish, and was afraid lest I be thought to be blushing at what I had not in fact heard. Robert left the Meeting immediately, but the faces as he went out seemed sympathetic, as much as anything. It seemed to me extraordinary that they could be well-acquainted with my subsidiary role as interpreter of the message, and yet hold the fault to be in me when things went so badly wrong. Certain of the brethren asked me to put a stop to the whole business of "tongues", but I persuaded them that Satan had special interest in perverting what was potentially so powerful—Satan had only left us alone in the past because we were doing *nothing*. In the gentlest way I hinted that our brother might unwittingly have laid himself open to malign influences—you might compare him to a badly-tuned receiver that was picking up wrong signals.

'I set myself the task of determining what was wrong—and if possible, before the next Sunday. Our absence from the Meeting would be as damaging as another false "tongue", and our authority could not withstand another episode. I deliberately freed myself from chores and paperwork, passing over as much as possible, so as to be able to keep a discreet eye on Robert's comings and goings. I watched his relationships in the station, whom he ate with in the canteen—but there seemed nothing out of the ordinary there. Tactfully I quizzed some of the young constables as to his behaviour in the station-house, but if they had noticed anything odd it could not be got at without my appearing to take an unusual interest—and I was sensitive to what might be insinuated behind my back. Robert himself evaded any attempt to draw him into conversation, could even be said to shun me. I felt the loneliness of the elect. I decided to go to the extent of following him. This was not easy, given the irregular hours and unpredictable visits of a detective-constable, so I resolved to wait for him where I could be certain he must return, at the station-barracks. The very first night, and by no means late in the night, I recognized him walking by the light of a street lamp. He was holding hands, rather tentatively I thought, with a young woman. He might almost be pestering her, half-turned toward her, leaning over her, talking very urgently and persuadingly, while she seemed to be pulling away. Eventually he gave up, put his arm around her waist, and they walked off in the opposite direction from the station-barracks. I followed discreetly after them, quite openly, but at a distance that made it unlikely that Robert would recognize me if he turned round. My relationship with him would not in any way have excluded his taking to himself a chaste young woman, so that you can say my inquiry was dispassionate. After six or seven streets they came to a semi-derelict Victorian tenement, went into the hall—I could see their outlines through the frosted glass of the inner door. A minute later a light went on in the dormer window of the attic. The lower casement was open, I suppose to air the room, but though it was a bitterly cold night they didn't shut it or close the curtains. I could see shadows on the ceiling—presumably they had a light near the floor. I think it was the light on the floor, together with the open window (which should have suggested that everything was above board) that gave me the idea that something was wrong, something not proper. I watched the moving shapes on the ceiling, hardly daring to interpret what they might mean. I feared to give way to my own thought, that Robert might have fallen into carnal desire. The doctrine I preach does not exclude sexual relations, provided they are an expression of the marital bond, but teaches that such relations are to be calm and infrequent, the energies of the soul retained till they discharge themselves in the leap toward Godhead. I remembered his muddied eye, and felt a great surge of grief. Could this be the source of infection, the point that fouled the clear waters of the Spirit? It was so obvious, you might say predictable, that a young man of his age should fall this way—but in Robert's case the normal categories were cancelled, there was no box into which you could fit him. When he stayed half an hour, then walked home disconsolate, even then when he passed me on the other side of the street, I felt (looking at his light, controlled form) that I was imposing on him some unhealthy fantasy of my own.

'The next day was difficult for me. My mother, noticing I was away from home even more than usual, began to insinuate that I was spending more time with Robert, that the work of the Meeting was "not sanctified", that there was "something more than normal" in my relationship with him. In the intervals of tedious chores I found myself praying "O Lord, let me discover the source of corruption—and let me uncover it *soon*." The day passed wretchedly. In the late afternoon, I came across (quite by chance) a "Register of prostitutes, with their places of operation", a file which two of the men were bringing up to date in the intervals between more pressing tasks. There were annotations in pencil against the tenement where Robert had been. The name of an occupant of the attic had been scored through, and against it written: "name or pseudonyms of present tenant unknown—said to be on the game, no controller—freelance?" *That* was where Robert had been—I found it hard to credit.

'I couldn't bear to watch that night—I needed time to adjust to what I had discovered. To my mother's surprise I arrived home early, and I could not but feel she was smirking, attributing it to her rebuke. My hang-dog expression must have given her the triumph of having made me feel guilty. All night I grieved over the problem of Robert. He evaded any attempt of mine to probe his state of mind, and in a way that communicated quite clearly his belief that I myself was a better subject for inquiry. I could not bring myself to tell him I had been spying on him. It was then that it came to me that there was another possible approach, through the girl. If I could somehow get her to desist, frighten her off, the situation might be saved. I was convinced it was not in Robert to *seek* corruption—somehow she must have inveigled him, and if she could be persuaded to stop, he would naturally revert to his former state.

'That Saturday night I watched *her* house, not the barracks. Robert seemed not to come near all night. I had impressed on him the importance of attending Sunday's meeting just the same, and for the sake of truth enduring what the Spirit might torment us with—no doubt he was struggling with his own distress. If it led him to examine his behaviour, I thought that would be no bad thing. The girl came back late, as if from a party. Her heels were higher than would have been comfortable for extensive street-walking, and there was more leg than anyone would want to expose to a November night. She smirked as she passed me standing there, and I conceived for her a violent, instant dislike. She moved her posterior exaggeratedly from side to side as she walked away from me, a gesture plainly intended to insult—I decided she had been drinking and would be invulnerable to any approach that night.

'In consequence, I went to the Sunday Meeting in dread, resolved to contribute nothing. Robert had come as I had told him, but there was some murmuring at my presenting myself there again. His "tongue" arrived like clockwork, at the opening of the free-prayer session, so fraudulently pure that I began to detest it. I hunched in my seat, determined to resist any impulse to interpret. I had my Bible open, and concentrated on reading one of the Psalms. I didn't dare to mouth the words for fear something might take over, but filled my mind with what I was reading. After a while the tension in the Meeting began to relax: there was to be no interpretation. Someone ventured a prayer, and in his generalized thanksgiving there was more than a hint of rejoicing that we had been spared another incident.

'I allowed myself to relax also, almost in tears at the thought that Robert might have reconsidered his position, even perhaps broken it off. Maybe I had been unjust to call the "tongue" in question this time. After two humiliations, it was understandable if my tortured feelings began to reject what had been the cause of their pain. The interpretation might well have been as pure, as edifying as it had always been. I even began to think his demeanour had regained some of its other-worldly abstraction.

'My eye fell on the text of Psalm 126: *"When the Lord turned again the captivity of Zion, we were like them that dream."* We too had been delivered from our captivity. The words so perfectly expressed my sense of gratitude that I thought I might venture, on the prompting of the Spirit, to read it to the Meeting. I had completed only the first sentence, when the interpretation came crashing in. This time I could hear it—howling, shrieking, animal-like grunts, bursts of obscenity, blasphemies. When it was over I stood appalled, mouth open, hardly daring to close my lips for fear of tasting the poison that had passed through them. The top of my stomach hurt as if I had vomited.

'There was no outcry. Someone seated me in a corner of the room and held my hand, which was very cold. The Bible which was clutched in my other hand was prised from my grip, and a sister began reading from the previous psalm, something sturdy and comforting: *"They that trust in the Lord shall be as Mount Zion, which cannot be removed, but abideth for ever."* Others sat around me, their eyes shut, whispering prayers of support. Someone more practical had made a cup of hot, sweet tea, and I was grateful to take it and purge my mouth. They took me home by car, and although I tried to stand alone at our front door, my mother could not have missed seeing how my companions waited as if expecting to support me. Of course she knew something was wrong: it was what she had been hoping for, for months. In her thanks to them for bringing me home there was so much dissembled triumph that I could have struck her.

'It was then that I conceived my plan for bringing matters to a conclusion. The incident of that morning had so violated me that I concluded that anything was permissible to break the evil that had taken hold on us. I would not reason with her or threaten her, as I had anticipated. I would give her the opportunity to leave him alone, or I would exact from her the penalty ordained in Israel for the punishment of harlots. I made my fever the excuse to take no Sunday dinner, and fasted all afternoon to put my resolve to the test, avoiding my mother by keeping to my room. Every meditation confirmed my decision: when Elijah vanquished the prophets of Baal on Mount Carmel he put them to the sword, so that they should no longer infect Israel. By the word of the Lord were the Amalekites destroyed, and all the peoples whose lust and sodomy polluted the land of Canaan. In a Godless city the law of man protected those whom the Law of God condemned.

'What validated my resolve was that every hour I grew stronger, more integrated. But I had not realized the extent of my righteous anger—it struck me great hammer-blows, beating my will into a sharp sword. I would become an instrument of the Law, the true Law. It was all so simple, free of the indirectness, the dubiety of other solutions.

'I knew that Robert was safe in the evening Meeting, which commenced at 8 p.m.—but I hardly expected to find *her* at home. Her hair hung in long, slatternly ringlets around her neck. Perhaps she had a vestigial aversion to plying her trade on Sundays: more likely she allowed herself one day off, like any law-abiding citizen. Her dress was negligent, but she hardly seemed to think it a reason for keeping me out. I was glad there had been no one to see me on the stairs. She slipped the door to behind me with the air of having made a catch—I presume she remembered me from the night before.

'There is a world of difference between taking a decision in principle, and piloting it through all the little shoals of detail, the rubs of particularity that may impede its progress. There are those, even in the Brotherhood, who would advocate "being flexible", "responding to circumstances". But I have seen too many good principles founder that way. I knew that I must guard myself against any touch of fellow-feeling that might spring up from our common humanity. Fortunately, her every action might have been calculated to arouse my animosity. She exaggerated her influence over Robert, claiming over him a power which I knew she could not have. There was a feline stench in the room that accorded well with her cat-and-mouse attitude toward him. You could have said I was trying to wrest a soul from a creature whose only interest in it was as a bauble for her own instinctual game. Three times I tried to alert her to the danger of her position, but she only returned to me the blank incomprehension of the predestinate damned. It became to me a matter of the utmost importance that she should have some inkling of the choice before her. "Either you let him go, or I will kill you," I said. "Now you wouldn't want to do that to me, dearie, would you?" she said, crossing the room to where I sat and standing over me, legs astraddle, negligé parted, so that I could see the pimples between her breasts, down past the navel to her strip of underclothing. In reaching up to fend her off, I touched her greasy, mouse-like hair as it hung over her shoulder. That touch did more for me than all my spiritual calculations put together. Through the greasy fuzz I felt the muscles of her throat. I rose to my feet and bore down on her throat with both hands, pressing my thumbs about her Adam's apple to obstruct the passage of any further vileness. I felt as the servants of Jehovah, putting down the priests of Baal. Dispassionate justice was expressed in every movement: I remember observing, as her eyes bulged from their sockets at the pressure on her throat, that the motion was like squeezing out a tube of toothpaste. She struggled surprisingly little; and the power in me held her upright till the last movements of her hands died away. She had not even tried to mark me with her nails, as if even in extremity her fingers recoiled from touching the holiness I then expressed. I lowered her on to the bed, taking care not to soil my knuckles with the sheets on which she had entertained her customers. After washing my hands at the little wash-basin beside the bed, I left the room, feeling regretful that prudence had made me cover the tap handles with a flannel, so as to leave no traces behind me. Similarly, I used no towel, lest I leave identifiable skin tissue. It seemed an improverishment that in this world it would be impolitic to proclaim the truth of what had happened.

'My mother met me at the door of our home. I felt a surge of affection at that passionate righteousness whose demands I had at last fulfilled. She was gratified at my spontaneous kiss, and did not even comment on my early arrival from the Meeting. Supper was not my re-heated dinner, as I had anticipated, but sausages and tomatoes freshly cooked. I ate with relish, and retired early to bed, at peace with myself, my sense of inadequacy purged, the clawed flesh behind my breast-bone exposed, salved, and healed.'

CHAPTER
TWENTY-FOUR

'Tribulation'—Care: the pun was simple and obvious. 'A member of some fanatic sect,' Lepage had said, 'giving themselves prophetic names. Presumably from the sorrows before the Last Day.' The problem that Cathcut had set aside, the temptation from which, with exemplary self-denial, he had withdrawn himself, had presented itself on his doorstep, this time with flashing eyes and floating hair. At whatever cost to his pride, he knew he must contact Lepage, stay with him throughout, and do his best to ensure that a process he himself had set in motion would stop short of disaster. He rushed downstairs with Care's writings in his hand, praying for a cruising taxi. A broad, ungainly woman waited for him in the street.

'I thought you'd be down sometime,' said Mrs Driscoll. 'I want a word about my daughter. . . . She *is* with you, isn't she?' she accused him, since Cathcut neither crumpled, nor made excuses.

He turned his attention to the swing-doors and double-locked them, checking them by pulling on the bar.

'. . . You've got her tucked away up there, and you're keeping her from her own mother.' She jerked her thumb inelegantly toward the roof, while Cathcut wondered how to get shot of her.

'Miss Driscoll is a free agent.'

'Oh, I know *you*. With your fancy manners and college ways. "Free agent", my foot! D'you think we're all stupid down here? Like as not, now you've lured her in, you've got her gagged and bound to the bed.'

The notion itself, the sheer inopportuneness of the attack, forced Cathcut to laugh.

'—Oh! You find that funny, do you? I'll make you laugh, my

boy, on the other side of your face. What will your Bishop say when he hears you like locking up young girls?'

Cathcut checked himself, and considered. 'I hope he'll say what I say—that you're an evil-minded, tyrannical old woman, whose daughter's best hope is to get away from you altogether. You know the saying, *"Leave the dead to bury their dead"*? I'll be pleased to repeat it to her.'

Mrs Driscoll stood transfixed, bound to the pavement by sheer weight of lard, while Cathcut made good his escape.

He calculated the cost of slipping round to the back shed for his cycle, of the necessary unlocking and re-locking, together with the unpredictability of that mode of progress, as against the time spent in sprinting, or rather, hobbling through several streets in a clerical cassock. He determined to hobble, and arrived at Seshton Police Station with only a split seam and a mud-spattered hem.

'Inspector Lepage?' No one knew where he was. 'Superintendent Care?' He seemed not to be answering. No doubt they would both be back in a moment—but could the duty sergeant take a message?

'I'll handle this,' Lepage said from behind him. The ridge of his nose was blue and white, with dark, cavernous eyes, as if he had been wandering for some hours without a coat. His suiting clung to him, and his trousers had lost their creases. They walked side by side towards Lepage's office.

'—Has someone been asking for you? Did they phone?'

'No one phoned me. But one of your men delivered this.' Cathcut passed over Care's writings.

Lepage stopped in the corridor under a subdued neon light, and held the sheets at arm's length. A mere cursory glance led him to run at speed to Care's office, with Cathcut trailing after. The door opened without resistance, the room was empty, save for a pervasive smell of balsam. A note had been propped on Care's typewriter.

'I should have known,' Lepage shouted. 'I should have known they'd stick together. I thought Evans had an interest, and could be trusted.'

'Evans brought the letter,' Cathcut said. 'He seemed distraught. As soon as he gave it to me, he ran off.'

'Distraught? He'll be more than distraught!' Lepage rang down to the car-pool to check if they had taken anything out, and then contacted Communications. 'Lepage speaking. Tell all cars to keep an eye open for Superintendent Care. He'll be on foot, and is wanted immediately at the station. Ask them to report as soon as they see him. And if anyone runs across Detective-Constable Evans, I want him brought to my office. By *force*, if necessary.' Lepage hastily slit open Care's note, glanced at it, then passed envelope and contents across to Cathcut.

It was addressed to Mrs Melissa Care. 'Zechariah 13,' the note read. '*I am that third part that shall be refined as silver is refined, and its dross purged away.*'

'What do you think?'

'It doesn't look good,' Cathcut said. But despite their shared alarm, he couldn't resist a guilty pleasure that Lepage had lost control, that he was capable of miscalculation—or even (if he had felt any sympathy for Care's predicament) of one of those disturbing accidents that prove, on reflection, to be half on purpose.

Lepage asked switchboard for the Chief Constable, and, while he waited, perused the detail of Care's confession. He looked increasingly like Savonarola before a burning.

The switchboard rang back: the Chief Constable was out playing golf with the Lord Lieutenant of the county, and couldn't be reached at present.

'In *this* weather,' Lepage exclaimed. 'No wonder we won the war!' He pushed Care's confession back to Cathcut. '—I don't know how you read *that*. But I'm not inclined to ask for road-blocks and a watch on the ports, at present.'

'I'm more afraid of something else,' Cathcut confirmed.

They walked across to the Murder Room, whose staff, with their bull's-eye map, neat piles of manila folders and reports, and their row of manned telephones, seemed to continue with a discreet momentum of their own, untroubled by recent events.

'Take every available man and woman off house-to-house calls, and get them looking for Superintendent Care. Let them start from where they are. I want every street combed, the cinemas checked, the parks, and especially, every place of worship.' They looked at Lepage with astonishment, as if he had proposed that government be abandoned for the sake of a lost child—then settled immediately into the presumption that their quarry had been found, and that Care was wanted for interviews. Since Lepage fended off all questions, they contented themselves with speculating about Cathcut.

'We'll visit the mother,' Lepage said to the clergyman in an undertone. 'It may be that he's gone back to the womb.'

He summoned up a squad car, and had the pair of them

dropped off at the corner of Care's street. They approached circumspectly, after an initial reconnoitre of surrounding gardens and the back alley.

Care's mother blenched at the sight of Lepage with a clergyman. Her roses still lay in a bush of lavender by the front door, though the wrapper had blown and caught on the stems of a pruned shrub.

'What's happened?' she cried. 'Has my son been hurt?'

'Is Superintendent Care with you, ma'am?' Lepage looked past her down the hall, and surveyed the ground and first-floor windows.

Especially with Cathcut present, she wasn't going to let on that there had been anything odd about their parting. 'I haven't seen him since early this morning. Didn't you find him at his Meeting?' Her fingers were working at the edges of her apron—but not with the anxiety of concealment.

'He's left a message for you.'

She took the envelope and withdrew the note, after first making clear, by turning over the packet, that she noticed it had already been opened. The message made her unyielding.

'Have you a Bible?'

'Of course.' She left them at the door, and returned with a heavy, leather-bound copy, black, with a brass clasp.

'Your department,' Lepage said, handing the Bible to Cathcut. 'Read it to me.'

Cathcut turned to Zechariah 13, scanned the opening verses, and then began reading aloud.

> 'And it shall come to pass in that day, that the prophets shall be ashamed every one of his vision, when he hath prophesied; neither shall they wear a rough garment to deceive:
> 'But he shall say, I am no prophet, I am an husbandman: for man taught me to keep cattle from my youth.
> 'And one shall say unto him, What are these wounds in thine hands? Then he shall answer, Those with which I was wounded in the house of my friends.'
> 'Awake, O sword, against my shepherd, and against the man that is my fellow, saith the Lord of hosts: smite the shepherd, and the sheep shall be scattered: and I will turn mine hand upon the little ones . . .'

Cathcut looked up, seeming very troubled. 'Ah,' he said, after a brief hesitation. 'I think I've got it. This is it.' He read with increased speed.

'... *And it shall come to pass, that in all the land, saith the Lord, two parts therein shall be cut off and die; but the third shall be left therein.*
'*And I will bring the third part through the fire, and will refine them as silver is refined, and will try them as gold is tried: they shall call on my name, and I will hear them: I will say, it is my people: and they shall say, The Lord is my God.*'

Cathcut closed the Bible and returned it to Lepage.

'There's nothing there,' Lepage said, handing it to Care's mother, who tucked it under her arm. 'It doesn't tell us where he is.'

'This is some kind of treasure-hunt, isn't it? From the church? Aren't you a bit old for playing games?'

'Your son is in trouble,' Cathcut said. 'We need to find him.'

For a moment, her eyes showed panic. 'What kind of trouble? Is he sick?'

Cathcut shook his head silently.

She took on the rigidity of a peg-doll, white, with tight-pressed lips. 'He's always been a trouble, that one. More than the rest put together. They all of them died young.'

By mutual consent the two men turned back down the garden path, Lepage pausing only to urge the mother that, if Care returned there, she should immediately ring the station.

Lepage led off down Seshton Hill at a jog, with Cathcut keeping up only by lifting his cassock well above his knees. The priest was desperate enough not to care what figure he cut, and even half-enjoyed a sense of abandon. But Lepage went uncomfortably close to the Driscoll home, before halting at a parked vehicle.

'I dumped the car here early this morning.'

Cathcut's face must have registered a pang.

'Don't worry. She turned me down. Get in.' He opened his nearside door for the priest, and sat adjusting his radio to a police frequency. The air crackled with voices; but nothing of any substance.

'The river,' Cathcut said quietly. 'Evans was shouting about the river. I heard him from half a street away.'

Lepage drove his car to a public telephone booth, leapt out, leaving the engine running, rang, then turned and motioned Cathcut to wind down his window. He propped open the door of the booth with his back, taking the receiver-cord to its full extension, so as to keep within earshot of his radio. 'Porson, please. . . . —Porson, get a couple of cars down by the river. One each side. We're searching for Care. And contact the army divers.' His message must have been sufficiently dramatic to preclude discussion.

Despite afternoon rain, the river had not markedly improved either in its speed or its odour. They searched the bank on either side, invading empty warehouses through holes that they enlarged in the corrugated iron with their boots, covering their clothing with great flakes of rust. They peered under jetties, checked inlets and sluices, and were eventually joined by three further teams, one on the near, and two on the far side of the river. They worked in silence, except when a team sought instructions on where to extend their search. Eventually, cloud closing-in brought on nightfall even earlier than expected. 'Radio for lights,' Lepage ordered. 'And turn those headlights on over the water.'

There was a shout thirty yards to their right, and two of the uniformed men drew a large object from the current, holding it against the footings of a wharf with a boat-hook. By torch-light, it proved to be a dead dog, a big sand-coloured retriever, floating on its side, with its belly bloated and its legs thrust out like sticks. The jaws were muzzled, and the feet had been fastened together front and back with electrical wire, which showed a flash of colour where the fur did not cover it, and a glint of bared copper. It had probably floated down some distance, hitting obstructions on its way, for the body was already frayed and gelatinous about the edges, from partial decomposition and the attacks of rats. Its eye had rotted, or been eaten out. It seemed to promise little future for a human corpse.

Against the sodium lights on the iron road-bridge Cathcut saw a figure leaning over, watching. For a moment he thought it was Care, about to jump. '*Rosmersholm!*' he shouted, running after Lepage, who had gone to move a vehicle so that it illuminated the main stream more effectively. Lepage turned at the sound, as though the priest had gone mad. '*Rosmersholm!*' Cathcut cried again, spluttering in the policeman's face. 'It's a play by Ibsen. An ex-clergyman who's lost his faith, and is implicated in his wife's suicide. —That doesn't matter. He jumps off a bridge.' He intoned a line. '"*Where I have sinned, there I must expiate*". He'll be at the flat: the house where they found the body.'

Without pausing to question the process by which Cathcut's conclusion was reached, Lepage ran to his own car, started its engine and released the clutch, leaving Cathcut to bundle himself in as best he could. He reversed at speed and drove them back toward the main trunk road up Seshton Hill, screeching tyres on a roundabout, and causing Cathcut to splay his Office Book across the near-side window in an effort to keep his seat. When the springs returned to equilibrium, Cathcut turned the pages of his tiny volume furiously, and with the help of passing street-lights began to read aloud.

'Some put their trust in chariots, and some in horses:
but we will remember the name of the Lord our God.'

'Not *"we"*,' Lepage said grimly. 'Leave me out.' Nevertheless, he turned on an overhead light. 'And lock that near-side door, unless your faith is perfect.' They took a right turn at speed, throwing Cathcut hard against the handle.

They came once again to the attic room; up five flights of stairs, feeling for bare treads with their feet, stumbling across landings. When Cathcut put his hand to where a switch should be, he touched only naked wires. The door on the topmost landing refused to open.

Lepage fished for his key-ring, and held up each key in turn to the window; but neighbouring buildings obstructed any light. He resorted to gauging their size with his fingers, chinking small metal melodiously. 'The door's bolted from inside,' he reported after some moments. 'He must have let himself in with keys we took from the landlord.'

At this confirmation of his guess, Cathcut's heart pounded still louder. He held Lepage's key turned in the lock, while the policeman butted several times with his shoulder. The door bowed, and yielded with a splintering of wood. Inside was completely dark, save for a crack of light from under an inner door.

'This one's locked too.' Cathcut felt around for a light-switch, flicked it on, but produced no light. 'I've got my hand on some kind of metal box. I think it's a coin-in-the slot. Do you happen to have a shilling?'

'Forget it,' Lepage said. 'The scene-of-crime team spent a small fortune, before they realized the landlord had rigged the meter. If you can help me with this door, there's candles and matches on the inside, on a shelf to your right.'

The door gave easily under their combined weight, and they tumbled into the room. Immediately, they were assailed by a smell of singed flesh, with a faint aromatic undertone, like incense. Care sat with his back toward them, over by the bed, with a single candle in a saucer on the mattress before him. His shadow spread across floor and wall. His head was sunk, his breathing loud and stertorous. As they rushed over to him, it quickened for six or seven rapid snortings, almost as if he had been frightened; and then subsided into its previous noisy rhythm.

His eyes were open, with oddly dilated pupils, like black ink in the candle-light; but they seemed not to focus. Lepage picked up one wrist and felt Care's pulse, then rummaged in his pockets. On the floor he discovered a medicine bottle, some three inches high, and read its label by the candle. When he shook it, it made no sound.

'"Doriden",' he exclaimed. 'Glutethimide. By the look of it'— he indicated two empty water tumblers which lay on their side by the bed—'he's taken enough to kill himself twice over. It should have been withdrawn from the market years ago.'

He inspected Care's hands again, turning their palms to the light so Cathcut might see. There were burn-marks around the cracks between each finger and down to the centre of his palms, as if he had passed each hand several times across a naked candle-flame. Between Care's spread thighs, on a patch of upholstery, Cathcut saw a dark, spreading stain, and smelt a strong tang of ammonia. Globules of liquid shone and trickled down the varnish of the chair-leg.

'My God!' Cathcut cried to Lepage in horror. 'Did I help you to do *that*?'

Lepage ignored him, turning Care's armchair preparatory to rolling the patient on to the floor. As he rocked and shifted the chair-legs, his attention was caught by a familiar black book, propped on the bed against a cardboard box. It lay open at the Book of Job, chapter 13; but the page had been mutilated, as if its owner expected no further use for it. An oblong had been drawn around two verses to highlight them, though at the cost of obliterating part of the preceding and successive verses. Lepage tugged Cathcut's elbow, and together they peered at the text.

> *Wherefore do I take my flesh in my teeth, and put my life in mine hand? Though he slay me, yet will I trust in him; but I will maintain mine own ways before him.*

The verses were placed so as to be immediately before the dying man, the last thing he looked at before losing consciousness. That was why his eyes had remained open.

'Help me,' Cathcut pleaded, tugging at Care's legs. 'Help me lay him out on the floor. Then I can use Holger-Nielsen—I learned it in the Scouts. It's vital to maintain breathing.'

Lepage put a hand on the priest's shoulder and pulled him back. 'Wait,' he said quietly. 'Let him be. What is there left for him? He's been wrong in his own terms, he's been inconsistent, so he's punished his shortcoming. I admire that.'

'It isn't *Christian*,' Cathcut said with feeling.

'Maybe not. But when have you done any one thing whole-heartedly?'

The priest looked grieved and ashamed. In the flickering light, Lepage had about him a curious, macabre elation.

'... Little man,' he said again, putting an arm round Cathcut's shoulder, 'don't you understand when you've got a victory? He's put himself to the stake for what he believes. It's better than lions and circuses.'

Cathcut shook him off, twisting shoulders and body. 'It isn't martyrdom, if it was for the wrong reasons. It's only sanctified self-slaughter. —Like *this*.'

'Let him be,' Lepage insisted once more. 'Let him sort it out with his God. If you succeed in keeping him alive, what would it be for? If he escapes being a vegetable, will he survive a life-sentence? They don't like religious maniacs inside, any more than sex-offenders. He'll count as both. Twenty years of being a certified lunatic, and every man's hand against him. What would there be left of him? Would he keep his faith? Would he remember what faith was? It's better as it is.'

'It's a disaster,' Cathcut said.

Lepage reached for Care's Bible and turned over several pages. 'Do you know how Job ends?' He read from the final chapter.

> '*I have heard of thee by the hearing of the ear: but now mine eye seeth thee. Wherefore I abhor myself, and repent in dust and ashes.*'

He laughed wryly, replacing the book against its box; but seemed close to tears.

They stood on either side of the dying man, waiting in the semi-darkness as the candle guttered, till his breathing grew steadily more shallow, faltered, and finally fell silent.